The fie[...]
which you[...]
phy." This[...]
ful laser b[...]
so tiny th[...]
photograp[...]
glow of a [...]

So look for the Zebra Hologram Heart whenever you buy a historical romance. It is a shimmering reflection of our guarantee that you'll find consistent quality between the covers!

PASSION'S TEMPTATION

A feeling of dizziness came over Regina. Tottering feebly, she leaned against Matt for support and was grateful when his strong arms grasped her.

Mistaking her swoon as another attempt to entice him, Matt's eyes hardened as his gaze met hers. His severity startled Regina, and she tried to squirm out of his embrace.

Keeping her pinned against him, he continued to stare darkly into her upturned face. He hadn't the will power to refuse her, but two could play her cunning little game. If she wanted to trap him into marriage by offering him her delectable body, then he'd accept her tempting bait—and leave her afterward without so much as a backward glance.

Regina wasn't expecting Matt's kiss, and when his lips suddenly pressed demandingly against hers, she was taken totally by surprise. She gasped for breath. Matt removed his mouth from hers only long enough for her to inhale deeply before he was once again kissing her forcefully. He entwined his fingers in her hair, keeping her lips against his.

She had fought against him and against her own desires, but now she could only surrender completely. . . .

Ida N.

LOVING TORMENT

ROCHELLE WAYNE

ZEBRA BOOKS
KENSINGTON PUBLISHING CORP.

ZEBRA BOOKS

are published by

Kensington Publishing Corp.
475 Park Avenue South
New York, NY 10016

First printing: February 1986

Printed in the United States of America

For Jim, my dear friend and conscientious agent.

Chapter One

A mote on the horizon separated into a fast-moving black stallion and a large white dog that had little trouble keeping up with the horse's long graceful gait. Astride the steed was a vivacious rider. Honey blond hair streamed from beneath her Spanish-style hat, which was held in place by chin straps, and the wind molded her white blouse to her body, outlining her feminine bosom. In her elegantly tailored leather riding skirt and high-topped boots, Regina Blakely was a fetching sight. She sat tall and erect in the saddle, holding the reins in one gauntleted hand, while the other seemed to keep time with the fluid movement of the steed she controlled.

In 1880 not many women rode alone on the range, but Regina was a skilled horsewoman who knew how to defend herself with the rifle she carried in a tooled-leather scabbard attached to her saddle.

Although Regina was lovely, she wasn't a classic beauty. It was her demeanor that made her beautiful. The proud lift of her chin projected an aura of elegance that women envied and men found sensual. Upon meeting Regina, men quickly realized that her appearance was not her most captivating asset; that was her spirit. They soon stopped admiring the color of her green eyes and became entranced by their lively expression. They toyed with the idea of making love to Regina, but invariably they became enthralled by her exciting vitality.

From her eighteenth to her twenty-first year, Regina was the most popular young lady in and around Albuquerque, New Mexico. She received numerous marriage proposals, but she turned down all of them. With the passing of time, the proposals began to dwindle, for the men in town and those on the nearby ranches came to believe that the lovely Miss Regina Blakely would never marry.

Regina had nothing against marriage. Indeed, she looked forward to her wedding day, indulging in the same fanciful dreams as most young women. But she would not wed just because it was expected of her. She would marry when she met the right man, and although she was now twenty-four years old, she still hadn't found the one who could win her heart.

However, as she rode up to the stable on her Black Diamond Ranch and turned her horse over to her head wrangler, marriage was not on her mind. She was concerned about a number of things that had to do with running her ranch, and she knew resolving them would not be easy. Her father had recently died, and his untimely death still had her quite upset. A heart attack, the doctor had said. But her father had always been so strong and healthy! How could he be so vibrantly alive one day and dead the next?

Hearing an approaching horse, Regina gazed down the road that led to the house. When she recognized the rider, she hurried to the hitching post to greet him. Seeing Regina waiting, Dan forced himself to smile as he waved to her, but he shook his head slightly for he regretted the purpose of his visit.

Daniel Butler was Regina's half brother. Her father had married his mother when Dan was a boy of eleven. Katherine Butler had been widowed two years when she'd met James Blakely, and against the advice of relatives and friends, she had married the dashing stranger. Katherine was aware that everyone believed he had married her for her money and for the beautiful, prosperous plantation, in Georgia, that she had inherited from her husband. But Katherine was blindly in love with the handsome James Blakely, and although she knew nothing of his past, she married him with no reservations whatsoever. She not only gave him her money and her plantation but also two daughters. Katherine named her first daughter Julie Anna, but she died giving birth to her second daughter, and it had been James Blakely who had named the baby Regina Charlene.

Halting his horse in front of the ranch house, Dan dismounted. He paused for a moment to admire his sister, finding her extremely lovely. Then, flinging the reins over the hitching post, he embraced her.

"How are you, Gina?" he asked, using the pet name he had given her when she was a baby.

"I'm all right," she replied, sounding quite the opposite.

Nodding toward the porch steps, he suggested, "Let's sit down. I need to talk to you."

Doing as he requested, she settled herself on the stoop; close by his side. Regina loved her brother. Although they had often been separated, he had always been in her thoughts, and it had delighted her when, two years ago, he had moved permanently to Albuquerque. But Regina and her father had always disagreed over Dan. James Blakely had considered his stepson a scoundrel. He hadn't even liked him when Dan was a boy for he had never been able to manipulate Katherine's son—and James Blakely disliked anyone he couldn't control. At the age of eighteen, when Dan had left the plantation to sow his wild oats, James Blakely had been well pleased to see him leave. Yet Blakely had feared that Daniel would someday return and claim the plantation which was rightfully his. Then, at the outbreak of the War Between the States, Daniel Butler had joined the Confederate Army, and James Blakely had sent his daughters to stay with Katherine's sister in St. Louis before offering his own services to the Confederacy. When the war had finally ended there was no plantation left for either man to claim. The elegant, columned home had been burned to the ground and the fields were barren.

Now Regina looked at her brother in puzzlement. Apparently something was bothering him. She touched his hand encouragingly, and smiling, he covered her hand with his. Daniel Butler was a handsome man. He had taken after his father, inheriting dark hair and eyes that were richly brown and dreamy. He was only a couple of inches taller than Regina, and his physique was slim and masculine.

"Gina," he began, "this afternoon I received an unexpected visit from Antonio Ramírez. He came to talk to me about your father."

Regina frowned. "Honestly, Dan! Must you always refer to him as "my father"? His name was James."

Dan sighed impatiently. "Let's not get into a discussion about my feelings toward James Blakely."

"If only you hadn't gone against his wishes and bought that saloon in town, maybe you and Papa could have found a way to become friends."

Dan laughed harshly. "If I had bought a church, your father and I would still have remained bitter enemies."

"That's because you're as stubborn as he was."

"Stubbornness had nothing to do with it," Dan answered firmly. Then, gently squeezing her hand, he asked, "Did you know James had business dealings with Ramírez?"

"No!" she exclaimed, astounded. "I thought Papa disliked Ramírez."

"He didn't especially dislike him; he simply thought himself superior to Ramírez. But when it came to money your father had a way of overlooking some things."

"What do you mean?" she asked.

"James borrowed money from Ramírez." Standing, Dan looked down at Regina and added disapprovingly, "James Blakely was a compulsive gambler."

"But Papa usually won!" Regina replied.

Dan shook his head. "No, he usually lost. He just never let you know about his losses."

Getting to her feet, Regina clutched his arm. "Dan, what are you trying to tell me?"

"I'm telling you that you are head over heels in debt to Antonio Ramírez."

"But there's enough money in the bank to cover Papa's debt."

"There is no money in the bank. Your father hadn't made any deposits for over three years."

"Then I'll get a loan on the ranch and the cattle," Regina declared.

"Not when you don't have a deed to the place."

"Of course there's a deed! Papa kept it in the safe in the study."

"It isn't there. Your father gave it to Ramírez for collateral."

Regina wanted to cry out that Dan was wrong, that Papa would never have gambled away their home! He had loved the ranch as dearly as she did. Instead, her knees weakening, Regina sunk to the porch steps.

"I don't believe it," she gasped. "Papa wouldn't do

11

something like this to me."

"Well, maybe you'll believe it when you have to pack up and get out of here."

"Get out?" she repeated tremulously.

"You have one month to pay the debt or leave." Dan sat down beside her. "When Blakely gave the deed to Ramírez, they had a legal paper drawn up which specified a certain date on which your father had to pay back the debt. If he failed to meet the deadline, this ranch would belong to Ramírez."

"But surely Papa had a way to pay Ramírez; otherwise he wouldn't have drawn up a paper stating when he must repay the money."

"Oh he had a way in mind," Dan answered bitterly. "He hoped to win the money gambling."

"Dan," she whispered raspingly, "what am I going to do?"

"You'll have to move in with Julie for a time," he replied gently.

"No!" she cried.

"You sure as hell can't stay with me! I live above a saloon."

Raising her chin, Regina's eyes gleamed with determination. "I won't lose the Black Diamond!"

"Gina," he said tenderly, "there's nothing you can do. If I had the money, I'd take care of the debt. But it would take a rich man to cover the cost, and I'm far from wealthy." Dan watched her lovingly. He believed that James Blakely had manipulated both his daughters. He had married Julie off to a man she didn't love, simply to get her out from under his roof. Julie was too much like Katherine Butler—but Regina had the looks and bearing of a Blakely. So James Blakely had tolerated his older daughter, while taking charge of the younger one.

Suddenly, Regina declared, "I'll go see Ramírez. If

necessary, I'll plead with him to extend the time to pay back Papa's loan."

"When do you plan to visit him?" Dan asked.

"Tonight," she answered.

"Alone?" he inquired. She nodded, and Dan grumbled, "You have no business riding by yourself at night! I would go with you but I need to get back to the saloon. Wait and go tomorrow during daylight."

"For goodness sakes, Dan!" she complained. "You know perfectly well that I can take care of myself. I can shoot as well as any man and better than most."

"All the same, I think you should take Juan or one of the ranch hands."

"After a full day of working on the ranch, Juan is tired and so are the men. I'll go alone." But seeing Dan's concern, she added quickly, "If it'll make you feel better, I'll take Blackie with me."

Glancing around, Dan asked, "Where is that likable mutt?"

"I'm sure he's somewhere close by." Standing, Regina called the name Blackie.

Immediately the enormously proportioned dog came bounding around the corner of the house. Going to Regina, he sat at her feet, looking up at her with worshipful eyes. Turning his head sideways, he whined softly. Blackie's hair was solid white. He had once belonged to a ranch hand known as Blackie. James Blakely had allowed the man to keep the dog because it had been trained to round up cattle, but Blackie had never given the animal a name. He had simply called him Dog. After a few months, when Blackie packed up and moved on, he had left his pet behind. At first people called him Blackie's dog, but eventually he became Blackie.

Petting the dog's huge head, Dan suggested, "Why don't you change his name? Calling a white dog Blackie

13

is a little erratic, don't you agree?"

Smiling, she responded pertly, "Well the dog doesn't mind, so why should I?"

Moving to his sister, Dan placed a hand beneath her chin, tilting her face upward. "I haven't seen you smile in over a month, not since your father died. And you have such a beautiful smile."

"You're prejudiced because you're my big brother."

"Prejudice has nothing to do with it. Gina, you are a very lovely woman." Leaning over, he kissed her cheek. "I need to get back to the saloon. Let me know what happens. Good luck with Ramírez."

"Thanks." She sighed. "But I have a feeling I'm going to need more than just luck to convince Ramírez to extend Papa's loan."

Entering the bedroom, Regina stepped to her mahogany wardrobe and opened the door. She had decided to go on horseback to Antonio Ramírez's ranch, so she took out one of her newer riding skirts and a long-sleeved silk blouse. Going to her bed, she sat down and placed the garments at her side. Sighing, she distractedly rubbed her fingers across the chenille spread. "Papa," she whispered, "why did you place the Black Diamond in jeopardy? You loved this ranch as much as I do." But had he? Or had she only taken that for granted? She tried to remember whether her father had ever come right out and said that he loved the ranch. Concentrating deeply, she couldn't recall a time when he'd actually done so.

Rising slowly, Regina went to the window, and drawing back the lace curtains, she gazed out into the night. Since her bedroom faced the corral, she could hear the soft neighing of the penned horses. She thought about the first time she had seen the ranch. She had loved her new home immediately.

After the war, James Blakely had joined his daughters in St. Louis. Knowing he was penniless, Katherine's sister had invited him to stay with her husband and herself until he could find a way to make a home for his daughters, but James Blakely had been miserable living with his in-laws. They had been too upright and religious for a man like him; and they had detested any form of gambling. Since his older brother owned a ranch a few miles from Albuquerque, he had decided the West was where he wanted to live and he had written to his brother telling him of his desperate circumstances.

Carl Blakely had sent money for the trip to Albuquerque, and James had conveniently moved himself and his daughters into Carl's home. Three years later when Carl Blakely had become ill and died, he'd left everything he owned to his brother.

Stepping away from the window, Regina slipped out of her clothes and, after a quick sponge bath, put on fresh riding togs. She left the bedroom and hurried down the hallway to the kitchen. Juan and his wife Luisa were sitting at the table talking, but as Regina entered, they halted their conversation. Juan and Luisa had worked on the ranch for years; they had been hired by Carl Blakely. Luisa ran the house, and Juan took care of all repairs and cooked the meals for the ranch hands.

Regina liked the two elderly servants, and smiling warmly, she asked, "Juan, will you please saddle my father's horse?"

Complying, Juan got to his feet. It was on his lips to advise the *señorita* not to ride by herself at night, but he suppressed the urge. She would do as she pleased, regardless of his objections.

As her husband left through the back door, Luisa

15

clicked her tongue against the roof of her mouth, a gesture she always used before chastening Regina. *"Señorita,* you should not ride alone after dark."

Leaving the kitchen, Regina called back to Luisa, "Don't worry, I'll be perfectly all right."

Rushing down the hallway, the young woman went to her father's study. Going directly to the gun cabinet, she removed the rifle which Juan had returned to it after her ride. Holding the Winchester familiarly, she then darted out of the room. At the front door, she remembered to grab her wide-brimmed hat from the wall rack before leaving the house.

Regina restrained the spirited stallion, making him walk at a leisurely pace, and as she rode across the quiet plains, she thought about Antonio Ramírez. He had bought the ranch bordering Regina's less than a year ago. She wasn't personally acquainted with him and had only caught glimpses of him in town. But she was aware that he had the reputation of being difficult to deal with, and she was afraid it was doubtful that she could persuade him to extend her father's debt.

Her thoughts on Antonio Ramírez, Regina didn't detect Blackie's sudden growl. But as his snarl deepened and grew more vicious, she became aware of the dog's warning.

Reining her horse beside a large boulder, she asked quietly, "What is it, Blackie? Do you hear something?" Cautiously, she removed the rifle from the scabbard on her saddle.

His hair bristling, Blackie leaped onto the boulder, stalking his way to the top. Cocking her rifle, Regina edged the stallion around the huge rock. The night was clear and she quickly spotted the three mounted men. They were some yards away from her, so she couldn't distinguish the words they spoke in hushed voices. She saw that two of the men had their pistols drawn and aimed at the third one. Uncertain of what she should do, Regina wished Blackie would come down from the boulder so they could simply move away. However, one of the armed men suddenly caught sight of the dog's white coat against the blackness of night, and he turned sharply toward the boulder.

Frightened that the man might shoot Blackie, Regina fired her rifle into the air, hoping only that the unexpected sound would throw off his aim. Instead, as the blast from Regina's rifle thundered across the landscape, the two armed men galloped off. Recocking her rifle, Regina held it on the remaining man and, with a slight pressure of her knees, urged the stallion forward. When she was only a few feet from the man, she halted her horse.

The moonlight shining down on Regina made her clearly visible, and taking in her alluring beauty, the stranger smiled admiringly. When he spoke his voice was deep and full, "Thank you, ma'am, for coming to my rescue."

The man was in the dark shadow of the boulder so Regina couldn't see him very well. Furthermore, he wore a black hat pulled low over his forehead so it was impossible for her to get a close look at his face. Although he was on horseback, she could make him out well enough to realize that he was tall and his physique was lean but solid.

Keeping her rifle aimed at him, she asked a little shakily, "Why were those men holding you at gunpoint?"

"They mistakenly thought they were going to rob me," he answered calmly.

"Mistakenly?" she asked. "It looked to me as though they would have been quite successful."

17

He moved forward, and she alertly raised her rifle. Stopping his horse, he lifted his hand and when he turned it over, she saw a small double-barreled derringer resting snugly in his palm. "There are two bullets in here," he explained. "I had one for each of them."

Noticing his empty holster, she glanced down at the ground and saw his pistol. "It seems they only thought they had you disarmed," she stated, a certain degree of admiration in her voice.

"When I travel I always keep this weapon in reserve," he told her, placing the derringer under his belt. Eying Regina's rifle, he proceeded carefully, "Ma'am, must you keep that gun pointed at me? Looking down a loaded barrel always makes me feel a little edgy."

Lowering her rifle, she said questioningly, "I didn't really come to your rescue after all, did I?"

He smiled, and the whiteness of his teeth showed in the darkness. "I don't suppose we'll ever know for sure. I only had two bullets, and I might have missed."

For some reason Regina had a feeling that this stranger was not a man who ever missed. Suddenly realizing it was fairly late, she said brusquely, "I must go."

"If you're going to town, I'll ride with you. That's where I was heading when I was unexpectedly delayed."

"I'm not on my way to town," she replied. Glancing up at the boulder, she called, "Come on Blackie."

The man looked on as the dog bounded from the rock and ran to his mistress. The stranger chuckled softly, and although he was curious, he decided not to ask why she called a white dog Blackie.

Slipping the rifle into the scabbard, Regina spoke hesitantly. "Good night, sir, and . . . and watch out for highwaymen."

18

As she began to ride away, he said, "I don't even know your name."

"Regina Blakely," she called over her shoulder before encouraging the stallion into a fast canter.

The man dismounted and picked up his pistol. Slipping it back into his holster, he looked in the direction that Regina had taken. Now that she was gone, he almost felt she had only been a figment of his imagination. Remounting, he smiled as he recalled her loveliness. No, she had definitely been real, he decided, and he knew he'd never forget the beautiful lady riding a black stallion and accompanied by a white dog named Blackie.

The ranch hands at the corrals, and the ones in front of the bunkhouse, stared at the woman riding up to Antonio Ramírez' home. Expertly handling the large black stallion, Regina sat it proudly and majestically, her blond hair touching her shoulders, and her riding skirt clinging seductively to her hips and her long legs. Oblivious to the admiring eyes of the men, Regina halted the horse next to the hitching post that ran the length of the veranda. Then, telling Blackie to stay, she walked up to the door, her strides long and determined. Her firm knock was answered almost immediately, and since she had expected the door to be opened by a servant, she was startled to see Antonio Ramírez standing before her.

The few times Regina had seen Ramírez in town, she had found him to be exceptionally attractive, and that night he looked quite handsome. Antonio was wearing a white shirt that fit snugly across his wide shoulders, and his trousers were black with silver trimming running vertically down the seam of each leg. He was in his early forties, but his dark hair didn't have a trace of gray.

"Mr. Ramírez," Regina began, "I am here to talk to you about my father's debt."

Stepping aside, he said, "Come in, *señorita.*" Taking her arm, he escorted her through the foyer and into the parlor. The room was enormous, and was decorated tastefully in Spanish décor.

Gesturing to the rose-colored sofa, he asked, "Would you like to sit down?"

Pausing in the center of the room, she replied, "No, thank you."

"A glass of wine, perhaps?" he inquired.

She shook her head. Deciding to get straight to the point, Regina declared, "Mr. Ramírez, I came to ask you to give me an extension on Papa's loan."

He smiled coldly. "I am sorry, *señorita.* I know no reason why I should."

"But, Mr. Ramírez, I have only now learned of Papa's debt. You must give me time to get the money together."

Still smiling, he asked, "How much time do you need?"

Hopeful now, she answered briskly, "I don't know. How much do I owe you?"

Throwing back his head, he laughed uproariously before inquiring, "You mean you do not know, *señorita?*"

"No," she answered, embarrassed. Why hadn't she remembered to ask Dan the extent of the debt?

"Ten thousand American dollars," he told her.

Regina's mouth dropped open, and she caught her breath deeply. "Ten thousand!" she gasped.

"Now, I will ask you again, Señorita Blakely, how much time do you need?" When she didn't answer, he continued almost gently. "It would take you years to pay back your *papá's* loan. Your ranch is no longer

20

turning a profit. What cattle you have left are poor specimens. James Blakely sold all his superior breeds. Gambling meant more to Señor Blakely than his ranch."

Certain of defeat, Regina asked, "Why do you want my home? You have more land than you need."

"Power, *señorita*. The more land I own, the more power I possess."

"Does power mean so much to you that you would evict me from my home without giving me an opportunity to pay back the money owed to you?"

Walking to the liquor cabinet, he poured two glasses of wine, then returned to her side. Handing Regina her drink, he said smoothly, "I have a proposition to offer you."

Accepting the glass, she asked warily, "What kind of proposition?"

His eyes traveling boldly over her sensual curves, he answered, "Become my mistress and I will let you keep your indebted ranch."

Instantly angered, she blurted out, "I'll never be your mistress or any man's!"

Totally collected, he took a sip of his wine before replying, "You're a very desirable woman, Señorita Blakely, and as my mistress you would reap many rewards. I have seen you in town on more than one occasion, and I have wanted you for a long time. I think very soon now you will belong to me."

Shoving her full glass of wine into his hand, she stated forcefully, "I wouldn't let you touch me! You're rude, offensive and a damned scoundrel!"

Laughing, Antonio went to the table placed in front of the sofa. Putting down the glasses, he replied lightly, *"Señorita,* you are a charming spitfire."

Whirling sharply, Regina began to stalk out of the room. Watching her, Antonio called, "Remember that

21

my proposition will stand for only one month. After that it will be too late for you to agree to my proposal because your ranch will already be mine."

Although Regina knew there was no foreseeable way for her to prevent Ramírez from foreclosing on her home, she nonetheless declared, "I wouldn't be so sure about that, Ramírez! You might not find it so easy to take my land!" Roughly she swung open the door, and darting outside, she slammed it closed.

Chapter Two

Julie Edwards watched her sister as she paced back and forth in front of their father's desk. Sitting on the sofa beside her husband, she had to restrain an impulse to leap to her feet and tell Regina that she didn't care whether James Blakely had gambled away the ranch. Why should she care? This home might hold precious memories for Regina, but not for her. From the day they had arrived, Julie's father had treated her as impersonally as he would a servant. She had been twelve years old when James Blakely had moved himself and his daughters to Albuquerque, and four short years later, at the tender age of sixteen, Julie had been married off to a man she didn't love.

Turning her gaze from her sister, Julie looked at the man at her side. Mace Edwards was thirty-one, short, and extremely thin; and he had now been married to Julie for ten years. Although he was very fond of his wife, she had been a big disappointment to him. He had wanted children, lots of them—especially sons—but Julie had remained barren. Now he had almost given up on having a family, and he very seldom bedded his wife. He believed marital relations had only one purpose, to conceive a child. Now, wishing his brother-in-law would arrive, Mace impatiently brushed his fingers through his hair. Perhaps if her husband had had a humorous and engaging personality, Julie might have learned to love him. But he lacked charm and wit, and although she respected him, she had not found him to be even remotely romantic.

It would have surprised Mace to know that their childlessness made Julie unhappier than it made him. If only she could have a baby, she felt she would have someone to shower with love. She would never let her child know what it was like to be unwanted or cast aside.

Returning her gaze to Regina, Julie sighed deeply. She, too, wished that Dan would hurry. She didn't know why he had called a family meeting. Probably because he wanted her and Mace to convince Regina to give up the Black Diamond and move in with them. Their home and ranch were small, but they could afford to take care of Regina. It was true that Julie had envied Regina their father's love, but she felt no resentment toward her sister. Indeed, she truly loved both Regina and Dan, for Julie was a gentle woman and a compassionate one. She was also very beautiful, but one had to look more closely to see her loveliness. Her beauty had never been given a chance to bloom so it lay dormant, waiting to be awakened. Her crowning glory was her hair. It was reddish brown, and when she released it from its confining bun, it fell in long waves to her hips. Her eyes were almond shaped, their color a soft brown. Long lashes and dark eyebrows, perfectly arched, set them off. Although her frame was small, she was very soft and feminine.

Suddenly, at the sound of heavy footsteps, they all looked toward the open doorway. As Dan ambled into the study, he removed his hat. Then he kissed each sister on the cheek and nodded a hello to Mace before stepping to the desk and placing his hat on it.

He asked Regina, "Did you see Ramírez last night?"

"Yes, and the man is insufferable!" she answered sharply.

"I take it that Ramírez wouldn't grant you an extension," Dan surmised.

"No," she replied, deciding not to tell her brother about Ramírez' rude proposition.

Moving around the desk, Dan sat in the leather-bound chair. Crossing his hands over his chest, he looked at Mace and Julie, explaining, "I asked both of you to be here because I think you two, as well as Regina, should know that I have come up with a plan that might save this ranch."

Regina instantly asked, "What is your plan?"

"Don't get your hopes up, little sister. It's a long shot, and there's only one chance in a hundred that it'll pay off." Reaching into his pocket, he removed a cheroot. After lighting it, he continued. "Matt Brolin is in town, and he's a friend of mine. I knew him before I moved to Albuquerque."

"Matt Brolin!" Mace exclaimed, a note of disgust in his voice.

"Do you know this Matt Brolin?" Regina asked Mace.

"I know of him. And his reputation is not an honorable one."

Firmly, Dan argued, "Matt Brolin is one of the most honest men I know."

"What does he have to do with your plan?" Regina wanted to know.

Smiling shrewdly, Dan replied, "Matt and Miguel Ordaz are good friends."

Stomping to the desk and placing his hands on the desktop, Mace stared angrily at Dan. "Miguel Ordaz is worse than Matt Brolin! I refuse to let my family be

25

associated with either man!"

Undisturbed by Mace's anger, Dan answered calmly, "Miguel Ordaz despises Antonio Ramírez, and he just might loan Regina ten thousand dollars. I intend to ask Matt to take me to Ordaz' hacienda; then I hope Matt will intervene on Regina's behalf and ask Miguel Ordaz for a loan."

"I forbid you to contact Ordaz!" Mace ordered.

Regina had never heard of Miguel Ordaz, but at the moment, she was not interested in his reputation. Going to Mace's side, she said firmly, "Mace, please stay out of this!"

"But, Regina, you don't understand," Mace explained testily. "Your brother wants to bring you into personal contact with men who are murderers and outlaws."

Looking at Dan, Regina asked, "Is that true?"

Dan shook his head. "Matt Brolin and Miguel Ordaz are not murderers or ruthless outlaws as Mace would like you to believe. They both have reputations which have been unfairly exaggerated by men such as our brother-in-law."

Offended, Mace moved back to the sofa and sat down. Where Dan was concerned, he had been in complete accord with James Blakely. Julie and Regina's brother was a worthless, shady rogue.

Rising, Dan decided, "I'll return to town and talk to Brolin." Stepping out from behind the desk, he went to Regina, and taking her hands into his, he warned her gently, "Gina, don't be too hopeful. That Ordaz will help you, is a helluva long shot." He kissed her cheek, then taking his hat, he walked out of the room.

Entering his saloon, Dan spotted Matt Brolin sitting at a table in the corner. Hastily, he made his way across the room, and upon reaching Matt, he paused. There

26

were two glasses and a bottle of whiskey on the table, but Matt didn't seem to be interested in drinking. He was sitting low in the chair, his legs stretched out and his feet resting on the chair across from him. His hat was pulled over his eyes, and, for a moment, Dan wondered if he was asleep.

Matt's voice was unemotional, "Either state your business, or get the hell away from my table."

"Is that any way to talk to a friend?" Dan chuckled.

Slowly, Matt pushed his hat back from his brow. Grinning, he replied, "Well, don't just stand there; sit down."

"I will as soon as you take your feet off my chair."

Removing his feet, Matt said, "Last night you asked me to meet you here. As you can see I showed up, but where in the hell have you been?"

Sitting, Dan answered, "I had to ride out to my sister's ranch." Leaning his elbows on the table, he proceeded eagerly, "I wanted you to meet me because I need to talk to you about my sister."

The night before, Matt had stopped, by chance, at Dan's saloon to have a drink before riding on. He hadn't seen or heard from Dan Butler in over three years. Happy to see each other, Matt and Dan had sat up half the night, drinking and rehashing old times.

Matt raised his eyebrows questioningly. "You want to talk to me about your sister?"

Studying him, Dan smiled. Although he hadn't seen Matt for years, the man hadn't changed. Matt Brolin was handsome in a rugged sensual way that women found attractive. His dark hair was worn to collar length, and his sideburns were long and full. His deep brown eyes were framed by black eyebrows, and his complexion was as dark as a Mexican's. The faded scar across his left cheekbone only added to the sensual aura he exuded.

27

As quickly as possible, Dan told Matt of Regina's present circumstances. When he had finished, Matt replied, "Your sister can't fight a man like Ramírez. Tell her to give up the ranch."

"Do you know Ramírez?" Dan asked.

"Our paths have crossed a few times," Matt answered.

Pouring himself a drink, Dan explained, "I have a plan to help my sister, but I'll need your help."

"What do you want me to do? Take on Ramírez and his men single-handed?" Matt grinned wryly.

"No, nothing quite that drastic," Dan replied good-humoredly.

"Then what can I do for you?" he queried.

Dan filled Matt's glass and, handing it to him, stated, "I remember you telling me once that you and Miguel Ordaz are good friends."

Understanding what he was leading up to, Matt grinned wisely. "Just what makes you think Miguel will help your sister."

"Because he despises Ramírez."

Arching an eyebrow, Matt prodded him. "Go on, there must be more to this."

"I'm hoping you will ask him to help her as a personal favor to you."

Matt shook his head. "I'm not traveling to Mexico to see Miguel. I'm on my way to Wyoming."

"Why are you going to Wyoming?" Dan asked.

"To buy a piece of land," he answered.

"Are you planning to settle down?"

Matt nodded. Then, placing his glass to his lips, he emptied it in one swallow.

"Can't you postpone your trip?"

"I could if I wanted to, but I don't."

Disappointed, Dan leaned back in his chair, sighing, "Without you, there's nothing I can do to help Regina."

Suddenly Matt sat up straight. Remembering the woman who had run off the two men intending to rob him, he asked anxiously, "Regina Blakely?"

Shocked that Matt knew her name, Dan answered tentatively, "She's my half sister, and that's why we have different last names. You don't know her, do you?"

Grinning, his friend replied, "Yeah, I know her. She rides a big black stallion and has a white dog."

"That's Regina, all right. But how in the hell did you meet her?"

"Quite by accident." Matt chuckled. He helped himself to another drink, then told Dan about his encounter with Regina before asking, "How much money does she owe Ramírez?"

"Ten thousand," he revealed.

Matt whistled softly. "Miguel dislikes Ramírez, but I don't know if he dislikes him ten thousand dollars worth."

"Will you help Regina?" Dan asked hopefully.

Matt nodded his consent. "Your sister helped me out last night, and I owe her a favor. Can you be ready to leave in the morning?"

"Sure," Dan replied.

"Good," Matt declared. "I want to get this business taken care of as soon as possible so I can be on my way to Wyoming."

Regina had been standing at the front window watching for Dan, and the moment she caught sight of him, she hastened outside. Pausing at the hitching post, she didn't even give him time to dismount before asking, "Is Matt Brolin going to help us?"

Swinging from the saddle, Dan answered happily, "Matt and I are leaving in the morning to ride to Mexico and see Ordaz."

Overjoyed, Regina clapped her hands, exclaiming, "Oh Dan! I can't believe it! He's really going to help save my ranch!"

Holding the bridle reins, Dan unconsciously toyed with them as he cautioned, "Gina, Brolin has a lot of influence with Ordaz, but he might not be able to convince him to loan you ten thousand dollars. I told you it was a long shot." Pleadingly, he added, "Honey, don't let yourself become too elated. If you do, you may be heading for a hard fall."

Regina nodded agreeably. Dan was right. Why should Miguel Ordaz help a woman he didn't even know? This was only a slim hope.

Dropping the reins over the hitching rail, Dan continued, "Why didn't you tell me about your encounter last night with Brolin and the men who tried to rob him?"

"You mean the man I met last night is Matt Brolin?" she gasped.

Nodding, Dan asked, "What did you think of him?"

"I didn't talk to him long enough to form an opinion." Hesitantly, she queried, "What is he like?"

"I don't know how to describe Brolin," he replied. "But I like and respect him."

Unable to subdue her curiosity, she asked, "Is he handsome? Last night I couldn't see him very well."

Dan chuckled. "Hell I don't know if he's what you'd call handsome, but Brolin's never had any problems getting women to fall for him. I guess ladies find him attractive."

"How old is he?"

Shrugging, Dan guessed, "He's somewhere around

30

thirty-two, maybe thirty-three." Watching her closely, he asked, "Why all the questions?"

"Well, if the man is going to help us, isn't it natural that I should be curious about him?" Regina replied casually, but in truth she hadn't been able to get Matt out of her mind. She couldn't understand why a man she had barely seen had made such a strong impression on her.

Leaning over, Dan kissed her lips lightly. "I have business to take care of before I can leave in the morning, so I need to hurry back to town." Taking the reins, and stepping to his horse, he mounted swiftly. Looking down at Regina, he ordered, "While I'm gone, stay away from Ramírez."

Regina experienced a touch of anxiety. "Please be careful!" she pleaded.

"I'll return in a few days," Dan promised. Then he rode away from the Black Diamond Ranch.

Regina was sitting alone on the front porch when she spotted a solitary rider approaching the house. Dusk was descending so she wasn't able to make out who he was. Rising from the pine rocker, she walked to the top step.

The man halted his horse and dismounted, flinging the reins over the hitching post. Sauntering to Regina, he tipped his black sombrero. "Miss Blakely?" he inquired.

Regina had never seen the young man before. Wondering who he could be, she answered vaguely, "Yes."

"My name is Santos Ramírez. My father is Antonio."

"Ramírez!" she exclaimed. "Get off my land! You are not welcome here!"

Instead of leaving, he moved closer to the porch

31

steps. "I have been away, and I only returned home this morning. Your brother is my friend, and I came here to tell you that I am sorry about what Papá is doing to you."

"You know Dan?" she asked. How many friends did her brother have that she knew nothing about? Matt Brolin, and now, Santos Ramírez.

"Sí," he answered. "Señorita, may I sit down and talk to you for a few minutes?"

"Of course," she consented. Regina sat on the top step and he joined her. "Mr. Ramírez, I apologize for my rudeness."

"Please call me Santos—and you have every right to be angry. Papá should have given you an extension, and he should not have insulted you."

Blushing, she breathed, "He told you about . . . about his proposition?"

Finding her flushed cheeks enticing, he smiled as he replied, "Sí, he told me. Now that I have seen you, I can understand why Papá found you so tempting."

Studying him, Regina was amazed by his strong sensuality. His smile was similar to his father's, but Santos' mother had been Apache. From her he had inherited his complexion, the straight black hair, and the high cheekbones. At the age of eighteen, Santos Ramírez was exceptionally good looking.

"Tell me about your father," Regina requested.

Reaching into his shirt pocket, he brought out a small cigar and match. "Do you mind if I smoke?"

"No, please do," she encouraged.

After lighting the cigar, he blew out the match before asking, "What do you want to know about Papá?"

"Anything," she responded, very curious about this man who planned to take her ranch. "My father said he was a Comanchero, was he?"

"Sí. He was a Comanchero for many years. They

32

needed a man with intelligence to lead them and Papá was that man."

"But why did he become a Comanchero? One would take him for one of the Spanish gentry."

"Papá's father was a wealthy man of the Spanish nobility. He had two sons, Papá being the youngest. My *abuelo,* my grandfather, owned a beautiful hacienda, but his oldest son took no interest in the land. He spent his time drinking and chasing *putas.* Sometimes he would be gone from the hacienda for weeks, even months, at a time. It was Papá who stayed home and helped my grandfather run the hacienda from sunup to sundown. When my grandfather took ill and was bedridden for weeks, Papá not only kept the hacienda operating, but at night he sat up with his ailing father. The day before my grandfather died, my uncle returned. He swore to his father that he was a changed man and begged him to forgive him for his years of negligence. His father had always loved him more than Papá, and he believed him because he wanted to. He did not change his will. He left his money and the hacienda to my uncle."

"He left Antonio nothing?" she exclaimed.

"Papá had the right to use the money in the estate, but it was controlled by my uncle. Papá left the hacienda and never returned. He became a Comanchero." Santos paused a moment before continuing. "He wanted to make enough money to buy land. He is obsessed with power. To Papá land represents power, and he believes if he can own enough land, it can never be taken from him."

"When did he meet your mother?" she asked.

"When he was a Comanchero. My mother was Apache. She died when I was four years old."

"Did he love her?"

Santos shrugged. "I don't think so, but I remember

33

that he was kind to her."

Sighing, she replied, "In a way, I feel sorry for your father."

He laughed humorously. *"Señorita,* do not waste your pity on Papá. There is no reason to feel sorry for him. He is a very prosperous man, and, yet, he has no qualms about making you homeless." Standing, he added, "Hate him. Love him. But do not pity him." Taking her hand, he brought it to his lips, kissing it gently. *"Adiós, señorita."* Going to his horse, he mounted, and touching the brim of his sombrero, he told her, "I will see you again, Regina Blakely."

Chapter Three

Rushing into the house, Juan called excitedly, *"Señorita! . . . señorita!"*

Hurrying from the study, Regina asked, "What is it?"

"Señor Butler, he is here!" Juan announced.

Darting outside, Regina saw Dan tying his horse to the hitching post. Hastening to his side and throwing herself into his arms, she cried, "Thank God, you're back!"

Hugging her, Dan said, "Honey, there's something I want you to see."

Stepping back, she asked, "What is it, Dan?"

Taking her hand, he ushered her to the narrow lane that led up to the ranch house. He placed an arm around her shoulders, then said, "I have a surprise for you. It'll be materializing at any moment."

Bewildered, Regina peered down the dirt lane. There was a small incline at the end of the road, and, suddenly, a large group of horsemen appeared over the crest. The impressive sight caused her to catch her breath. She couldn't tell how many riders were approaching, but to Regina they looked like an army.

Chuckling at her look of wonder, Dan explained,

"Miguel Ordaz and his men."

"Ordaz!" Regina breathed.

"Gina, your ranch is safe," Dan told her. "Miguel Ordaz is more powerful than Ramírez."

Astounded, Regina watched the riders enter the narrow lane two abreast. As they drew nearer, Regina noticed the man riding beside the huge Mexican that she surmised to be Ordaz. She was sure the man at his side was Matt Brolin.

Arriving, Miguel Ordaz pulled up his white stallion as his men halted behind him. Dismounting, he went to Regina and, taking her hand, kissed it lightly. "Señorita Blakely," he said in a deep, pleasant voice.

"Mr. Ordaz," Regina began, "I don't know what to say. How do I thank you?"

"No thanks is necessary. I consider it an honor to help a beautiful *señorita.*"

Regina smiled warmly and decided immediately that she liked Miguel Ordaz regardless of his reputation. She knew Mace believed Ordaz had no values, but intuitively, Regina sensed that he was a man of integrity.

Miguel Ordaz was in his late forties, but his age was indiscernible. He had the physique of a man years younger, and as he removed his wide sombrero, Regina noticed that his full head of hair had hardly any gray. His wrinkle-free face smiled at Regina, and the whiteness of his teeth contrasted brightly against his dark complexion.

Miguel Ordaz was not handsome. He had never been handsome, not even in his youth. His eyes were too small for his broad face, and his black mustache curled up at the corners of his mouth, lending him a villainous appearance. But Miguel Ordaz was not ruthless, for an honest man had nothing to fear from him. He lived by his own rules, and with good cause, his enemies feared him. He could order a man's death without hesitation, but according to his rules, he never killed unjustly.

"Regina," Dan began, "Miguel has offered to loan you ten thousand dollars. He came back with Matt and me because he wants to hand Ramírez the money himself."

"Mr. Ordaz," Regina said gratefully, "I promise you that as soon as I can possibly manage it, I will pay you back in full."

Miguel smiled pleasantly. "Tomorrow I will pay a visit to Ramírez, and I promise you, he will bother you no more. Trust me, Señorita Blakely."

Looking deeply into his eyes, she answered, "I do trust you."

"*Señorita,* is it all right if my men and I set up camp beside the bunkhouse?"

"Yes, of course. But, Mr. Ordaz, you are welcome to stay in the house. I have a guest room."

"*Gracias,* but I will stay with my vaqueros."

Regina could no longer keep her gaze from Matt Brolin, so trying to appear nonchalant, she inched her way closer to his horse, and slowly raised her eyes.

Matt was sitting leisurely, one arm resting across the pommel of his saddle. He had a lit cigarette in his mouth, but sensing he was being observed, he removed the cigarette and lowered his gaze. Meeting Regina's eyes, he smiled roguishly. Dressed in black and with his pistol worn low on his hip, he looked extremely dangerous, much like a man who would draw his gun at the slightest provocation.

Tipping his hat, Matt nodded. "Howdy, ma'am." Conspicuously, his dark eyes roamed over the soft curves that her thin cotton dress accentuated.

"Mr. Brolin," she began, trying to appear completely composed, but she had been very aware of his intense scrutiny, "I also want to thank you for all your help."

37

"You're welcome," he replied carelessly, his piercing gaze now centered on her face. He was finding Regina refreshingly pretty.

Moving away from Matt and facing Miguel, Regina extended an invitation. "Mr. Ordaz, I hope you will be my guest for dinner."

"Gracias, señorita," Miguel replied.

Turning back to Matt, she added, "You are invited too, Mr. Brolin."

"Thank you, ma'am, but I've already made plans with your brother to ride into town." As he declined, Matt tugged gently on the bridle reins.

Disappointed that Matt Brolin wouldn't be a dinner guest, Regina sighed deeply as she watched him ride toward the bunkhouse.

Before leaving to go to town with Matt, Dan informed Miguel that he'd return in the morning to ride with him to Ramírez' ranch. The confrontation between Ordaz and Ramírez was one meeting Dan had no intention of missing.

Somewhat later, Mace and Julie stopped at the ranch, and Regina insisted that they stay for dinner. But the conversation at Regina's table was strained and uncomfortable.

Mace Edwards was not at ease with a man like Miguel Ordaz. He had always lived a quiet and respectable life, and had socialized with small ranchers like himself. He knew Miguel was looked up to by many Mexicans and that they believed him beyond reproach, but to Mace, Miguel was no better than a bandit. He found it very difficult to be civil to a man he considered totally without scruples.

Miguel was aware of Mace's obvious dislike for him,

but he found the man's hostility amusing and gave him only a passing regard. It was Julie who occupied his thoughts. Although she did nothing to draw a man's attention to her beauty, Miguel had detected her loveliness, and he'd been enthralled by Regina's quiet and reserved sister. He wondered if any man had ever aroused her passion. Chuckling inwardly, he decided that Mrs. Edwards had never once experienced sexual ecstasy, and if she remained married to Mace, he knew she never would. What a waste, he thought. A woman as beautiful as Regina's sister was made for love. How he wished he could be the one to turn the cold *señora* into a passionate wildcat. If Miguel had been a younger man, he would have found a way to capture Julie, and in his bed her slumbering passion would have been awakened.

When dinner was over, Miguel pulled out Regina's chair as she rose to her feet. *"Gracias, señorita* for the repast," he said cordially. "But if you will please excuse me, I must check on my vaqueros."

"I'll walk with you to the porch," Regina offered.

As Regina strolled to the front door beside Miguel, Mace and Julie remained seated. Watching them leave, Mace told his wife, "I don't understand how your sister can socialize so freely with a man like Ordaz."

Deciding not to get into a discussion with her husband about Regina, Julie suggested, "Why don't you go to the study and have a glass of brandy? I'll help Luisa with the dishes."

When Mace took her advice, Julie stared numbly down at the table. She sighed, and unexpected tears rolled down her cheeks. Puzzled, she wondered why she was crying.

Julie was too naïve to understand her sudden tears, but Miguel Ordaz could have told her why she was weeping. Julie was a woman unfulfilled.

As Miguel and Regina stepped onto the porch, she happened to glance in the direction of the corral. The darkness of night didn't prevent her from recognizing Matt Brolin. He was standing by the gate, observing the black stallion that was proudly galloping behind the circular fence.

Following Regina's gaze, Miguel informed her, "Señor Brolin told me about the night he met you. I think maybe he is very impressed with you."

"He is?" she asked instantly, confused as to why she thought it important to have made a good impression on Matt Brolin.

Laughing lightly, Miguel advised, "Why don't you go talk to him, *señorita?*" Tipping his sombrero and bidding her good night, Miguel walked off the porch and headed in the direction of his vaqueros.

Slowly Regina moved down the steps, and as she drew closer to Matt, her pulse began to quicken. She wondered why she felt so apprehensive about approaching this man whom she barely knew. Why had she suddenly become intimidated by him? That first night when they had met by chance, his presence certainly hadn't made her uneasy. But that had been before she'd seen him in daylight and had become aware of his sexual appeal.

Sensing Regina's approach, Matt turned away from the corral to watch her. He couldn't help but admire the sensual sway of her rounded hips as she walked up to stand at his side.

"Good evening, Miss Blakely," he said, touching the brim of his black hat.

"I was surprised to see that you had already returned from town."

40

"I didn't see any reason to linger," he answered lazily. Crossing his arms on the top of the fence, he continued to watch the stallion. "He's a magnificent animal," he murmured.

"He belonged to my father," Regina replied, her eyes following his. "The stallion's name is Midnight."

Matt chuckled, causing Regina to turn away from the stallion and look at him with puzzlement. "I'm sorry," Matt apologized, "but considering the dog's name, I thought you probably called the horse White Cloud or some similar name."

Regina smiled amiably. "Dan thinks I should change Blackie's name, maybe I'll take his advice."

"You don't want to do that. It'll just confuse the poor dog."

"I suppose you're right," she agreed. Enjoying his presence immensely, Regina watched Matt as he reached into his pocket and brought out a cheroot and a match. He struck the match against the fence, and as he lit the cigar, she studied him closely. He isn't exactly handsome, she decided, but he's so ruggedly attractive that just looking at him makes me feel wonderfully strange inside. She wondered how he had gotten the scar on his cheek. Apparently it had been made years ago because the scar was only vaguely noticeable.

Hoping for a tidbit, the stallion trotted over to them. Snorting loudly, he nudged his nose against Matt's shoulder. Laughing, the man reached over the fence and patted the horse.

As she observed Matt with the stallion, Regina was suddenly reminded of Mace telling her that Matt was a murderer and an outlaw. Surely Mace had been wrong! Matt certainly didn't seem like a ruthless criminal. Hoping she wasn't behaving too forwardly, she asked tentatively, "Mr. Brolin, how do you make a living?"

She could tell her question took him off guard, and

facing her, he stammered, "Didn't . . . didn't your brother tell you?"

"No," she answered.

"At present I'm a retired bounty hunter," he replied flatly.

"A bounty hunter!" she gasped.

"Does the profession shock you?" he asked, his tone defensive.

"I don't know," she said hesitantly. "I . . . I never met a bounty hunter before."

"I'm also an ex-convict," he told her none too gently.

Had Mace been right? Was Matt really a murderer and an outlaw? Dropping her gaze from his, she mumbled, "I'm sorry, Mr. Brolin. I didn't mean to pry."

"No. I'm the one who should apologize," he assured her hastily. "I guess I'm too touchy about my life."

A strained silence came between them as they both went back to watching the stallion who was once again prancing around the corral.

Thinking over what Matt had told her, Regina sensed intuitively that Matt was an honest and compassionate man in spite of his past. She felt if he'd open up and talk to her about himself, he would probably prove that she was right.

"Why does Mr. Ordaz despise Antonio Ramírez?" Regina asked curiously.

Matt took a long drag on his cigar before replying, "You're full of questions tonight, aren't you, Miss Blakely?"

His uninformative attitude was beginning to perturb her. "I learned a long time ago that the best way to get answers is to ask questions."

He was quiet for so long that she was sure he wasn't going to let her know about Ordaz and Ramírez, but finally he said, "Ramírez used to be a Comanchero, and Miguel hates Comancheros. Their personal war with each other goes back a long way."

"I like Mr. Ordaz," Regina stated simply.

Matt smiled, and she was glad to see that his mood had lightened. "I like him too," he replied, so quietly that she barely heard him.

Neighing, and moving proudly, the stallion trotted back to the fence. This time he went to Regina, and once more hoping for a handout, he nudged her shoulder with his nose.

The stallion's solid nudge sent Regina stumbling toward Matt, and he caught her in his arms to keep her from falling.

Finding herself in Matt's strong embrace caused a thrill to run through Regina, startling her. Why did his closeness feel so good? And why did she feel as though she belonged in his arms? Responding to Regina's tempting body pressed against his, Matt's firm hold tightened as he drew her even closer. She lifted her face to his; she wanted his lips on hers with every fiber of her being.

Matt's better judgment warned him to release her, to put Regina Blakely completely out of his thoughts. His future was in Wyoming, and hers was right here on this ranch. He couldn't let himself fall in love with her. He had worked too many years to save for his own ranch to let anyone interfere with his plans. Not even a woman as desirable as Regina!

Regina could see his indecision, and although she couldn't understand his inner conflict, she murmured pleadingly, "Matt, please kiss me."

Her sensual, but sweet, plea was more than Matt could resist, and his lips came down on hers with a force so demanding that his kiss was almost brutal.

His demanding kiss aroused Regina, and sliding her arms about his neck, she completely surrendered herself to him. As her lips parted, Matt's tongue entered her mouth, exploring and savoring her sweetness, while with one arm he encircled her waist, drawing her thighs flush to his so she could feel his hard desire pressed against her.

The stallion neighed again, and the horse's intrusion brought Matt back to his senses. As his prospective ranch in Wyoming crossed his mind, Matt released Regina with unexpected abruptness.

"Matt, what's wrong?" she asked, her knees weak from his electrifying kiss.

"Regina, I'll be leaving sometime tomorrow," he said with a calmness he was far from feeling. "Let's not start something we can't finish."

"But, Matt . . ." she began, wanting to be back in his arms.

"Good night, Miss Blakely," he said curtly, and turning swiftly, he headed toward the bunkhouse where Miguel's vaqueros had bedded down.

Staying by the corral, Regina watched his sudden retreat. Why had he kissed her so intensely, only to leave her so rudely?

The stallion edged himself closer to the fence, and Regina faced him so that she could place her arms around his powerful neck. For years she had turned down marriage proposals waiting for the man who was right for her. She strongly suspected that Matt Brolin was that man, but she had a depressing feeling that she had found him only to lose him.

After helping Luisa with the dishes, Julie decided to step outside for a breath of cool air. As she walked onto the front porch, a refreshing breeze greeted her, and sitting in the rocking chair, she undid the top button of her high-necked dress. Rocking gently, Julie closed her eyes. She felt very depressed. *If only I could have a baby,* she thought. *A child would bring me so much joy. Why must I be barren?*

"Señora Edwards." Miguel had suddenly walked up the short flight of steps.

Startled, Julie hurriedly fastened the button on her dress. "Mr. Ordaz," she stammered.

Sitting on the top step, Miguel removed his sombrero. Placing it beside him, he apologized, "I am sorry if I startled you."

Flustered, she replied, "That's all right." She made an attempt to compose herself, then proceeded, "If you're looking for my sister, I heard her come into the house a few minutes ago. I think she's in her bedroom, if you want I'll—"

Interrupting, he said, "I was not looking for Señorita Blakely. I was only taking a walk when I happened to see you sitting here by yourself. When I stepped up to the porch, you appeared to be very deep in thought."

"I was merely resting," she answered breathlessly.

Smiling, he asked, *"Señora,* do I make you uneasy?"

Fidgeting, she replied, "A little perhaps." Actually Julie was completely awed by this powerful man. She found his huge physique overwhelming and his reputation shocking. She was sure he was uncivilized, and that no woman was safe in his presence. She wanted desperately to get up and flee into the house, but her legs felt too weak to support her.

"Señora Edwards, please do not be frightened," he said tenderly.

Julie looked at him with surprise. She had no idea that her feelings were so obvious.

"I am not a monster," he continued. "I do not molest women, or chop off the heads of little children."

Unexpectedly, Julie found herself smiling. "I never pictured you as quite that ruthless," she answered.

45

"Do not judge a man by his reputation. Reputations have a way of becoming more legend than truth."

"And what is the truth?" Julie asked impetuously, shocking herself with her boldness.

"Behind the legend lies a lonely man."

"Lonely?" Julie couldn't imagine a man like Miguel Ordaz being lonely.

"Sí, Señora. Every day I am surrounded by my people. They love me very much, and I also love them. Yet, I am lonely." Noticing her expression of surprise, he asked, "You do not understand how a man can be lonely when he is loved?"

"No!" she cried. "I do understand how you feel! I am also loved, yet I am so desperately lonely!" Julie could feel a sudden blush rise to her cheeks. How could she have been so forward? She was thankful the blackness of night concealed her embarrassment.

"When my wife and I married, we were very young," Miguel began quietly, his voice easing Julie's discomfort. "She died shortly after our child was born, and I gave all my love to my daughter Rosa."

"You have a daughter?" she inquired.

Somberly, he replied, *"Sí,* I did. She was very beautiful and kind. But God took my Rosa. Perhaps to punish me."

"Oh no, Mr. Ordaz! I don't believe God takes our loved ones to punish us."

Leaning back against the post, he sighed, "I lost my daughter two years ago, and since then I have felt an emptiness, loneliness." He paused before changing the subject, *"Señora,* you speak of my reputation. What do you hear about me?"

Once again feeling uneasy, Julie stammered, "I only know what my husband has told me. Your hacienda is so large that it is like a village. You rule over your people as though you are their lord and master. When-

46

ever it suits you, you take the law into your own hands, and more than once you have ordered a man's execution."

Sí, Señora, many times I have seen men hanged. But you must consider that in Mexico, we do not live the way you live here. The New Mexico territory and the entire West will soon be very civilized. You have good laws and just ones. But in Mexico, men like myself must protect their people because there is no law to shelter them. But I am not a tyrant, *Señora.*" Sighing distinctly, he added, "I am only a man."

They remained silent for a moment; then, impulsively, Julie asked, "Why didn't you remarry?"

Shrugging his wide shoulders, he answered, "I do not know. Perhaps as time passed I became too set in my ways to change my life for a woman. But now I wish I had taken myself a wife. I am a rich man, yet I have no heir to inherit my wealth."

"But it isn't too late, Mr. Ordaz. You can still marry."

Chuckling, he answered, "You flatter me, *Señora.* At my age, I should start a family?"

Daringly, Julie asked, "Why not?"

"Señora Edwards, you are very good for an old man's ego."

Smiling coquettishly, she replied, "Mr. Ordaz, you aren't old. You're the kind of man who will never grow old." Julie had never flirted in her life, but she was happily doing so with Miguel Ordaz. And, surprisingly, she was enjoying every minute of it.

His deep laughter was jovial. "Such charming flattery coming from one so young and beautiful. *Señora,* I will cherish your generous compliment."

"Young and beautiful?" Julie asked teasingly. "Now who is being the flatterer?"

Studying her, Miguel queried, "Could it be, *Señora,*

that you are unaware of your beauty?"

Blushing, she answered, "My sister is the one who is beautiful."

"*Si*, Señorita Blakely is a very lovely woman. But why do you ignore the beauty God has given you?"

Before Julie could reply, Mace stepped out onto the porch. He hadn't expected to find his wife conversing with Miguel Ordaz, and he stared at them with astonishment.

Rising, Miguel said warmly, "*Buenas noches, Señora Edwards.*" He picked up his sombrero, and without bothering to acknowledge Mace's presence, he walked away.

Glaring at Julie, Mace demanded gruffly, "Why were you speaking alone with that man?"

Leaning back in the chair, Julie smiled at her husband. "Oh, Mace, we have misjudged the man. Miguel Ordaz is so kind!"

Flabbergasted, he stared at his wife. "Good Lord, you have taken leave of your senses!"

Chapter Four

Riding speedily toward Ramírez' ranch, Ordaz and his men were a threatening spectacle. But Antonio had been forewarned of their arrival, and as they rode up to his home, he and two of his men were on the porch waiting. As Miguel drew nearer, Antonio recognized Matt riding on the huge Mexican's right and Dan on his left.

Roughly, Miguel and the others pulled up their horses. The two men standing beside Antonio eyed Miguel cautiously. Matt judged them to be hired gunmen.

The moment the horses came to a stop, a group of Antonio's men walked around from the bunkhouse and the remainder of his vaqueros suddenly rode in from the direction of the corrals. Quickly they surrounded Ordaz and his men.

Chuckling, Miguel asked, "You were expecting me, *sí, señor?*"

"If you value your life," Antonio warned, "you'll get off my land!"

"My life!" Miguel exclaimed heartily. *"Amigo,* is that any way to welcome an old friend?"

Stepping forward, the taller of the two gunmen hissed, "Listen to me, Ordaz, you're outnumbered. So why don't you be smart and take Mr. Ramírez's advice?"

"Outnumbered?" Miguel questioned. "I think not, *Señor.*"

Suddenly, hoofbeats pounded at the entrance to the ranch, and the rest of Miguel's vaqueros materialized. Joining the others, they circled Antonio's men.

Tearing his gaze from Miguel's large group of vaqueros, the tall gunman said coldly, "If you're lookin' for a shootout, you're the first son of a bitch who'll die!"

Miguel's grin was close to a sneer. "You will find out, *Señor,* that I do not like to be called a son of a bitch."

The man stepped forward, but Antonio grabbed his arm. "Take another step, Dawson, and Ordaz will kill you!" Looking at Miguel, Antonio offered, "Come inside, and we'll have a glass of brandy." Cordially, he added, "Señor Brolin and Señor Butler, I'm sure you'll wish to join us."

The three men dismounted. Then Miguel reached up and removed his saddlebags, handing them to Dan. Taking his rifle, he held it at his side as he trailed the others into the house. The two gunmen followed cautiously.

Going to his study, Antonio walked briskly to his desk. Matt stepped into the room, but remained by the open door. Leaning against the wall, he nodded to Dan, conveying the message that he was to do the same. Confused, Dan moved to the other side of the doorway as Ordaz and the two gunmen entered the study.

Miguel halted abruptly, then swerving smoothly, he struck the butt of his rifle across Dawson's forehead, knocking him to the floor.

Swiftly, the other man reached for his pistol, but Matt instantly had his gun drawn. "Go ahead, gun-

slinger," Matt warned, "I need the target practice."
Carefully, the man let his hand drop to his side.

Dan looked on with amazement. Considering how
leisurely Matt had been leaning against the wall, Dan
wondered how he had managed to get his gun out so
damned fast.

Dawson wiped at the blood flowing from his cut
forehead as he looked fearfully up at the huge
Mexican. When he made an attempt to get to his feet,
Miguel quickly placed his foot on the man's hand.

"My God!" Dawson moaned. "If you break my
hand, I'm dead! I make my livin' with my gun."

"And you have many enemies, *sí?*" Miguel asked.

"Yeah! Hell, yeah!" Dawson muttered anxiously.

"If you very humbly apologize for calling me a son of
a bitch, maybe, *Señor,* I will not break your hand."

"All right! All right!" Dawson cried.

"I am waiting for my apology, *Señor,* and I'm not a
patient man." Miguel sneered.

"Okay!" Dawson yelled. Then, softening his tone, he
said, "I'm sorry I called you a son of a bitch."

Leaning his weight on the man's hand, Miguel asked,
"And what is my name?"

Grimacing with pain, the gunman answered hastily,
"Mr. Ordaz."

"Then, *Señor,*" Miguel stated calmly, "you should
say, I am sorry, Mr. Ordaz."

"I'm sorry, Mr. Ordaz! I'm sorry!" Dawson begged.

Miguel removed his foot; then, knowing Matt still
had his pistol drawn, he turned his back on the man
and sauntered casually to the desk. Looking at
Antonio, he said cheerfully, "Now that the pleasantries
are behind us, *amigo,* shall we get down to business?"

Glaring, Antonio ordered, "Get that sniveling
imbecile out of here!"

Quickly the other gunman hurried to Dawson and

helped him to his feet, and leaning on his comrade, he stumbled out of the door.

Shoving the door closed, Matt slipped his gun back into its holster.

"Come on over, *amigos*," Miguel called heartily, "and join us for brandy."

Antonio opened the bottle of brandy, then filled four glasses. He handed one glass to Matt and the other to Dan, but when he reached for the third one, Miguel swiftly grabbed the bottle, tilted it to his mouth, and helped himself to a large drink. Sitting in the chair, he remarked, "*Amigo,* you buy only the best liquor." Miguel hated Comancheros—he had witnessed their destructiveness and cruelty—and Antonio Ramírez had once been their leader. Miguel's deep resentment of Ramírez made him enjoy egging the man on.

Controlling his anger, Antonio took the chair behind the desk. He did not drink his brandy but sat silently, staring at Ordaz.

After swallowing another generous amount of brandy, Miguel told him, "My business with you will not take very long—which is good, because the sight of you turns my stomach."

A nerve twitched at the corner of Antonio's mouth as he clutched the arms of his chair. He didn't know why Ordaz had left his hacienda to visit him. He had believed when he had moved to Albuquerque that he would never again come into contact with the threatening Mexican. He did not understand why Dan Butler was riding with Miguel Ordaz.

Dan handed Miguel the saddlebags, and opening them, Ordaz removed a large stack of bills. Placing the money on the desk, he said, "Señorita Blakely's debt is paid in full. Now, if you will be so kind as to give me the deed, I will leave."

So Miss Blakely was his reason for being here. Of

course, that explained Butler's presence. Antonio pushed back his chair and, rising to his feet, walked across the room. He removed a large oil painting to reveal a wall safe. Quickly he turned the combination lock, and reaching inside, he brought out the deed to Regina's ranch. Returning, he handed it to Miguel.

Miguel examined the official document with care, then helped himself to another drink before standing. Placing the bottle on the desk, he then said, "Let us hope, Ramírez, that we do not meet again."

As Matt and Dan followed Miguel to the door, Antonio stated threateningly, "Ordaz, I promise you, we will meet again. And when we do, I will kill you!"

Without commenting, Miguel left the study with Matt and Dan.

Mace was at Regina's ranch when Miguel and the others returned, and he looked on in silence as Dan told Regina that her home was now secure. He was relieved to hear that the Black Diamond would remain in her hands, for his own ranch was smaller and less profitable and he expected, in time, to own Regina's property. He was certain that as soon as Regina faced all the difficulties connected with running a spread of this size, she would gladly hand over the deed to him. Regina was a very attractive young woman, and Mace was certain she'd soon marry and leave the ranch to live with her husband. Then the Black Diamond would belong exclusively to Julie and to him.

When Miguel asked Regina if they could talk privately, Mace wondered why the man wanted to speak with her alone. He didn't trust Miguel Ordaz, and after Regina had led Miguel into the study, Mace walked quietly to the closed door to eavesdrop.

Going to the small safe located in the corner of the

53

study, Regina knelt and placed the deed inside it. Then she rose and turned to face Miguel. Smiling, she asked, "How can I ever thank you?"

"Señorita, no thanks is necessary."

Perusing him, she replied, "My brother-in-law believes you are no better than a bandit, but he is so wrong."

"Do not let my act mislead you, when I find it imperative, I can be very cruel."

Nodding, she answered wisely, "Perhaps, but you could only be cruel to those who deserve it."

Miguel went to the chair in front of the desk, and before sitting down, he gestured to the one behind it. *"Señorita,* sit down. We need to talk."

Doing as he requested, Regina replied, "Mr. Ordaz, you sound so serious. Is something wrong?"

Trying to think of the correct words to use, Miguel's eyes roamed vacantly over the room. He glanced at the rifles hanging above the fireplace and the huge gun chest located against the far wall. Deciding the best approach was a direct one, he stated bluntly, *"Señorita,* you must find yourself a husband—and you must find him soon."

"What?" she gasped.

"You need a man to run this ranch," he explained.

Standing outside the study door, Mace leaned in closer, listening to their every word. Damn Ordaz! Why in the hell couldn't he mind his own business?

"I can run this ranch alone," Regina answered firmly.

"Then you will lose the Black Diamond, *"Señorita."*

"Why do you think that?" she asked.

"You are a woman living in a land that is still partially untamed. A woman alone cannot survive as a rancher in this part of the country. You need a man's protection. Also, *Señorita,* running a spread as large as

54

this one is work for a man. Your ranch hands and your foreman, it will not be easy for them to take orders from a woman."

"Well, they have been doing so recently." Regina said sternly.

Miguel lifted his huge frame, and leaning over the desk, he rested on the palms of his hands. Looking Regina straight in the eyes, he replied authoritatively, "I insist that you listen to me. The best protection for yourself and your ranch is a husband."

"But I'm not in love with anyone!" she exclaimed.

Sitting back down, Miguel shrugged. "Sometimes, *Señorita,* love comes after marriage."

"Mr. Ordaz," she began impatiently, "this conversation is a waste of time. I am not romantically involved, so there is no one for me to marry."

Removing his sombrero, Miguel placed it in his lap. Toying with its brim, he suggested tentatively, "Would you consider marrying Matt Brolin?"

"Matt!" she blurted out, obviously astounded.

"Why not?" he questioned.

"But, Mr. Ordaz . . ." she stammered.

Leaning forward, he eyed her sternly, "I have ten thousand dollars invested in your ranch, which gives me the right to advise you."

"And what exactly is your advice?" she asked, although it took much effort to keep her voice on an even keel.

"Marry Señor Brolin," he replied calmly.

Mace whirled away from the closed door. He had heard enough. So Miguel wanted Regina to marry Matt Brolin. Raging inwardly, Mace stomped out of the house. If she took Miguel's advice and married Brolin, then there was no hope of him ever owning the Black Diamond!

Regina rose from her chair, and this time she was the

one to lean on the desktop to stare into Miguel's eyes, "Mr. Ordaz, if you are implying that I should try to entrap Matt, then my answer to you is a firm no! When I marry it will be for one reason only!"

"Love?" he queried, raising his eyebrows.

"Of course!" she answered firmly.

"Sit down, *Señorita,*" he requested gently. As she returned to her chair, he told her, "I am sorry if I offended you. It was not done intentionally."

Forgiving him, Regina smiled. "Mr. Ordaz, I'm sure you were only trying to help me, and I certainly do not find the thought of marrying Matt Brolin offensive, quite the contrary. But basically I guess I'm too honest to trap him, or any man, into marriage." Placing her elbows on the desktop, she cupped her chin in her hands and asked inquisitively, "I thought Mr. Brolin was your friend, so why would you want me to entrap him?"

"Matt and I are very close friends. But I think, *Señorita,* that you would be good for Matt."

"Maybe he doesn't share your opinion," she muttered regretfully, recalling his brusque departure the night before.

Grinning, Miguel replied, "You and Matt will have two months together, and much can happen between two people in that amount of time."

Sitting up straight and looking at him confusedly, she questioned, sharply, "What are you talking about? Matt and I won't have two months together. In fact, he's leaving today for Wyoming."

"He will not be leaving, *Señorita.* This morning, I had a long talk with Matt, and after much persuasion on my part, I have convinced Matt to stay until he has your ranch running smoothly. He did not want to stay, but he did finally agree to remain for two months."

"You don't want him to go to Wyoming, do you?" she asked.

"No," he admitted.

"Why is he moving to Wyoming?"

"He plans to buy some land and build a ranch."

"But why in Wyoming?"

"He thinks maybe his reputation will not follow him there."

"Why are you so set against his leaving?"

Somberly, Miguel revealed, "I have no family left, but Matt is like a younger brother to me. If he moves to Wyoming, I am afraid that I might never see him again." Miguel sighed heavily, then continued. "I have no family to love, but I love Matt as though he were truly a brother."

"So you talked him into staying here, hoping that Matt would fall in love with me and knowing if Matt is living on this ranch, he won't be so far away from you," she surmised.

Pleadingly, he questioned, *"Señorita,* is it so wrong for me to feel that way?"

"No, Mr. Ordaz, it isn't exactly wrong, but you can't run his life for him."

"I know, *señorita,"* he conceded. "But you do need Matt's help, and he will put your ranch in order." Smiling hopefully, he added, "And maybe you and Matt will fall in love, *sí?"*

Remembering the passionate kiss she and Matt had shared, Regina sighed dreamily, "Yes, maybe we will."

Miguel left the house intending to find Matt, and as he walked outside, he saw Julie drive up in a buckboard. He went to assist her and, taking the horse's reins, tied them to the hitching rail. As she stood to step down from the wagon, he hurried to her side. Putting his strong hands on her waist, he lifted her into the air and then placed her on her feet.

Smiling down into her face, Miguel said warmly, "Señora Edwards, it is good to see you again."

Finding his powerful presence overwhelming, Julie said breathlessly, "I was on my way home from town, and I thought I'd stop by and see if my husband is here." Was that really true? she wondered suddenly, or had she been hoping to see Miguel? Abashed by her own thoughts, she asked uneasily, "Do you know if Mace is in the house?"

"He was earlier, but I think he left."

"As long as I'm here, I suppose I'll visit with my sister." Julie started to walk to the porch, but touching her arm, Miguel halted her. *"Señora,* please don't leave." The sun's rays shone on Julie's reddish brown hair, causing it to shine with a shimmering radiancy. As her large eyes looked up at Miguel, they mysteriously softened with an expression similar to love. A sudden blush appeared in her cheeks, contrasting beautifully with her pale complexion. Miguel caught his breath in admiration. Removing his hand from her arm, he spoke tenderly, "You are as lovely as an angel."

Embarrassed, she glanced away as she stammered, "Th . . . thank you, Mr. Ordaz."

Once again, he touched her arm. Shyly, she looked up at him. *"Señora,* today I will be leaving." His hold tightened as he added, "But I will come back someday soon and see Señorita Blakely. Very much, I hope I will also see you." Julie was very aware of his hand touching her arm, and surprisingly, she found his touch pleasing.

Impulsively, she replied, "But, Mr. Ordaz, why would you want to see me? I am a married woman!" Embarrassed by her outburst, Julie stepped back, and stumbling over her words, she said quickly, "Forgive me for being . . . so forward."

"Someone as lovely as an angel, should not be so

unhappy," Ordaz murmured sympathetically.

Trying to conceal the truth, Julie replied, "I am not unhappy. I have given you the wrong impression."

"You and Señor Edwards have been married many years, *sí?*"

"Yes," she answered, puzzled by his question.

"Yet you have no children. Do you believe a child would make you happy?"

Fleetingly, Julie knew she should reproach the man for probing into her personal life, but instead, she cried sincerely, "Yes . . . oh yes!"

Cautiously, he moved closer. He was afraid to move too fast, afraid he would frighten her, causing her to run away. Being small, Julie barely came to his shoulders, and due to his height, she had to lift her head to see into his eyes. Although Miguel was not handsome, his looks were not intimidating. The expression in his eyes could be cold and ruthless, but it could also be tender. And it was with extreme tenderness that he studied Julie's upturned face. He stepped even closer, and his brawny physique towered over her delicate frame.

"Are you in love with Señor Edwards?" he asked.

Taken aback by his question, she answered hesitantly, "Yes . . . of course I love my husband."

"A woman can feel love for a brother or a friend, but she should be in love with the man who shares her bed."

Blushing, Julie inhaled sharply. Seeing her discomfort, Miguel continued hastily, "I sometimes forget that most *gringas* are taught from early childhood that love between a man and woman is degrading and should be kept behind locked doors."

Julie felt flushed, and she brushed her hand across her warm brow. "Mr. Ordaz," she pleaded, "this conversation must cease immediately."

Miguel smiled. "I can see in your eyes that you do not

59

love Señor Edwards. Believe me, *Señora,* if I were a younger man, I would not let your husband stand in my way." His smile broadening, he then said, *"Adios,* my lovely angel."

Stunned, Julie watched him as his long strides carried him in the direction of the bunkhouse.

Chapter Five

It was late afternoon before Matt decided to talk to Regina. Luisa let him into the house, then showed him into the study where he found Regina sitting at her father's desk going over some papers. Upon hearing him enter, she glanced up, and he strode across the room, smiling as he asked, "What are you doing?"

Regina wished his presence didn't have such a strong affect on her. She wondered why she couldn't see his smile as nothing more than a friendly gesture. Why must she notice that his grin was slightly crooked, that it had a boyish appeal capable of melting a woman's heart.

"I'm examining Papa's ledgers," she explained, her pulse quickening as he drew closer.

Moving around the desk, he stood at her side and looked over her shoulder, to study the open book. His closeness disturbed her, made her feel flushed and a little uncomfortable. She thought about their intimate embrace the night before, and remembering the thrill of having his arms about her, she wanted desperately to stand up and draw him so close that their bodies would be flush.

"From what I have already read," Matt stated flatly,

"it looks like your father kept his records incompetently."

Surprised, she turned her head to look up into his dark eyes. "What are you saying?"

Stepping back from her chair, he declared evenly, "I'm saying that your father apparently did not keep his records straight." He hesitated, then continued. "It looks like this job is going to be harder than I thought. It's going to take a lot of work to get this ranch in proper order."

Resenting his attitude, she said peevishly, "Mr. Brolin, I did not ask you to take this job, and as far as I'm concerned you can leave anytime you wish."

He quirked an eyebrow, and Regina wished the gesture didn't make him look so charming. How could she conceivably stay perturbed with him when she found him so irresistible?"

"Miss Blakely," he began tolerantly, "I am here as a favor to Miguel, and I will see this job completed."

"Oh?" she quipped. "Do you suppose you can complete everything in only two months, since there is apparently so much to do?"

He shrugged nonchalantly. "I told Miguel that I'd stay for two months, and I intend to keep my word." Then he grinned devilishly. "After that, little darlin', you're on your own."

"Will you leave for Wyoming?" she asked.

He looked at her questioningly. "How did you know I was planning to go to Wyoming?"

"Dan told me about it this morning, and before Mr. Ordaz left, he mentioned it to me." Hesitantly, she continued, "Mr. Brolin, I'm sorry that you had to postpone your trip. Mr. Ordaz shouldn't have imposed on you."

Ambling around the desk and sitting in the chair across from her, he studied Regina with an expression she couldn't fathom.

Matt knew it wasn't Regina's fault that he was still here instead of on his way to Wyoming. It was Miguel who had insisted that he stay, and he didn't really blame Miguel. The man had a lot of money invested in this ranch, and there was little chance of it being paid back if someone didn't step in and straighten out the mess James Blakely had made of everything. Taking careful note of Regina's beauty, Matt sighed deeply. It was going to be damned hard to be in her tempting company for two months without becoming emotionally involved with her. If he and Regina were to fall in love, would she give up her ranch and go with him to Wyoming, where nothing awaited them except a piece of vacant land? That would be a great sacrifice to expect any woman to make, especially one who was used to living in relative luxury. Deciding it would be best to keep some distance between himself and the enticing Regina Blakely, he said formally, "Miss Blakely, there's a combination lock on the safe. Write down the combination for me."

Taking a piece of paper from the desk drawer, Regina jotted down the combination, then handed it to Matt.

Taking the slip of paper, he folded it and put it into his pocket. "Miss Blakely—" he began.

Interrupting, Regina asked, "If we're going to be working together, don't you think we should be on a first-name basis?"

"Who said we'd be working together?" Matt remarked dryly. He sure as hell wasn't about to have Regina as a constant companion. His will power could be stretched only so far.

"Of course we'll be working with each other," Regina insisted. "This does happen to be my ranch."

Leaning back in his chair, Matt replied, "Miss

Blakely, why don't you oversee the cooking and house-cleaning and let me take care of business?"

Standing and glaring at him, Regina snapped, "Mr. Brolin, you are impertinent. How dare you insinuate that I belong strictly in the house!"

"Don't you?" he asked coldly.

"I have always taken an interest in this ranch," she replied angrily.

"Do you know why it's been run so badly?" he asked.

"Operating the ranch was Papa's job, and he never bothered to show me how to take care of the paper-work involved. But he was more interested in gambling than being a rancher, and that's why this ranch is no longer turning a profit." She hurried around the desk to stand beside Matt's chair. Imploringly, she continued, "Mr. Brolin, I'm sure I can learn all there is to know about running the Black Diamond. Will you please teach me?"

"Why?" he questioned. "You have an honest and reliable foreman, he'll be able to take care of this ranch for you."

"You don't understand!" she pleaded. "I love this ranch, it means everything to me! The only way I can ever be sure that I'll never lose my home is to learn how to run this spread myself!"

"This ranch means that much to you?" he asked carefully.

"Yes!" she cried.

Matt looked away from Regina and stared thoughtfully across the room. His intuition had been right. This ranch commanded Regina's loyalty, and he seriously doubted if she'd ever love a man as much as she loved her home.

"Matt," she murmured, using his first name, "will you teach me?"

"I'll think about it," he mumbled.

64

Deciding not to pressure him, Regina replied, "I'll leave you alone so that you can look over Papa's records."

She turned to leave, but he stopped her by saying, "Miss Blakely, hereafter, if you should come to the study at night, you will knock on the door and wait to be invited inside."

"Why?" she demanded.

"I intend to move into this room. The sofa will suffice as a bed." Stretching out his long legs and reclining farther in the chair, he glanced up at her with a cocky grin. "I always sleep nude, and if you were to barge in some night, it might prove to be a trifle embarrassing."

Regina was taken off guard by his brazen remark. "You . . . you sleep nude?"

His brown eyes twinkling, he suggested, "It's very unrestrained, very comfortable. You should try sleeping that way yourself."

"How do you know I don't?" she quipped saucily, taking him by surprise. Then she walked away from him and left the room.

It was dusk when Matt left the ranch to ride into town. He had made the decision to visit Dan's saloon on the spur of the moment, and putting away his paperwork, he had hurried out of the study to head straight for the stables. The solution to his problem occurred to him all at once. The best way to put Regina Blakely out of his thoughts was to find another woman—the kind of woman who wouldn't seek emotional ties, one who would simply satisfy the ache that had been in his loins since he had kissed Regina. He needed a prostitute, and he knew Dan had four of them working for him.

As usual, Dan's saloon was crowded, and as Matt stepped inside, he had to maneuver his way past the customers to make his way to the bar. Spotting Dan talking to the bartender, he joined him.

Pouring Matt a glass of whiskey, Dan inquired, "When are you leaving for Wyoming?"

"In two months," Matt answered flatly.

"Why the delay?"

"Miguel asked me to stay on and get Regina's ranch running smoothly."

Surprised, Dan raised his eyebrows, exclaiming, "You agreed to stay? Why?"

Picking up his glass, Matt downed the shot of whiskey. "Damned if I know why."

Dan was tempted to delve deeper into Matt's reason for staying, but knowing Matt wouldn't take kindly to his probing, he decided to change the subject. "Is there any special reason why you came to town? Are you looking for a card game?"

Shaking his head, Matt smiled slyly. "What I'm lookin' for isn't a game of cards."

Comprehending, Dan grinned. "Let me introduce you to Claire." Nodding toward the piano, he added, "That's her over there."

Turning, Matt watched Claire as she talked to the man playing a lively tune on the piano. She was a buxom woman, and her flaming red hair was piled high on top of her head in a mass of tight curls. As Matt turned back to the bar to pour himself another drink, he caught sight of the woman descending the stairs.

"Who is she?" he asked.

Following Matt's gaze, Dan replied, "That's Dolly. Do you prefer her to Claire?"

Matt nodded, "Yeah, I sure do."

"Dolly!" Dan called loudly.

Hearing her name, Dolly looked over at them, and smiling, she headed toward the bar. Dolly was a tall, slim woman with blond hair that fell smoothly to her shoulders.

As she drew nearer, Dan remarked, "She looks a lot like Regina, doesn't she?"

"I hadn't noticed," Matt answered too quickly.

Guessing the reason behind Matt's hasty denial, Dan replied shrewdly, "The hell you didn't notice."

With her short red skirt swaying provocatively, Dolly paused in front of Dan and Matt. "Did you want to see me, boss?"

"I'd like you to meet a good friend of mine," Dan commented. "This is Matt Brolin."

Dolly's green eyes traveled boldly over Matt's strong, lean frame, letting her vision linger on the bulge in his tight black trousers. Slowly she transferred her intense scrutiny to his face, and his sensual handsomeness caused her pulse to race with anticipation. "Matt Brolin," she murmured invitingly, "why don't we take a bottle up to my room where we can be alone?"

Studying Dolly, Matt suddenly found himself comparing her with Regina. Dolly's makeup was applied heavily, and the smell of her cheap cologne was overwhelming. Thinking of Regina's natural beauty, and recalling the light, tantalizing aroma of her perfume, Matt swerved back to the bar and lifted his glass.

"Matt?" Dolly pressed. "Don't you want to come up to my room?"

"Maybe later," he mumbled, his turned back dismissing her.

Disappointed, Dolly walked away and Dan asked, "Is something bothering you, Matt?"

He shook his head. "No, I'm just not in the mood for Dolly."

"Well you were definitely in the mood when you came in here," Dan argued.

"I changed my mind, all right?" Matt spat short-temperedly. He downed his shot of whiskey, then slammed the glass down on the bar. He'd been a fool to think a prostitute could ease the longing he had for Regina. By God, he wanted Regina Blakely and no other woman would do!

"Matt," Dan began curiously, "why does moving to Wyoming mean so much to you?"

Matt's eyes looked sharply into Dan's. He wasn't used to explaining himself and usually resented anyone prying into his affairs, but he liked Dan Butler. As the hardness went out of his eyes, he answered evenly, "It's not Wyoming that means so much to me. I just happened to pick Wyoming. I could just have easily settled for Colorado, or even Montana. I've never had a permanent residence, so I have no roots to tie me to one particular place."

"Then it's the ranch you intend to build that is important to you?" Dan queried.

Matt nodded. "I want a place that I can call home."

"I never dreamed having a home meant that much to you."

"Don't we usually want what we've never had?" Matt responded, looking at Dan questioningly. He filled his glass, then drank the whiskey in one swallow. Placing the glass on the bar, he nodded. "See you around, Butler."

Using long strides, Matt moved toward the swinging doors. When he was halfway across the room, Dolly caught up to him. Clutching his arm, she asked anxiously, "You aren't leaving, are you?"

"I need a good night's sleep, I have a full day facing me tomorrow." Cuffing her gently on the chin, he smiled charmingly. "Maybe some other time, Dolly."

Returning to the ranch, Matt stabled his horse. It was fairly late and the night was quiet. The lights in the bunkhouse were extinguished for the ranch hands had already retired, but Matt headed in the direction of the house. Blackie heard his approach and bounded from the front porch. Seeing the huge dog coming straight toward him, Matt halted, and when Blackie playfully jumped up on him, he patted the animal's head. He was already quite taken with the dog and had spent part of the day making friends with him. Tail wagging, Blackie once again leaped up, and his large paws pounded against Matt's chest.

Chuckling, Matt ordered fondly, "Down, boy."

Obeying, Blackie sat on his haunches, and looking up at Matt, he whined softly.

As Matt resumed his walk to the house, Blackie followed him, trotting close behind. Taking the porch steps in one long stride, Matt glanced back down at the dog. "See you tomorrow, Blackie," he said.

Quietly, Matt moved down the hallway to the study. When he noticed a light shining under the door, he wondered if he'd forgotten to turn off the lamp before he left. He swung open the door.

Regina was standing in front of the bookcase when Matt entered. Her back was turned, but hearing him enter, she whirled about.

The unexpected sight of Regina dressed in a flowing, sheer negligée, caused Matt's steps to falter. For a moment, he was stunned by her seductive beauty; then regaining his composure, he closed the door before walking farther into the room.

"Matt," she explained hastily, using his first name without conscious thought, "Juan told me you had ridden into town. If I had known that I might see you, I would have dressed more fittingly. I wanted to read awhile before sleeping, so I came here to get a book."

"You owe me no explanation," he replied evenly. "This is your home, and you have every right to dress as

69

you please." He looked away from her deliberately and sauntered toward the desk. My God, she was tempting enough in a dress or riding clothes, but to see Regina in a flimsy night gown was almost more than he could bear. The ache in his loins became even more uncomfortable.

Lifting the brandy bottle from the desktop, he wrenched it open. Taking a glass, he filled it.

"Mind if I join you?" Regina asked, walking over to stand beside him.

He got a whiff of her perfume; it smelled as sweet as lilacs. "Do you drink hard liquor?" he queried, keeping his tone even.

"Papa was a brandy drinker, and I used to join him for a drink occasionally."

Pouring her brandy, he turned to hand her the glass, but as he did so, his arm brushed across her soft breasts. Tensing, Matt took a couple of steps to the side.

Accepting her glass, she smiled enticingly as she raised it. "Here's to better times."

"Better times?" he pondered.

"When the Black Diamond will be prosperous once again." She was puzzled to see a frown flicker across his face. "Did I say something wrong?"

"Of course not," he said firmly. He raised his glass. "Here's to your ranch, Miss Blakely. May it reign supreme."

"And we must also drink to your future ranch," she added, although she wished with all her heart that he wasn't planning to go away.

He placed his glass to his lips and downed his drink. Joining him, Regina finished her brandy in one swallow.

Taking her glass, he placed it with his on the desk. "It's getting late, Miss Blakely, don't you think we should turn in for the night?" If she stayed in this room one minute longer, he just might forget that she was his friend's sister, as well as a lady, and ravish her with or without her permission.

"I wish you'd call me Regina," she pleaded, unaware of why he wanted her to leave.

"All right!" he agreed impatiently. "I'll call you Regina." His eyes piercing hers, he demanded, "Regina, go to bed!"

Piqued, she snapped, "Well, you don't have to be so rude!"

"And you don't have to run around the house half-naked!"

"You just told me how I dressed was my own business!" she reminded him sharply.

Reacting impulsively, he reached out and grabbed her wrist, jerking her close. "You innocent little fool! Don't you realize that dressing gown is almost transparent? Do you have any idea how damned tempting you are? Just how much do you think a man can take?"

Regina knew she should find his remarks in bad taste and reproach him, but instead she was thrilled. He wanted her! Apparently, he wanted her so badly that he could barely control his emotions!

"Matt," she whispered, her green eyes glazed with desire, "don't you know how I feel about you?" She pulled her wrist free of his grip, then daringly slid her arms about his neck, bringing his lips down on hers.

Matt's restrained passion exploded, and he drew her to him so tightly that her body was molded to his. His mouth opened over hers, and as his tongue probed between her teeth, his hands moved to her buttocks pinning her thighs against his firm manhood.

Feeling his hardness pinpointed excitingly against the softness between her legs, Regina experienced a longing so intense that she couldn't stop the moan that came from deep in her throat.

A loud knock on the door broke them apart, and trying to compose himself, Matt called testily, "Who is it?"

Opening the door a crack, and peeking inside the room, Luisa said timidly, *"Señorita,* Juan and I are retiring for the night." Opening the door a little wider, and edging herself around it, her eyes traveled over Regina's flimsy dressing gown. Protectively, she said, "And, *señorita,* I think before I go to bed, maybe I will see you to your room."

Regina looked hopefully at Matt, wanting desperately for him to ask her not to leave.

"You had better go with Luisa," he declared.

"But, Matt . . ." she argued.

"Good night, Regina," he said with finality.

"Good night, Matt," she mumbled. Confused and angry, she followed Luisa out of the room.

Matt poured himself another drink, downing it immediately. He was falling in love with Regina. He could feel it, he could sense it! But the knowledge brought him no pleasure, only a disturbing restlessness. Regina Blakely, heir to the Black Diamond, which would soon be prosperous again. And what did he have to offer her? A piece of land he hadn't even purchased yet? Marry me, Regina, he daydreamed bitterly. Marry me and give up your ranch so that you can run off with me to Wyoming and endure the pioneer life! Matt laughed harshly, deciding his resolution to keep a distance between himself and Regina was still the best answer. All he had to do was find a way to avoid her.

Chapter Six

Regina awoke early the next morning, and certain that Matt would begin teaching her about the ranch, she hurried out of bed. She was sure that Matt would want her to accompany him on the range, so she removed her riding apparel from the wardrobe. Hastily she slipped into her suede skirt and a long-sleeved plaid blouse, also donning the fringed vest that matched her skirt. Then she stepped to the vanity table and brushed her blond hair with brisk strokes. Having finished, she hurried to the bed, sat on the edge, and slipped into her boots. Anxious to spend the day with Matt, her steps were lively as she moved across the floor. Remembering to grab her wide-brimmed, suede hat from the top of the wardrobe, she darted out of the room and down the hall to the study. Finding the door standing open, she glanced into the room, but Matt wasn't there. Wondering where he could be, she decided to ask Luisa if she had seen him.

Regina hurried to the kitchen, but Luisa was not in evidence. As she turned to rush in the direction of the parlor, Juan entered through the back door.

"Have you seen Matt?" Regina asked him.

"Señor Brolin left at dawn," he answered.

"Where did he go?" she exclaimed, her heart suddenly thumping. Surely Matt hadn't left for good! He'd promised Miguel Ordaz he'd stay for two months!

"He said he would be on the west range until noon," Juan replied.

Regina sighed with relief. "Will you please saddle Midnight for me?" she requested, deciding to ride out and find Matt.

"Are you going to town?" Juan wanted to know.

Her green eyes shining brightly and her cheeks glowing with vitality, Regina explained, "No, I plan to spend the day with Matt." Her voice ringing with excitement, she continued, "Matt's going to teach me how to run this ranch!"

Regina noticed the look of disapproval that appeared on Juan's wrinkled face. She should have known he would be against the idea. He was a man and most likely believed a woman's place was in the home. Men! They could be an insufferable lot!

When Juan made no move to leave, she reminded him firmly, "My horse? Will you saddle him for me?"

"*Sí, señorita,*" he conceded hesitantly.

As Juan walked out the back door, Regina grabbed the coffeepot from the stove. She'd have a cup of coffee before leaving, but she was much too excited to eat breakfast.

Regina made a striking picture as she rode her sleek black stallion across the rolling plains. Wanting to feel the wind blowing through her hair, she removed her hat, and the thong tied under her chin kept it from falling. Regina longed to give Midnight free rein and race over the landscape, but Blackie was accompanying her, so she kept the spirited stallion at a steady gallop.

The Rio Grande, which flowed through the western portion of Blakely land, made the west range a fertile, grassy area bordered by ponderosa pines and spruces.

A short distance from the grazing cattle, Matt and the foreman were standing together and discussing business. When they became aware of Regina's approach, Matt told the foreman that he'd talk to him later; then he moved away to meet her.

Pulling up the stallion, Regina dismounted quickly, and as Matt walked up to her, she asked pertly, "Why did you leave at dawn? Couldn't you have waited until a more decent hour?"

"I like to get an early start," he answered somewhat impatiently. He wished Regina wasn't looking so damned beautiful.

Smiling, she said briskly, "Well, I'm ready to start learning."

"Regina, I only intend to stay two months, which means I won't have time to teach you about ranching." His voice was apologetic, but he was determined to stick to his decision to avoid her company whenever possible.

"But you promised!" she blurted, although she knew he had never actually made a commitment.

"I told you that I'd think about it," he put in quickly. "Well, I thought about it and decided I don't have time."

"But, Matt—"

"Regina," he began testily, "your foreman is a trustworthy and competent man. He can run this ranch for you very sufficiently."

"What if he should decide to quit?" she argued. "I have no guarantee that he'll remain here permanently!"

"There are no guarantees in life, Regina," Matt remarked with an aloofness he didn't really feel.

Desperate, she reached out and grasped his arm.

75

"Matt, you must help me! There's so much I need to learn!"

"For instance?" he questioned.

Releasing her hold on his arm, she cried, "Everything!"

"Everything, Regina?" He grinned indolently. "Shall I begin by teaching you how to rope and tie a steer? And then, of course, you can learn how to brand him." Stepping to her horse, he took the reins and handed them to her, saying curtly, "I have a lot of work to do, so why don't you go back home?"

"Why don't you go to the devil, Matt Brolin!" she spat out angrily. Jerking the reins from his hand, she mounted and dug her heels sharply into the stallion's sides, causing the beast to take off with a sudden start.

Matt watched Regina until she disappeared over a grassy incline. He despised himself for treating her curtly. She had been so happy, and he had totally shattered her mood. He didn't think it was a mistake for her to take an interest in the ranch and to want to learn more about it, although a foreman would always be essential to handle certain jobs. There was no reason why she couldn't successfully operate her own ranch. He had refused to help her strictly because he was trying to avoid her. He didn't want to fall in love with Regina and he was determined to keep a safe distance between them.

Regina had never felt so angry, but she wasn't sure whether she was more upset with Matt or with herself. Matt's ambivalence was enough to drive her to anger, but, all the same, she was annoyed at herself for letting him hurt her so deeply.

Suddenly, catching sight of a man riding in her direction, Regina halted the stallion. As the rider drew closer, she recognized him. "Oh no!" she groaned.

"Considering the mood I'm in, I don't need a confrontation with Antonio Ramírez!"

Stopping his horse alongside Regina's, Antonio flashed a friendly smile. *"Buenos días, señorita."*

Her expression revealing her dislike, Regina asked, "Is there any special reason why you're on my land?"

"I was looking for you. Your house servant told me where you had gone."

"Mr. Ramírez," she stated coldly, "if this is a social call, then I think I should tell you that I have no wish to see you."

"Señorita Blakely," he said cheerfully, "can't we let bygones be bygones? Your papa gave me the deed to this ranch as collateral. To me it was merely a business arrangement. I would not remain prosperous very long if I allowed sentiment to interfere with business. You asked for an extension, and I turned you down. It would not have been wise on my part if I had agreed to your terms."

"Perhaps," Regina replied irritably. "Are you now planning to tell me that propositioning me was also business?"

"No, *señorita,* I do not intend to tell you that was business. But I did come here to apologize. I am usually a gentleman, but that night I behaved very rudely. I am truly sorry, and I hope very much that you will forgive me."

Regina wasn't sure that he was sincere. "Mr. Ramírez, let's just forget about that night, shall we?"

"Does that mean you are harboring no hard feelings and accept my apology?"

"Let's just say, I'm willing to give you the benefit of the doubt."

Offering her his hand, he said genially, "Let us be friends, *señorita."* When Regina obviously hesitated, he proceeded, "Perhaps the term *friends* implies more than you want to give, so let us be . . . civil acquaintances?"

Regina smiled, although she hadn't intended to do so. Antonio Ramírez's charms were hard to resist so, giving him her hand, she consented, "Very well, Mr. Ramírez, we will be civil acquaintances."

He shook her hand gently, then released it. "Are you returning to the house?" he asked.

"Yes," she answered.

"May I ride with you?"

Regina agreed, and as they started their horses into a brisk walk, Antonio said, "I understand that Matt Brolin is now working for you."

"He isn't exactly working for me," she specified. "Miguel Ordaz asked him to stay temporarily until the ranch is in order. It seems as though Papa made a mess of everything. You were right that night when you told me Papa cared more about his gambling than his ranch."

Encouragingly, he told her, "Do not worry, *señorita*. Señor Brolin knows what he is doing. He will get your ranch back up to its potential. You would be wise to listen to his advice."

"Advice!" she said bitterly. "I can't very well take his advice when he refuses to tell me anything."

He looked at her uncertainly. "He will not advise you?"

"No," she replied peevishly. "I have never met a man so stubborn, obstinate, and . . . and bullheaded!"

Laughing heartily, Antonio agreed, *"Sí,* that sounds like Señor Brolin. He is all you say and much more."

"How well do you know Matt?" she asked curiously.

"Well enough to know that he is not a man I would care to cross."

His uninformative reply perturbed Regina. She was

78

irritated because men were so close-mouthed. Suddenly, feeling terribly depressed, Regina sighed deeply.

Noticing her discontent, Antonio asked tenderly, "Are you unhappy about something, *señorita?*"

"I'm not especially unhappy," she found herself confiding. "I'm just very upset."

"Would you care to tell me about it?"

"Antonio," she began, unconsciously aware that their short acquaintance had already led to a first-name basis, "I know very little about how a ranch is supposed to operate. I used to plead with Uncle Carl to teach me, but he never took me seriously. Then after my uncle died, I told Papa that I wanted to learn, but he always put me off, promising that someday he'd get around to teaching me. I foolishly believed that Matt Brolin would help me, but he's even worse than Uncle Carl and Papa were."

"Worse?" Antonio asked.

"Yes!" she said firmly. "Matt told me I should oversee the cooking and house cleaning. It's quite obvious where he believes a woman belongs!"

Antonio suppressed an urge to laugh because he was certain that Regina would be offended and think he was making fun of her. *"Señorita,"* he began, "the night you came to my house, I treated you unfairly, and I would like to prove that I am sincerely sorry."

"I don't understand," she answered, confused.

"Let me make amends by teaching you everything you need to learn about ranching."

Regina was amazed. "Do you really mean it?" she exclaimed.

Chuckling, and admiring her enthusiasm, he assured her, *"Sí,* I am very serious."

"Antonio." This time she caught herself and hesitantly, inquired, "May I call you Antonio?"

"Please do, *señorita.*"

"And you must call me Regina," she told him before asking hastily, "When can you start teaching me?"

"I do not have too much spare time, but I should be able to give you at least two afternoons a week. Will that be all right?"

"That'll do just fine," she answered. Then, smiling brightly, she added, "And thank you very much."

Antonio was totally entranced by Regina's enticing loveliness, and he replied graciously, "You are more than welcome, but, believe me, having your charming company two afternoons a week will be a pleasure."

It was fairly late in the evening when Regina left her bedroom and walked down the hall to the study with determined strides. It wasn't until she raised her hand to knock on the closed door that she hesitated and letting her hand drop to her side, apprehensively paced back and forth. Don't be such a coward, she told herself. What you plan to do isn't wrong. Antonio said that he'd help you and you very gratefully accepted his kind offer, so why are you afraid to tell Matt that Antonio will be teaching you about ranching? After all, it is Matt's fault that you turned to Antonio for help. If Matt hadn't so rudely refused to teach you, then you wouldn't have been compelled to turn to someone else for assistance.

The hall wasn't carpeted, and as Regina continued pacing, her hard-soled slippers clicked against the polished hardwood floor. When the study door opened suddenly, Regina's steps halted abruptly as Matt stepped into the hall.

"I suppose you have a good reason for pacing back and forth in front of this room."

"Matt, I need to . . . to talk to you." She hesitated, her eyes trailing intently over his attractive frame. She wondered if he had been preparing to retire because his beige shirt was unbuttoned and hanging outside his dark trousers.

"All right." He complied, moving aside so that she could step into the study.

Determined not to let him intimidate her, Regina raised her chin proudly, and as she walked past him, she clutched her long skirt so it wouldn't brush against his legs.

Leaving the door ajar, Matt followed her into the room. Regina paused in front of the desk, and joining her, Matt leaned back against the desk top, crossing his arms over his chest. Eying her curiously, he asked, "What do you need to talk to me about?"

Taking a deep breath, Regina explained, "This morning, after you so rudely dismissed me, I ran into Antonio Ramírez on my way back to the house. He has offered to teach me about ranching. I thought you should be informed of that. Should you see him at the ranch, you'll know his reason for being here."

When Matt didn't respond, but merely continued to watch her, she proceeded, "If you have any objection to Antonio's presence, I think you should state it now."

He shrugged insouciantly. "It's none of my business, but I don't think Miguel would approve."

"Well, Miguel Ordaz is in Mexico, so I can't very well ask him his opinion, can I?" she pointed out impatiently.

"I guess not," he mumbled.

His aloofness was upsetting her, but Regina tried to keep her voice steady. "What exactly do you think of Antonio Ramírez?"

"At times, he can be tolerable," Matt grumbled.

"Then, apparently you don't dislike him as much as Mr. Ordaz does?"

Moving lithely, Matt went behind the desk and sat in

the chair. "Miguel has his own reasons for not liking Ramírez, and in my estimation, they are valid reasons. Ramírez was a Comanchero, and Comancheros are ruthless outlaws."

"But Mr. Ramírez only became a Comanchero because he was wronged by his father."

"I know all about Ramírez's inheritance," Matt broke in testily. "Life has been unfair to a lot of men, but they didn't use it as an excuse to become Comancheros."

"Do you disapprove of Mr. Ramírez?" she queried.

"It's not my place to approve or disapprove of him," Matt replied flatly. "If you don't mind, Regina, I've had a long day and I'd like to get some sleep."

His rude dismissal made her bristle, and she had to bite back a retort. "Good night, Matt," she said icily, as she turned haughtily toward the door.

Standing, Matt called softly, "Regina?"

She paused to look back at him. "Yes?"

"Good night, and sweet dreams," he said with deep tenderness.

She smiled faintly, wishing she understood how he could be so impersonal one minute, then so warm the next. "Thank you," she murmured, and not knowing what else to say, she left the room.

Chapter Seven

Sitting obediently beside the buckboard, Blackie waited for Matt and Juan to come out of the Donaldsons' Mercantile. When the men had left the ranch to ride into town, Blackie had taken it upon himself to accompany them. Juan had ordered him to stay home, but Matt had told Juan to let the dog come along as he would only be in town a short time, and when he left to return to the ranch, he'd take Blackie with him.

As Matt and Juan stepped out of the store, their arms filled with packages, Blackie stood and greeted them by wagging his bushy tail. After they had placed the bundles in the rear of the buckboard, Matt told Juan, "I'm gonna head back to the ranch, but if you want, you can stay in town."

Grinning widely, Juan answered, "I think maybe I will have a couple of drinks at Señor Butler's saloon. It will take Señor Donaldson a little while longer to fill the rest of our order."

Stepping to his horse, and taking the bridle reins from the hitching post, Matt said, "I'll see you later." He started to mount, but catching sight of Dan leading his horse across the street, he paused to wait for him.

"Are you riding back to the ranch?" Dan asked, as he

petted Blackie who had run to his side.

"I was thinking about it," Matt grinned.

"Mind if I ride with you? I thought I'd visit Regina, then ride over and see Julie. They don't come to town very often, so I never see as much of them as I'd like."

Mounting his horse, Matt said, his tone unintentionally tinged with irritation, "Well, I don't know if Regina will be home. She might be off somewhere with Antonio Ramírez."

"Ramírez!" Dan exclaimed, getting on his horse. "What in the hell would she be doing with Ramírez?"

"Ask her," Matt replied flatly, guiding his horse into the street.

Riding alongside him, Dan remarked firmly, "You're damned right, I'll ask her. I can't understand Regina. Why would she associate with a man like Ramírez?"

Matt grinned lazily. "You've been listening to Miguel, and where Ramírez is concerned, Miguel is more than a little biased. Ramírez isn't all bad, he's just a hard man to understand."

Curious, Dan wanted to question Matt about Ramírez, but Matt urged his horse into a fast canter, and Dan knew him well enough to know he had said all he intended to say about Antonio Ramírez.

With Blackie following closely, Dan and Matt rode out of town and into the rolling plains. The vast landscape was filled with large clusters of sagebrush, giving the area a gray-green hue.

The weather was pleasant, and as they rode at a leisurely pace, Matt talked to Dan about the Black Diamond.

Suddenly, Blackie's ears rose alertly, and a deep growl sounded from his throat before he took off across the plains, running so speedily that he was only a white streak.

"What do you think's wrong with him?" Dan asked,

watching the dog fading into the distance.

Matt shrugged. "I don't know, but I think we'd better follow him."

Turning their horses, and sending them into a run, they headed after Blackie. They had ridden only a couple of minutes when they came upon the dog. He was crouched a short distance from a huge clump of sagebrush. The sounds of mens' voices and the muffled cry of a woman caused Matt and Dan to urge their horses forward with caution. Swiftly, Matt removed his pistol from its holster, while Dan slipped his rifle from the scabbard on his saddle. As they drew steadily closer, they could make out a buckboard and four saddled horses on the other side of the thick sagebrush.

All at once, the woman's muffled cry became a piercing scream, and, bounding powerfully, Blackie soared over the sagebrush. His large paws hit the dirt only inches from where the woman lay on the ground. One man was kneeling between her legs, and three other men had her pinned down. Her dress was torn and disheveled, and her skirt and petticoats had been shoved up to her waist. The man kneeling between her spread legs had his trousers and undershorts down around his knees.

Moving with lightning speed, Blackie lurched, and the animal's large body hit the man full force, sending him plunging to the ground. His legs were tangled in his lowered pants, and he squirmed awkwardly as he attempted to fight off the huge dog. One of the men holding the woman jumped to his feet and drew his pistol. He aimed it at Blackie, but before he could fire, a gunshot exploded and his weapon flew from his hand.

Grimacing and checking his fingers, which had been slightly injured when Matt had shot the pistol out of his hand, the man turned sharply to find two men holding him and the others at gunpoint.

"Blackie!" Matt shouted.

Hearing his name, the dog backed away from his victim, whose arms were bleeding from the animal's sharp teeth. With difficulty, the man got to his feet and pulled up his trousers.

Gesturing with his pistol, Matt ordered the three men to join their comrade and to keep their hands in the air and away from their guns. Then he told Dan to check on the woman.

Replacing his rifle in its scabbard, Dan dismounted and hurried to her. She was still lying on the ground, and her skirts were in disarray. Hastily, Dan pulled down her petticoats and skirt. Her arms were folded across her face, and her body shook with violent sobs. She was hysterical, and when Dan tried to uncross her arms, she struck out at him. Her arms now flaying wildly, she tried to rake her finger nails over his face. Capturing her hands, Dan said strongly, "Ma'am, I'm not going to hurt you . . . you're safe. No one will harm you . . . everything is all right . . ."

Her large blue eyes stared hysterically into Dan's, but gradually he could see understanding come to her face.

"My father," she pleaded hoarsely. "Please check on my father."

Glancing about, Dan saw a body sprawled close to the buckboard. The woman sat up and watched fearfully as Dan hurried to her father. He returned quickly, and kneeling beside her, he said gently, "I'm sorry, ma'am, but he's dead."

Crying heavily, she sobbed, "They killed my father! . . . They shot him!"

Dan placed his hands on her shoulders to help her to her feet, but, as he did, she flung herself into his arms. Holding her close, Dan wished he could find a way to comfort her, but what could he possibly say or do?

Gripping her firmly, Dan drew her to a standing position. She was small, and she had to look up to see into his eyes. "Th . . . thank you," she murmured.

For a moment, Dan studied her upturned face. She wasn't especially pretty, but she had a certain quality about her that was attractive.

The young man who had been about to rape the woman when Blackie had intervened, whispered to the man standing next to him, "Chuck, you have two pistols. When I count to three, you draw your left gun and I'll draw the right one. We'll both take the guy on his horse, the other man isn't armed."

Matt was perfectly aware that the man was whispering orders to his friend, but his set expression didn't change. He was about to warn them not to try anything foolish when, quickly, the young man counted softly to three. The two men dropped their arms and drew the guns.

Reacting defensively, Matt shot twice, hitting one man and then the other before either had time to fire his drawn weapon.

Dan rushed to the fallen men to see if they were still alive. Glancing at Matt, he told him, "The guy Blackie attacked is dead, but the other one isn't."

"Let's get these sons of bitches to the sheriff," Matt replied, his tone dry. He derived no pleasure from killing the young man, but he felt he had been given no other choice. Looking at the helpless woman, and seeing the bruises on her arms and face, Matt decided he didn't care that one of her attackers was now dead.

Leaving the sheriff's office, Matt and Dan escorted the young woman, whose name they had learned was Susan Chandler, to the dining room that was actually a part of Dan's saloon. It had a separate street entrance from the bar and they went in that way. Ushering her to a table, Matt pulled out a chair for her while Dan went into the kitchen to fetch three cups of coffee.

Returning to Matt and Susan with the cups of steaming coffee, Dan remarked with annoyance as he sat down, "Lisa, my waitress, was in the kitchen and she told me she's quitting next week. I'm going to be in a bind if I can't find someone to replace her before she leaves." Looking at Susan apologetically, he continued, "I'm sorry, Miss Chandler. I shouldn't be complaining about business at a time like this." She smiled timidly, assuring him that he owed her no apologies.

Matt and Dan had already told the sheriff everything that had happened, and while they had done so the sheriff's wife had taken Susan to her home, where the young woman had taken a bath and changed clothes. Then, refreshed, she had returned to the sheriff's office so that she could provide the sheriff with any further information he might require.

Sighing heavily, Dan said to Matt, "It's too bad that guy you killed was Robert Selman, Jr."

The men who had also attacked Susan had told the sheriff that the dead man was Robert Selman's son. Dan had never met Robert Selman, but the man's name was well known in the West. He owned a large and prosperous ranch outside of Santa Fe. His son, and the men who had been traveling with him, had taken a trip to Mexico and were on their way home when they had run across Susan and her father traveling in their rickety old buckboard.

Matt took a sip of his coffee before replying calmly, "If Selman wants to avenge his son's death, I'll oblige him."

"I've heard a lot about Selman," Dan explained, "and I don't think he's the kind to face you man to man.

He sounds like the type who'd shoot you in the back, or hire someone to do the job for him."

"Oh, Mr. Brolin!" Susan gasped. "I hope I haven't caused you problems!"

"I'm not worried about myself," Matt replied gently, "but I am concerned about you. After your father's burial, what do you plan to do? You said at the sheriff's office that you and your father weren't headed for any place in particular, and you also said that you are very low on funds."

Folding her hands on the table, Susan took a deep breath, then let it out slowly. "As you already know, my father was a doctor. He had a good practice at our hometown in southern Texas. But he'd taken to drinking, and because he was always under the influence, his patients stopped trusting him. Another doctor moved into town, and, naturally, everyone started going to him. Father had been drinking heavily for two years before he finally made the decision to quit. He'd been cold sober for six months by the time we decided to move to a place where no one would know about his . . . his problem. By that time we had very little money. Most of our possessions had been sold to support father's drinking habit, and the only income we'd had for more than a year had been the small amount of money I could make by taking in sewing. But we loaded up the old buckboard and left, hoping to find a small town where a doctor might be needed."

"Do you have any family back home?" asked Dan.

"I have a married sister. Her husband is a blacksmith."

"If you need some money to get back home," Dan began, "I'll be happy to offer you whatever you need. If you like, you can consider it a loan, and pay me back whenever you can arrange it."

Susan sighed deeply. "Thank you very much, Mr.

Butler, but I don't know yet what I want to do."

As an idea suddenly occurred to Dan, he suggested, "Miss Chandler, while you are deciding what you want to do, why don't you come to work for me here in the restaurant. As you know, next week I'll be needing a waitress."

"Mr. Butler, thank you. I'll very gratefully accept your offer of a job. Is there a boardinghouse in town?"

"Yes, there is," he answered. "But I have extra rooms above the saloon, and you can rent one of them if you like."

"Live above a saloon?" Susan asked incredulously, her cheeks blushing a bright red.

Flustered, and feeling a little embarrassed, Dan stammered, "Excuse me, Miss Chandler, but I guess I didn't . . . didn't stop to think."

Suppressing a grin, Matt stood. "I'll go over to the boardinghouse and see if Miss Rainey has a vacancy."

He was gone only a few minutes before returning to announce that Miss Rainey's boardinghouse was filled, but that as soon as one of her boarders moved out, she'd let Miss Chandler know.

"Well," Susan began, wondering what life above a saloon would be like, "I suppose I'll have to rent a room from you, Mr. Butler."

Standing and pulling out Susan's chair as she rose to her feet, Dan replied, "I'll take you to your room, then see that your horse and buckboard are taken care of. I'll also have your luggage brought up."

Pausing beside Dan, Susan turned to look at Matt and smiled. "Thank you again, Mr. Brolin, for all your help."

"You're welcome, ma'am," he said softly, somewhat embarrassed. Mumbling a hasty goodbye, he left the restaurant to find Blackie waiting for him outside the door. Reaching down to pet the dog's head, Matt remarked fondly, "Come on boy, let's go home." The moment the words crossed his lips, he wondered why he had so easily referred to the Black Diamond as home. It wasn't his home, it was Regina's. His home didn't exist, it was still waiting to be built.

It was three days later when Robert Selman made his appearance at the Black Diamond. Regina was in her bedroom when she heard horses in the lane that led up to the house. She moved quickly down the hallway as Matt suddenly emerged from the study. Neither realizing the other's presence, they collided.

As Matt grasped her shoulders to steady her, Regina asked, "Do you suppose Miguel Ordaz has returned?"

Releasing his hold on her and heading toward the front door, Matt replied, "I doubt it. Miguel said he wouldn't be back for a few months."

Hurrying to keep up with Matt's long strides, Regina said, "Maybe it's Antonio and his ranch hands."

Opening the front door, Matt stepped aside, and Regina moved past him onto the porch. Walking behind her, Matt watched a large group of horsemen ride up to the ranch house. He noticed a buckboard drawn by a pair of horses, and catching sight of the coffin in the rear of the wagon, Matt knew he was about to meet Robert Selman.

He walked slowly down the porch steps as Robert Selman brought his horse to a halt. Selman was an imposing figure of a man. He was dressed in the customary linen duster worn by cattlemen, but his bearing and his handsome mount set him apart from the men riding with him.

"My name is Robert Selman, and I'm looking for

Matt Brolin," Selman said stiffly.

"You don't have to look any farther," Matt replied calmly.

A cold look of deranged hatred came into Selman's eyes as he glared at Matt. Frightened for Matt's safety, Regina went down the steps to stand by his side.

Matt hadn't told her about Susan Chandler, but the day after Susan had been attacked, Dan had come to the ranch and he'd told Regina everything that had happened.

"Brolin," Selman rasped, "why did you kill my son?"

"I'm sure you read the sheriff's report, and you already know why your son died."

"Lies!" Selman spat harshly. "That report is nothing but lies made up by you, Butler, and that Chandler girl! The men who were with my son told me what really took place. After you let your dog maul my boy, you killed him. It was an act of cold-blooded murder!"

Refusing to argue with the man, Matt said evenly, "Selman, I'm sure you came here to have your say, so just say it and then get the hell off this property."

"Someday I'm going to see you dead, Brolin!" Selman threatened, his eyes bulging with rage. "I don't know how or when, but I promise you that you will die for murdering my son. I will not rest until justice has been done and my boy's death has been avenged."

Jerking his horse's reins, he turned the animal sharply, dug his heels into its sides, and rode past his men. They turned to follow him.

Watching them ride away, Regina grasped Matt's arm, her fingers unintentionally digging into his flesh. "Oh, Matt!" she groaned. "Selman meant what he said!"

He glanced down at his arm, and realizing that she was gripping him, she removed her hand. Calmly, he told her, "This isn't the first time I've been threatened, and it probably won't be the last."

"Matt, you must be very cautious!" Regina declared.

He grinned, and she had the feeling that he was finding her advice foolish. "I don't intend to spend my days looking vigilantly over my shoulder." He moved away and began climbing the porch steps, but before reaching the top, he paused to look back at Regina. "By the way, have you had your first lesson yet?"

"Lesson?" she repeated faintly, wondering how Matt could have taken Selmen's threat so casually.

"With Ramírez," he explained.

"Yes, he came over yesterday afternoon while you were on the range."

"How did the lesson go?"

"Just fine," she mumbled.

His eyes held hers for a moment, and she wished she knew what he was thinking. Turning abruptly and taking the remaining two steps in one stride, Matt said hastily, "I have work to do in the study." He crossed the porch and went into the house.

Sighing discontentedly, Regina sat on the bottom porch step, and placing her elbows on her knees, she cupped her chin in her hands. She had the depressing feeling that Matt was trying to avoid her, but as hard as she tried, she couldn't figure out why he had decided to shun her company.

Chapter Eight

Irritably, Susan threw off her covers and rose from the bed. She had been trying to fall asleep for the past two hours, but the raucous hubbub that drifted upstairs from the saloon area had made sleep difficult to achieve. She lit the lamp beside her bed; then, grabbing her robe, she quickly slipped it on over her cotton nightgown.

She had been staying in this dreadful room now for four days and nights, during which time she had managed to get very little sleep. If Miss Rainey's boardinghouse didn't soon have a vacancy, she was afraid she might collapse from total exhaustion. She desperately needed a good night's rest, and she was miserable in her present surroundings. Susan had always thought saloons quite distasteful, and she detested the four women who were employed by Dan. She knew they were prostitutes, and she considered their profession degrading, as well as abhorrent.

In the four days she had resided in Dan's establishment, she had found only one pleasant aspect to being there; and that had been Dan Butler himself. Susan had become hopelessly enamored with Dan, but she wasn't sure whether he shared her feelings. Sometimes when he was showing her special attention, she would begin to think that maybe he was falling in love with her, but at other times he treated her politely but distantly.

Suddenly, Susan heard Claire's shrill laughter coming from the hallway, and she cringed when she detected Dan's jovial laughter mingling with Claire's. It had become apparent to Susan that Dan's and Claire's relationship was not strictly businesslike.

Susan frowned as she wondered how a gentleman as suave and debonair as Dan Butler could keep intimate company with a woman like Claire. Obviously, where his sexual drives were concerned, Dan had no qualms about the type of woman who shared his bed. She couldn't understand why he was involved with a woman like Claire instead of one who would make him a good and loyal wife.

Susan's face suddenly brightened as she realized that Dan had no way of knowing that she was in love with him. If he knew, she decided quickly, then surely he'd no longer associate with Claire! He'd be faithful to her, and when they married, there would be no reason for him to turn to strumpets to satisfy his masculine needs.

Fastening her robe, Susan hurried toward her closed door. This is one night Dan Butler will not be spending his time with Claire, Susan thought determinedly. I'll tell him of my true feelings, and he, in turn, will profess his own love!

As she opened the door, Dan and Claire were strolling past her room. Dan had one arm over Claire's shoulders, and tucked in the other was a bottle of brandy.

Their steps came to an abrupt stop as, together, they turned to look questioningly at Susan.

"Dan," Susan said softly, using his Christian name for the first time, "may I please talk to you for a moment?"

95

Dan had been drinking. He didn't usually drink to excess, but tonight he had overindulged. Realizing he was in no condition to visit with Susan, he replied in a slurred voice, "Can't it wait until tomorrow?"

"No, I must see you at once," Susan answered firmly, secretly admiring the man she had come to love. He was dressed elegantly in tight-fitting trousers and a tailored vest beneath which he wore a ruffled linen shirt, now partially unbuttoned to reveal the dark hairs that grew thickly over his manly chest.

Claire did not like Susan Chandler. Considering the drastic differences in their social status, she hadn't expected Susan to behave warmly toward her, but she deeply resented Susan's superior attitude and felt it was totally uncalled for.

Sliding her arm around Dan's waist in a familiar fashion that made Susan's blood boil, Claire taunted her huskily, "Sorry, dearie, but tonight he's all mine."

Susan's eyes traveled critically over Claire's skimpy and gaudy gown as she replied frigidly, "I wasn't speaking to you, I was talking to your employer." Looking pleadingly at Dan, she continued, "Will you please come into my room so that we can talk privately?"

"All right," Dan agreed, wishing his mind wasn't quite so muddled from brandy. Stepping away from Claire, he told her, "Go back downstairs, I'll join you in a few minutes."

"Be careful, boss," Claire warned. "Black widows have been known to devour their lovers."

As Dan staggered into the room, Susan cast an icy stare at Claire. "Your humor is as pathetic as you are," Susan sneered, before slamming the door closed.

The loud bang caused Dan to turn with a start. Due to his tipsy condition, the womens' biting remarks had completely escaped his notice.

"There's a draft in the hall, and sometimes it makes the door slam," Susan lied coolly.

"What do you need to talk to me about?" Dan asked, once again wishing for a clearer head.

Moving to stand close to him, she looked up into his face. He is such a handsome man, she thought, and I love him so much! Truly I do! She lowered her gaze. Now that she had him in her room where they were completely alone, she began to lose her confidence. Oh, what would she do if she were to confess her love only to have him turn her away? His rejection would shatter her world and break her heart. Just imagining a rebuff brought tears to her eyes.

Dan rubbed a hand across his brow as though it might help clear his jumbled thoughts. When Susan's eyes remained downcast, he placed his fingers beneath her chin, tilting her face upward. The sight of her tears surprised him. "Miss Chandler, what's wrong?" he asked anxiously.

She clutched his hand tightly in hers. "Please call me Susan."

"Did something happen to frighten you, Susan? Did some man come up here to your room?" Upset, he pulled his hand free of hers. The thought of a customer barging into Susan's room made Dan's temper flare. "By God, just tell me who he is, and I'll personally beat him to a pulp!"

Oh, he does care! Susan thought delightedly. Why else would he react so angrily at the mere thought of some man insulting me?

Dan wasn't sure why he felt so protective of Susan. Maybe it was because he was used to protecting two younger sisters, or perhaps it was simply because Susan was a lady alone with no one to fend for her.

"No one came to my room," Susan assured him. She reached for the brandy bottle that he was still holding, and taking it from his hand, she walked over and placed it on the dresser. Turning and looking at him, she smiled happily. He loved her! She was positive that he did. "Dan," she began strongly, "I asked you to come into my room because I have something to tell you. Dan, my darling, I am in love with you!"

Dan was still unable to think clearly, but Susan's declaration came as a shock. He hadn't had the slightest inkling that she was falling in love with him. He was very fond of Susan, but that was as far as his feelings for her went.

Susan waited expectantly, and when Dan suddenly moved toward her, she was sure that he planned to embrace her.

Pausing in front of Susan, Dan reached instead for the brandy bottle. Wrenching the cap from the bottle, he tilted it to his mouth and took more than a generous swallow. "Susan," he said gently, "maybe you only think you're in love with me. After all, you've only known me for a very short time."

Shattered, because he hadn't said that he loved her, Susan cried wretchedly, "Oh, I've made a fool of myself! I'm so ashamed!"

Dan helped himself to another drink before placing the bottle on the dresser. Susan was moving away from him, and as he reached for her, he lost his balance and stumbled. Damn! he thought, I am in no fit condition to handle such a delicate siuation! He made another attempt to catch her, and this time he was successful. Placing his hands on her shoulders, he turned her so she was facing him. Her sad face touched him deeply. "You did not make a fool of yourself, and you have no reason to feel ashamed. That a woman as nice as you could be in love with a no good bum like me is more than I deserve."

Desperate to win Dan's love, she threw herself into

his arms, and slipping her arms about his neck, she pleaded, "Kiss me, Dan! . . . Please, kiss me!"

Dan hesitated, his better judgment warning him that would be a mistake. Susan was a genuine lady, and he should not trifle with her affections. Yet, as her soft body clung to his, he could feel his maleness responding, even though his muddled reasoning seemed to be telling him to beware of Susan's inveigling charms.

He gazed down into her face. Her large blue eyes were still moist with tears, and her long auburn hair was falling seductively over her shoulders. Although Susan was not especially beautiful, she was attractive and very feminine. If Dan had been in complete control of his faculties, he might have been able to refuse Susan's tempting offer, but the brandy had weakened his defenses. One arm tightened around her waist as, suddenly, his lips sought hers. He entwined his fingers into her flowing hair, pressing her mouth closer to his.

Dan's rapturous kiss sent Susan's thoughts swirling, and surrendering willingly, she parted her lips so that he could intensify their lingering kiss. With his lips still on hers, Dan swept her into his arms and carried her to the bed. Placing her on her feet beside it, he whispered thickly, "Susan, you're so desirable." Then, with anxious hands, he began to remove her robe.

Susan had always believed it was wrong for a woman to give herself to a man before matrimony, but her mind wasn't working logically. Furthermore, she feared if she refused him, he might never return. Surely, if he made love to her, he would then behave as a gentleman and ask her to marry him.

He removed her robe, heedlessly letting it fall to the floor. Then he adeptly undid the tiny buttons on the bodice of her nightgown. Gently pushing aside the soft material, he slipped it from her shoulders, and that garment dropped onto the fallen robe.

He bent his head, and his lips relished her full breasts, his tongue flickering over each nipple.

A feeling of ecstasy came over Susan, and curling her fingers into his dark hair, she urged his mouth even closer, loving the pleasure he was giving her. Dan's passion was now aroused beyond his control, and thinking only of giving and receiving sexual enjoyment, he eased her onto the bed.

Still feeling the effects of the brandy, Dan undressed a little precariously. Susan's eyes glazed as she watched him disrobe. Awed by his solid, masculine physique, she slowly lowered her gaze. She had never seen a man totally unclothed, and she was a bit frightened.

Going to Susan, and lying beside her, Dan drew her into his arms. If he had been sober, he would have sensed her fear and would have calmed her anxieties. But he was only conscious of his physical need, which was burning intensely.

As Dan moved over her, afraid, Susan stiffened. For a fleeting moment she considered pushing him away, but she quickly decided not to risk losing him. She parted her legs so he could enter her and then closed her eyes, dreading the pain she knew would soon follow.

Penetrating her swiftly, and taking her virginity, Dan shoved his thighs against hers. Susan cried out softly, but her discomfort was short-lived, and the feel of him inside her soon evoked pleasing sensations. He began to thrust himself against her, slowly at first, then with vigor. Susan responded rapturously and lifted her thighs up and down, welcoming his probes.

Clinging to her, Dan kissed her lips, the hollow of her throat, and her breasts. Drowning in total bliss, Susan moaned and sighed heavily in response to his fondling. But Dan's fulfillment came to him explosively, and his frame trembled as he achieved sexual release. Breathing heavily, he remained on top of her for a moment before moving to lie at her side.

Susan smiled contentedly as she snuggled close to him. Now he would most assuredly tell her that he loved her. When Dan remained silent, she raised up on one elbow to look down into his face. She started to ask him if something was wrong, but his deep, even breathing told her that Dan was sound asleep.

It's because of the brandy, she thought resentfully. He's sleeping off a drunk, just like father always did! Well, when we're married, there will be no more boozing . . . or saloons . . . or loose, immoral women! Dan will live a respectable life! I will see to it—personally!

Dan awoke slowly the next day. He was first conscious of the headache that pounded mercilessly at his temples. Frowning, he put a hand to his brow, massaging it gently. Hangovers could be brutal, and apparently he had a dilly! He opened his eyes drowsily, and the bright sunlight filtering across the bed from the open window glared into his face. Rolling onto his side, he turned away from the radiant light. Why hadn't he remembered to draw the drapes last night?

With his face now turned away from the glaring light, Dan once again attempted to open his eyes. It took a moment for his vision to clear, and when his eyes focused on Susan sitting rigidly in a chair placed beside the bed, Dan came fully awake. Sitting upright with a sudden start, he glanced fleetingly at his surroundings. He was shocked to find himself in Susan's bedroom. He had a quilt placed over him, but he didn't need to raise the cover to know that he was totally naked.

Susan had been up for hours, waiting anxiously for him to awaken. She knew Dan's schedule well enough to know that he liked to keep late hours and preferred to sleep until noon. That was another part of his life-style that she intended to change. Susan was a firm believer in early to bed and early to rise. If a man was ever in need of a good woman's guidance, she was certain Dan Butler was that man!

She smiled brightly. "Good morning, darling. Or perhaps I should say good afternoon. It's almost one o'clock, you know."

"It is?" he mumbled, still dumfounded at finding himself in Susan's bed. What in the hell had happened last night? His head ached, and he found it extremely difficult to concentrate. Slowly, he began to remember bits and pieces, but his recollections were cloudy.

"Susan," he began carefully, "exactly what happened last night?"

Gaping incredulously, she asked sharply, "You don't remember?"

"Well . . . not everything," he stammered.

She had never been so humiliated! She had given this man her heart and body, and he didn't even remember! Bounding to her feet and glaring at him, she said angrily, "Dan Butler, you are a beast and . . . and a heartless scoundrel!"

He started to get up, but remembering he was nude, he realized he couldn't very well leave the bed to calm her.

Susan had neatly folded his clothes and placed them at the foot of the bed. Now, grabbing them, she flung them at him. "Get dressed; then leave my room!" she ordered, turning her back so that he could have privacy.

Dan threw off the quilt, and the sight of blood on the white sheets made him grimace. It was evident that last night he had seduced a virgin. Feeling like a cad, he slipped hastily into his clothes. When he was fully dressed, he stepped to Susan, and placing his hands on her shoulders, he drew her around to face him.

"Susan, I'm sorry," he murmured.

"Sorry?" she remarked sharply. "Is that all you have to say?"

His head was still pounding terribly, and his mouth felt as dry as cotton. He certainly didn't feel up to soothing Susan's wounded pride. When he was feeling better and had more time to think about what had happened, perhaps then he and Susan could talk things over.

"Is that all you have to say?" she demanded again.

"What do you want me to say?" he asked, more harshly than he had intended.

Oh, she had been a fool to believe he would marry her simply because he'd taken her virginity! He was a cad, a villain! She wished she didn't love him because she wanted to despise him!

Stepping away from Dan, and lifting her chin proudly, Susan said quite calmly, "Miss Rainey talked to me this morning while you were asleep. One of her boarders moved out yesterday. I will leave your establishment this afternoon and move into her house. She also told me that she needs help because there is so much cleaning and cooking to be done, and I have decided to work for her. You will have to find another waitress."

He certainly didn't feel like arguing with her, so he nodded agreeably. "Do you need help moving?"

"I can manage quite well, thank you," she said smugly.

She was upset and angry. Dan couldn't very well blame her. Last night he had taken advantage of her innocence, and to make matters worse, he was now treating her unfairly. But he was very fond of Susan. He didn't want their friendship to end on a bitter note; in fact, he didn't want it to end at all. However, this was

103

not the time to pressure her. Surely, later she would be more agreeable and less hostile.

"Will you have dinner with me tonight?" he asked, hoping she'd accept his invitation so he could start making amends.

Susan was tempted to say yes, but she decided she shouldn't forgive him so easily. He must be made to realize that she was not the kind of woman to be taken lightly.

"I do not wish to have dinner with you tonight or any other night," she responded coldly. Walking quickly to the door and opening it, she said formally, "Good day, Mr. Butler."

Dan's face clouded with regret. "Susan, please . . ." he began helplessly, his words suddenly fading. Then, deciding there was nothing more he could do to get back into her good graces, he strode to the open door and left the room.

Susan listened to the sound of his footsteps diminish as he strode down the long hallway, and recalling the pain and regret she had seen on his face, she murmured confidently, "You'll come back to me, Dan Butler, and when you do, you'll ask me to be your wife."

Chapter Nine

Regina wondered how it was possible for two people to share the same house and see as little of each other as she and Matt did. She concluded that Matt avoided her on purpose. He had been staying at the ranch now for almost two months, and during that time he seemed to go out of his way to make certain that she never had the chance to engage him in conversation.

Yet the ranch hands liked and respected him, and he ran the place expertly. During the day he stayed on the range from sunup to sundown, and at night he closed himself in the study, taking his evening meals in the privacy of his room while he worked diligently on James Blakely's books. To Regina it seemed that Matt considered the study his own private domain, so when he sent word that he wished to see her there, she was amazed.

It was late evening and Regina was in her bedroom when Luisa brought her Matt's message. Regina gave her hair a quick brushing; then she rushed out of the bedroom and down the hall to the study. The door was closed so she knocked lightly on it. Matt called for her to come in, and she stepped into the room, closing the door behind her.

He was sitting at the desk, his dark head bent over a stack of papers as he jotted down numerous figures. Not bothering to look up, he nodded toward the chair in front of the desk. "Sit down, please. I'll be right with you."

Complying, Regina moved to the chair, sitting on the very edge. She waited expectantly for Matt to explain why he had sent for her, but he was concentrating on his work.

Compelling herself to remain patient, Regina slid to the back of the chair and, resting her elbows on the arms, folded her hands beneath her chin. Her gaze centered on Matt, she studied him intently. First, she examined his hair. It was thick and wavy, and the color was a deep, rich brown. His eyes were lowered, revealing that his lashes were black and extremely long. Matt's complexion was so dark that she wondered if he might be part Mexican. That would explain his close relationship with Miguel Ordaz. Scrutinizing him at her leisure, she slowly moved her gaze to his mouth. His lips were full but firm, and recalling how thrilling it had been to have his mouth relishing hers, Regina's heart ached to once again know the rapture of his kiss. The lamp on the desk shone on his face, illuminating the scar on his cheek. The disfigurement should have marred his looks, but it didn't. If anything, it made him appear more sensual.

Pushing back his chair, Matt rose to his feet, and closing the tally ledger, he picked it up. Regina continued to watch him as he stepped over to the safe. She was amazed that a man as tall as Matt could move so gracefully. He was lean, but his shoulders were wide and his arms were visibly strong. She didn't turn away her gaze as he knelt in front of the safe, placing the ledger inside, and when he stood upright, her eyes took in the shape of his long legs and his narrow hips.

Suddenly Regina remembered that Dan had told her Matt never had trouble getting a woman. She could easily see why. His masculinity was so blatant it couldn't possibly escape a woman's notice.

He moved back to the desk, and still studying him, Regina told herself that he wasn't elegantly handsome. That's why he's so attractive, she mused. He's so ruggedly sensual that when a woman is with him, she knows she's in the presence of a man.

Returning to his chair, Matt leaned back against the soft leather upholstery, and giving Regina his full attention, he said, "Before Miguel left, he told me that he'll send you a herd of cattle. Most of your own cattle are poor specimens, but the ones Miguel are giving you are top grade. And among them will be a prize bull."

Surprised, Regina exclaimed, "But I already owe Mr. Ordaz so much, how can I possibly accept more?"

"He told me to tell you he would add the cost of the cattle to the money you owe him. You need not consider his gift charity."

Regina emitted a worried sigh. "I'll be so far in debt to Mr. Ordaz that I may never be able to pay him back in full."

"Of course you'll be able to repay him," Matt told her with confidence. "Before long this ranch will be as profitable as it was when it was operated by Carl Blakely."

She smiled gratefully. "Thanks to you and Miguel Ordaz."

Grinning wryly, he replied, "What are friends for?"

"Are we friends, Matt?" she asked impulsively.

"I hope so," he responded, watching her dubiously. "Why do you ask?"

"Matt," she began hesitantly, deciding to clear the air, "sometimes I get the distinct feeling that you want to avoid me, and friends don't try to elude each other."

107

"I've been very busy," he said evasively.

"I don't think that is why we seldom see each other," she replied, speaking her mind. "I'm afraid it's because . . . because . . ."

"Because?" he coaxed.

She lowered her gaze for a moment, and when she once again looked up at him, he was concerned by the hurt he saw in her eyes. "I'm afraid it's because you don't especially like me." Regina had tried not to think about that fear, but she hadn't been able to deny it.

Her answer surprised Matt. Not like her? He not only liked her, he admired and respected her. "That isn't true," he quickly assured her. "Regina, I like you very much."

"Then why do you usually treat me so curtly?" she asked pleadingly.

"If I have hurt your feelings, Regina, believe me, it wasn't done intentionally. It's just that . . . well, I have a lot on my mind."

Regina now knew that he was going to evade the issue. Why, she wondered, must he be so elusive?

"How are your lessons with Ramírez coming along?" Matt asked, purposely changing the subject.

"Antonio has taught me a lot," she answered, accepting his decision to turn their conversation away from himself.

"I'll be leaving soon," he announced calmly, his statement taking Regina by surprise.

"Why?" she breathed, already dreading his departure. He'll ride out of my life, she thought depressingly, and I'll never see him again!

"My two months are almost up," he explained.

"Can't you stay longer?" she pleaded.

"There's no reason for me to stay," he replied. "Regina, don't worry so much. Your ranch is running smoothly. Listen to your foreman and take his advice.

He can be trusted."

She longed to cry out to Matt that her ranch was not the reason why she needed him to stay. She didn't want him to leave because she had fallen in love with him. But, apparently, he didn't share her feelings, and if she were to tell him of her love, her confession would probably only make him uncomfortable. He might even feel sorry for her, and she knew she couldn't bear it if he were to pity her. Holding tenaciously to her pride, Regina asked collectedly, "When do you plan to leave?"

"I don't know for sure, but probably within the next couple of days. There are a few loose strings I must tie up before I move on."

"I'll miss you," she murmured, immediately wishing she could withdraw the words she had spoken so naturally. If she wasn't careful, she'd soon be blurting out that she loved him. Fidgeting, Regina rose from her chair and walked lethargically to the window. She pulled back the lace curtain and glanced out at the night. Lamps burned in the distant bunkhouses, and the open window allowed the sounds of night to drift into the room. She listened vaguely to the faraway cry of a coyote, to the periodic neighing of the horses penned in the corral. Matt would soon be leaving, and he would take her heart with him. It seemed ironic that she could be in love with a man who hadn't the slightest idea that she cared so much about him!

Sitting in a relaxed way, Matt watched her closely. He wondered what she was thinking about.

Sighing heavily, Regina leaned her face against the window pane. It felt cool against her flushed cheek. Her mood was gloomy, and speaking wistfully, she reminisced. "When Papa went into town to play cards, he usually took the buggy. Midnight isn't the ideal horse to pull a carriage, so Papa never used him. When

109

he left, I'd saddle Midnight and ride for hours. I know every acre of this land. I'd watch the cattle grazing in the twilight, and admire the landscape. The range is so beautiful at night, so peaceful. Alone, and surrounded by the mysteries of night, I would often try to imagine the man who would someday come into my life and sweep me off my feet."

"I should think your nights would have been filled with prospective suitors," Matt commented.

Regina smiled shyly. "I had my fair share of beaus."

"Did you fall in love with any of them?"

"No," she whispered. "Not one of them was right for me."

"What kind of man is right for you, Regina?" he asked. His question sounded casual, but Matt was waiting intensely for her answer.

You are the right man, Regina felt like replying. Instead, she murmured, "I'm not sure."

Detecting a note of sadness in her voice, Matt left his chair and walked over to stand close to her. "You sound unhappy," he said caringly. "I should think you'd be overjoyed to know that your ranch is secure."

No longer able to suppress her feelings, she blurted irritably, "Damn this ranch! Do you think my home is all I care about?"

Her anger catching Matt off guard, he stammered, "No, of course I don't think that."

"Then why do you act as though this ranch is all I live for?" she demanded testily.

"You once told me that your land means everything to you," he reminded her. "It was the night you asked me to teach you about ranching."

"I didn't mean that the way it sounded," she tried to explain. "My ranch does mean a great deal to me, but, Matt, it isn't the most important thing in my life!"

"Then what is?" he asked so quietly that she barely

heard him.

"You are!" she cried, not caring if she made him feel uncomfortable, or if he pitied her. She loved him so strongly that she could no longer keep her feelings suppressed.

Taken aback, Matt was silent for a moment. Mistaking his silence for a rebuff, Regina whirled sharply, intending to leave the room in hate, but Matt's hand clutched her arm. "Regina, what are you saying?" he asked thickly.

Fighting back tears, she replied softly, "I want you, Matt."

His body tensed, causing his grip on her arm to tighten. "Regina," he uttered heavily, "don't say that you want me unless you mean it."

"But I do want you, Matt! Desperately!" she cried, the plea in her eyes melting Matt's firm resolution not to let Regina into his heart.

Fiercely, he drew her into his arms, pinning her against him so tightly that the contours of her body were molded to his. Then he kissed her forcefully, his lips searing hers. Regina's head was spinning with ecstasy, and her body trembled with desire for him.

Sending fleeting kisses across her face, Matt murmured hoarsely, "Regina, you're so beautiful. God, how I want to make love to you!"

Regina had never been with a man, but she knew only Matt could satisfy the longing that his kiss had awakened within her.

"Yes," she whispered raspingly. "Make love to me, Matt. Make me your own."

"Regina, my sweet darling," he groaned, lifting her into his arms.

He didn't know whether Luisa and Juan had retired, but he wanted Regina so powerfully that, at the moment, he didn't care. Carrying her to the study door,

111

he managed to turn the doorknob. Then he carried her swiftly down the hall and into her room. After placing her on her feet and turning back to lock the door, he gathered Regina into his embrace, his mouth taking desperate possession of hers, his hands moving to her soft buttocks and pressing her thighs to his.

Regina could feel his firm arousal through her petticoat and skirt, and the hardness of him excited her, causing her to press against him. She was aware that Matt's breathing quickened with passion as he reached for the tiny pearl buttons at the bodice of her gown. He undid them quickly and, pushing aside the material, slipped a hand beneath her chemise. His warm palm traveled smoothly over one breast and then the other, its touch a flickering spark, igniting a desire that spread hotly through Regina.

Anxious to see Regina's bared beauty, Matt hastily helped her out of her dress and petticoat. As she stepped out of her shoes, he slipped the narrow straps of her chemise over her shoulders. Wanting to free her breasts so that he could touch them again, Regina quickly removed the undergarment, letting it fall carelessly to the floor.

Swiftly Matt bent his head to kiss her full mounds, suckling and biting lightly at their taut nipples. Loving the pleasure his mouth was giving her, Regina placed one hand to the back of his head, encouraging him to continue. Then, once again, his lips sought hers, kissing her demandingly before he suddenly lifted her into his arms and carried her to the bed. The covers had been drawn back earlier, and he laid her down gently on the crisp sheets. She still wore her lace pantalets so Matt took them off slowly to reveal all of her seductive body.

Dropping the undergarment onto the floor, he then leaned over Regina and placed his lips on the golden vee between her legs. Such intimacy caused Regina to flinch, but his caress was fleeting for, standing upright, Matt began to disrobe.

Regina watched boldly as Matt shed his clothes and when he stood before her completely nude, she lowered her eyes to his stiff maleness. Its hardness amazed her. Longing to touch him there, as he joined her she moved her hand to his erection.

Her gentle touch caused Matt to groan, "Regina . . . Regina."

Realizing her touch had the same power over him that his had over her, she let her fingers encircle his throbbing maleness. Then, grasping him firmly, she moved her hand up and down.

Matt pulled her closer, his mouth crushing hers, and as her lips opened beneath his, his tongue tasted her sweetness. She slid her hands upward so she could wrap them about his neck while he continued to kiss her, his hand exploring her body, his fingers sending warm and tingling sensations through her entire being.

Then he moved over her and, to avoid prolonging her pain, drove into her powerfully. Regina gasped, but as he slowly moved circularly within her, his inserted maleness seemed to fill her. Gradually she began to experience thrills of pleasure, and sensing this, Matt urged her legs around his waist. His deeper penetration provoked such delightful sensations in Regina that she murmured tremulously, "Matt, my darling, I love you."

Matt chuckled and embraced her forcefully. "Sweetheart, the best is yet to come."

"Then I will lose my mind and never be the same again."

"That's true, my sweet innocent. You will never again be the same. You are now a woman." Pulling her thighs upward, and holding them tightly against his, he continued huskily, "And I have never wanted a woman

113

as much as I want you."

"You have me, darling," she whispered in his ear.

He rose to his knees and thrust his maleness into her even deeper.

Gliding gloriously into love's wonderful bliss, Regina welcomed the sensuous pleasure Matt was giving her, a pleasure that, until now, she had not known. Clinging tightly to Matt, Regina surrendered her body, heart, and soul to the man she loved.

The pillows were propped against the oak headboard of Regina's bed, and Matt was leaning back against them. Resting one arm over Regina's shoulders he kept her snuggled close to his side as his thoughts ran deeply. He was still amazed that Regina had given herself to him so sweetly and unselfishly. Had he been wrong all this time to think that she would be unwilling to give up her ranch for him? If he were to ask her, would she leave with him for Wyoming? A concerned frown crossed his face. He couldn't expect her to make such a sacrifice. It would be unfair to demand that she leave a comfortable and secure life when he had nothing to offer her but hardship.

For years Matt had worked and saved in order to buy his own ranch, but for the first time, he now began to wonder if having his own ranch was really so important. Was it more important to him than Regina? Did her comfort and security mean more than his dream of owning his own tract of land? He knew these questions couldn't be answered right now. He would have to give them a lot of thought. If he were to marry Regina, to stay here on her ranch, would he grow to feel that this land was a part of him or would he resent working on a ranch that wasn't truly his? Could he just proceed with his original plan to move to Wyoming?

The bedside lamp was burning, and lowering his eyes, Matt studied Regina as she stirred to look up into his face. No, he thought. Realizing how much he needed her, he knew he could not leave her. She has come to mean too much to me, he thought. I think I fell in love with her the first moment I saw her. He smiled faintly at the memory of Regina riding out from behind the boulder and holding a rifle on him—beautiful lady on a black stallion with a white dog called Blackie. Her sudden appearance had astounded him, and when she'd vanished as quickly as she had appeared, he had thought he'd never see her again.

"Where are your thoughts?" Regina asked curiously.

Matt chuckled softly. "I was just remembering the first time I saw you." He was tempted to tell her that he had fallen in love with her at that moment, but he decided to wait until he had everything clear in his mind before speaking about love and their future. He knew he was going to ask her to marry him; however, he wasn't sure whether he wanted them to move to Wyoming or remain at the Black Diamond.

Placing her head on Matt's shoulder, Regina cuddled against him. She sighed. She had hoped he would tell her that he loved her. She wanted desperately to declare her true feelings, but she was still wary of how he might respond.

Bending his head, Matt kissed her forehead; then, moving away from her and swinging his legs over the side of the bed, he said, "I'd better go back to the study before we fall asleep. I can just imagine Luisa's shock if she were to come in here in the morning and find us in bed together."

Regina knew he was right. It was best that he leave, but she wished with all her heart that he could stay.

Matt dressed hastily, then leaned over the bed and gave Regina an intense and lingering kiss. "I'll see you

115

in the morning," he whispered.

"Good night, Matt," she murmured, fighting back an urge to ask him if he still planned to go to Wyoming. If only he'd ask her to go with him! . . . She'd gladly hand over the deed to the ranch to Julie and Mace and accompany Matt to the ends of the earth just to be at his side!

"Good night, darling," he replied warmly. Smiling, he winked at her before he moved away from the bedside and left the room.

Taking one of the pillows propped against the headboard, Regina placed it beneath her head. She clutched it tightly as she murmured intensely, "Oh Matt, please . . . please don't desert me! I love you so much!"

Chapter Ten

Sitting at the kitchen table, Julie watched Mace finish eating his breakfast. Taking his napkin, he wiped his mouth, then took a large swig of his coffee. As he placed the cup back on the table, he glanced at his wife. When his gaze met hers, Julie lowered her eyes. Mace studied her, wondering why she had been acting so strangely for the last couple of months. Thinking back, he decided her peculiar behavior had started about the same time Miguel Ordaz had visited the Black Diamond. But what in the world could Ordaz have to do with Julie's present mood? Dismissing the timing of her change as merely coincidental, he took another sip of his coffee.

Julie sighed pensively. She wished Mace would leave the house so she could get started on her morning chores. She wanted to be busy, because only when she was working steadily could she seem to avoid this feeling of melancholy. Julie didn't understand why she was depressed. Her life had been the same for the past ten years, so why did it now seem unbearable? Yet as hard as she had tried, she had been unable to put

Miguel Ordaz out of her mind. It was terribly wrong for her to feel such an attraction for a man who wasn't her husband, but no man had ever made her feel so exceptional and desirable! Miguel Ordaz was a powerful man, yet he had treated her as though she were someone special. Toying with her coffee cup, Julie cast Mace a fleeting glance, once again wishing he would go about his work. Why was he procrastinating?

Leaning back in his chair, Mace looked about the room, mentally comparing it to the Blakely home. It wasn't right that he and Julie lived in this three-room cabin while Regina had the ranch house all to herself. Mace didn't bother to remind himself that he could afford to enlarge his home if he so desired, although at one time he had planned to expand his house. That had been a few years back when he'd still hoped to have sons. He now saw no reason to enlarge a house that would never be filled with children. To do so would involve useless expense. But the spacious Blakely home was already built, and he firmly believed that he and Julie had as much right to reside there as Regina. Damn James Blakely for leaving everything to Regina! Well, if it was within his power, he'd see to it that very soon he and Julie would be living in the Blakely home—and that he'd be in charge of the Black Diamond.

Mace knew that Matt Brolin had only agreed to stay for two months. That time was almost up. Surely, within a few days, he'd be moving on. Then, it would be only a matter of time before Regina would decide to deed the ranch to him. Mace could not conceive of a woman effectively running a spread as large as the Black Diamond. With Matt Brolin out of the picture, he was certain Regina would be compelled to turn to him for assistance. He smiled spitefully. Regina Blakely was in for a rude awakening! When she came to him to ask for his help, he'd flatly refuse. He'd let her know that he believed the ranch should belong to Julie and himself. James Blakely had been a fool to leave his property to a woman! But, of course, Regina was his sister-in-law, so he'd inform her that all she had to do was sign the deed over to him and he'd promise her a home at the Black Diamond for as long as she desired. He'd be sure to point out to her that eventually she'd wish to marry, so she would not hold tenaciously to the ranch because someday she would leave it to live with her future husband.

Thoughts of Regina's prospective marriage recalled Miguel Ordaz' advice that she trap Matt Brolin, which brought Mace back to his reason for procrastinating on this morning. He needed to question Julie about her sister. If Regina hoped to marry Brolin, he was certain that she would have confided in Julie.

Looking at his wife, Mace asked with a feigned casualness, "Have you talked to Regina lately?"

"Yes, I saw her the other day," Julie answered.

"Did she say anything about Brolin?" he questioned, and he held his breath as he waited for Julie's reply.

Standing, and stacking the dishes, Julie murmured, "No, she didn't mention him at all. Why do you ask?"

"No special reason," Mace mumbled evasively, getting to his feet. Meanwhile he gloated inwardly, thinking that apparently the ploy Regina and Ordaz intended to use to trap Matt Brolin into marriage had failed! Smiling with relief, he continued, "I have some work to do with the hands this morning, but in the afternoon, I'll be going into town. Do you need me to pick up anything for you?"

"No, thank you," Julie replied, and as she turned to

119

carry the dishes to the counter, Mace leaned over and kissed her cheek. This token of affection startled Julie. Mace very seldom kissed her.

Smiling, he went to the front door and, grabbing his hat from the wall rack, stepped outside. He was still grinning largely as he moved across the porch and down the short flight of steps. Heading toward his bunkhouse, Mace was mentally picturing the Black Diamond and his own ranch as one spread. His land bordered the northern part of Regina's spread so he planned to combine the two properties. His future ranch would be even larger than Antonio Ramírez'. Mace was certain that very soon he'd be the richest and most prosperous rancher in New Mexico.

Entering Dan's saloon, Matt looked about, hoping to catch sight of Dan. Failing to locate him, he strolled across to the bar. "Where's Butler?" he asked the bartender.

"He said he was riding out to see his sister," he replied.

"Regina?" Matt specified.

Nodding, the man answered, "Yeah, I think she's the one he was planning to visit."

Matt had ridden into town directly from the range, which was why he hadn't run into Dan.

"Give me a beer," he ordered, placing a few coins on the bar.

Taking the filled mug, Matt sauntered to the table by the front window. Pulling out a chair, he sat down, and immediately his thoughts turned to Regina. He hadn't seen her since last night when she had so beautifully surrendered her love to him. This morning he had left the house before daybreak to ride out to the range. He had purposely departed early to avoid seeing Regina. He'd needed time to think. He had ridden to the east range, and sitting beneath a large cottonwood, he had watched the sun climb over the horizon. After giving his future and Regina's much thought, he had finally decided not to go to Wyoming if Regina agreed to marry him. Her happiness was more important to him than his own spread in Wyoming; Matt believed Regina would never truly be happy living anywhere except on her ranch. He could only hope that, in time, Regina's land would come to mean as much to him as it did to her.

Lifting his mug, he took a big drink of beer. He'd stayed away from Regina all day, and if he left now, it would be close to dusk before he reached the ranch. He had come to town solely to see Dan, so he could ask him to ride out to the Black Diamond later in the evening. He planned to ask Regina to marry him, and he wanted Dan to celebrate their engagement with them. Finishing his beer, Matt was about to get to his feet when Mace stepped into the saloon.

Seeing Matt, Mace smiled and called out, "Brolin, I'll get us some beer."

"I was just about to leave," Matt explained.

"You can stay and have one drink with me, can't you?" Mace asked hopefully. He desperately wanted to question Matt, to find out for himself exactly when the man intended to leave.

Conceding reluctantly, Matt agreed, "Sure, I have time for one more."

Quickly Mace ordered their drinks and, carrying the two mugs over to the table, sat down across from Matt. After helping himself to a generous swallow of beer, Mace stated in a friendly manner, "Well, I suppose you'll be leaving soon." When Matt didn't respond,

Mace pressed him. "When do you plan to leave?"

Matt preferred not to reveal his new plans to Mace, but the man's question had put him on the spot. He felt as though he should talk seriously to Regina before confiding in Mace, but he seemed to have no alternative but to tell Mace his intentions. Matt did not even consider telling Mace a lie because deceitfulness was a fault he could not tolerate, not in himself or in others. "I might not be leaving," he told Mace.

Mace had been about to take a drink of beer, but he lowered the mug to the table. "What?"

"I might not leave," Matt repeated.

"Why not?" Mace questioned, his jovial mood plunging.

Matt answered honestly. "I plan to ask Regina to marry me, and, if she agrees, we'll live on her ranch."

Mace paled, and his hand trembled as he lifted the heavy mug to his mouth. He took three enormous swallows before putting the mug back down. He was seething inwardly. Damn Regina, and damn Ordaz! he thought. So their deceitful scheme to manipulate Brolin had been successful after all! Well, he'd personally see that their plan failed. "You've been made into a fool," Mace said cynically, eying Matt speculatively.

Tensing, Matt replied menacingly, "Edwards, you'd better have a good explanation for what you just said!"

Mace smirked. "Oh, I have an explanation all right! On the same day that Ordaz paid off Regina's debt, he and Regina had a long, private conversation in the study. I didn't trust Ordaz, so I went to the study door and listened to what they were saying."

Matt frowned. He found Mace's sneaky maneuver disgusting.

"Ordaz seemed to be quite worried about the ten

thousand dollars he had invested in Regina's ranch. He does intend to be paid back with interest, doesn't he?"

"I don't see that his arrangement with Regina is any of your business," Matt replied impatiently.

"You shouldn't be so quick to guard Regina's and Ordaz' business arrangement, because they apparently don't give a damn about your best interest. Miguel Ordaz is a very devious man. He came up with the perfect solution to save Regina's ranch and guarantee his investment. He told Regina that all she had to do in order to secure her future, and the future of the Black Diamond, was to trap you into marriage." Mace sneered as he continued, "And, since you plan to ask Regina to marry you, obviously their conspiracy was successful." Mace was pleased to see barely controlled rage flicker dangerously in Matt's eyes. Getting to his feet, Mace told him calmly, "Think over what I told you, Brolin. Give it a lot of thought before you propose to Regina." Wanting to put even more emphasis on what he had maliciously told Matt, he leaned over and placed his hands on the table. His face only inches from Matt's, he pressed the issue, "I know Regina, and, believe me, the Black Diamond is all she cares about. She's just like her father was. Neither of them ever gave a damn about anyone, only themselves!"

Staring into Mace's eyes with a deadly coldness, Matt warned, "Get the hell away from me, Edwards!"

Backing up, Mace said hastily, "Regina made a fool of you, Brolin. She's not in love with you. Why do you think she's stayed unmarried so long? Because she isn't capable of loving any man, that's why! She's married to a goddamned piece of land!"

Flinging open the swinging doors, Mace darted outside. Then, turning back, he peeked into the saloon, and detecting Matt's silent anger, he smiled with satisfaction. He hurried to his horse and mounted. There was not a shred of doubt in Mace's mind that Brolin wouldn't be asking Regina to marry him.

Sitting on the porch steps, Dan watched Regina closely as she rocked back and forth in the pine rocker. He was deeply curious as to where her thoughts were. She had been unusually quiet and preoccupied.

Sighing heavily, Regina noticed that the sun was dipping farther into the west. Why had Matt stayed away all day? He had left so early that she hadn't even had a chance to see him before he rode out to the range. She had watched for his return all day, but only a few minutes ago, her foreman had informed her that Matt had gone into town. That information had been devastating to Regina. Apparently, Matt was still purposely avoiding her. After the love they had shared last night, how could he continue to treat her so coldly? Didn't he love her at all?

"Regina, is something bothering you?" Dan asked gently.

Tearing her thoughts away from Matt, Regina looked over at Dan. Should she take her brother into her confidence? She desperately needed to talk to someone. But, no, she'd wait until she saw Matt again. Maybe she was worrying needlessly. Matt might have a perfectly logical reason for staying away all day. It might have nothing to do with his feelings for her. Surely, he'd return soon and take her into his arms and tell her that he loved her!

"Regina?" Dan called softly when she made no reply to his inquiry.

Clearing her mind, Regina forced a smile. "I'm sorry, Dan. I seem to be lost in daydreams."

"Is everything all right?" he asked.

"Yes, everything is fine," she replied, suppressing her doubts. Then, wanting to turn the conversation away from herself, she queried, "By the way, how is Susan Chandler?"

"I'm not sure," he mumbled, his face suddenly troubled.

"Did something happen to her?" Regina asked, seeing Dan's worried look.

"Yes, I'm afraid so," he muttered, feeling guilty. Dan had brought Susan to the Black Diamond a couple of days after she had come to town, and now he asked, "What is your opinion of Susan?"

"I don't really know her well enough to give you an opinion. But she seemed very nice. Why do you ask, Dan? Did something happen between the two of you?"

He nodded a little reluctantly, "When she moved into Miss Rainey's boardinghouse and decided to work for Miss Rainey, it was because of me."

"Well, I can easily see why she chose to live at the boardinghouse, but why did she decide not to work at the restaurant?"

"She doesn't want to come into contact with me."

"But why?" Regina exclaimed. "When she was here at the ranch, she talked very highly of you. In fact, I got the feeling that she might be falling in love with you."

Standing, Dan leaned back against the porch railing, and crossing his arms over his chest, he replied regretfully, "Regina, the night before Susan moved out, I took advantage of her." His voice heavy with self-condemnation, he told Regina what had happened that night. Then he finished by saying, "She hasn't spoken to me since she moved into the boardinghouse, not for almost two months."

"Have you tried to see her?" Regina asked.

125

"I made several attempts to get in touch with her, but she flatly refused to cooperate." He shrugged, adding, "So finally I gave up."

"But you still feel terribly guilty, don't you?" Regina sensed his disturbance.

"I can't forgive myself for what I did to her," he admitted.

"It wasn't all your fault, Dan," Regina said firmly. "Besides, she should agree to see you and give you the opportunity to apologize."

"Apologize?" Dan raised his eyebrows. "I owe her more than an apology."

"What do you mean?" Regina asked carefully, hoping he wasn't leading up to what she feared.

"I owe her a marriage proposal," he answered quietly.

Regina had been afraid that Dan was contemplating marriage. Hurrying to her feet, she moved over to stand at his side. "Dan," she began urgently, "you can't marry Susan just because you feel obligated to do so! You would be doing an injustice to both of you. You must marry for love and for no other reason." Clutching his arm, she asked anxiously, "Are you in love with her?"

"I had hoped she'd start seeing me again so we'd have a chance to get to know each other better."

"Don't avoid my question!" Regina demanded testily. "Do you love her?"

"I don't know," he mumbled honestly.

"Dan, promise me you won't ask her to marry you until you know for sure that you love her!"

Now wishing to make light of the situation, he smiled as he answered, "I never knew you were such a romantic. What do you know about love, little sister?"

"I know that love should be the only basis for marriage," she breathed, as Matt's face flashed briefly in her mind.

"Are you saying you'd never marry for any reason other than love?"

Her voice intense, she declared, "I would never marry a man unless I sincerely loved him."

Chapter Eleven

Matt switched from beer to whiskey, and for over two hours he occupied the same table in Dan's saloon. He drank steadily, consuming one shot of whiskey after another, a deep and bitter resentment building in him. Regina had coldly tried to trick him into marriage, and he had almost fallen into her cunning trap.

His expression concealing his inner turmoil, Matt's thoughts turned to Miguel Ordaz. He supposed he should be just as disgusted with Miguel as he was with Regina, but he wasn't. Matt and Miguel had been close friends for too many years, and Matt understood how the man thought. Matt didn't doubt that when Miguel advised Regina to tempt him, he'd had Matt's best interest at heart. More than once, Miguel had made it perfectly clear that he was firmly against Matt moving to Wyoming. He wanted Matt to settle down, marry, and live fairly close to his hacienda so that they could visit each other frequently. Matt wholeheartedly agreed with Mace's analysis of Miguel Ordaz. The huge Mexican could indeed be devious, but Matt knew the man loved him like a brother. Still it had been a foolish mistake on Miguel's part to encourage Regina to use her feminine wiles to entrap him into marriage.

Matt's short, throaty laugh was harsh. Miguel probably had even believed that he and Regina would fall in love. Well, Miguel, old friend, Matt thought bitterly, you were partly right. I responded to Regina's tempting charms and fell in love with her.

Matt wondered if he should confront Miguel with what Mace had told him. He considered doing so for a moment, then decided to hell with it. There was no reason to bring up the unpleasant matter with Miguel. If he did, the man would only feel apologetic and perhaps remorseful. Matt owed Miguel too much to reproach him simply because he had given Regina foolish advice.

Matt had no animosity for Miguel Ordaz, but a slow burning resentment of Regina seared his heart.

He thought back to the night he had walked into the study to find her standing at the bookcase wearing a revealing negligée. Had she purposely planned that encounter, knowing how tempting and seductive she would appear? Hadn't she encouraged their embrace? Had that, too, been coldly calculated? Then, last night, she had once again taken the initiative when she had told him that she wanted him. Had that been only another ploy? Well, if it had, she had almost succeeded. Only his chance meeting with Mace had deterred him from proposing marriage.

Matt wished he could believe that Mace hadn't spoken the truth, but he couldn't think of one logical reason for the man to lie.

Once again, Matt filled his shot glass from the whiskey bottle on the table. He downed the drink in one quick swallow and, relaxing, leaned back in his chair. He shrugged his shoulders, telling himself he didn't give a damn about Regina's deceitfulness. So she wasn't the caring and honest woman he had thought her to be; now that he could see her as she truly was, he was certain that he'd get over her with relative ease. In a couple of days, his work here would be completed. Since he had promised Miguel that he'd visit him before going to Wyoming, he would do so. Then he would head for Wyoming and build his ranch. Nothing that had happened had changed his plans for the future; they had merely been temporarily delayed.

A sudden movement at his side caught Matt's eye, and glancing up, he saw Dolly standing next to his table. "Mind if I join you?" she asked, smiling invitingly.

Matt's eyes boldly took in the sensual curves which her flashy gown accentuated. Suddenly finding Dolly quite desirable, Matt inwardly cursed himself for letting his need for Regina cause him to turn away from her that first night when Dan had introduced them. He'd seen Dolly several times since then, but although she had made it very clear that he could have her anytime he wished, Matt had continued to reject her invitations. Recalling all the times he had refused Dolly, Matt smiled bitterly. Deep inside, he had wanted Regina so badly he had actually convinced himself that no other woman could possibly satisfy his craving. Well, he was no longer blindly enamored of Miss Blakely, and the best cure for what now ailed him was Dolly's very lovely and willing body. At least with Dolly there would be no trickery, no deceitfulness; she was for sale and made no bones about it.

Matt smirked bitterly. Regina Blakely was also for sale, but her price was not dollars, she demanded a man's pride, his self-esteem and dignity! Well, her price was too damned high and he wasn't buying!

Pushing back his chair, Matt patted his lap as he smiled at Dolly. "Of course you can join me, and don't bother to pull up a chair. You can set your pretty behind right here."

Dolly was pleasantly startled by Matt's suggestion. For the past two months she had tried to get Matt Brolin to want her. She could hardly believe that he was, at last, willing.

Sitting on Matt's lap, and sliding her arm about his neck, she whispered, "Let's go up to my room."

Matt chuckled, and moving a hand to her soft thigh, he replied, "After a while, but first let's have a couple of drinks."

Dolly agreed reluctantly. She was afraid if they waited too long something might happen to prevent Matt from sharing her bed.

Matt poured her a shot of whiskey, handed it to her, then took the bottle for himself. "To what shall we drink?" he asked.

Smiling, she answered, "To us?"

"Here's to you, Dolly," Matt toasted, raising his bottle.

"And to you, Matt Brolin," she responded.

As Dan entered his saloon, he was surprised to see Dolly sitting on Matt's lap. He had been aware of the times Matt had declined Dolly's sensual propositions. He started to go to their table, but changed his mind and headed toward the bar, making his way past tables filled with customers, most of them engrossed in games of poker or keno.

Facing the back of the bar, Dan's eyes traveled over the Trail Dust Saloon sign that hung between two framed pictures, one a sketch of a nude woman and the other a painting of an Indian buffalo hunt. Although his gaze seemed to be examining the sign and the bordering pictures, Dan wasn't really seeing them. His stare was vacant, but his thoughts were filled. He had always suspected Regina was Matt's reason for continually turning down Dolly. Dan had come to believe

131

that Matt might be falling in love with Regina, and he had hoped that Regina was also in love with Matt. He was certain that no two people could be more ideal for each other.

Hearing Dolly's sudden laughter mingling with Matt's, Dan turned and glanced toward their table just as Dolly bent her head to kiss Matt full on the lips.

Looking away, Dan frowned with disappointment. I guess I was wrong about Matt and Regina, he thought regretfully. He told his bartender to pour him a shot of whiskey, and as he polished off the drink in one swallow, Dan decided that when it came to love his speculations weren't worth a damn.

Regina halted the black stallion in front of the saloon. As she noticed Matt's horse tied to the hitching rail, anger sparked in her green eyes. When night had descended and Matt still hadn't returned, Regina had begun to fear that something might have happened to him. She hadn't forgotten Robert Selman's threat on Matt's life! Unable to stay home where she had nothing to do but worry, she had decided to search for Matt.

Now, seeing Matt's horse outside the Trail Dust Saloon, Regina knew that Matt was perfectly all right. Her worry had been for naught. How could he be so inconsiderate? Surely he must realize she would be concerned when he didn't come home!

Dismounting, she flung Midnight's reins over the rail. She was determined to give Matt a piece of her mind!

Stepping to the swinging doors, Regina pushed them open, then gasped at the sight that confronted her. Matt had one arm about Dolly's waist and was escorting her up the stairway to the rooms above. Hearing Regina's gasp, he turned to look behind him, and for a tense moment, his eyes met Regina's. Then, whirling, she darted outside.

Standing at the bar, Dan had witnessed Regina's entrance, and as she was fleeing, he hurried after her. When he reached the doors, however, he felt Matt's hand descend on his shoulder.

"I'll take care of this!" Matt stated, his tone leaving no room for argument.

Dan stepped aside, and Matt flung open the doors, leaving as quickly as Regina had. Dan's brow furrowed thoughtfully. Apparently, he had been wrong to think there was nothing personal between Regina and Matt. But, if there was something, then what in the hell was Matt doing with Dolly? He glanced up the stairway. Dolly was still standing where Matt had rudely left her, disappointment on her face.

Regina was about to mount her stallion when Matt walked up behind her. Placing her foot in the stirrup, she ignored his presence as she swung herself into the saddle and jerked the reins, but Matt quickly grabbed the horse's harness, halting her retreat.

"You shouldn't ride alone at night," he said, wondering why he still cared about her safety. "If you'll wait, I'll escort you to the ranch."

Scowling, she snapped, "Your lady friend is waiting for you. Go back to her and stay the hell away from me!"

Matt studied her critically. So she was actually going to pretend that she was jealous! Damn it, didn't she ever run out of deceitful little schemes?

"Let go of my horse!" Regina demanded sharply.

Matt released his hold, and turning the stallion, Regina dug her heels into Midnight's sides, sending him into a fast gallop.

Matt swerved to return to the saloon, but upon seeing Dan poised in front of the doors, he came to an

133

unexpected halt.

"If you don't go after her," Dan began, "then I will. She has no business riding by herself this time of night."

Matt started to flippantly inform Dan that he could have the honor, but he suddenly realized he had lost his desire for Dolly and for whiskey. Was Regina the cause of his sudden disinterest in Dolly and booze? By God, what kind of damned witchery did she practice? Fuming, he grabbed his horse's reins and remarked testily, "I'll catch up to her and make sure she gets home safely!"

As Matt was mounting up, Dan asked hesitantly, "Matt, is something going on between you and Regina?"

"There's not one damned thing between your sister and me that's worth discussing!" Matt replied sourly.

"I don't believe you, Brolin," Dan argued.

Refusing to comment, Matt slapped the reins against his horse's neck and headed in the same direction Regina had taken.

Once outside the town limits, Regina gave Midnight free rein, letting him run as fast as he pleased. As she raced across the landscape on the stallion's broad back, the night air whipped about her, making her long blond tresses stream behind her. She tried not to cry, but she was hurting so badly that she couldn't stop some tears from falling.

Matt didn't love her, and now she was sure that he never would. She had given away her heart, only to have it broken! Oh Matt . . . Matt! she cried silently, her love for him a torment. I don't think I will ever get over losing you!

Grasping the reins in one hand, Regina wiped at her

tears in an attempt to clear her vision. But the effort was a useless one, for by this time she was crying so hard that new tears kept flooding her eyes.

If Regina hadn't been blinded by her tears, she might have spotted the small gopher hole in the stallion's path and directed him safely around the gaping hazard. Fortunately, Midnight's hoof barely grazed the outer edge of the hole, but the mishap forced the animal off stride, causing him to stumble.

The stallion whinnied, and a powerful tremor racked his body as he limped to an awkward halt.

Regina loved Midnight, and she desperately hoped that his injury wasn't serious as she hastily dismounted. He was holding his weight off his front right leg. Kneeling, Regina reached toward him. His nostrils flaring, he snorted powerfully, backing away from her touch.

"Midnight," she pleaded desperately, "please let me check your leg!" What would she do if it were broken? Could she bring herself to shoot him? I can't kill an animal that I love! she thought, although in the deep recesses of her mind, she knew the animal would have to be destroyed if his leg was broken. Once again, she made a careful attempt to check his leg, but as before, Midnight drew away.

Her heart breaking over Matt's betrayal and Midnight's injury, Regina stopped kneeling and sat on the earth. Raising her knees, she folded her arms across them, and pillowing her head, she began to sob uncontrollably. Limping slightly, the stallion edged closer, and lowering his huge head, he nudged his nose against Regina's bowed shoulder.

Regina was crying so heavily that she didn't hear Matt's arrival. He was puzzled to find her sitting on the ground, and, apparently, quite upset. Could he have

135

been wrong? Had her jealousy been real? Could it be that she was in love with him? If her actions had been insincere, there was no reason for her to continue her deceitfulness out here in the middle of nowhere. Suddenly aware that Regina's deep, tearing sobs were caused by real pain, Matt dismounted swiftly.

Was he the reason behind her tears? Was she hurting so terribly because of him? Hurrying to Regina, he silently pleaded with her to give him just one sign that she truly loved him. By God, if she did he'd take care of the rest!

Hearing footsteps, Regina looked up quickly, surprised to see that Matt had followed her.

"Regina, what's wrong?" he asked, then waited anxiously for her answer.

How desperately she longed to throw herself into his arms and beg him to love her! But holding onto her pride, she answered, "It's Midnight. He stumbled, and I'm afraid his leg might be broken."

Matt's hurt was visible for only a fleeting moment before he concealed it. It happened so quickly that Regina never saw his pain.

She's crying over a horse!, Matt thought bitterly. And I was actually foolish enough to think she might be crying over me!

His resentment toward Regina now stronger than ever, Matt went to the stallion and knelt in front of him. Midnight's reins were trailing the ground so Matt grasped them firmly, holding the horse in place as he ran a hand over the animal's leg. He examined Midnight's injury with extreme care. When he stood upright, Regina hurried to his side.

"Is his leg broken?" she asked fearfully.

Matt shook his head. "No, it isn't broken. He'll be all right, but it'll be a few days before you can ride him."

136

Regina sighed with relief. "Thank goodness, he wasn't seriously injured." She stepped up to Midnight and, wrapping her arms about the horse's neck, hugged him affectionately.

Matt looked on for a moment before stating brusquely, "Let's go. We'll have to ride double."

Fighting her need to fling herself into Matt's arms, Regina walked over to his horse, and Matt quickly stepped to her side, intending to help her mount. But Midnight's accident and Matt's dalliance with Dolly had taken their toll on Regina. A feeling of dizziness came over her, and she leaned toward Matt for support. His strong arms grasped her, and overcoming her sudden weakness, Regina looked up at him.

Mistaking her swoon for another attempt to entice him, Matt's eyes hardened as his gaze met hers. The severity in his glance startled Regina, and she tried to squirm out of his embrace. But keeping her pinned against him, he continued to stare darkly into her upturned face. Then, against his own volition, his body began to respond to hers. Knowing he hadn't the will power to refuse her, he decided that two could play her cunning little game. If she wanted to trap him into marriage by offering him her very delectable body, then he'd accept her tempting bait, but when it was time for him to move on, he'd leave her without so much as a backward glance.

Regina wasn't expecting Matt's kiss, and when his lips suddenly pressed against hers with demanding force, she gasped for breath. Matt removed his mouth from hers long enough to allow her to inhale deeply before he once again kissed her forcefully. He entwined his fingers in her hair, keeping his lips against hers. Surrendering, Regina laced her arms about his neck, and her mouth parted beneath his so that he could deepen their kiss. She clung tightly to Matt, and as his heated kiss continued, an intense longing overwhelmed her.

Matt lowered his lips to her neck, as his fingers undid the buttons on her blouse. Then pushing aside the material, and bending his head, he sent fleeting kisses over the soft fullness of her breasts. Within moments he was lifting her into his arms and carrying her to the shelter afforded by a towering tree. Gently, he laid her on a bed of grass, and, positioning himself beside her, drew her close.

Matt impatiently drew her skirt up to her thighs as, leaning over her, his lips sought hers. His tongue darted into her mouth at the same instant his hand slipped beneath her undergarment to cup her warm mound, and this intimate caress caused Regina to moan with desire. She longed to tell Matt how dearly she loved him, but his own deep silence dissuaded her from doing so.

The pain in his loins demanding release, Matt rose swiftly to his knees and quickly removed Regina's skirt and undergarment. The moon's golden rays shone on Regina's fair skin, and Matt's eyes roamed hungrily over her, finally touching on the blond triangle between her thighs. She was so beautiful and so desirable!

Unbuckling his holster, Matt placed it on the ground. As he shed his trousers, Regina watched him. She wished she could read his thoughts, but his face was inscrutable.

Without changing his expression, he placed himself between her legs and, slipping his arm about her waist, brought her thighs into contact with his. He entered her swiftly, filling Regina with rapturous pleasure.

Matt's lips crushed hers as he began to move inside her, and lifting her hips, she matched her movements perfectly with his.

138

Overcome with love, Regina murmured provocatively, "Oh Matt . . . Matt, my darling, I need you."

You need me to run your damned ranch! Matt thought, enraged. His anger surging, he pounded into her roughly and aggressively. Matt's unbridled passion aroused Regina, and she responded with total abandonment. Her fervent response excited Matt, and holding her thighs flush to his, he achieved a potent release.

A deep sigh came from Regina as, embracing him, she also found the peak of pleasure.

Remaining in her arms, Matt relaxed for a moment, while his rapid breathing slowed to normal.

Regina waited hopefully for him to tell her that he loved her, but instead he stood and slipped into his trousers. Her disappointment was so great that she felt her heart would break.

Keeping his eyes averted from hers, he strapped on his gun belt. "You'd better get dressed," he advised, his voice void of warmth. "We need to get back to the ranch so Juan can tend to Midnight's leg." When she made no reply, he looked down at her.

Not wanting Matt to see her suffering, Regina rolled onto her side.

"Regina," he said impatiently, "your horse is in pain."

So am I! she thought wretchedly, but when he turned away and walked over to the horses, Regina arose and got dressed. Then she stepped over to his horse, and he assisted her into the saddle.

As he swung himself up behind her, she pleaded, "Matt, something is wrong. Please tell me what it is!"

"Nothing is wrong," he declared short-temperedly. "I'm just tired and need a good night's sleep."

"But, Matt—" she began.

He silenced her sharply. "Regina, say no more!"

Guiding his horse over to the stallion, he leaned over and grabbed Midnight's reins. Then they rode to the ranch without speaking. Deeply involved in their own turbulent thoughts, they both wondered how it was possible to continue to love someone who was capable of such callous betrayal.

Chapter Twelve

At daybreak, Regina was still tossing restlessly. Hoping she'd eventually fall asleep, she remained in bed as the sun continued its ascent into the sky. Finally, realizing her anxieties were too great to allow her the luxury of sleep, Regina got up, dressed, and went to the kitchen for breakfast.

When she sat down at the table, Luisa placed a plate of eggs and bacon in front of her. Regina took one look at the food and knew that her inner turmoil had not only deprived her of sleep but of her appetite as well. How could she conceivably eat or sleep until she knew exactly where she stood with Matt? Pushing aside her plate, Regina's mind worked feverishly as she sipped her coffee.

Noticing that Luisa was on her way out of the kitchen with the pot of coffee, Regina asked her where she was going. Luisa quickly told her that Señor Brolin had asked her earlier to bring his coffee to the study. Regina was surprised to learn that Matt was still in the house. Why hadn't he ridden out to the range? She had never known him not to leave by daybreak. Was she his reason for lingering? Did he stay home to talk to her about their future? Was he planning to ask her to marry him? Hope surging rapidly, Regina informed Luisa that she'd take Matt his coffee, but the servant's answer completely shattered Regina's expectations. Luisa stated reluctantly that Señor Brolin had given explicit instructions; he did not want to see anyone, especially Miss Blakely.

Disappointed, as well as crestfallen, Regina returned to her bedroom. She had never felt more apprehensive, and she spent the next two hours pacing back and forth. Surely Matt would soon send word that he wished to see her! He couldn't possibly intend to leave for Wyoming without even discussing their relationship! No, he would talk to her, and when he did? . . . Would he ask her to leave with him? Would he tell her that he loved her? Or was he destined to ride out of her life? Oh Matt, please . . . please don't leave me! Regina silently begged.

Suddenly, Luisa knocked on Regina's door. *"Señorita?"*

Praying frantically that Matt had sent for her, Regina swung open the door. Holding her breath with anticipation, she asked, "Yes, Luisa?"

"Señor Ramírez is here," the woman announced.

Her elation dissipating, Regina replied, "But this isn't the day for my lesson. Why does Antonio wish to see me?"

"I do not know," Luisa answered. "He is waiting in the parlor."

"Very well, Luisa. Tell Mr. Ramírez I'll be right there." The servant left, and Regina went to her dresser. Peering into the mirror, she studied her reflection as she brushed her hair. Taking a rose-colored ribbon that matched the shade of her dress, Regina used it to hold back her blond tresses. Then she stepped back from the mirror to make one final appraisal of herself. If Regina had been vain, she would have admired the way her gown complemented her full breasts, small waist, and curvaceous hips, but in her unselfconscious way she simply decided she looked perfectly all right to receive company.

Leaving her bedroom, Regina headed for the parlor, but as she passed by the study, she hesitated and glanced warily at the closed door. She wanted to fling it open, rush into the room, and throw herself into Matt's arms! But fearing rejection, she by-passed the study and continued down the hall and into the foyer. The parlor was located across from the entryway so Regina could see Antonio sitting on the sofa.

As she stepped into the room, he rose promptly, greeting her by lifting her hand to his lips and kissing it softly.

Smiling, Regina said cordially, "Good morning, Antonio."

"Morning?" he questioned. *"Señorita,* it is past noon."

"It is?" she pondered. "My goodness, today I seem to have lost all track of time." She studied him for a moment, finding him extremely attractive. He was garbed in black trousers trimmed in gold thread, and a matching vest beneath which he wore a ruffled white shirt. "Would you like a cup of tea or perhaps a glass of wine?" she asked courteously.

"No, thank you, *señorita."* Antonio declined her offer graciously.

Watching him, Regina waited. She was curious about why he had come.

"I suppose you are wondering why I have paid you this unexpected visit. Please except my apology for intruding without first sending a message asking for your permission."

Hastily, Regina informed him, "Antonio, you owe me no apology. You are always welcome in my home."

"Gracias, señorita. You are very generous," he replied. Then, with a somewhat nervous sigh, Antonio moved a short way from Regina. He couldn't understand why he was feeling as apprehensive as a young suitor about to ask his first love for her hand in matrimony. He was a mature man well into his forties, with a grown son; so why did he feel so unsure of himself? Hadn't self-assurance always been one of his strong points? So why was he now so full of uncertainty? It is because I've never truly been in love before, Antonio decided. Love makes even the most powerful man vulnerable.

Turning his back to Regina, Antonio placed his hands on his hips, and shifting his weight to one foot, he glanced thoughtfully about the room while he contemplated the best way to ask Regina to marry him. The Blakely parlor was decorated tastefully in a Spanish décor, but the colorful furnishings were not seen by Antonio. He was concentrating so deeply on his marriage proposal that his eyes surveyed the room without actually seeing the woven rugs, the dark oak furniture, or the expensive knickknacks placed artistically about the room.

"Antonio?" Regina asked. "Is something wrong?"

Her voice caused him to whirl about, and admiring her loveliness, he approached her. Taking both of her hands in his, Antonio gazed down into Regina's emerald green eyes. *"Señorita,"* he murmured, "you are very beautiful."

Blushing slightly, she responded, "Thank you, Antonio."

His hold on her hands tightened as he continued, "Regina, these last couple of months, we have spent much time together. I have come to know you very well, and I not only respect you, but I also. . . ."

"Yes, Antonio?" She encouraged him, never imagin-

144

ing his intent.

"I have also fallen in love with you. Regina, I came here today to ask you to marry me," he confessed. Then, holding his breath, he awaited her answer.

Regina was taken totally by surprise. She had never dreamed that Antonio Ramírez might be in love with her. Yet she was very fond of Antonio, so she took no pleasure in answering, "I'm sorry, but I can't marry you."

"I realize you do not love me, *señorita,*" he said urgently, "but sometimes love comes after marriage."

"So I have been told," Regina murmured, recalling the advice Miguel Ordaz had once given her concerning matrimony. Antonio was still holding her hands, so gently squeezing his hands with hers, Regina explained tenderly, "Antonio, I am already in love."

Emitting a deep sigh, he relinquished her hands as he asked softly, "Señor Brolin?"

Nodding, Regina answered somberly, "Yes, I'm in love with Matt."

Detecting her sadness, Antonio queried, "This love, it does not make you happy, *señorita?*"

"Oh, Antonio," she began intensely, "I could be ecstatically happy if only . . . if only—"

"If only Señor Brolin loved you in return?" Antonio guessed. Studying Regina tenderly, he proceeded, "If Matt Brolin does not love you, then he is a fool."

"I don't know whether or not he loves me," Regina admitted. "Sometimes, I believe he does, but at other times I'm sure he doesn't care about me at all."

Antonio resented losing Regina to a man who did not appreciate her, but he suddenly remembered that Matt would soon be leaving for Wyoming. He might still win the heart of the woman he loved. With Matt Brolin out of Regina's life, he could pursue her without competition. It was only a matter of time before Regina would be his wife.

Conceding to fate with a humility that he wasn't truly feeling, Antonio placed his hands on Regina's shoulders and asked gently, *"Señorita,* will you please kiss me goodbye?"

"But, Antonio, this isn't goodbye. We can still be friends, can't we?" she pleaded.

"Of course we can be friends," he replied quickly. "And forgive my rude conduct. I should not have asked for a kiss. But I love you, Regina, and a kiss would soothe my aching heart." Antonio was certain she'd agree to kiss him. Following his touching plea, how could she possibly refuse?

Responding as he knew she would, Regina slipped her arms about his neck and brought his lips down on hers. Antonio knew it would be a mistake for him to turn their kiss into one of passion. He was sure Regina would pull away from him, so he kept their embrace tender in the hope that she'd allow their kiss to linger. Antonio was extremely gentle as he encircled Regina with his arms and drew her closer. The embrace stirred no desire in Regina, but she liked Antonio and felt badly about rejecting his love. Only compassion for him compelled her to remain in his arms.

Emerging from the study, Matt left the door ajar as he walked down the hallway. He was on his way to the kitchen to ask Luisa where he could find Regina, but detecting voices coming from the parlor, he headed in that direction. He had no ulterior motive for moving soundlessly. Because of his precarious past, it had become second nature for Matt to walk with graceful, light steps.

He reached the parlor at the same moment that Regina slipped her arms about Antonio, and his face darkened with fury as he watched Antonio draw her into his embrace. Then, swerving swiftly, Matt hurried back down the hall and into the study. In his anger and resentment, he wanted to slam the door shut, but he didn't want Regina and Antonio to know he had witnessed their lover's embrace so he closed it quietly.

Striding to the desk, he sat down in the leather-bound chair. There was a bottle of brandy on the desktop, and grabbing it, Matt wrenched it open. Not bothering to use a glass, he tilted the bottle to his mouth and took a large swallow of the potent liquor.

My God, how many times was he going to let Regina make a fool of him? Why did he keep letting her pull the wool over his eyes?

After giving Regina's behavior hours of thought, Matt had finally decided to confront her with what Mace had told him. He had been willing to give her the benefit of the doubt, to allow her to tell her side of the story, thinking that perhaps Mace had misconstrued what he had overheard between Miguel and Regina.

Now Matt frowned bitterly, deciding that Mace hadn't been wrong after all. Apparently, Regina Blakely was as conniving as Mace had led him to believe. He wondered if Antonio Ramírez was her ace in the hole. If she lost the cunning game she was playing with him, did she plan to keep Ramírez in reserve? Picturing the embrace he had just witnessed, he remembered it had been Regina who had made the first move. She had initiated the kiss, not Antonio. Perhaps she realized that with Ramírez for a husband her ranch would definitely be secure.

Matt took another swallow of brandy; then replacing the cap, he set the bottle on the desk. To hell with Regina Blakely and her Black Diamond spread, he was going to Wyoming, and the sooner the better! The best way to get Regina out of his thoughts was to put distance between them. Determined to leave immediately, Matt rose from the chair and walked quickly across the room. Stepping into the hall, he closed the door loudly so that Regina and Antonio would be warned of his approach.

Regina had just bid Antonio good day, and she was stepping away from the front door when Matt entered the foyer. At the sight of him she stopped abruptly, and her heart pounded heavily as her gaze met his. But seeing only cold aloofness in the eyes staring into hers, Regina lowered her own. Matt's dark brown trousers were skin tight, and his tan shirt was partially unbuttoned. Looking at his lean, strong frame made Regina long to feel his body next to hers. He wore his holster low on his hip, tied securely to his thigh, and the leather gun belt that rested snugly below his waist made his male bulge more prominent. As her eyes centered on his maleness, Regina felt an ache spreading between her thighs.

"Regina," Matt began calmly, willfully keeping his composure, "I'll be leaving in a few minutes."

"Wh . . . what?" she gasped, hoping she hadn't heard him correctly.

"I'm leaving," he repeated.

"You mean for good?" she gasped. Oh, surely he meant he was only riding into town!

"My work here is completed," he answered flatly. "There's no reason for me to linger."

"Can't you stay until tomorrow morning?" Regina pleaded, wishing frantically to delay his departure even for a night!

"I'll be packed and gone in about fifteen minutes," he announced brusquely. She was puzzled to see anger flickering brightly in his dark eyes as he added bluntly, "Let's say goodbye now, shall we? I'm sure you plan to try to convince me to stay, but I'm leaving. There's

148

nothing you can say or do to change my mind."

Her heart breaking, Regina cried, "How can you leave me this way? Don't my feelings mean anything to you?"

Matt laughed harshly. "Regina, I know all about your so-called "feelings," and to be perfectly honest, darlin', I don't give a damn how you feel!"

Turning smoothly, he left Regina and hurried down the hallway to return to the study.

His cold severity shocked Regina into believing that he cared nothing about her. The man she loved with all her heart and soul did not love her. In fact, he had acted as though he didn't even like her. Trying to hold back her tears, Regina fled to her bedroom, determined to remain there until Matt was gone. She intended to stay out of his sight so he couldn't see how badly he had hurt her. Alone with her grief, Regina fell across the bed. She wished that she did not love Matt because she could not understand his cruel behavior.

Susan wrung her hands nervously as she stood across the street from the Trail Dust Saloon. She was trying to gather the courage to walk inside the establishment and ask for Dan, but never in her eighteen years of life had she entered a saloon! When she had rented a room from Dan, she had always used the rear stairway because it led into the back of the restaurant, whereas the front staircase descended into the saloon.

Perspiration accumulated on the palms of her hands, and distractedly, she wiped them on her skirt. It had now been almost two months since she had last talked to Dan. Following their disagreement, he had come several times to the boardinghouse, but she had flatly refused to see him. Susan had believed that Dan's guilt would continue to plague him and so he would persist in his efforts to contact her. Much to her disappointment, after three weeks of being turned away, he stopped seeking her out. Susan hadn't counted on Dan giving up so easily. She'd had every intention of forgiving him eventually. She had only wanted to prove that she was not a woman to be taken lightly. Now she had come to realize that if she didn't make the next move toward a reconciliation, she would lose Dan permanently.

Lifting the skirt of her long dress, Susan stepped off the wooden sidewalk and began to cross the dusty street. Her gaze fixed on the saloon, she raised her chin haughtily as she mentally rehearsed her approaching meeting with Dan. She had decided to behave like a lady who has been wronged, but at the same time to act as though she were the one who should ask for forgiveness. *That is the way I feel,* Susan told her conscience. *I was done a terrible injustice, and although I should despise Dan Butler, I feel no animosity toward him. Furthermore it is quite true that, in a way, I have treated him unfairly. But I still love him, and if I play my cards very carefully, he'll soon be asking me to marry him.*

Upon reaching the entrance of the Trail Dust Saloon, Susan smiled triumphantly. She was thinking that as soon as she became Mrs. Dan Butler that sinful business would be sold. Her smile widened as she envisioned a for sale sign nailed above the swinging doors. Then she took a hesitant step toward the doors of the saloon. Her courage was beginning to falter, and she wasn't sure if she actually had the nerve to enter. *I must!* she told herself. *My whole future depends on this meeting with Dan!*

Cautiously, she glanced about. She didn't want any of the friends she'd made since she'd moved into Miss Rainey's boardinghouse to see her entering a saloon.

150

Since there was no one close by, she took advantage of the nearly deserted street and darted inside.

Without looking left or right, she headed straight for the bar and informed the bartender that she wished to see Dan Butler. Pointing toward a door at the back of the room, he told her that Mr. Butler was in his office. It was early afternoon, and the saloon wasn't crowded, but the few patrons at the bar stared incredulously at Susan as she walked swiftly toward Dan's office. It was unusual to see a lady in a saloon, especially an unescorted one.

Pausing at the closed door, Susan knocked.

"Come in," Dan called out in response. Entering, and closing the door behind her, Susan saw Dan sitting at his desk, surrounded by paperwork. Putting down his pen, Dan glanced up.

"Susan!" he gasped, obviously startled to see her. Rising and hurrying around the desk, he went to her side. "You shouldn't have come here," he said caringly. "If you had sent a message, I'd have come to you."

Susan glowed inwardly. He still cared about her! Why else would he be so considerate?

"Dan," she began softly, lowering her eyes modestly, "I came here to ask you to please forgive me."

Dan was astounded. "Forgive you? Susan, I am the one who should be pleading for forgiveness."

Keeping her eyes downcast she murmured, "I suppose you are right, but, Dan, I have treated you unfairly." She raised her gaze to his, and he was distressed to see tears glistening in her eyes. "Surely you must realize that I believe what happened between us was wrong! I feel so ashamed! I know I could never bring myself to marry! I wouldn't feel right about going to my husband . . . dishonored."

Dan had never been more aggravated with himself. He wondered why in the hell he had gotten involved in such a situation? He had always made it a point to avoid virgins, but he considered himself a man of honor and he'd not shirk his duty.

Gently he grasped Susan's shoulders, and studying her tenderly, he replied, "I cannot undo what has already been done. God knows, I would if I could. We must try to forget that night and start over."

"What are you saying?" she asked fearfully. Her heart pounded rapidly because she feared he was planning to tell her that he had no intention of continuing their relationship!

"I'm trying to ask your permission to pay court. I think that's the correct terminology." He grinned.

"You want to court me?" she asked happily.

"Yes, but as a gentleman," he quickly assured her.

Susan was victorious! Dan wanted to court her, and she was sure his courtship would lead to matrimony.

"Well?" Dan pressed with a smile. "May I call on you?"

Her eyes shining radiantly, Susan answered, "Yes, of course you may!"

Chapter Thirteen

Regina remained in her bedroom until late afternoon before finally deciding to go into town to see Dan, but as she removed her riding clothes from the mahogany wardrobe, her thoughts were on Matt. Why had he treated her so coldly? What had she done to make him hurt her so deeply?

Dressing quickly and leaving the room, she hurried into the kitchen. Seeing Luisa sitting at the table and peeling potatoes for dinner, she told her, "I'm going into town."

Luisa turned her plump frame toward Regina. "But it is too late, it will be dark before you can return."

"I plan to spend the night in town. I'll take a room at the hotel."

"Why must you go into town, *señorita?*" she questioned.

"I want to be with Dan," Regina answered solemnly. "I need to see my brother." She strove for control, but she desperately needed to be close to someone she loved, who loved her in return. Surely Dan's presence would make her feel better and perhaps seeing him would ease this terrible pain that losing Matt had created.

"Where is Juan?" Regina asked, but the question had scarcely passed her lips before he entered the kitchen through the back door. "Juan," Regina began, "will you saddle a horse for me? I'm going to town."

"Sí, señorita." He nodded.

"How is Midnight's leg?" she inquired.

"It is healing very well, but it will still be a few days before you can ride him."

As Juan walked out the door to carry out Regina's instructions, Luisa said, "Señor Brolin, he left a couple of hours ago." She sighed heavily. "I will miss him. Señor Brolin is a very nice man, sí?"

"Did . . . did he leave a message for me?" Regina asked hesitantly, at the same time wondering why she couldn't make herself face the truth. Matt cared nothing about her, so why did she keep grasping at straws?

"No, señorita," Luisa replied.

Regina left the kitchen quickly so that Luisa couldn't see her hurt and disappointment. Going to the study, she took her Winchester from the gun cabinet; then as she crossed the room, she paused and looked about. Matt's presence was everywhere. His bottle of brandy was still on the desktop, and the ashtray held a partially smoked cheroot. Inhaling, she could even detect the scent of his shaving lotion. "Oh, Matt! . . . Matt!" she moaned tearfully. Resuming her steps, she rushed out of the study and headed for her bedroom to pack an overnight bag.

As she was leaving the house, Juan appeared from the direction of the stables, leading a saddled horse. "I do not think you should ride into town alone," he mumbled as she hurried to meet him.

Pausing at the horse's side, Regina reached up and slipped her rifle into the scabbard. She then attached her bag to the saddle. "I'll be fine," she assured Juan.

As he helped her mount, he grumbled, "I still do not like you riding alone." He wondered why he even bothered to state his objections. Didn't Señorita Blakely always do as she pleased, regardless of his advice?

Sending the horse into a gallop, Regina called over her shoulder, "I'll be back tomorrow."

Sitting at a table with Dan in his restaurant, Regina stared at the food on her plate. She had no appetite so she picked up her fork and toyed with the potatoes. The room was fairly crowded, and she absentmindedly listened to the sounds of people dining and talking to each other.

Eying Regina closely, Dan suddenly asked, "Do you want to talk about it?"

"What?" she asked vacantly.

"Do you want to talk about it?" he repeated. "Obviously, something is troubling you."

Putting down her fork, Regina murmured sadly, "Oh Dan, I'm so terribly depressed."

"Because of Matt Brolin?" he queried.

"How did you know?"

He smiled tenderly. "I suspected something was going on between you two." Dan reached over and placed a hand over hers. "Are you in love with him?"

"Yes," she whispered.

He squeezed her hand affectionately. Then, releasing it, he asked softly, "Does he love you?"

Tears shone in her eyes as she replied. "No. Matt doesn't love me."

"Are you sure?" Dan pressed.

She nodded somberly. "I don't understand Matt. He's so complex and ambivalent. You've known him longer than I have. Has he always been the way he

155

is now?"

"I'm not that closely acquainted with him. As far as I know, there are only two people who are close to Matt. Miguel and José."

"Who is José?" Regina asked.

"An old Mexican who befriended Matt years ago. I don't know the story behind their friendship. But I do remember Matt once telling me that José means a great deal to him."

"Where is José?"

"I think he's working on a ranch outside of Santa Fe. He works for Alan Garrett. If I remember correctly, Matt once worked for Garrett himself."

"Before he became a bounty hunter?"

Dan nodded. "I think so."

"When was Matt in prison?"

"I don't know," Dan replied.

"Do you know why he was sent to prison?"

"No," he answered.

Regina sighed discontently. "Why am I asking all these questions about Matt? It's foolish to be so curious about a man I'll probably never see again. He's on his way to Wyoming, and here I sit with him still in my heart and on my mind."

"He's not on his way to Wyoming—at least not at the moment."

"Wh . . . what do you mean?" she stammered.

"He's spending the night in town. He has a room at the hotel."

"How do you know?"

"He was at the saloon earlier, and he told me he wasn't leaving town until tomorrow morning." Reading Regina's thoughts, Dan advised, "Gina, don't go see him. When he was at the saloon, he was hitting the whiskey pretty hard."

"But, Dan, I must talk to him!" she declared intensely.

"Why?" he insisted gently.

"I want him to explain . . . explain . . ." Her voice faded.

"Explain what?" Dan encouraged.

Regina couldn't continue. How could she conceivably tell her brother why Matt owed her an explanation? She certainly didn't want Dan to know everything that had happened. If Dan knew of the truth, he might very well feel it was his duty to confront Matt, and knowing her brother, she feared he would insist that Matt marry her. She didn't want to become Matt's wife because he was pressed into a wedding.

Regina said brusquely, "Thanks for the dinner, but if you'll excuse me, I need to get back to the hotel."

Dan's arm shot across the table, and he grasped her hand to keep her from leaving. "You're planning to go to Matt, aren't you?" he demanded quietly. She didn't reply, but he could see the truth in her eyes. "Gina, I don't think that is a wise move. You've lived a relatively sheltered life, and you don't understand how liquor can affect a man. I don't know what happened between you and Matt, but I do know he was downing one shot of whiskey after another—and I'm sure you were the reason behind his drinking."

Forcefully, Regina pulled her hand free, and standing, she remarked firmly, "Dan, I know you mean well, but you must realize that I'm a grown woman. I can handle my life where men are concerned."

"But Matt Brolin isn't just any man," he reminded her.

"Yes, I know," she murmured. Stepping to Dan's side of the table, she bent over and kissed his cheek. "Good night," she mumbled hastily. Then she hurried across the dining-room floor.

Watching Regina leave, Dan's first impulse was to go after her, but he decided against it. He waited a moment, then pushed back his chair and got to his feet. Taking long strides, he walked through the dining room and outside. He still believed Matt and Regina belonged together, and he hoped that everything would work out between them.

Upon entering the hotel lobby, Regina stepped quickly to the desk and asked the clerk which room Matt was occupying. Then she hurried to the stairway and climbed it swiftly. Her pulse was racing at the thought of seeing Matt. Only moments before, she had believed that she would never see him again!

The hallway was dim, and as Regina darted around a corner, she collided with a man who had been heading for the stairway. The collison caused her to lose her balance, and she would have fallen if a pair of strong hands had not grabbed her shoulders to steady her.

Regina glanced up to thank the man for his support, but recognizing the dark eyes staring into hers, she gasped, "Matt!"

Tightening his hold, he pulled her closer. "What in the hell are you doing here?" he demanded harshly.

"I . . . I have a room for the night," she answered hesitantly, wary of his foul mood.

Turning her loose, he stepped back and started to brush past her, but she clutched his arm.

"Matt," she pleaded, "I must talk to you! Let's go someplace where we can be alone."

He smiled, but the expression in his eyes was cold. He believed she was continuing her deceitful little game by following him to town and checking into the hotel. My God, he thought, doesn't her conniving little mind ever run out of ploys? Mistaking her motive as one last desperate effort to inveigle him, his smile widened devilishly. The goods she was offering were desirable, so he might as well accept them.

"Your room or mine?" he asked, quirking an eyebrow.

"We can use my room," she decided, never imagining the path his thoughts had taken.

Impetuously, she grabbed his hand, leading him further down the hall. When they reached her room, she released him so that she could take the key from the pocket of her skirt and unlock the door.

The small room was sparsely furnished, its one window open. A gentle breeze blew the lace curtains, causing them to billow. Matt followed Regina into the room as she crossed over to the night table to put down the key, and when she reached toward the lamp to raise the flame, he suddenly jerked her into his arms so violently that Regina's long hair flew wildly across her face.

Then his lips descended on hers, and he drew her close, pressing her thighs to his. Just as the feel of his firm manhood made desire flood Regina's senses, Matt turned her loose so abruptly that she tottered for a moment before regaining her balance.

She looked on in puzzlement as he suddenly took off his gun belt and placed it on a nearby chair, but when he began unbuttoning his shirt, she asked raspingly, "Matt, why are you undressing?"

"Why aren't you?" he quipped.

"Matt, I asked you to my room so that we could talk. I didn't bring you here because I wanted us to . . ." She was too flustered to continue.

He stopped unbuttoning his shirt. "Talk?" he said questioningly. He felt like telling her that he knew damned well the only conversation she wanted from

159

him was a marriage proposal. To hell with it, he thought. He reached for his gun belt and picked it up. He was sick and tired of her schemes.

Impulsively, Regina stepped to his side, and taking the gun belt, she placed it back on the chair. She didn't know why he was leaving her room, or why he was behaving so strangely. She only knew that she loved him, and if this was to be their last night together, then she'd keep what little time was left.

"Don't leave," she whispered, throwing away her pride.

Looking directly at her, he replied, "You know what will happen if I stay."

"Yes, I know," she admitted softly. "But I want it to happen."

There was a battle raging within Matt, one part of him said he must leave, another urged him to stay. After all, he thought, what did he have to lose by spending this one night with her? He was aware of Regina's cunning game so she couldn't trap him. But he still wanted her, and, by God, he'd have her one last time!

Setting his hands on her shoulders, he grasped her firmly, and bending his head, he placed his lips on hers. His kiss, tender at first, grew steadily more intense. Regina's arms encircled his neck, and drawing her into his embrace, Matt held her close.

As he showered her face with brief kisses, he murmured, "Regina, I want you."

"Yes, Matt," she replied shakily. "I want you too. Darling, I want you desperately!"

Stepping back, he began to take off his clothes, and Regina also undressed. Anxious to be together, they disrobed quickly, letting their garments fall carelessly to the floor, and the moment that Regina was naked, Matt pulled her back into his arms.

As their bare flesh touched, Regina felt his hard

desire pressing against her womanhood. Wanting him inside her, she pushed her thighs to his, and taking her hand, he led her to the bed. He drew back the covers, then eased her onto the clean sheets and lay beside her. Leaning over her, he caressed her shoulders and her breasts with his lips, and Regina moaned fervently as his tongue flickered over her nipples, his mouth suckling and nibbling gently.

Then his hand moved downward, finding the softness between her velvety thighs. Demandingly, his mouth crushed against hers as his fingers probed in and out, causing Regina to cry out softly with intense yearning. Returning his passionate kiss, her hips began to arch toward Matt's magic touch.

"Regina . . . Regina," he groaned thickly, moving over her. Slipping an arm under her, he elevated her thighs and placed his mouth on hers as his manhood entered her warm, feminine depths. Thrusting against her, he whispered, "Regina, love me . . . love me."

Regina's passion soared, and her hips circled against him provocatively, her sensual movements further arousing Matt. Placing her legs about his waist, he drove into her aggressively. His deep penetration excited Regina, and clinging tightly, she drove herself into his hard thrusts.

Momentarily melded by love's heated bliss, Regina and Matt were swept away on a tide of tempestuous ecstasy.

Raising herself onto one elbow, Regina studied Matt's face as he lay quietly beside her. Brushing her finger across his scar, she asked, "What happened?"

"I was cut with a knife," he answered.

"When?" she wanted to know.

"It was a long time ago," he mumbled.

"How old were you?"

"Seventeen," he replied.

"Were you in a fight?"

He chuckled briefly. "Don't you ever run out of questions?"

"Tell me how it happened and I'll stop questioning you."

"I chose the wrong man to rob. He kicked my pistol out of my hand and had his knife at my throat before I even knew what had happened. He slashed my cheek so I would have a permanent reminder that robbery doesn't always pay off. And, by God, what he did worked! That was the first and last time I ever tried to rob anyone."

Regina was amazed that Matt was actually talking about himself. He had always been so secretive, yet there was so much she wanted to know about this man she loved.

"The man who cut your cheek, did you ever see him again?"

"Quite a few times. It was Miguel Ordaz."

Astounded, she gasped, "Ordaz!"

"After that little incident, we became good friends."

Snuggling against him, she urged him on. "Tell me more about your life, Matt."

"Why in the hell do you want to know about my life?" he asked curtly.

His question took her by surprise, and she stammered uneasily, "I'm . . . I'm very curious."

Again, he asked, "Why should you be curious about me?"

Aggravated by his doubting questions, she asked in frustration, "Honestly, Matt, must you be so difficult?"

"I don't like to talk about myself," he mumbled gruffly.

She wanted to plead with him to confide in her and

162

to trust her. She longed desperately to become emotionally close to him. But what does it matter? she reminded herself. He'll leave in the morning, and I'll never see him again. The thought of losing Matt tore painfully at her heart. Could she possibly persuade him to stay? If I don't at least try, she decided, I'll never forgive myself!

"Matt," she began anxiously, "I don't want you to go to Wyoming."

Regina was still snuggled against him, and she didn't see the bitter frown that hardened his features as, mistaking her reason for wanting him to stay, he said firmly, "Regina, don't start pressuring me. I'm leaving, and there's nothing you can say or do to change my mind."

"But, Matt—" she began.

"Damn it, Regina!" he seethed. "Can't you leave well enough alone?"

Her own anger surging, she sat up and remarked sharply, "You are the most impossible man I have ever met!"

The cover had fallen away, and the tempting sight of Regina's bared bosom aroused Matt's passion. Grasping her, he drew her down to his side, and bending his head, he kissed her soft breasts. The touch of his lips reawakened Regina's desire. She entwined her fingers in his dark hair and pressed him even closer. Sliding his body upward, he placed his mouth over hers and kissed her deeply. "Regina," he whispered, "I want to make love to you again."

"Yes, Matt," she said urgently. She needed him desperately.

Placing his large frame over hers, he penetrated her suddenly and swiftly. Believing this was the last time he'd make love to Regina, Matt's frustration made him pound into her roughly, but his demanding thrusting excited Regina and she instantly matched his rapid rhythm. They reached their ultimate pleasure simultaneously, Regina trembled as tingling chills ran up and down her spine, and Matt moaning as he released his seed inside her.

As they gradually left their sensual cocoon, Regina longed for Matt to whisper loving words, but instead he shifted so he lay at her side. How can I love a man who treats me so unfairly? Regina asked herself.

The whiskey Matt had consumed earlier was beginning to make him drowsy, and giving in to his fatigue, he closed his eyes. As he drifted into sleep, Matt wondered how long it would take for him to get over Regina Blakely.

Lying close to Matt, Regina waited patiently for him to speak, but when he remained silent, she raised up to look into his face.

She wasn't perturbed to see that he had fallen asleep; she was looking forward to spending the night sleeping next to him. Thoughtfully, she studied him as he slept soundly. Her eyes trailed lovingly over his high forehead, his prominent cheekbones, and his sensual lips. She lowered her head and kissed his mouth with extreme gentleness. "I love you, Matt," she whispered very softly. "Please don't leave me! If you must go to Wyoming, take me with you . . . please!"

Reaching over Matt, Regina turned down the wick of the lamp until the flame was out. Then, carefully so she wouldn't awaken Matt, she cuddled close to his side, placing one leg over his, her arm across his chest. As she nestled her head on his shoulder, Matt, halfway between sleep and consciousness, slipped his arm around her, drawing her closer.

Regina loved his nearness, and although it took her a long time to fall asleep, she relished every minute that she lay in the arms of the man she adored.

Dawn was still an hour away when Matt's absence caused Regina to awaken. The room was dark, but she could hear Matt slipping into his clothes. Sitting up, she lit the kerosene lamp, and the flame brightened the room.

Astounded, she watched Matt tuck his shirt into his pants. If she hadn't awakened, he would have left without saying goodbye! Oh, Matt! Why . . . why? she thought.

Going to the bed, he sat down and began to put on his boots. Regina clutched his arm and cried out, "Matt, what are you doing?"

He answered flippantly. "What does it look like I'm doing?" It hurt him to leave Regina, but he'd be damned if he'd let her see his pain. He supposed he could stay, marry her, and run the Black Diamond. But, damn it, he had his pride, and he wanted to hold on to it, regardless of the cost!

Rising, he stepped to the chair, picked up his gun belt, and strapped it around his slim hips.

Regina had to force herself not to beg him to stay, but valuing her dignity, she suppressed the desperate pleas she would have made.

He walked over to the table and took the key. Holding it in his hand, he stared at it for a moment as he debated one last time with himself. Should he leave, or should he stay? Did Regina mean more to him than his pride? Yes, he decided intensely, I love her more than anything, but I won't marry a woman who isn't in love with me! Not even if that woman is Regina Blakely!

Regina sensed that Matt was trying to decide whether or not to leave, and she awaited his next move

165

with bated breath.

Slowly, he turned to face her. The cold expression in his eyes told her his decision and her heart sank.

"Goodbye, Regina," he mumbled.

He waited a moment for her to reply, unaware that she couldn't bring herself to say goodbye to him. Then he strode to the door and unlocked it. He turned around and pitched the key onto the bed. It landed beside Regina's leg, and, numbly, she picked it up. As her world fell apart, she stared vacantly at the key nestled in her palm.

Matt, meanwhile, stood in the open doorway, studying her intently. Say you love me, Regina! he pleaded silently. Tell me you love me, and for God's sake, make me believe you!

Regina's heart was crying out to Matt that she loved him, but she was hurting so terribly that she could make no response to his silent plea.

Encircling the key with her fingers, Regina slowly raised her gaze to Matt's, but deciding to leave, he had already stepped out of the room. Regina glanced up just in time to see the door close behind him.

Staring at the closed door that represented the end of her dreams, Regina waited for tears to come, but they did not. Until this moment, Regina had not known that it was possible to hurt too deeply to cry.

Chapter Fourteen

Two months had passed since Matt had left Albuquerque, and from the day of his departure, one tragedy after another had befallen Regina. They began to descend upon her the morning Juan and Luisa, wearing apologetic faces, had informed Regina that they had a little money saved and wished to return to Mexico and buy a small place of their own.

Although they had given Regina a month's notice, she had been unable to find a qualified couple to take their place. Consequently when one of the wranglers, an elderly man, had offered to take Juan's job as cook for the ranch hands, Regina had gladly accepted his offer.

Next her trusted foreman, while in town, had been shot and killed during a poker game. Suddenly, all his responsibilities had become Regina's. She now kept the tally ledger that Matt had worked on so diligently. Unfortunately, she had stopped taking lessons from Antonio—knowing that he was in love with her had made her feel too uncomfortable—and he hadn't gotten around to teaching her how to keep the tally ledger. Regina found the ledger terribly complicated. The ranch hands were continually asking all sorts of confusing questions of the already flustered Regina. Should they roundup the calves from the west range and brand them? Did she want the calves returned to the range or corraled? Did she think the cattle on the east range were ready for market? Regina's response to their inquiries was usually a muddled, "I don't know. What do you think?"

Desperate, she offered the foreman's job to every hand on the ranch, but they all declined. Some were Mexicans and unable to read English, let alone cipher, so the tally ledger would be as much a mystery to them as it was to Regina. A few of the less honest hands considered Regina's offer. It seemed to provide an opportunity to take advantage of her inexperience. But they knew she was protected by Miguel Ordaz, and their fear of the threatening Mexican was stronger than their greed.

Finally, Regina decided to ask Mace for help, but on the very day she had planned to visit him, she received an urgent message from Julie, telling her to come to the ranch immediately.

Arriving at Julie's home, Regina learned that Mace had been accidentally killed. He had been thrown from his horse, and the fall had broken his neck. Devastated, Regina wondered how many more disasters were forthcoming.

Regina paced the study, and finding her black mourning dress cumbersome, she impatiently jerked the long skirt out of the way as she paused beside the desk. There was a look of desperation in her eyes as she gazed down at the brandy bottle on the desktop. She reached toward it but brusquely whirled away.

"I need a drink!" she remarked to herself. "But if I start, I may never stop!"

She knew she should check on Julie. She hadn't looked in on her since Mace's funeral service had ended three hours ago. As soon as they had returned from the service, Julie had enclosed herself in Regina's guest room. Regina turned to leave the study, but changing her mind, she went to the large leather-bound chair behind the desk.

Sitting, she said vaguely, "I'll check on her later." She leaned back against the soft upholstery and sighed deeply. "What will I do?" she cried, anguish in her voice.

For a long time, Regina sat numbly, her eyes glazed with desperation. Finally, she leaned forward and placed her elbows on the desktop, resting her head in her palms. Her nerves were stretched to their limit, and she was on the verge of panicking. A shudder racked her body as she thought about the sickness that had struck her the last three mornings. It wasn't until the first spell had passed that Regina realized her time of the month was now weeks overdue. She was pregnant, and the father of her child was somewhere in Wyoming!

Aroused by the sounds of horses approaching, Regina rose from her chair and hurried out of the study. Opening the front door, she smiled for the first time in ages when she saw Miguel Ordaz and his vaqueros.

Halting his white stallion at the hitching post, Miguel dismounted and walked briskly to the porch. As he entered the house, he removed his sombrero and said cordially, *"Buenas tardes, señorita."*

"Miguel!" Regina cried in her joy at seeing him spontaneously using his first name. "I'm so happy you're here!" She didn't believe there was any way that Miguel could help her, but the sight of his friendly face lifted her spirits.

169

Pleased by her warm response, Ordaz smiled tenderly, and bending over, he kissed her cheek. "Is it all right if I tell my vaqueros to go to the bunkhouse?"

"Yes, of course," she answered.

Stepping to the open door, he relayed the order to his men; then, turning back to Regina, he suggested, "Let us go to the study so that we can talk in comfort."

Regina led the way, and he followed her down the hall and into the room. Returning to her chair, she sat down.

Hanging his sombrero on the hat rack beside the door, Miguel sauntered to the desk. He poured two glasses of brandy, and then said, "When in town, I had a long talk with Señor Butler." Handing her one of the glasses, he continued, "He told me about Señor Edwards' accident and also about the problems you are having with the ranch." As Miguel eased his huge frame onto the chair across from the desk, he noticed Regina wasn't drinking. "Drink the brandy. It will make you feel better," he said.

Putting down her glass, Regina shook her head. She was afraid if she took so much as a swallow, she would then continue to drink until she reached the state of oblivion.

"I will see if I can find you a reliable foreman," Miguel began, "and I am sure that in time you will locate qualified house servants." Studying Regina's worried face, he said reassuringly, *"Señorita,* I will help you and soon your troubles will be over, *sí?"*

"No!" she blurted out impulsively. "They will not be over!"

"Why?" he asked urgently. "What is wrong, *señorita?*

"I can't tell you!" she moaned. "I'm too ashamed!"

Placing his glass on the desk, Miguel rose swiftly. Moving to Regina, he placed his large hands on her shoulders, drawing her to her feet. "Shame?" he

170

repeated. "What kind of shame?" When she made no reply, he demanded firmly, "Answer me!"

"I can't!" she declared firmly. Then suddenly, hard sobs shook her body.

Guessing the cause of her distress, Miguel asked gently, "You are with child, *si?*"

Covering her face with her hands, she admitted it with a nod.

Tenderly, he took her into his arms. Regina had been uncertain of his reaction, but she hadn't been expecting such sweet tenderness. Needing to be comforted, she allowed him to hold her close.

"Señor Brolin?" he asked softly.

Unable to find her voice, she nodded.

"He will marry you," Miguel stated calmly.

Stepping out of Ordaz' embrace, she looked up into his face. "How can he possibly marry me? He's in Wyoming."

"No, *señorita*. All this time, he has been at my hacienda. He is now in town with your brother at the saloon."

"But why didn't he go to Wyoming?" she asked, astounded that Matt was actually in Albuquerque.

"I made him promise that he would visit me before he left for Wyoming. His visit, it has lasted for two months."

"Why did he stay so long?" she exclaimed.

Studying her closely, Miguel answered, "Because Wyoming is too many miles away from the woman he loves."

Miguel had hoped his words would comfort her, but instead she seemed depressed and mumbled, "He doesn't love me."

"I do not agree. Nonetheless, he will marry you."

"If I force him into marriage, he'll despise me," Regina murmured.

171

"You and Matt must protect the innocent baby you carry," Miguel said firmly; then whirling about, he strode across the floor. Taking his sombrero, he opened the door.

"Where are you going?" Regina asked.

"I will talk to Matt, and I promise you, by this time tomorrow you will be married."

Before Regina could protest, he was gone.

It was late afternoon, and the saloon was almost empty except for two customers at the bar and the four men playing cards in the far corner.

Dan and Matt were sitting at the table by the front window. Absently, Matt stared out at the street. Periodically, a rider or a buckboard would pass by, but at this time of day the town was usually quiet.

Dan took a drink of his beer. "Mace was never one of my favorite people," he mumbled, "but I'm sorry he's dead."

Pushing his hat back from his brow, Matt drew his gaze away from the window. Looking at Dan, he asked, "Do you think your sister will be all right?"

Nodding, Dan replied, "I'm sure she will. Julie never loved Mace. Maybe now she can find the right man and fall in love."

"If she didn't love Mace, why did she marry him?"

"Because James Blakely told her to." Dan sneered, not trying to conceal his resentment. "Blakely never cared anything about Julie. She's to much like our mother Katherine, and Blakely only married Mother for her money and property."

"How did he feel about Regina?" asked Matt, wondering why he should even care.

"Blakely was incapable of love, so he possessed Regina. He tried to make her a replica of himself, but

172

Regina's too warm and compassionate. Although Blakely tried like hell, he couldn't change her."

Matt snickered, but he made no comment. Obviously, Dan was not aware of the cunning and underhanded game that his sister had been playing.

"I'll get us some more beer," Dan offered, but as he started to rise, the front doors swung open and Miguel barged into the saloon. Going to their table, he said to Matt, *"Amigo,* I must talk to you."

"All right," Matt agreed warily. He knew that Miguel had ridden out to visit Regina, and he hoped that she wasn't the reason why Miguel was intent on speaking to him. Matt planned to leave early in the morning for Wyoming, but he suddenly had a strange feeling that Miguel was about to upset his plans.

Once again Dan started to get up, but Miguel's large hand landed on his shoulder and prevented him from standing. "You are Señorita Blakely's brother, and you will take part in this conversation."

"Miguel," Matt remarked impatiently, "what in the hell is going on?"

Turning, Miguel called to the bartender, "Bring a bottle of whiskey and three glasses."

The bartender brought the order, and when he left, Miguel poured whiskey into the glasses. Lifting one, he said heartily, "A toast, *amigos!"*

"What are we toasting?" questioned Matt.

"Señorita Blakely's upcoming marriage," Miguel replied. Raising his glass, he said, "Stand, *amigos,* and let us toast."

Stunned, Dan got slowly to his feet, but Matt remained seated. "Sorry, Miguel," Matt began sourly, "but I won't drink to Regina's marriage."

"But, *amigo!"* Miguel exclaimed. "The groom should drink a toast to his lovely bride!"

"Groom!" Matt raged. "Damn it, Miguel! I'm not

marrying Regina!"

Pulling up a chair, Miguel sat down. Slowly, Dan returned to his own chair, and, astounded, he stared at the huge Mexican.

In a flash, Miguel had his pistol drawn. Aiming it at Matt, he said, "You will marry Señorita Blakely."

Grinning, Matt stated calmly, "Who in the hell do you think you're foolin'? You won't kill me."

"No, *amigo,* I will not kill you. But if you try to get up, I will shoot you in the leg so that you cannot run away. Tomorrow morning you will marry the *señorita* if I have to keep you here all night at gunpoint."

Crossing his arms on the table, Matt leaned closer to Miguel. "Why, damn it?" he demanded.

"She carries your child," Miguel answered softly.

Miguel watched Matt carefully. At first he could read no discernible expression on his face. Then, gradually, a gleam came into his eyes, and a smile started at the very corners of his mouth, broadening expansively.

"A baby?" Matt choked out.

Roaring with laughter, Miguel returned his pistol to its holster. "Forgive me, Matt, for drawing my gun, but I was not sure of your reaction."

Turning his attention to Dan, Matt asked, "You knew nothing about this?"

"Regina never breathed a word of it to me," Dan answered. He knew he should be angry at Matt, but he wasn't. He still believed that Regina and Matt were perfect for each other.

Looking at Miguel, Matt asked, "How is she?"

"She is upset, but that is to be expected. She is an unmarried woman in the family way. It is a good thing, *amigo,* that you postponed your trip to Wyoming."

174

"Why haven't you gone to Wyoming?" Dan questioned.

When Matt didn't reply, Miguel chuckled, "Why do you think, *amigo?* Your sister, she is a captivating woman. A man would not find her easy to forget."

"I tried, Miguel," Matt admitted quietly. "I tried like hell to forget her."

"But you need no longer try. Soon she will be your *esposa* and the *madre* of your child."

Chapter Fifteen

Feeling terribly restless, Regina paced across her bedroom floor, then walked to the window and pulled back the curtain to look outside. It was late in the day, and as she turned back to the room she noticed the long shadows that fell across it. Going to the bed, she sat down and toyed nervously with the soft quilt folded neatly at the foot. What was taking Miguel so long? Had he talked to Matt? Did Matt now despise her? Apprehensive, Regina rose from the bed and once again began pacing. Suddenly, she halted.

"Maybe Miguel will bring Matt to the ranch!" she gasped out.

Hurrying to the dresser and seating herself on the velvet-covered stool, she peered into the mirror. She quickly opened a drawer and took out a small jar. Removing the lid, she dabbed rouge on her cheeks. Then she intently studied her reflection. Stress had taken its toll. Lack of sleep made her eyes appear harsh, and loss of weight caused her high cheekbones to seem extremely prominent.

Perhaps, Regina thought, if I wear my hair down, I won't look so . . . so severe. Hurriedly she took the pins from her blond tresses, letting them fall to her shoulders. Then she stood before the mirror and studied her appearance. She had exchanged her mourning dress for a mint green gown which had tiny gold threads woven into its material. The neckline was cut low and revealed the fullness of her breasts.

Sighing disconsolately, she turned from the looking glass and walked to the window. The setting sun was casting a lustrous glow across the open sky.

"Why am I being so foolish?" she asked herself. "Matt probably won't even notice how I look." She held her cheek against the lace curtain and considered begging Matt to be kind, but pride had been bred into Regina. Stepping back from the window, she raised her chin defiantly. "I will not humble myself!" she swore aloud. "This pregnancy is just as much his fault as mine!"

Suddenly, Regina heard Matt call her name, and her hand flew to her heart. Thinking his unannounced arrival was due to anger, she backed across the room until the foot of the bed was between her and the closed door at which she was staring.

Matt called again, "Regina . . . Regina!" She could tell by the sound of his voice that he was nearing her room.

Swinging open the bedroom door, Matt entered, but he halted abruptly when his eyes fell upon Regina. Would she rush into his arms? Did she love him at all? He waited anxiously, hoping she would give him a sign that she cared.

The sight of Matt set Regina's heart to pounding, but unable to read his thoughts, she raised her chin stubbornly, refusing to be intimidated. She had her pride and dignity to protect; she would pretend that his presence was unimportant. Child or no child, she would not beg him to marry her! Concealing her true feelings behind a frown, she said crossly, "Don't you know how to knock?"

He didn't answer. Mistaking his silence for anger, Regina whirled from the foot of the bed and walked to the center of the room. Facing him, she remarked, "I thought you were going to Wyoming."

He closed the door, then, leaning back against it, looked at her with an expression that was inscrutable. Dispassionately, he said, "It's fortunate for you, ma'am, that I'm not in Wyoming."

"Oh?" she responded, trying to sound uncaring.

"You'd be minus one necessary husband," he explained calmly.

Determined to keep her true feelings hidden, Regina said coolly, "Indeed? Well, if Miguel told you that I want to marry you, then you have been misinformed."

In two quick strides he was at her side, clutching her arms tenaciously. The savage fury in his dark eyes was frightening. "My child will not be born a bastard!" he declared loudly. "If need be, madam, I'll publicly drag you to church!"

"You wouldn't dare!" she retorted.

"Try me, Regina!" he challenged. "Just try me!"

She walked away from him and went to the dresser. Why can't we communicate civilly? she thought. Why must our relationship be so stormy? It's because he doesn't love me, she decided. And now, because he feels honor bound to marry me, he probably despises me. Pulling out the vanity stool, she sat down. As the mirror picked up his reflection, she tried to find warmth in his eyes, but their expression was icy. "Matt," she began uneasily, "I didn't exactly plan what has happened."

Striking out at her verbally, he shouted, "You got just what you wanted! A husband!"

Springing to her feet, she seethed, "Are you implying that I wanted to become pregnant?"

178

"Didn't you?" he raged.

Shocked, as well as hurt, Regina cried, "No, of course not! Matt, why would you even think such a thing?"

"I have my reasons," he mumbled.

For a long moment they stared at each other, the tension heavy between them in the quiet room. Then, turning unexpectedly, Matt opened the door. Glancing back at Regina, he said evenly, "I've already talked to the reverend. I'll pick you up in the mforning at ten o'clock." His dark eyes hardened. "And, Regina, you had better be ready."

Telling herself that she no longer loved this man who could treat her so harshly, Regina gave her head a petulant toss before haughtily raising her chin. "Don't tell me what to do, Matt Brolin!" she said icily.

In spite of Matt's anger, he had never found her more desirable than he did at this moment. "Regina," he said gruffly, "you can get to me more than any woman ever has." In one swift move, he shoved the door closed and secured the small bolt. Quickly he was at her side, lifting her in his arms.

"Put me down!" she demanded, fighting against him.

Carrying her to the bed, he laid her on the soft mattress, and his body covered hers, trapping her beneath him. She made an effort to protest, but instantly, his mouth was on hers. She tried to turn her face away, but he forcefully pried her lips apart, making her accept his fervent kiss.

"Regina," Matt whispered, his voice edged with a vague note of pleading, "I want to make love to you."

As she became more and more aware of the feel of his hardness between her thighs, uncontrollable desire overwhelmed Regina.

His breathing heavy with passion, Matt said huskily, "Regina, you want me as much as I want you."

She longed to tell him that she didn't want him, but she couldn't force the denial past her lips.

"Admit it," he insisted.

Surrendering, she sighed, "I want you." She wished that she had the strength to refuse him, but she realized she still loved him. How can I possibly turn him away when he's my heart and my very soul?

Lying at her side, Matt took her hand and guided it downward so that she touched him. Even through his trousers, she could feel how hard he was, feel the electrifying desire her touch sent through Matt's entire being. With deep yearning, he conquered her lips with his, kissing her demandingly.

Moments later, both drugged with passion, they rose from the bed and quickly removed their restrictive clothing. Then, eager for him to make love to her, Regina returned to the bed, holding out her arms to him. Going into her embrace, Matt immediately eased his erection into her womanhood.

As he penetrated her, Regina writhed and moaned with unrestrained desire. "Matt . . . Matt . . ." she purred in his ear.

Clasping her buttocks in his hands, Matt pulled her against him and, responding, Regina entwined her ankles over his back.

Driving himself deep into her, Matt breathed hoarsely, "I wonder if you have any idea how good you feel to a man."

Suddenly his lips were on hers, and when his tongue began exploring the inside of her mouth, his kiss ignited a burning longing through Regina that bordered on the ecstatic. Losing herself in their lovemaking, she answered Matt's passion and within moments they achieved utter fulfillment.

Rolling to Regina's side, Matt stretched out on the bed. She waited for him to say something, but he didn't seem to be interested in talking. Unsure of what she should say or do, Regina remained silent. She desperately wanted to tell him how she felt, but she was afraid he might reject her love.

She was unaware that Matt was feeling bitter. His bitterness was not aimed at Regina, but at himself, for once again, he had succumbed to her tempting charms. My God, had he no will power where she was concerned? he wondered. He knew her to be a cold, calculating woman, yet he continued to love her. She had set her trap, and he had fallen into it—and she had caught him with the oldest trick in the book!

Holding his emotions in check, Matt rose hastily and began to dress. Reaching for the quilt at the foot of the bed, Regina pulled it up and spread it over herself.

Although Matt's sudden cold detachment was paining her, she said collectedly, "Matt, you don't have to marry me if you don't want to."

"Don't you think I know that?" he asked, sitting on the edge of the bed. He studied her for a moment, wondering why she had reminded him of his options. Shrugging off that speculation, he said calmly, "I told you, my child will not be born a bastard." Quickly he put on his boots; then he rose and walked across the room. Reaching the door, he released the bolt. Then he turned back to Regina. "As I said earlier, I'll pick you up at ten o'clock in the morning."

He stepped out of the room, and the moment he closed the door, Regina gave in to the tears she had been keeping suppressed.

Julie's steps were sluggish as she walked out onto Regina's front porch. Crossing to the short flight of steps, she sat down. Her eyes were dull as she stared into the dark shadows. She could hear voices coming

181

from the bunkhouse and, periodically, the soft neighing of horses. She folded her hands in her lap, clenching them tightly. Sighing, she glanced up at the stars shining brilliantly against the black sky.

Hearing someone approach, Julie sat upright. As the visitor came within her view, she said with surprise, "Mr. Ordaz!"

Tenderly, he replied, "Señora Edwards." Removing his wide sombrero, Miguel sat on the steps beside her. Taking her small hand into his, he said gently, "Señora, please accept my deepest sympathies."

Timidly, she pulled her hand free. "Thank you," she answered.

"Is there anything I can do?" he asked.

She could see he was deeply concerned about her, and touched by his kindness, Julie burst into tears. Her sudden distress disturbed Miguel. Uncertain of how he should console such a gentle lady, he awkwardly patted her trembling shoulder.

"Angel," he shispered soothingly, "sometimes it is good to cry."

Somehow, she was suddenly in his arms. Holding her close, he allowed her to weep until, finally, her deep sobs became soft whimpers. Then, tenderly, Miguel released her. Reaching into his pocket, he brought out a colorful bandanna and wiped the tears from her face.

"Mr. Ordaz," she said softly, "no man has ever treated me so compassionately. You make me feel so special."

"You are very special," he murmured deeply. "You are an angel."

"Believe me, Mr. Ordaz, I'm not what you think I am. You have the wrong impression."

"Perhaps, but to me you are an angel." Placing his hand under her chin, he tilted her face up to his. "I am a stubborn man. Do not try to change my mind."

182

His kindness made fresh tears stream from her eyes, but she thought Miguel Ordaz a very wonderful and compassionate man.

"Why are you weeping?" he asked softly.

Reverting her gaze from his, she stammered shyly, "You are so kind and considerate."

"And that makes you cry?" he asked, somewhat confused.

Keeping her eyes turned away, she murmured, "I'm sorry, I shouldn't be so emotional. I am behaving foolishly."

"Look at me," he ordered gently.

Julie turned and looked into his dark eyes. Carefully, he placed a hand over hers. His touch disturbed her in a strange way, causing her to grow tense. Understanding her discomfort, Miguel thoughtfully removed his hand. Moving his large frame to the other side of the step, he told her firmly, "Someday, when your time of mourning has passed, I will not be so considerate." Not giving her time to reproach him, he asked quickly, "Did Señorita Blakely tell you she is getting married?"

"Yes, she did!" Julie replied irritably.

"Why does her marriage upset you?" he queried.

"My sister and I are in mourning, yet she has the bad taste to marry the day after Mace's funeral! I can't—"

Interrupting, Miguel touched her arm as he said, "Señora, please. Do not be so quick to pass judgment."

Holding out her hands as though she were pleading, Julie frowned touchingly. "I told you that I'm no angel."

Smiling tenderly, he asked, "Did your sister tell you why she is marrying Señor Brolin?"

"No," she replied. "Regina came into my room and informed me that she's getting married in the morning. Before I could try to reason with her, she left."

Miguel looked directly at Julie. "Señora, why do you

183

suppose your sister is marrying so quickly and while she is still in mourning? Mace Edwards was her brother-in-law. She would not marry so soon without good cause."

Julie considered his question, then she inhaled sharply. "Oh no!" she gasped. Her eyes opened extraordinarily wide as she stared at Miguel. Breathlessly, she cried, "Surely . . . she isn't? . . ."

"Ask your sister," he answered evasively.

"Oh, Regina . . . no!" Julie moaned.

"Do not be so distressed. Señor Brolin and your sister will find happiness together." Miguel chuckled softly, adding, "Sharing the same bed night after night will make them forget their differences."

"But, Mr. Ordaz," Julie argued, "considering Mr. Brolin's past, I'm afraid he is not the right man for Regina."

Rising, Miguel picked up his sombrero. Placing it on his head, he replied, "Señor Brolin is a good man, and he loves Señorita Blakely." Kneeling in front of Julie, he continued, "Promise me, *señora,* that you will give him a chance to prove himself. Life has seldom been kind to Matt Brolin, but, perhaps, *señora,* you will be kind."

Impulsively, she grasped his hand. Julie's brown eyes glowed as she answered, "Yes, Mr. Ordaz, I promise I'll be kind to Mr. Brolin. If you say he is a good man, then I believe you."

Guiding her hand to his lips, he kissed it fleetingly. The touch of his lips sent a tingling sensation through her entire body. She had never experienced such a mysterious thrill, and, confused, she pulled her hand from his. Trying to cover her uneasiness, she stammered, "Mr. Ordaz, why did you come back to Albuquerque?"

"To check on your sister, and *señora,* I hoped very

much to see you again." Standing, he tipped his hat. *"Buenas noches,* Angel," he said tenderly, before turning and walking toward the bunkhouse.

Julie watched him until he disappeared into the darkness of night. There was a radiant glow on her face, but she was innocent as to the reason why.

Chapter Sixteen

Dan and Miguel were Matt and Regina's guests for dinner. Little was being said at the table, but the long periods of silence did not make anyone uneasy. Their friendships were too close and secure for a lapse in conversation to cause any discomfort. Due to Julie's good cooking, the meal was deliciously prepared. Regina had pleaded with her sister to join them for dinner, but because she was still in mourning, Julie had refused to socialize.

Staring down at her plate of food, from which little had been eaten, Regina found herself counting time. I have been married for seven hours, she thought, and my husband has barely spoken a word to me. As she reached for her glass of wine, the crystal chandelier hanging above the table made the gold band on her finger shine brightly. Studying it, Regina wondered how Matt had acquired a wedding ring on such short notice.

Feeling Matt's eyes on her, she drew her gaze from the ring and looked at her husband. It seemed strange to see Matt occupying the chair at the head of the table. Strange . . . but comforting.

Regina tried to understand Matt's expression, but

she wasn't able to analyze his mood. Then, suddenly, their eyes locked with compelling intensity, and Regina's pulse raced. I want him, she thought with burning desire. I want him right now; this very minute!

Just then, Dan and Miguel pushed back their chairs, the movement breaking the spell of Matt's gaze. Going to his sister, Dan leaned over and kissed her cheek.

"Be happy, Gina," he whispered.

"I'm sure I will be," she murmured, smiling tenderly.

Miguel stepped to Regina's chair. *"Señora,"* he began, "I plan to leave early in the morning, and I will have no chance to see Señora Edwards. Will you please tell her I said goodbye and that I hope someday soon to see her again?" Detecting puzzlement on Regina's face, he asked, "Are you surprised that I want to see your sister?"

"Well, yes I am," Regina replied.

"Señora Edwards is a beautiful woman, but a very lonely one. She touches my heart."

"But her husband hasn't been gone long enough for Julie to feel loneliness," Regina reasoned.

"She has been lonely for many years," he replied.

Standing, Matt shoved his chair under the table, remarking testily, "Not all marriages are made in heaven, Regina!" Striding to her chair, he placed his hands on its arms, and leaning over he looked darkly into her green eyes. "Surely you haven't already forgotten the little masquerade we acted out in church this morning."

Matt's cutting remark wounded Regina deeply, but before she could respond, Dan said reproachfully, "Matt, that's a hell of a thing to say!"

Stopping the argument that was about to develop, Miguel grasped Dan's arm, saying firmly, *"Señor,* do not interfere."

Dan nodded, deciding it was best that he stay out of

187

Matt and Regina's business. "I think I'll head back to town," he said briskly.

"Si, amigo," Miguel replied. "And I will go to the bunkhouse."

Stepping back from Regina's chair, Matt said to Miguel, "I'll walk out with you. I want to go to the bunkhouse and have a talk with the men."

Regina watched the men head out of the dining room. Then she stacked the plates and carried them into the kitchen, where she found Julie waiting to wash the dishes. She offered to help, but Julie refused her assistance, telling her that it was her wedding night and she shouldn't be doing chores. As she was leaving the kitchen, Regina remembered to give Julie Miguel's message. Then, needing a breath of fresh air, Regina walked out onto the porch. She started to sit on the pine rocker, but just then she noticed a lone rider approaching the house so she paused by the steps and watched him draw closer.

Recognizing the man on horseback, she smiled warmly, and, as he pulled up his horse, she said politely, "Antonio, what a pleasant surprise."

Dismounting and draping the reins over the hitching post, he joined Regina. "I just came from town where I heard a rumor that you and Señor Brolin were married this morning."

"It's not a rumor," she assured him.

He looked disappointed. "Then it is true?"

"Yes, it is," she replied.

Antonio sighed regretfully. It was not easy to lose the woman he loved, but he controlled his hurt feelings and said evenly, "I wish you much happiness."

"Thank you, Antonio," she murmured. Suddenly remembering Miguel's presence, Regina gripped Antonio's arm, saying intensely, "Miguel Ordaz is here!" If the two men were to come face to face, Regina feared what might happen.

Understanding her concern, Antonio said hastily, "I will not stay, Regina."

Neither of them heard Matt's quiet steps as he approached the porch from the direction of the bunk-house, but upon seeing Regina with Antonio, Matt's eyes narrowed with jealous suspicion. Regina's hand was still on Antonio's arm, and Matt watched as Antonio placed a hand over hers.

"You must leave here before he sees you!" Regina cried.

Overhearing Regina's plea, Matt presumed that she was referring to him not to Miguel.

Antonio leaned over and brushed his lips across Regina's cheek. "I will see you later," he promised. As he moved away from her to walk to his horse, he spotted Matt poised at the bottom of the steps.

Suddenly aware of Matt's presence, Regina was startled, and she said tentatively, "Matt . . . I didn't hear you approach."

Antonio descended the steps, saying, *"Señor,* you are a very lucky man."

When Matt offered no reply, Antonio shrugged, then went to his horse and mounted.

As Ramírez was riding away from the house, Matt stepped onto the porch. He started to brush past Regina but hesitated when she asked, "Where are you going?"

"I have work to do in the study," he mumbled, then strode into the house.

A moment later, Regina followed. Slowly, she walked down the hall and into her bedroom. Going to the bed, she sat down. She found Matt's impersonal attitude terribly depressing. Sighing heavily, she reached for the nightgown placed at the foot of the bed. Then she slipped out of her dress and stepped to the

189

wash basin. After taking a thorough sponge bath, she donned the nightgown, and, moving to the dresser, she picked up her brush and gave her hair a hundred brisk strokes. Finally, taking a bottle of perfume, she dabbed a drop of the scent behind each ear.

When she drew back the covers and lay down, she placed her hand on her stomach and thought about the life growing inside her. A small smile tugged at the corners of her mouth as she continued to think about the baby. Matt's baby, she reminded herself, thrilled at the prospect of having his child.

Her spirits lifting, Regina told herself that surely she and Matt would work things out. She loved him so, and somehow she'd make him love her in return. She knew he was bitter about giving up his plan to build his own ranch, but, with time, she hoped the Black Diamond would come to mean as much to him as it did to her.

Wanting Matt to join her, and praying their wedding night would be tender and beautiful, she looked at the closed door, mentally willing Matt to open it. But the door to Regina's bedroom remained closed throughout the night. Matt had chosen to remain in the study.

Ordaz and his men were camped outside the bunk-house. Miguel, with his vaqueros, was sitting beside a fire when he noticed Julie approaching. Putting down his coffee cup, he rose hastily to his feet, and as he went to meet her, he called, "*Señora,* are you looking for your sister, or perhaps Señor Brolin?"

When he paused at her side, Julie drew a nervous breath. "No. I came to see you."

Grinning widely, he replied, "Angel, I am pleased."

"Regina gave me your message, and I couldn't let you leave without saying goodbye. You have been so kind to me."

As he gazed down into her large brown eyes, Miguel was reminded of a wild timid doe, ready to take flight at any unexpected moment. "Señora, you are very thoughtful," he said gently.

Rising on tiptoe, Julie impulsively planted a fleeting kiss on his cheek. Then, shocked by her brazen behavior, she stepped back from him. "I . . . I hope to see you . . . when you return."

"Angel, you will see me again if I have to move heaven and earth to get here."

Julie's smile was so radiant that her beauty momentarily stunned Miguel. Taking one last look at him, she lifted the hem of her long skirt and, turning, fled to the house.

Regina had tossed all night, finally falling asleep after the sun had risen. When, at mid-morning, the door to her bedroom was opened roughly, she sat up in bed, startled. She was apprehensive when she saw Matt standing in the doorway, nonetheless her husband's appearance filled her with desire. Matt's well-fitted black pants outlined his slim hips and long legs, and the colorful bandanna he wore loosely tied around his neck gave him a jaunty air.

"Get dressed," Matt said flatly. "I must talk to you—in the study."

His attitude astounded Regina. He had left her alone on their wedding night, and apparently he did not intend to explain why.

"Where did you stay last night?" she asked firmly.

"The study," he answered.

"But why?" she pleaded.

"Why not?" he rapped out.

"You're my husband, and your place is here with

me!" she declared.

"Husband?" A bitter smile crossed his lips as a picture of Regina with Antonio flashed in his mind.

Quickly, Regina got out of bed and hurried to his side. "Matt, we'll never find compatibility in this marriage until you stop being so unreasonable."

"Compatibility?" His tone was sarcastic.

"Do you find the word humorous?" she asked, feeling perturbed.

"I find this whole farce of a marriage humorous," he remarked dryly.

Losing her temper, Regina blurted angrily, "You're free to leave this marriage anytime it suits you!"

Swiftly, he reached out and clutched her shoulders. Drawing her close, he said, "Madam, it suits me right now, but, damn it, I intend to be a father to my child!"

Regina looked deeply into his dark eyes. He despises me! she thought despondently. Because of me he gave up his lifetime dream of having his own ranch! He'll never forgive me for this pregnancy. For a moment, she considered asking Matt if he wanted her to deed the Black Diamond to Dan and Julie so she'd be free to go to Wyoming with him. But, no, she couldn't leave! In her present condition, the trip would be too strenuous.

Deciding not to bicker with him, she went to her wardrobe and took out a dressing gown. Slipping it on, she reminded him, "Didn't you say that you wanted to talk to me in the study?"

He left the room, and she followed him down the hall. In the study, she walked to the chair facing the desk, and sat down. "What do you want to talk about?" she asked.

Going to the safe, Matt opened it. He took out the tally ledger and dropped it on the desk in front of Regina. Pointing at it, he said sternly, "I want to talk to you about this."

192

"The tally ledger?" she asked, baffled.

"Why hasn't it been kept up to date?" he demanded testily.

"Because I wasn't sure how to keep it correctly," she explained. "Antonio hadn't taught me how to—"

His jealousy surging, Matt interrupted, "Were you too busy inveigling him? Is that why he didn't have the time to explain the ledger?"

Regina was so shocked by his harsh accusation that she simply stared at him. When she had regained her poise, she replied with barely controlled rage, "He didn't explain the ledger to me because shortly after you left I discontinued the lessons."

Her answer surprised Matt. He stammered, "Why... why did you stop them?"

Should she tell Matt that Antonio was in love with her? Uncertain of how he would take the revelation, Regina decided not to say anything. "I simply chose to stop the lessons," she answered evasively. "Why is not important."

He studied her carefully. Why had she avoided his question? What kind of game was she playing now, and what part did Antonio play in her scheme? he asked himself. Why had she wanted Antonio to leave last night before Matt saw him? If only she were honest!... Matt could not tolerate deceitfulness. Only if Regina were truthful with him could they find a way to make their marriage work. His dark eyes observed her, and the more he thought of her dishonesty, the stronger his resentment grew.

His hard scrutiny made Regina uneasy, and she muttered vaguely, "I was going to ask Mace for help but he died."

"How very inconsiderate of him!" Matt retorted, his bitterness making him react unfairly.

Regina hadn't meant the statement to sound unfeel-

193

ing, and Matt's cruel response made her temper flare. She bounded to her feet, intending to lash out at him verbally. However, the sudden movement made her feel faint. The room began to tilt, and, losing her balance, she fell against Matt.

Lifting her, he carried her to the sofa and gently laid her down. As he knelt beside her, he asked with concern, "Are you all right?"

"Yes," she sighed weakly. "It's my condition. I shouldn't have stood up so quickly."

"Regina," he said sincerely, "I'm sorry. What I said about Mace was uncalled for." He hesitated a moment before remarking quietly, "We must stop this continual bickering."

"I couldn't agree more," she answered.

His eyes met hers and held. She wished desperately that she could read his thoughts. "Matt," she implored, "please tell me what you are thinking about?"

Answering, he replied, "I was thinking about this marriage and our child."

When he didn't continue, she coaxed, "And?"

"Regina, I don't want our child to grow up believing his parents can barely tolerate each other."

Tolerate! She wanted to cry. Oh, Matt, is that how you feel about me, when I love you so dearly?

"So, for the child's sake," Matt was saying, "we have to find a way to make the most of this marriage. But it will take time. I must learn to lose the bitterness I'm feeling and try to put my thoughts into perspective."

The word *bitterness* tore hurtfully into Regina's heart. Had this ranch in Wyoming meant so much to him?

"In the mean time," Matt explained, "I'll run your ranch, and, from now on, I'll try my damnedest to be civil."

"Civil!" she cried, holding back tears.

194

Standing upright, Matt went to the desk and picked up the tally ledger. Looking back at Regina, he said calmly, "Don't ask for more, because at present civility is all I'm capable of giving you." Striding to the door, he added brusquely, "I'll take the ledger to the bunkhouse and see if any of the men can come up with correct figures." Before she could reply, he left the room.

Chapter Seventeen

During the weeks that followed, Matt abided by his pledge to be civil. However, his attitude bothered Regina, and she retaliated with cold politeness.

Meanwhile Julie had become aware that Regina and Matt did not occupy the same bedroom. More than once she had attempted to broach the subject to her sister, but Regina always cut her off brusquely. For some reason that Julie couldn't understand, Regina absolutely refused to discuss her marriage.

Matt soon had Regina's ranch running smoothly. The hands liked and respected him, and harmony was restored. The Black Diamond was now secure and prosperous, yet Regina had never been so unhappy.

Loving Matt, yet believing that he didn't love her was heartbreaking, and Regina's sadness had prompted her once again to saddle Midnight and take moonlight rides with Blackie. Following dinner, Matt never failed to close himself in the study. When he did, Regina sought consolation from the land she loved so dearly.

Returning home from one of her nightly rides, she was surprised to find a strange buckboard standing in front of the house. Wondering who was visiting, she quickly unsaddled the stallion and turned him loose in the corral; then she hurried into the house.

Upon entering the parlor, Regina was puzzled to find an elderly man and two children sitting on the sofa. Matt was standing in front of the unlit fireplace, one arm resting on the mantel. For a fleeting moment, it crossed Regina's mind that Matt never stood in any fashion except casually. Julie was sitting on the chair facing the couch, and when her sister appeared she got to her feet.

"Regina," Julie began, "we have been waiting for you." Looking at the children with tenderness, she continued, "I would like you to meet María and Cortés."

Glancing at the children, Regina smiled warmly.

Julie continued her introductions, "And this is José Carénas."

The man had his sombrero on his lap, and as he stood he accidentally dropped it. When he reached down to pick it up, Regina noticed that his hands were shaking. Apparently, the man was upset. "Señora Brolin," he mumbled, his eyes not quite meeting hers.

The man's name seemed vaguely familiar to Regina, and trying to remember where she had heard it, she suddenly recalled Dan mentioning that Matt had a close friend called José. Turning to Matt, she looked at him questioningly.

"I have known José for many years," Matt explained. "María and Cortés are his niece and nephew. Their mother was a good friend of mine." Stepping away from the fireplace, Matt proceeded, "José wants to talk to me alone. Why don't you take the children into the kitchen and give them something to eat?"

Moving to the sofa, Regina knelt in front of María and Cortés. Although she was smiling, her eyes studied them concernedly. They were much too thin, and they looked very tired. Regina's heart went out to them, and she wished she could gather them into her arms.

"Would you and your brother like to come with me to the kitchen?" she asked María.

The girl nodded slowly, and taking her brother's hand, she helped him from the sofa. María, who was fourteen years old, was a pretty girl. Her hair, black as a raven's, fell to her hips in long full waves, and her brown eyes looked extraordinarily large because her oval face was entirely too thin and pallid. The two-year-old Cortés didn't have strikingly dark hair like his sister's. His was a rich chestnut color that matched his eyes. He was a handsome boy, but like María, he looked undernourished.

As Regina and Julie led the children from the parlor, José said to Matt, "Your wife, she is very beautiful."

His voice sounded cheerful, but Matt could see the worry on his aged face. José had already informed Matt that María and Cortés were now orphans, so Matt believed the older man was concerned for them and grieving for his sister, their mother. José had loved her. Matt hadn't seen José in over four years, but their friendship had been a close one and Matt was still very fond of the older man.

"How did you know where to find me?" Matt inquired.

Sitting on the edge of the sofa, José placed his sombrero at his side. "Miguel Ordaz sent me to you, *amigo.*"

Matt sat down on the chair facing the sofa. Watching José speculatively, he asked, "Something is wrong, isn't it?"

"Sí," he nodded.

"Why did Miguel send you here?"

The old man sighed heavily. "It is a long story."

Encouraging him gently, Matt said quietly, "Start at the beginning and tell me what has happened."

Running a hand across his brow, José leaned back

on the sofa and tried to relax. "I am still working for Señor Garrett, but I decided to take a trip to Mexico to visit Rosita. I had not seen my sister in a long time."

Interrupting, Matt asked, "Did she remarry?"

"No, amigo."

"But her husband has been dead for over six years, and the boy Cortés couldn't be more than two."

Once again, José sighed deeply. "Rosita did not marry Cortés' father."

"That doesn't sound like Rosita. She wasn't that kind of woman."

"No, *señor,* she was not," he agreed, and Matt was puzzled to hear a tinge of anger in his voice. "But, one night, she took a man to her bed. A man she loved. On one of my visits, she told me she was going to have a child."

"Did she tell you who the father was?" Matt asked.

"Sí. I told her I would hunt him down and bring him back, that he would marry her or I would kill him. But Rosita did not want me to find him. She said what had happened between them that night had been her fault. The man had stopped by her home for a short visit, but Rosita had given him much whiskey. She had loved him for many years, and she wanted him, if only for a night."

Matt rose to his feet very slowly, and moving as if he were in a trance, he returned to the fireplace. Placing his elbow on the mantel, he stared into the unlit hearth. He spoke so quietly that José could barely hear him, "I was that man, wasn't I?"

"Sí, amigo," José mumbled.

Matt's shoulders slumped, and leaning his head on his hand, he groaned, "If I had known, I'd have married her. I wasn't in love with Rosita, but I liked her. Believe me, José. I liked and respected her."

"I believe you, *amigo."*

199

Turning to face José, Matt asked, "How did she die?"

"She took sick. From what María has told me, she had a high fever for many days." Rising, José walked to Matt's side. "When Rosita found out she was going to have a child, she moved away from the village where she had lived all her life. She bought a small hut, many miles away. It was as you say . . . all alone?"

"Secluded," Matt put in.

"*Sí, amigo.* I did not know where she had moved, so I went to Miguel Ordaz and asked him to help me find Rosita. After searching for many days, we came upon her hut. Rosita, she was very ill and died a few minutes after we arrived. When Rosita had first come down sick, María had tried to go for help, but their horse had shied away from her and run off. They were too many miles from help for María to walk. She nursed her *madre,* but Rosita grew weaker and weaker. Without the horse, María could not go for supplies so their store of food grew smaller and smaller. From what María has told me, she tried to stretch the food, but finally it was almost gone. When Miguel and I found them, María and Cortés were weak from . . . from how you say, not enough to eat?"

"Malnutrition." Matt answered.

"We took María and Cortés to Miguel's hacienda. When I told Miguel everything I knew, he said I should bring Cortés to you because you are his *papá.*"

"And María?" he questioned.

"I ask you, *amigo*—no, I beg you—please do not separate her from her little brother."

Matt placed a hand on his old friend's shoulder. "You don't need to beg. The children belong together."

Suddenly, a deep sob shook José's slender frame. "María, she has nightmares."

"What kind of nightmares?" Matt asked.

"In her sleep, she cries for food because she is so hungry."

"My God!" Matt whispered.

"María, she went without food so that her little brother could eat. Cortés is only a baby, and he did not understand why she gave him such small amounts. He would beg his sister to give him more."

"Don't José," Matt pleaded. "Don't tell me any more."

Bowing his head, José mumbled, *"Sí, amigo.* I understand."

"Why did Rosita move out into the middle of nowhere?"

Raising his gaze, José answered, "Why do you think, *señor?* To hide her shame."

Swerving, Matt struck his fist against the mantel. "Damn it!" he raged. "If only I had known!"

"Do not blame yourself. Rosita should have let me find you."

"Why didn't you go against her wishes and come to me?" Matt demanded.

José shrugged. "I wish I had, *amigo."* Touching Matt's arm, he asked, "Will you take care of María and Cortés?"

"I'll have to discuss all this with my wife," he answered.

Matt led José into the kitchen, where he asked Julie to fix the man something to eat; then he told Regina that he needed to talk to her.

They returned to the parlor, and Regina sat on the sofa while Matt took the chair facing her. Watching him curiously, Regina asked, "Why did Mr. Carénas come here?"

"Because of the children," he replied.

She raised her eyebrows questioningly. "The children?"

201

"Cortés is my son," Matt said evenly.

For a moment, Regina was too stunned to speak. She could only stare at Matt. "Your son!" she exclaimed raspingly.

Quickly, Matt told her everything he had learned from José. As his story unfolded, Regina's heart ached for María and Cortés, and when Matt finished his explanation, tears were sparkling in her eyes.

"Do you want us to take the children into our home?" she asked softly.

"Regina, how can we turn them away?"

"We can't." She sighed. She knew accepting María and Cortés was a big step, but there was no way she could possibly turn her back on two helpless children.

Matt was grateful to Regina. He admired her compassion and he found himself questioning how a woman as kind as she could have coldly set out to entrap him. Going to her, he took her hand and helped her to her feet. Keeping her hand in his, he said, "Are you sure you want to do this?"

"Yes, of course," she assured him. "Matt, Cortés is your son. He belongs with his father, and María should not be separated from her brother."

Releasing her hand, he brushed his fingers through his hair, and when his eyes met hers, Regina was touched to see a trace of tears in them. "My God, Regina!" he groaned, as the initial shock of learning about Cortés began to wear off. "I have a two-year-old son!"

Regina longed to take him into her arms and help him through this difficult time, but Matt had kept their marriage so impersonal that she felt too insecure to attempt to console him.

"Let's go to the kitchen and let José know that the children can stay," Regina suggested, and agreeing, Matt stepped aside so that she could precede him.

The others were seated at the kitchen table, and Julie was holding Cortés on her lap. Looking fondly at José, Matt smiled. "My wife has something to tell you."

"Sí, señora?" José looked at Regina.

"Mr. Carénas, the children are more than welcome to stay with us," she said warmly. "We have a large home, and we're only too happy to share it with María and Cortés."

"Gracias, señora," he replied gratefully, and his hand trembled as he brushed away tears of relief. Now he could return to Alan Garrett's ranch with his heart at peace and his mind at rest.

Surprised, but pleased, Julie exclaimed, "How wonderful! We're going to have children in the house." Hugging Cortés, she asked him, "Do you want to live here with us?"

"He does not speak English, *señora,*" María explained.

"That's all right," Julie replied. "He's very young and will learn quickly."

Matt moved over to Julie and Cortés and lifted the boy from her lap. Holding him, he studied the child intently before embracing him. "From now on, you will be called Cort," he announced; then he added emotionally, "Cort Brolin, my son."

Shocked, Julie caught her breath sharply, as María asked, "You are my brother's papá?"

Matt stepped to María, and placing his hand on her thin shoulder, he replied, "Yes, María. I am his father. And if you'll let me, I'll try to be a father to you."

Quickly, Maria looked at José. Smiling, he nodded to her encouragingly.

"I understand that it will take time, María," Matt told her tenderly. He turned his gaze to Regina, hoping she would help him reassure the girl.

Understanding his unspoken plea, Regina moved to stand at Matt's side, and gazing down at María, she said sincerely, "I hope we will become very good friends."

"Gracias, señora," María murmured, her heart pounding with joy. She and her brother had a home! And Señor and Señora Brolin were so nice!

Cortés missed Rosita, and suddenly Regina reminded him of his mother, which prompted him to reach out to her.

Smiling, Regina took him from Matt. Instantly, his arms were about her neck and his head was nestled against her soft shoulder. Holding him close, Regina's lips brushed across his chestnut curls.

Matt touched her arm, and she looked up into his face. "Thank you, Regina," he whispered, and the expression in his eyes told her he was truly grateful.

With the children in the house, Matt no longer closed himself in the study, and Regina stopped taking her nightly rides. Matt and Regina began spending their evenings with María and Cort. As the weeks passed, family gatherings in the parlor after dinner became a nightly event.

Having children in the house to love and care for was just the medicine Julie needed. Her husband's untimely death and her years of unhappiness began to fade, and she soon woke up each morning looking forward to spending the day with María and Cort.

It was easy for Regina to learn to love the children. María was an exceptionally sweet girl, and as Regina had hoped, they became good friends. She enjoyed María's company immensely, and when she took her shopping for a new wardrobe, Regina had found the affair as exciting as María did. And Cort was a joy to Regina. Knowing he was Matt's son made him all the more precious to her.

María and Cort brought a warmth he had never known into Matt's life, and, like Regina, he quickly learned to love them.

While dressing for dinner, Regina noticed that her gown was a little tight at the waistline. Soon she would need to start wearing the dresses that she and Julie had made. They were designed to expand with her increasing pregnancy.

Dan had been invited to dinner, so upon leaving her bedroom, Regina went to the parlor where she knew she would find everyone. Pausing in the doorway, she looked about the room. María was sitting on the sofa beside Julie, who was teaching her embroidery, and the young girl's head was bent over her work. Dan and Matt were occupying the two chairs that faced the sofa, while Blackie lay at Matt's feet. Cort's arms were wrapped about the dog's neck, and his face was buried in Blackie's thick fur.

"Matt," Julie complained, "do something with Cort. He's going to get dog hairs all over him."

Leaning forward, Matt gave his son a gentle pat on his rounded bottom. "Get off the dog," he mumbled.

Although Cort couldn't yet totally comprehend English, he instinctively understood his father's command. The boy's weight was now normal for his age, and getting to his chubby legs, he stuck out his bottom lip, apparently on the verge of crying.

Chuckling, Dan held out his arms to Cort. "Come here," he said. Instantly, the child went to Dan and snuggled into his lap.

None of them were aware of Regina's presence, and remaining unobserved, she continued to watch the warm scene. Everything would be so perfect, she thought depressingly, if only Matt and I were truly

205

husband and wife in every sense of the word!

María finished embroidering a rose on a doily and showed it to Julie.

"That's very good," Julie praised. "Show it to Matt."

Proudly, María took her work of art to Matt, and examining it closely, he exclaimed, "It's very beautiful, honey."

"*Gra—*" she began, but determined to speak English exclusively, she corrected herself. "Thank you."

Wanting to share in his father's attention, Cort climbed down from Dan's lap and promptly plopped himself into Matt's.

Catching sight of Regina, Julie told her, "Dinner should be ready in thirty minutes."

"Regina, would you like a glass of sherry?" Matt asked cordially.

She shook her head, and not wanting her mood to be observed, she turned away. Going to the front door, she rushed outside.

Dan followed, and stepping out to the porch, he found Regina sitting on the top step. Joining her, he draped an arm over her shoulders. "Gina, what's wrong?" he asked tenderly.

She sighed forlornly. "Oh Dan, I could be so happy if only . . . if only Matt loved me."

Drawing her closer, he murmured soothingly, "Maybe he does love you."

"No," Regina argued softly. "He can barely tolerate me, and he'll never forgive me for this pregnancy. Because of me he had to give up his dream of owning his own ranch."

"The fact that you're pregnant is just as much Matt's fault as yours. And as far as his own ranch is concerned, he has the Black Diamond. So where in the hell does he get off treating you unfairly?"

"Please, Dan," she pleaded, "don't get upset with Matt."

Dan frowned thoughtfully. "I don't know what's bothering Matt, but I suspect it's something more than your pregnancy and losing his ranch."

Regina shrugged. "Perhaps, but Matt keeps his thoughts to himself." Wanting to change the subject of their discussion, she asked, "How is Susan?"

"She's fine," Dan answered.

"You have been dating her for quite some time now. Are you still considering marriage?"

"Yes," he mumbled. "Eventually, I'll get around to proposing."

Amused, Regina smiled. "Dan, you make it sound as though it were something to dread."

"I've been a bachelor for thirty-eight years, and it's going to be difficult to give up my freedom. And Susan is twenty years younger than I am so our age difference might cause problems."

"If you love each other, age shouldn't be a factor." Watching him closely, she asked skeptically, "You do love Susan, don't you?"

"Of course," he muttered hastily. "But, Gina, you must realize that there are different kinds of love."

"But a passionate love is the only emotion that is inspiring!" Regina declared intensely.

Cocking an eyebrow, Dan queried teasingly, "What happened to make you such an expert on love?"

"I met Matt Brolin," she whispered.

Chapter Eighteen

Stepping out the back door, Julie emptied the dish pan, letting the sudsy water splash onto the ground. When she returned to the kitchen, she put the pan on the counter, and going to the large cast-iron stove, she removed the coffeepot and, opening the cupboard door, reached inside for a cup.

"Mind if I join you?" Matt asked.

Julie hadn't heard him enter the kitchen, and she was a little startled. Turning to face him, she smiled sincerely.

"I'd love some company."

Ambling to the table, Matt pulled out a chair and sat down. He watched Julie as she filled two cups with coffee.

Julie placed his coffee before him and asked, "Where are the children?"

"They're on the front porch with Regina," he answered. Hesitating, he broached the subject he wanted to discuss with Julie. "I need to talk to you about your ranch."

"My ranch?" she asked.

"Would you consider selling it?"

Julie was surprised. "I don't know. I hadn't thought

about it. It's my home."

"Nonsense," Matt remarked. "Your home is here with us. Surely you aren't thinking about living there alone."

"Do you want to purchase it?" she inquired.

"I'd like to, if you'll sell it to me. I have some money saved that I had planned to use to buy land in Wyoming."

"But why do you want my ranch? You have the Black Diamond, and this ranch is much larger than mine."

"Cort," he explained. "This ranch belongs rightfully to the child Regina carries. I want Cort to have an inheritance."

"I see," Julie replied. "And I agree with you."

"Then you'll sell?"

"Yes, I will," she decided.

"I intend to make you a fair offer."

Julie smiled pleasantly. "Matt, I'm sure you have an adequate amount saved; otherwise, you wouldn't have asked me to sell. I'm sure whatever amount you offer will be more than fair."

Taking a drink of his coffee, Matt studied her over the rim of his cup. He wondered why he hadn't noticed before how lovely she was. "When Regina and I first married, I had a very strong feeling that you didn't especially like me. Now, I could swear that you're my ally."

"It wasn't that I disliked you," Julie said quickly. "I didn't approve of your reputation. But Mr. Ordaz asked me to be kind to you, and I promised him that I would."

"Kind?" Matt suppressed a grin.

Wishing she hadn't been so rash as to use the word *kind,* Julie blushed. "I'm sorry. I didn't mean to sound as though Mr. Ordaz and I thought you were in need of charity."

"Don't be embarrassed," Matt told her tenderly. "Your kindness has been greatly appreciated." Studying her intently, he said approvingly, "You like Miguel, don't you?"

Her blush deepening, she murmured, "Yes, I do. He's such a gentle and compassionate man."

Eyes twinkling, Matt then asked, "Did he tell you not to judge me by my reputation?"

Nodding, Julie replied, "When the children arrived and I saw the way you took them to heart, I knew you were an honorable man." Smiling, she added, "I do so enjoy having María and Cort in the house."

"So do I," Matt commented happily, his eyes shining with pride.

Holding Cort on her lap, Regina sat on the porch steps beside María. Dusk was falling, but María was clearly visible. The girl seemed tired, and Regina wondered if she was getting enough rest.

"María," she began, "have you been sleeping well?"

"Yes, of course," María murmured, keeping her eyes turned away from Regina. She hadn't told the truth, and she felt bad about lying. She was plagued by nightmares, but, so far, she had managed to keep Matt and Regina from learning of the frightening dreams. She didn't want them to worry, nor did she want them to think that she was acting like a silly child.

Spotting a rider arriving, Regina peered down the lane leading up to the ranch house. When she recognized the visitor, she smiled happily. "It's Santos," she announced. "My goodness, I haven't seen him in months."

Santos waved to them and spurred his horse into a gallop. Within seconds he pulled up at the hitching post and dismounted. Removing his black sombrero, he went to Regina. Taking her hand, he kissed it lightly. *"Señora,* how have you been?" he inquired politely.

"Fine, thank you," she replied.

Santos glanced at Cort, who was still sitting on Regina's lap, and then brushed his fingers through the child's curly locks. Next he turned his attention to María. Lifting her hand, he placed a kiss upon it, bowing slightly as he did so. "You must be María," he surmised. "Señor Butler told me all about you and your brother."

María wanted to answer, but she couldn't find her voice. She had taken one look at Santos and had lost her young heart to him.

"I haven't seen you in ages," Regina remarked. "Where have you been?"

"I have been in Mexico," he answered.

"Not riding with Comancheros, I hope," she stated disapprovingly.

His expression cunning, he questioned, *"Señora,* why would I ride with Comancheros?" Then, smiling boyishly, he explained, "I visited with relatives."

"When did you get back?" Regina asked.

"This afternoon. I stopped in town and had a few drinks with your brother. Now, I am on my way home, but I wanted to stop by and pay my respects."

Gesturing to the steps, she suggested, "Sit down and talk to us for a while."

Complying, he sat on the second step. Santos had an engaging and humorous personality, and his amusing conversation soon had Regina and María laughing. When Santos rose to leave, Regina invited him to come back soon.

"I will, *señora,"* he replied, leaning over to place a kiss on Regina's cheek. Then he looked into Cort's sleepy eyes and said, "I think I have kept him up past his bedtime." Turning to María, Santos brushed his lips across her brow. "Good night, *Señorita."*

María's young face glowed with love as she replied softly, "Good night, Santos."

The young man strode to his horse and mounted, touching the brim of his hat before turning his mount.

When he had ridden out of sight, María sighed. "He is so beautiful!"

Regina smiled. "María, men are not beautiful. They are handsome."

The girl shook her head. "No. Santos is beautiful."

"You're quite taken with him, aren't you?"

"When I grow up," María declared intensely, "I'm going to marry Santos!"

Regina did not take what María said lightly. Knowing it was wiser to respect the young girl's dream, she answered, "If you want to marry Santos, then I hope that someday you will."

Fidgeting, Cort complained drowsily, "Sleepy . . . me sleepy."

He moved his head so that he could look up into Regina's face, and she kissed his cheek. "I guess we'd better put this little one to bed," she told María.

Carrying Cort to his bedroom, Regina, with María's help, prepared the child for bed. When he was tucked in, Regina bent over and placed a kiss on his brow. Cort's response was a big yawn which made her laugh. In response to her laughter, Cort grinned up at her, and she noticed that his smile resembled Matt's.

When Regina reached toward the lamp to turn down the wick, María stopped her by asking, "Regina?"

Turning away from the lamp, and facing María, Regina replied, "Yes?"

"May Cort and I call you Mama?" the girl pleaded.

For a moment, Regina was too filled with emotion to answer. Then, her eyes misty, she said earnestly,

212

"María, I'd be honored to have you and Cort call me Mama. I want to be a mother to you both. I really do."

Sitting up, Cort mumbled sweetly, "Night, Mama."

Leaning over, Regina hugged him affectionately, before tucking him back into bed. Then she turned to María and embraced her. Feeling extremely happy, Regina asked enthusiastically, "Do you know that soon you two will have a brand new brother or sister?"

Regina's pregnancy was beginning to show, and lowering her eyes to Regina's waistline, María smiled. "Yes, I know. I can hardly wait. Will you let me help take care of the baby?"

"Yes, of course." Studying María fondly, Regina murmured, "You're such a sweet . . . young lady." Suddenly, spotting Matt standing in the open doorway, Regina stammered, "How . . . how long have you been here?"

Smiling wryly, he answered, "Long enough to know you just became a mother."

María fled into Matt's arms, and Regina found herself envying the girl. If only she had the right to embrace Matt so freely!

"I also want to call you Papa," María happily informed him.

As Matt hugged María and told her how glad he was that she wanted him for a father, Regina slipped out of the room.

Returning to the front porch, Regina strolled to the railing, placed her hands on it, and breathed deeply. She belonged to the children now, and they belonged to her. She was elated! How was it possible for two children to bring so much happiness into her life? If she had Matt's love, everything would be perfect!

Stepping outside, Matt went to Regina and stood at her side. Neither of them spoke for a moment. It was

Matt who broke the strained silence. "You love those kids, don't you?"

"Yes," she whispered.

"Would your father have loved them?"

"No," she replied, puzzled by his question.

"Then you aren't really like him, are you?"

"Why do you ask?"

"Mace once told me that you and James Blakely were two of a kind."

"Why did he tell you that?" she wanted to know.

"It's not important," Matt mumbled evasively. Changing the subject, he asked, "Regina, how have you been feeling?"

"Feeling?" she repeated vaguely, still wondering why Mace had made such an untrue statement.

A little self-consciously, he explained, "What with the baby and all."

"I've been feeling fine," she answered.

His gaze dropping to her stomach, he replied, "You're beginning to look . . . Well, you look . . ."

Laughing spontaneously, Regina finished for him, "Pregnant?"

He grinned. "Yes, pregnant."

"Matt," she said impulsively, "do you want a boy or a girl?"

"I don't care," he answered truthfully. "Either one will do quite nicely. Which do you want?"

"I don't care either. I just want our baby to be healthy."

"Our baby," he repeated softly. "The way you said that, it sounded so natural."

"Well, it is ours," she replied firmly.

"I know, but you and I don't seem to belong with the word *our.*"

Moving from his side, Regina went to the pine

214

rocker and sat down. He doesn't want to share his life with me, or his bed or even his child, she thought, depressed. The sky was clear, and although it was nighttime, she could make Matt out easily. She wished she could understand this man who was her husband and the father of her unborn child. Rocking the chair gently, she said suddenly, "Matt, tell me about yourself." She seriously doubted that he would do so, but where was the harm in asking.

Sitting sideways on the porch railing, he looked at her from across the porch. "What do you want to know?"

"Why don't you tell me about your parents? Are they still living?" Regina inquired, amazed that he hadn't refused to discuss his life with her.

He shrugged. "Damned if I know."

"You don't know?" she cried.

"I never knew who they were. I was born in Memphis, or I guess I was. The orphanage in Memphis found me on the doorstep. I was in a basket, with a note pinned to my blanket. It simply read: 'His name is Matthew and he's two weeks old.'"

"You were raised in an orphanage?" she asked.

"Until I was twelve," he answered.

"Were you adopted?"

"No," he muttered. "I was never adopted. No one wanted to adopt a child whose parents could have been of any nationality. When I was twelve, I left the orphanage by running away."

"Where did you go?"

"Not very far. I hung around the waterfront, and by doing odd jobs, I managed to make enough to eat. I slept wherever I could find a place, usually in the back of some saloon. After six weeks of living like a street urchin, I met Silas Brolin. He was a big, strapping man who worked on the river boats. For some reason, he took a liking to me. He said he was fed up with cotton barges and asked me if I wanted to head west with him. Hell, I jumped at the chance. It was Silas who told me to take his last name."

"Did you go west?" she asked.

"Yeah, we sure did. But Silas had spent most of his life on boats, and he couldn't stay in one place for very long. So we did a helluva lot of traveling."

"How did you support yourselves?"

"Mostly by taking any jobs we could find. Silas wasn't what you would call an honorable man, and he didn't always stay within the law. He and three other men decided to rustle some cattle from a drive out of El Paso. They planned to take the stolen cattle down into Mexico."

"Did you go with them?"

He nodded. "Silas and two of his friends were killed. The other man and I were arrested. I went to prison for two years."

"How old were you?"

"Fifteen," Matt answered.

"Fifteen!" she exclaimed. "How could the law send a fifteen-year-old boy to prison?"

"I rustled cattle and I was carrying a gun. As far as they were concerned, I broke the law like a man so I could take my punishment like a man." Reaching into his pocket, he took out a cigar and a match. He struck the match on the railing and lit the cigar. "When I was released from prison, I was seventeen years old. I stole a horse and headed down into Mexico. I was broke, hungry, and desperate. That was when I tried to rob Miguel. After he slashed my cheek, he took me to his hacienda." Matt chuckled humorously, before continuing. "He told me if I was going to survive in this land, I

216

had a lot to learn, most importantly, how to handle a gun."

"It was Miguel who taught you to shoot?"

"Yes, but when I became as good as my teacher, he decided it was time for me to learn a trade. Miguel is a friend of Alan Garrett, so he sent me to his ranch. Garrett gave me a job and tutored me at night. All I know about ranching, and most of my schooling, I learned from Alan Garrett. It was at Garrett's I met José."

"You and José became good friends?"

"The best. I think a lot of that old man."

"But how did you become a bounty hunter?"

"I stayed at Garrett's until I was twenty-two, then I headed out on my own. In a small town in Texas, I got into a gunfight and shot a man. That was the first time I killed anyone. After the shooting, the sheriff went through his wanted posters and he found out there was a bounty on the man I shot. Instead of going to prison, I got a pat on the shoulder and fifty dollars."

"And a brand new career," Regina declared a little disapprovingly.

"I never hunted a man who didn't deserve to be hunted," Matt replied firmly.

"When did you decide that you wanted to be a rancher?"

"I knew when I was living with Garrett that someday I wanted to have my own ranch. It took me years to save up the money for it." He became quiet, and Regina wondered if he was thinking that because of her he'd given up his dream. Moving away from the railing, he said abruptly, "I have some paperwork to take care of."

She wanted to ask him to stay and talk to her, but she didn't. "Good night, Matt," she murmured.

"Good night, Regina," he replied, before going into

217

the house.

Remaining in the chair, Regina rocked back and forth as she gazed up at the stars that glowed brilliantly against the dark sky. The past few months had brought many changes in her life. Soon she would have a child. The mere thought of her baby thrilled Regina. She enjoyed having Julie back at the ranch, and María and Cort were bright rays of sunshine. But tonight, Matt had gone beyond cold politeness and had spoken warmly to her.

Within moments she decided it was time to go to bed. As she entered the house and walked down the hallway, she noticed that a light was burning in the study. She was tempted to stop and talk to Matt, but afraid he might think she was pressuring him, she dismissed the idea. At María's door, Regina stopped, intending only to check on her, but the girl was tossing fitfully in her sleep. Concerned, Regina hurried into the room and, going to the lamp, lit it.

Sitting on the edge of the bed, she placed her hands on María's shoulders, shaking her gently, "Wake up, honey . . . wake up," she said soothingly.

María tried to fight her way back to consciousness, but the nightmare held her like a vise. "I'm hungry . . . I'm hungry . . ." she moaned.

"María!" Regina said strongly. "Wake up!"

Matt poked his head into the bedroom. "What's wrong?"

"She's having a bad dream," Regina explained.

Moving to the side of the bed, Matt said hastily, "José told me that she'd been having nightmares." He bent over and touched María's shoulder, then shook her firmly. "María, wake up," he said sharply.

The girl's eyelids fluttered open, and for a moment, she was confused. "Wh . . . what happened?" she

218

asked, her voice muddled.

"You were having a bad dream," Regina told her.

"I'm sorry," María apologized demurely. "Forgive me for disturbing you."

"Forgive you?" Regina grasped the girl's hand. "Darling, Matt and I are just thankful that we were here to help you."

"María," Matt said compassionately, "you and Cort are safe, and neither of you will ever go hungry again."

The girl smiled timidly. "I think I can go back to sleep."

"Are you sure?" Regina insisted gently. "If you want me to, I'll stay with you for a while."

As María was declining Regina's offer, Matt asked, "Would you like a glass of warm milk?"

"No, thank you," María answered, grateful that these two people were her foster parents.

Regina kissed María's cheek, and, standing, she murmured, "Good night."

Stepping closer to the bed, Matt leaned down and also kissed the girl's cheek. "Good night, honey," he said.

He extinguished the lamp, then turned to follow Regina out of the room, but she had already left. Matt crossed the floor quickly, and as he stepped into the hallway, Regina was entering her own bedroom.

"Regina," he called softly.

Pausing in the open doorway, she waited for him to reach her. "Yes, Matt?"

"I . . . I just wanted to tell you good night," he stammered. Then, for the first time since he and Regina had been married, he looked at her passionately.

Seeing desire in his eyes, she waited breathlessly for him to draw her into his arms. But troublesome doubts assailed Matt and he swerved sharply and returned to the study.

Disappointed, Regina went into her bedroom, where she slipped into a soft, sheer gown and a matching peignoir. Then, sitting at her vanity table, she brushed her hair, the blond tresses fanning radiantly about her face.

Regina's thoughts were turbulent as she recalled the naked desire she had detected in Matt's eyes. He had wanted her! There was not a shred of doubt in her mind. Oh Matt, why did you turn away? she thought. I wish I could understand the force that drives you!

Suddenly she decided that she would go to him. If he wouldn't make the first move, she would. Regina stood and crossed the room with determined strides, but suddenly she hesitated at the closed door of her bedroom. What if he refuses my love? she wondered apprehensively. Am I emotionally strong enough to withstand such a heartbreaking rejection?

"No!" she moaned. "I'm not strong enough! If he spurns my affections, his rebuff will destroy me!"

Her hand trembled as she reached for the doorknob and turned it. Please, Matt! she pleaded silently. Don't turn me away! I love you so much!

Alone in the study, Matt paced restlessly back and forth, asking himself why he hadn't taken Regina into his arms. Why must his damnable pride always win out? She was his wife and he loved her, so why couldn't he let the past rest? If he did, he and Regina could start over again. Maybe she didn't love him now, but that didn't mean that she wouldn't love him in the future. He had to have her! My God, he couldn't continue to live in the same house with Regina and not make love with her! She was too beautiful, too desirable, and he had never needed a woman as badly as he needed Regina!

Deciding to confront her, he stepped swiftly to the study door and swung it open. Regina, who had been about to knock on the door, was shocked to come face to face with Matt. He was also startled to see Regina, and for a few moments, they just stared at each other.

Finally, drawing her gaze from his, Regina's eyes traveled over Matt's strong, lean frame. His beige shirt was partially unbuttoned, revealing the dark hairs that grew abundantly across his chest, and his snug tan trousers revealed his growing desire. A fiery hunger for him consumed Regina.

Meanwhile the sight of Regina's shadowed loveliness had electrified Matt, for the pink negligée silhouetted her soft, well-endowed curves. Moving with incredible speed, Matt's arm shot out and grasped her around the waist to pull her against him. Then his lips claimed hers with a kiss so demanding Regina's knees weakened.

Sweeping her into his arms, Matt carried her down the hall and into the bedroom. He lowered her onto the bed, and joining her, his lips conquered hers.

"Regina," he groaned huskily, kissing her forehead, her cheeks, and then her slender neck.

Regina's heart was pounding. She could hardly believe that she was actually in the arms of the man she loved so ecstatically.

"I want you, Regina," Matt whispered tremulously.

"Yes, darling," she murmured intensely. "I want you too, Matt."

Anxious to make love to her, Matt began discarding his apparel and Regina followed suit, disposing of her peignoir, but Matt impeded her movements by clutching her arm and pulling her against his now-naked frame.

"I'll undress you," he told her thickly, before kissing

221

her passionately.

He removed her nightgown slowly so that he could admire her bared beauty inch by enticing inch. As he gently brushed the slight swell of her stomach, he thought about the child safe in it's mother's womb. Then he eased her down onto the bed, his masculine frame covering hers, and using his knee, he parted her ivory thighs. Quickly he entered her warm depths, and as his hips moved back and forth, Regina's thighs converged with Matt's welcoming his forceful thrusts.

Withdrawing unexpectedly, Matt turned onto his back, and gripping Regina about the waist, he placed her on top of him. Regina had never made love in this position, and she was a little confused, but aware of her inexperience, Matt guided her down onto his manhood. Sliding easily into her moist softness, his hands still on her waist, he lifted her up and down. Following his lead, Regina rode him with ease.

Within moments, Matt again changed their position so he could reassume the dominant role. Urging Regina to cross her legs over his back, he thrust against her with such vigor that they simultaneously entered a private world of complete pleasure.

As they gradually returned to reality, Matt's lips covered hers, and his kiss was deep and lingering. Shifting to lie at her side, he encouraged her to snuggle against him. Then they fell silent, each waiting for the other one to speak.

"Regina," Matt finally said, "do you remember the day I told you I had a lot of bitterness to lose?"

Recalling that morning vividly, she answered, "I remember it very well." Why did losing your ranch make you so bitter? Doesn't our home mean anything to you? she thought.

For a moment, Matt considered telling Regina that

he was aware of her conspiracy with Miguel. That had made him bitter. But he decided to let the past die; the future was all that really mattered. "I'm no longer bitter, Regina," he murmured, and he knew it was the truth. His resentment was completely gone, but where Regina's love was concerned, he still felt very insecure.

She longed to encourage him to talk about his past bitterness and to discuss the dream he'd had of owning his own ranch. But she was afraid if she pressed him to do so, his resentment might be revived.

"Regina, the night we were married you were visited by Antonio, and I overheard you tell him to leave before I could see him. Why didn't you want me to know he was here?" As soon as he'd asked, Matt was annoyed with himself. Hadn't he just decided to let the past die? Why in hell had he brought it back to life? It's because of my damned jealousy! he admitted to himself. Jealousy was a new emotion to Matt and one he had coped with badly.

Recalling the incident to which Matt had referred, Regina explained, "I didn't warn Antonio to leave because of you. I didn't want Miguel to see him. Considering the animosity between those two, I was afraid of what might happen if they met."

"Miguel!" Matt exclaimed, wondering why he hadn't considered the possibility that she had referred to Miguel instead of himself. He had been mistaken about Regina, badly mistaken. Was that the only time he had misjudged her? Once again, he thought seriously of taking her into his confidence, of explaining everything to her. Again he rejected the idea, deciding to forget the past and start anew.

"Darlin'," he said gently, drawing her closer, "I want this marriage to succeed." He was very close to confessing his love, but he held himself back, intending to

223

wait until he felt that her feelings were as strong as his.

Smiling happily, Regina answered, "I want our marriage to work too." She wished he would tell her that he loved her, but she felt that in time he would. Maybe he didn't love her now, but someday she was sure she'd find a way to win Matt Brolin's heart.

Chapter Nineteen

The security and the loving environment at the ranch brought María's nightmares to an end. Although she was happy now, she was a quiet girl who usually kept her thoughts to herself. However, one night Regina found her standing alone on the porch and gazing dreamily down the lane that led to the house, and sensed that María was hoping Santos would make one of his unexpected visits. Realizing how much María looked forward to seeing him, Regina promptly invited Santos to dinner. Thereafter, to María's joy, Santos Ramírez became a frequent dinner guest.

Cort was an energetic child, full of vitality and zest, yet he was also an adorable child. Regina couldn't have loved him more if he had been her natural son.

When Regina informed Matt that she wanted them to legally adopt María and Cort, she had been pleased by his enthusiastic agreement. Apparently, having a family meant a great deal to Matt, and Regina was almost certain that he had fully recovered from not following his plan to build his own ranch.

Regina and Matt were now happy together, the only cloud hovering over their marriage being the insecurity each felt concerning the other's love. Yet neither brought up the subject so as weeks passed they found it more difficult to bring this problem into the open. Eventually they both decided to leave well enough alone, neither wanting to say or do anything that might jeopardize their happy, yet perilous, relationship.

The day was exceedingly warm, and as Matt dismounted, he drew an arm across his perspiring brow. Having worked for eight hours straight, he was looking forward to a bath and a nap before dinner. As he reached up to unstrap the cinch of his saddle, he heard riders approaching and stepped back to look behind him. Recognizing Dan and Miguel, Matt grinned and walked over to greet them.

As he and Dan dismounted, Miguel called out loudly, *"Amigo!"*

Cheerfully, Matt asked, "What in the hell are you doing back in these parts?"

"My vaqueros and I, we got here this morning. My men are in town at Señor Butler's saloon. I cannot stay, *amigo.* But I wanted to ride out and pay my respects to you and your family."

Raising an eyebrow, Matt asked with a twinkle in his eyes. "Did you have one particular family member in mind?"

Miguel's sudden laughter was deep and full. "How is Señora Edwards?" he inquired.

"She's fine. But why can't you stay? Regina and Julie will be disappointed."

A harsh look appeared on Miguel's face. "I am looking for three men," he answered menacingly.

Realizing there was trouble, Matt asked, "What happened?"

"These three *gringos,* they came upon a small *granja* not too many miles from my hacienda, and they

226

murdered the whole family. But the girl, she lived long enough to tell me what happened. The *hombres* broke into her home, killed her parents and two brothers. Then they raped her many times. When they finished with the *señorita,* she was stabbed and left for dead." Miguel paused, before adding somberly, "Matt, the *señorita,* she was only twelve years old."

"My God!" Matt moaned.

"My vaqueros and I, we have tracked them this far."

"Do you think they're still around here somewhere?" Matt asked.

"I think so, *amigo.* We lost their trail a ways out of Albuquerque, but I will find their tracks again."

"I'm going with you," Matt stated.

Smiling, Miguel replied, "I was hoping very much that you would."

"Come on," Matt said, "let's go let Regina and Julie know what's happening."

Briskly the three men headed toward the house, and as they neared the front porch, María opened the door and stepped outside.

"Where are Regina and Julie?" Matt asked her.

"They rode over to Aunt Julie's ranch."

"Why did they go over there?" Matt inquired.

"Aunt Julie has some canned preserves in her pantry, and she and Mama went to get them."

"Amigo," Miguel began, "I think maybe we should ride to Señora Edwards' ranch. With those three *hombres* around somewhere, it is not safe for the ladies to be alone."

"Are any of the ranch hands over there?" Dan asked Matt.

"No. Except for the ones here, they're all on the east range. There's no one at that ranch except Regina and Julie." Matt's eyes met Miguel's, and a foreboding chill went through him. "My God!" he groaned. "Let's get

227

the hell over there!"

Awkwardly, Regina stepped down from the buckboard, and picking up her rifle, she remarked resignedly, "I'm about as graceful as an ox."

As she removed the empty basket from the buckboard, Julie examined her sister's obviously pregnant body. "You still have two more months," she said, while considering Regina's size. All at once, Julie's eyes gleamed. "Maybe you're going to have twins!"

"Twins!" Regina exclaimed. "You know I definitely do feel enough movement for more than one baby."

"Maybe you should say something to the doctor," Julie suggested.

Shrugging off the possibility of twins, Regina reached into the buckboard for her rifle. "No, I'm sure there's only one," she answered. "No one in our family has ever had twins."

"What about Matt's family?" Julie asked.

As she strolled toward the front porch, Regina replied, "Matt has no knowledge of his family." Suddenly experiencing a feeling of uneasiness, she said briskly, "Let's get the preserves. This place is so empty, it gives me the creeps."

Quickly Julie led the way into the house. The kitchen and living area were actually in one room, but they were separated by a partial wall constructed of logs. The side facing the parlor was decorated with pictures. On the kitchen side, Julie had hung pots and pans so they were conveniently close to the large wood-burning stove.

Following Julie into the kitchen, Regina propped her rifle against the table leg. Julie opened the pantry door and handed her the basket. "How many jars should we take?" she asked.

"As many as the basket will hold," Regina decided. "You know how the children love preserves."

Reaching into the pantry, Julie picked up two jars. As she turned to place them in the basket, she noticed a sudden movement behind Regina. Her eyes widened with fright, and the preserves slipped from her hands, the jars hitting the floor and shattering.

Whirling, Regina looked behind her. The three men stood in the doorway. They were unkempt and loathsome, and when she saw the expressions on their faces, a strangled sound escaped from Regina. She dropped the basket and instinctively wrapped her arms across her swelling stomach in a futile attempt to protect her unborn child.

The man who stepped forward was extremely obese, and his smile exposed yellow, decaying teeth. "We been followin' you gals, wonderin' where you was headin'. Sure was sweet of ya to bring us here where it's nice and private. We was beginnin' to think we'd have to stop ya out yonder somewhere and throw ya on the ground to stick it to ya."

The man's beady eyes traveled over Regina, and his ghastly laugh sent chills through her.

"Looks like someone has already done it," he commented.

The other two men then moved swiftly, roughly grasping Julie's arms and jerking her toward them.

"Leave her alone!" Regina shouted.

The huge man laughed again. "You two can have that one. I'll take this one here."

His statement struck Regina like a blow. "Oh God . . . no!" she screamed. Her hands still clutching her stomach, she begged, "Please . . . please don't do anything to harm my baby!"

With the strength that comes from desperation, Julie pulled free of the men holding her, and grabbing at the

229

huge man's arm, she pleaded, "Please don't hurt my sister or her baby . . . you can have me! I won't fight you . . . I'll even be willing if that's what you want! But please spare my sister and her baby . . . please!"

The large man backhanded Julie across the face. The powerful blow knocked her to the floor, and the other two men immediately grasped her arms and began to drag her into the living room.

As he watched his companions haul Julie away, the monstrous man laughed. At that moment, Regina dashed for the table, intending to grab her rifle, but her pregnant state slowed her down, and before she could reach it, the man's hands were on her shoulders. Turning her roughly, he drew back his arm. Regina saw the blow coming, and she tried to bring up her arm to shield herself. But he was too fast. His fist struck her firmly across the chin.

The solid blow sent her whirling, and she fell heavily against the corner of the table. Its sharp edge dug painfully into her stomach, creating excruciating pain in Regina's womb. Moaning agonizingly, she nearly strangled on the bile that rose in her throat. An ear-splitting ringing roared through her head before she was mercifully engulfed in total blackness. Her knees buckled, and she dropped to the floor.

Laughing, the burly man checked the back door to make sure it was locked. Then he hurried to the front door and pushed home the bolt. He grinned sadistically as he watched his friends wrestle with Julie. Finally, one man grabbed her arms, pinning them over her head on the floor.

"Get them clothes off her!" the huge man ordered. "She's gonna pleasure all three of us!"

The man kneeling beside Julie asked, "What happened to the other one?"

230

"She's in thar on the kitchen floor. I reckon she'll soon be givin' birth, if'n she don't die first."

His words penetrated Julie's fear and revulsion, and she screamed piercingly, "Oh God! . . . Regina!"

As the three riders reined in their horses a short distance from the house, the large white stallion snorted loudly. Miguel rubbed his hand alongside his steed's neck.

"Quieto, Diablo," he whispered soothingly. Then, certain they had found the men he had been pursuing, he warned Matt cautiously, *"Amigo,* you must remain calm."

Matt stared at the three horses standing beside Regina's buckboard, and a nerve twitched violently at his temple. Fear for Regina and for his unborn child gripped his heart like a steel vise.

"We had best leave the horses here," Miguel began. "We do not want them to hear us coming."

Hastily, the three men dismounted. Dan watched as Miguel removed his rifle from its scabbard and then, moving to the other side of his mount, grasped a double-barreled shotgun as well.

"What in the hell are you planning to do with that?" Dan asked.

"We may need it, *amigo.* Come on; let's go."

Stealthily, they stalked toward the silent ranch house. As they drew nearer, they heard a man's deep laughter then, once again, silence. Quietly, they crept to the window facing the front of the house. The shutters were closed but not secured, and Matt noticed a small crack between them.

Dreading what he might be forced to witness, Matt peeked through the crack. He could see a huge man

231

standing in front of the door, staring across the room. Following the man's gaze, Matt looked to the right, and lowering his eyes he spied Julie on the floor. One man pinning her arms over her head while the other one knelt at her side. Their voices carried through the window.

"Get them clothes off her! She's gonna pleasure all three of us!"

"What happened to the other one?"

"She's in thar on the kitchen floor. I reckon she'll soon be givin' birth, if'n she don't die first."

Miguel grabbed Matt, pulling him away from the window just as Julie let out a piercing scream. "Oh God! . . . Regina!"

Using the strength in his powerful arms, Miguel restrained Matt, and aware of his friend's rage, he warned him quietly, *"Amigo,* if you do something rash, it could cost the women their lives."

Roughly, Matt flung off Miguel's grip. He took a deep breath and then answered, "I'm all right." Drawing his pistol, he continued, "I'm sure they have both doors barred, so lets find some other way to get inside."

"We have no time to lose," Miguel replied. "Where is everyone located?"

"There's a big son of a bitch standing in front of the door. To his right is Julie. The other two have her down on the floor. One's kneeling beside her, and the other is holding her arms over her head."

"Check and see if they are still in the same positions," Miguel ordered.

Quickly, Matt looked back through the narrow crack. "Yeah, only the one kneeling is ripping off Julie's dress."

With murderous rage flashing in his eyes, Miguel

handed his shot gun to Dan. "Cock both barrels!" he instructed. "When I give you the signal, empty both chambers into the front door." To Matt, he continued, "You take the one kneeling, and I will take the other one."

"What about the man standing in front of the door?" Dan asked.

Miguel grinned sardonically. "When you release both triggers on that shotgun, there will be little left of the son of a bitch."

Hastily Miguel and Matt took their places beside the door, one on each side. Both men made a quick check of their weapons. Meanwhile Dan positioned himself facing the front door, and cocking both barrels, he aimed the gun. Miguel raised his arm, then let it drop. Pressing both triggers, Dan discharged two barrels of deadly buckshot into the closed door. At the thunderous explosion of the gun, the door buckled inward, sending buckshot and splinters flying into the room.

The fat man had no time to react before the heavy wooden door slammed into his chest, thrusting him across the room and throwing him against the log partition. As he hit the floor, flying splinters dug into his body and face, but the man never felt them. He was dead.

Dashing into the room, Miguel aimed his rifle at the man who had been holding Julie's arms. The outlaw got halfway to his feet, before Miguel's fatal bullet penetrated his chest. Matt, meanwhile, had pivoted toward the other man and had ended his life with one accurate shot. He then made a beeline for the kitchen.

Dan hurried to Julie, and kneeling beside his sister, he drew her into his arms. Crying hysterically, she clung to him. Everything had happened too fast for Julie to realize how she had been rescued. She had only been aware that Dan's arms were suddenly reaching for her. Now, upon hearing someone walk up to them, she released her hold on her brother. Looking up, she saw Ordaz and gasped, "Miguel!"

Dan was startled when Julie suddenly pushed out of his arms. Weakly she tried to rise, but her legs failed to support her and she dropped to her knees. Determined, she attempted to stand again, but this time Miguel grasped her shoulders and pulled her into his embrace.

Throwing her arms around him, she placed her head on his shoulder, and with tears streaming unrestrainedly down her cheeks, she cried, "Miguel, don't leave me!"

Hugging her tightly, he murmured, "My little angel, I will never again leave you. I swear by all that's holy, I will never leave you."

Quickly Dan got to his feet. If his thoughts hadn't suddenly turned to Regina, he'd have been shocked by the touching scene between Julie and Miguel.

Remembering her sister when Dan headed for the kitchen, Julie stepped out of Miguel's arms and hastily followed her brother. They came to an abrupt halt when they saw Matt sitting on the floor with Regina held close to his chest.

Blood saturated Regina's skirt.

"I'll get the doctor!" Dan cried. Turning, he fled from the room.

"Also get the sheriff!" Miguel called after him.

Julie moaned deeply, and her hand flew to her mouth to hold back a scream. She went quickly to her sister and Matt. Kneeling, she touched Matt's arm, and only then did he become aware of her presence.

Tightening his hold on Regina, he groaned, "My God, what did that son of a bitch do to her?"

As consciousness returned to her, Regina moved her head back and forth. Then, suddenly, she was stabbed

234

by sharp pain.

"Regina!" Matt gasped. "Honey! . . . oh God, Regina!"

Focusing with difficulty, Regina looked into her husband's face, but the torturous pain again cut into her and she grabbed her stomach. Her cry of anguish broke Matt's heart.

"Our baby! . . . oh Matt, he killed our baby!"

Chapter Twenty

Miguel kicked the jagged pieces of the destroyed door out of his way. When he stood in the doorway to look outside, the flickering glow from the kerosene lamp made his shadow fall across the porch. He did not move as he watched Matt pace around the yard.

Stepping up behind Miguel, Dan suggested, "Maybe we should be out there with him."

Shaking his head, the older man answered, *"No, amigo.* Matt, he is a man who wishes to be alone."

Glancing in the direction of the bedroom, Dan said impatiently, "What's taking so long? The doctor has been in there for hours."

Miguel was about to reply when Julie opened the bedroom door. She paused a moment, unconsciously toying with the safety pin she had used to repair the torn bodice of her dress. Then, sighing wearily, she wiped her perspiring brow and slowly went to Miguel and Dan.

Ordaz opened his arms, and Julie practically fell into his embrace. Supporting her, he kissed her pale cheek. "My angel, you are so tired," he whispered.

Holding on to Miguel's strength as if it were her life line, she moaned, "Oh Miguel . . . I wish . . ."

"You wish what?" he coaxed gently.

Julie's voice quivered, and she sensed that she was close to hysteria. "I wish I could just stay here in your arms, where I feel so safe and protected."

He placed his lips on her warm brow before answering, "You must go to Matt."

Trembling, Julie muttered against his broad shoulder, "Dear God, how do I tell him?"

"Is Gina all right?" Dan asked urgently.

Julie left Miguel's comforting arms, and looking at her brother, she answered so weakly that he barely heard her, "I don't know."

Miguel gently reminded her, "Matt, he is outside. Do not keep him waiting."

Stumbling over the sharp pieces of wood, Julie made her way outside. Matt was standing next to the unhitched buckboard and he saw her the moment she stepped onto the porch. His body grew taut, and his heart pounded with fear. Clasping her hands together tightly to prevent them from trembling, Julie walked over to him.

When she paused in front of him, he asked, "Is she alive?"

Looking into his strained face, Julie answered, "Yes, she's alive."

"And the baby?"

For an instant, Julie's eyes closed, and she felt as though she were going to faint. When Matt clutched her shoulders and steadied her, she forced herself to look at him again, but unable to compose herself, she began to cry. "Twins! . . . oh God, Matt . . . two babies . . . two little babies!"

Urgently, he demanded, "Are they alive?" When she didn't reply, he shook her roughly. "Answer me, Julie!"

"Please!" she pleaded. "Let me go!"

He released her brusquely, and stumbling backward,

Julie covered her face with her hands. "We lost both of them!" she cried. "I'm sorry . . . oh Matt, I'm so sorry!"

Whirling swiftly, Matt slammed his fist against the side of the buckboard. Then he kept hitting it over and over again, the solid wood bruising his hands, making them crack and bleed.

Rushing from the house, Miguel grabbed Matt's arms and forcefully pulled him away from the buckboard. But Matt broke free of his hold. To Julie, he said, "Did we lose sons or daughters?"

Moving closer to Matt, she answered sympathetically, "A boy and a girl."

Matt's body sagged, and as Julie reached for him he went into her arms. Then Miguel encircled them both in his large embrace, murmuring, *"Amigo,* my heart breaks for you and Regina."

For a long time, Matt allowed himself to be held by them. Then drawing away, he asked quietly, "Were they born dead?"

Julie had to swallow hard before finding her voice. "The girl was stillborn, but the boy lived for a few minutes."

"A few minutes!" Matt choked out.

Julie's sobs punctuated her words, "He lived long enough for his mother to hold him . . . and kiss him . . . and tell him that she loved him. . . . The baby died in Regina's arms."

Once again, Matt whirled toward the buckboard, but this time he simply fell against it. "Regina," he moaned, "God help us!"

Stepping to Matt, Miguel touched his shoulder. Their friendship was so deep that there was no need for words. Willingly, Matt let the huge Mexican embrace him again, but when the doctor and Dan came out of the house, Matt hurried to them. "How is Regina?" he asked.

Obviously fatigued, Dr. Henderson brushed his fingers through his thick gray hair and sighed before answering, "There seem to be no internal injuries and the bleeding has stopped."

"May I see her?" Matt asked.

Nodding, the doctor answered, "Yes, of course. But, at the moment, she's asleep."

Matt turned toward the house, but stopped abruptly. He cleared his throat, and his voice was strong as he requested, "Miguel, will you ride into town and talk to the reverend? Please take care of all the arrangements for me. And, Dan, will you take Julie home?"

"But, Matt . . ." Julie protested.

"Please don't argue with me. I'll rest easier knowing you're there with María and Cort." Looking at Dr. Henderson, Matt asked, "When can Regina be moved?"

"You can take her home tomorrow. Just make sure the buckboard is well padded and that you take it very easy."

Matt's slim frame suddenly jerked awkwardly and he rasped out, "Where are the babies?"

"In the second bedroom," the doctor answered.

Reeling unsteadily, Matt walked toward the house. Julie noticed that his rigid steps had no resemblance to his usual graceful gait.

When Matt arrived at Regina's room, he opened the door and, looking inside, saw that she was sleeping. Quietly he closed the door and walked deliberately to the other bedroom to see his children.

Dawn was breaking over the quiet plains, and the golden rays of the rising sun shone through the window, falling across Matt's troubled face as he sat beside Regina's bed. His eyes were tired and bloodshot. Again he examined the ugly bruise on her chin as he tenderly brushed his fingers across her cheek. In a whisper, he confessed to the sleeping Regina, "I love you . . . oh, God, how I love you."

Then, fatigued, he leaned back in the chair, straightening his cramped legs in an attempt to achieve some degree of comfort. Finally, folding his arms across his chest, he gave in to his weariness and closed his eyes.

He was not aware that he had dozed off until he became conscious of Regina's feeble whisper.

"Matt."

Immediately wakening, he sat upright, and leaned toward the bed. "I'm right here, Regina."

Slowly, she opened her eyes. At first, her thoughts were muddled, and she felt confused as she tried to shake off her drowsiness. But, suddenly, reality took over, tearing cruelly into her heart.

"Our babies!" she groaned.

Regina's grief-stricken face filled Matt's heart with compassion, and an uncomfortable silence fell between them. The quiet was eerie.

Suddenly, Regina said softly, "I want the babies named after my parents." She sounded as though she were in complete control, but actually she was on the brink of hysteria.

Matt rested his head on the palms of his hands, and staring down at the floor, he mumbled, "What were their full names?"

"James Raymond and Katherine Ann."

Matt was amazed by Regina's emotional strength. My God, he thought, she's so strong that she doesn't even need me! But when Regina released a heartrending cry, he realized he was wrong. She needed him as much as he needed her.

Bolting from the chair, he lay beside her and took her into his arms. "Oh, Matt!" she cried. "Our babies . . .

our precious babies!"

He held her tightly, placing her head against his shoulder. Then, his voice breaking, he murmured consolingly, "Regina, we still have María and Cort. Thank God, we have them."

When Matt brought his horse to a halt beside the buckboard in front of Julie's home, Ted Lucas, who was standing on the porch, walked down the steps to greet him. Ted and his wife Hannah owned a small ranch north of Regina's. They had been Carl Blakely's friends, and although they hadn't especially liked James Blakely, they were fond of his daughters. Early that morning, they had learned of Regina's terrible loss and had ridden over to offer their condolences and to help in any way they could. Matt had asked them to stay with Regina until he returned from the cemetery in town.

"Mr. Lucas," Matt said, dismounting, "I want to thank you and your wife for staying with Regina."

When the older man offered Matt his hand, Matt shook it firmly, willing himself to remain composed. He had just come from burying his babies, and he didn't feel like shaking hands. He wanted to shout his anger and grief to the heavens, to find relief from the pain that was gnawing away at him.

"Hannah and me," Mr. Lucas began, "we've always thought a lot of Miss Regina." Removing his hat, he brushed his fingers through his graying hair, then said hesitantly, "Mr. Brolin?"

"The name's Matt."

"And I'm Ted," Lucas responded. "I know this is a bad time for you, but I was wonderin' if next month I could ride over and talk business with you."

Matt nodded. "Of course." Turning, he strolled to

241

the house. He went directly to the bedroom and knocked lightly on the closed door.

"Come in," he heard Mrs. Lucas call softly.

As Matt entered the room, the elderly, plump woman rose from her chair. He nodded politely to her before looking at Regina. Seeing that his wife was asleep, Matt moved quietly to the bed.

"Thank you, ma'am, for staying with Regina," Matt said in a lowered voice.

Mrs. Lucas responded in a hushed tone, "My heart just breaks for her. And for you, too, Mr. Brolin. God bless you both."

Her sympathy made Matt glance away and fight for control. "Thank you," he replied humbly.

Moving quietly, Hannah Lucas went to his side and placed her hand on his arm. "If you should need Ted or me, don't hesitate to send for us."

His gaze sought hers. "You're very kind, Mrs. Lucas," he murmured.

Patting his arm gently, the motherly woman smiled. "Please call me Hannah," she said, and patting his arm one final time, she left the room.

Carefully, Matt sat on the edge of the bed beside Regina. Reaching over, he caressed the long blond hair that framed her lovely face.

"Regina," he said gently. "Honey, wake up. It's time to go home."

Regina stirred fretfully, and as she was leaving the peaceful state of sleep, she moaned pitifully, "My babies . . ." Then, slowly, her eyelids fluttered open.

Matt leaned over and kissed her forehead, and wrapping her arms about his neck, she pleaded, "Hold me . . . please hold me!"

As he gathered her into his embrace, she began to cry. "Oh Matt, I want my babies!" she said.

He rocked her back and forth, his face next to hers,

and as deep sobs shook his lean frame, he murmured, "Regina, I'm so sorry. We lost them! God help us! We lost them!"

Suddenly, all the heartache Matt had been suppressing forced its way to the surface. His sorrow tore at him. Sharing his grief, Regina drew him closer, and together, they cried for their children.

Chapter Twenty-One

Courage and stamina had been born and bred into Regina, so as she recovered physically, she recovered emotionally. Matt's inner strength, embedded in him from early childhood, carried him through his time of sorrow. But the tragedy of losing the twins left a permanent scar on their hearts.

The Black Diamond now had a foreman. Ted Lucas had wanted to ask Matt for the job, and Matt had gladly offered him the position. For months he had been searching for a reliable and qualified man to fill the job.

Ted had feared that Matt would renege on his offer if he found that his prospective foreman hadn't been able to make his own ranch prosper. But Ted Lucas was an honest man, and he'd told Matt that his ranch was on the verge of ruin so he was seeking employment out of necessity. To Ted's surprise, Matt hadn't thought him incompetent because his ranch had failed. Matt had known that Ted had suffered more than his share of bad luck.

Offering Ted his hand, he had promised him the job, and after they'd enjoyed a glass of brandy, he had asked Ted if he thought Mrs. Lucas might be interested in accepting the position of housekeeper and cook. In that case, if they preferred, the Lucases would be more than welcome to stay in the servants' quarters, thus sparing themselves numerous trips back and forth from one ranch to the other. Within a few days, Ted and Hannah Lucas had closed up their house, sold their small herd of cattle, and moved to the Black Diamond.

As he entered the parlor, Miguel saw Julie standing by the window, gazing outside.

Sighing, she turned toward the sofa when, out of the corner of her eye, she glimpsed Miguel. She smiled, his vibrant presence, as always, making her feel flushed.

"Mr. Ordaz," she said.

Miguel instantly moved to her side. He had now been staying at the Black Diamond for over a month. Knowing Matt would need his help through this time of tragedy, he had tried to relieve Matt of many responsibilities. Although Miguel had seen Julie quite often, he hadn't attempted to engage her in personal conversation. He had waited for the appropriate time. Now, as he gazed down into her beautiful brown eyes, he decided to speak openly with her. "Why do you feel it necessary to address me as Mr. Ordaz? That tragic afternoon at your home when you went into my arms, you called me Miguel." He paused, then asked urgently, "Have you had a change of heart?"

"No . . . no, of course not," she replied, somewhat flustered.

Miguel placed his hands on her small shoulders and asked gently, "Angel, could it be that you are afraid of me?"

She reminded him of a frightened child when she replied with touching honesty, "Yes!"

245

"But why?" he prompted tenderly.

"Miguel, we hardly know each other, and yet . . ."

"*Sí?*" he encouraged.

Taking a deep breath, Julie declared, "Yet I am completely obsessed with you!"

He drew her into his powerful arms, hugging her tightly, and joy rang in resonant voice as he proclaimed, "Angel, it is not an obsession. It is love!"

Squirming out of his arms, she protested, "No, it can't be love. I haven't known you long enough to love you."

"Does love have a time limit?" Miguel asked archly.

"Well . . . I always . . . thought it did," Julie stammered.

With extreme tenderness, Miguel took her into his arms. Julie had never kissed any man except her husband, and as Miguel's lips came down on hers, she innocently expected his kiss to be similar to Mace's. His touch was gentle the way she imagined it would be. Then, suddenly, his arms tightened around her, and his lips still on hers, he whispered, "Angel, I love you."

Julie gasped as he crushed her body to him, while forcefully prying her mouth open with his lips and tongue. Miguel's demanding and savage kiss made Julie feel faint, and she would have fallen had he not been holding her. But her passionless marriage to Mace rendered her incapable of returning Miguel's fervent embrace.

Releasing her, he said softly, "Do not be afraid to lose your inhibitions. Love is beautiful when it is shared."

If Julie had stopped to think, her shyness would have prevented her from confessing, "But, Miguel, I've always considered that part of marriage a man's pleasure and a woman's duty."

Miguel grinned. "Angel, you have much to learn, but

I will enjoy teaching you."

"Teaching me?" She blushed.

"I once promised you that I would never leave you. I intend to honor my promise, but I cannot stay with you unless we are married."

"Married!" she exclaimed. "But my time of mourning hasn't passed."

"*Señora,*" he explained impatiently, "do not place so much importance on tradition. I want to marry you, but I cannot stay away from my hacienda indefinitely." He paused for a moment, then asked, "Will you marry me?"

Julie walked to the center of the room. Not acknowledging his proposal, because she was uncertain of her answer, she paused to reposition a porcelain figurine that had somehow been moved from its rightful place.

Sternly, Miguel suddenly demanded, "*Señora,* I wait an answer!"

He had never before raised his voice to her, and, startled, Julie nearly knocked over the expensive figurine she had been replacing. Stepping back from the table, her eyes opened wide and she stared at Miguel in surprise.

Swiftly, he crossed the room, and clutching her shoulders, he commanded, "My answer, *Señora.*"

Awed by his overwhelming presence, she asked hesitantly, "May I have time to think over your proposal?"

"No," he answered shortly. "I have desired you from the first moment I saw you, and I now love you very much. I want you to marry me, Angel, and I want your answer. I will not leave this room, nor will you, until you have said yes or no."

"Miguel," she began shakily, wanting to be totally honest with him, "I . . . I am frightened."

Gently, he asked, "Is it the physical side of marriage with me that frightens you?"

247

Lowering her eyes, she whispered, "Yes."

"Why?" he asked.

When she didn't respond, he put a hand under her chin and turned her face to his. "Why?" he asked again.

Mustering her courage, Julie said sincerely, "Oh, Miguel, you are such a vibrant man! I'm so afraid I won't be able to please you!" Then she grew deathly pale. How could she have spoken so brazenly?

He smiled warmly. "When the time is right, Angel you will please me very much."

"But, Miguel, what if I don't?" she asked.

He answered with certainty. "You will."

"I'm not sure that I'm in love with you," she mumbled hesitantly.

"I think maybe you do love me, *señora,*" Miguel said quietly.

Julie studied him closely. Should she marry him? She hardly knew this man, and she was wary of his strong masculinity; yet he could touch her heart with his tenderness.

Julie was not even aware that the words had passed her lips until she heard herself saying, "Yes, Miguel. I will marry you."

Smiling, he lifted her into his arms, and whooping loudly, he vigorously whirled her about. When his joy turned into jovial laughter, overcome by his excitement, Julie lost her usual reserve and her laughter mingled with his.

At last, placing her on her feet, Miguel said briskly, "We will be married soon. Now, Angel, I must share my good news with my vaqueros. I will return shortly." He hurried across the room, but stopped suddenly. Hastening back to Julie, he promptly pulled her into his arms and kissed her enthusiastically.

Then, not wanting to take his eyes from her, he backed across the parlor, grinning broadly and saying,

248

"Angel, you have made me very happy." When he bumped into a chair and lost his balance he remarked heartily, *"Señora,* you are marrying a clumsy ox!"

Dan pushed aside his plate, leaving the slice of apple pie untouched. He glanced across the table and his gaze met Susan's. She was watching him inquisitively, wondering where his thoughts were. He had invited her to dinner at his restaurant, and although it had been a pleasant meal, Dan had seemed worried and preoccupied.

He had told Susan that Miguel and Julie were getting married, and believing their engagement might be the reason for his perplexing behavior, she asked, "Dan, do you have reservations about Julie marrying Mr. Ordaz?"

"No, of course not," he answered quickly. "I think Miguel and Julie will be very happy."

Tentatively, she probed further. "But something is bothering you, isn't it?" She hoped Dan's strange mood was not provoked by their relationship.

"Nothing is bothering me," Dan assured her, evading the truth, for he was indeed troubled. Miguel and Julie's engagement had made him guiltily aware that he had kept Susan dangling far too long. He owed her a commitment that was now overdue, but giving up his bachelorhood was not easy for Dan. His independence was dear to him; nonetheless, he intended to marry Susan and he was determined to be a good husband. In his own way, he loved her very much, and he was certain that she cared for him. There was no foreseeable reason why their marriage couldn't succeed.

Reaching across the table, Dan slipped his hand into Susan's. "I asked you to dinner tonight for a very special reason," he murmured.

Sensing a marriage proposal, Susan's blue eyes sparkled. She had waited long and patiently for this moment. "Yes, Dan?" she responded demurely.

"Susan, I want you to marry me," Dan said tenderly.

Inwardly Susan felt triumphant! "Dan, I . . . I don't know what to say," she stammered deceptively. "You've taken me totally by surprise."

Smiling warmly, he replied, "Why don't you just say that you'll marry me?"

"Of course, I'll marry you!" Her eyes gleamed. Holding tightly to his hand, she continued, "When do you want to be married?"

"Well, I think we should wait until after Julie and Miguel's wedding. They are getting married next month, so why don't we plan on a month later?"

"All right," Susan concurred. She was finding it extremely difficult to control her elation. She had finally won the man she loved and she felt like shouting victoriously.

Releasing her hand and pushing back his chair, Dan asked, "Are you ready to leave?"

Susan placed her napkin on the table. She was disappointed that Dan apparently wished to end the evening. They had just become engaged! Why hadn't he planned a more romantic interlude? But perhaps she was being too hasty. Maybe he was going to take her on a buggy ride so they could talk about their future.

Moving behind Susan, Dan pulled out her chair. As she rose, she smoothed the soft folds of the blue frock which fitted her curves to perfection. Then Dan placed her hand in the crook of his arm and escorted her from the restaurant. As he turned in the direction of the boardinghouse, Susan held back.

"What's wrong?" he asked, puzzled.

The sidewalk was fairly crowded, and people brushed past them as Susan stared with hurt eyes into

250

Dan's handsome face. Tonight he looked especially elegant in his dark suit and white linen shirt. Aware that they were blocking traffic, Dan maneuvered her around the corner of the restaurant, and pausing in the shadowy alley, he asked her once again, "Susan, is something wrong?"

She replied dejectedly, "Dan, we just became engaged, and yet . . ."

"Go on," he encouraged.

"And yet you act as though this night were like any other."

Understanding her hurt, he mumbled regretfully, "Susan, I'm sorry."

Studying him, she analyzed his behavior. "The kind of women you associate with make you this way. You aren't used to dealing with ladies who expect to be romantically wooed."

Gently grasping her shoulders, he gazed down into her sad face. "I suppose you're right. Forgive me, Susan?"

Smiling ruefully, she whispered, "Dan Butler, what am I going to do with you?"

He grinned boyishly. "Teach me to be more considerate and chivalrous?" he asked as he drew her closer and, bending his head, touched his lips to hers.

Now that he had proposed to her, Susan wanted to make love to him again. She hadn't forgotten the rapture she had found in Dan's passionate embrace. Taking him by surprise, she slid her arms about his neck, and pressing her thighs against his male hardness, she quickly turned their chaste kiss into one of passion.

Holding her close, he murmured, "Susan, you'd better save that kind of kiss for our wedding night."

"Why?" she said innocently, although she knew exactly what he was trying to say.

"Because if you kiss me like that again, I'm going to take you to my room and ravish you," he threatened playfully.

"Promise?" she asked saucily.

"You have my word as a gentleman," Dan retorted.

"Well, in that case, Mr. Butler, I think I shall kiss you again and again until you keep your promise."

"I never break a promise," Dan declared, moving his hands down her back to her soft buttocks so he could press her against him. Then their lips met in a heated kiss that made their pulses race with uncontrollable desire.

In the alley, there was a rear stairway that led to the second floor of Dan's establishment. They hurriedly climbed it and entered the building. The hubbub from the saloon drifted upstairs, the sounds following them as they darted down the narrow hallway to Dan's quarters. Opening the door, Dan stepped back so Susan could enter first. Then he followed her inside and closed the heavy door, drowning out the raucous activity downstairs.

Quickly, he lit a lamp and it brightened the dark interior of his sitting room, which was furnished with masculine simplicity. Then, he took Susan's hand and led her to the bedroom. Gathering her into his arms, he kissed her long and hard. As their desire grew he undressed her, caressing her with his hands and lips as he did so. Then, pulling back the bed covers, Dan urged Susan to lie down. While she waited eagerly for him to join her, he undressed hastily, tossing his clothes haphazardly onto a chair. Naked, he entered her embrace, his strong frame covering hers.

Susan melted beneath Dan's fervent kisses which burned a trail over her face, her throat, and her breasts. And when his hardness slid into her, she moaned aloud with pleasure.

"Dan . . . darling!" she cried, her voice quaking with desire. Then, clinging to her love, Susan glided blissfully into erotic paradise.

Snuggled intimately in Dan's gentle arms, Susan emitted a deep sigh of contentment. Soon she and Dan would be married, and she could hardly wait for their life together to begin.

"Dan?" she murmured.

"Yes," he replied. He lit the bedside lamp and adjusted the flame.

"When will you put the saloon up for sale?" she asked. She knew he might put up an argument, but she was dead set on getting her way. She did not want the saloon to be a part of their lives.

Leaning back against the oak headboard, he looked down at Susan who was still cuddled close to him. "What did you say?" he asked, frowning.

She sat up, and holding the sheet over her bare breasts, she repeated, "When do you plan to sell the saloon?"

"I do not intend to sell it," he replied inflexibly.

"But I insist that you get rid of it!" Susan demanded.

"I'm not selling the saloon," he said firmly.

"But, Dan," she countered, "surely you don't plan to be the proprietor of this saloon after we are married!".

"Why not?" he wanted to know.

"A married man has no business managing such an establishment and . . . and associating with prostitutes!"

"The saloon is my livelihood," Dan declared testily. "Just how do you expect me to support us if I sell my business?"

"You can keep the restaurant," Susan replied quickly.

"The restaurant doesn't even provide one quarter of my income. The saloon brings in most of the money. If we try to live off the restaurant, we'll be practically destitute."

"Surely you're exaggerating," Susan said short-temperedly.

"Maybe," Dan admitted. "But that's beside the point. I'm not selling the saloon and that's final."

"And do you expect me to live here?" Susan bristled. Am I supposed to raise our children above a saloon?"

"Susan, you're acting very childish," Dan chided. "I own a vacant lot at the edge of town, and I plan to build a house on it. Until it's built we'll have to live here."

"And after the house is built?" Susan asked suspiciously.

Confused, Dan muttered, "What do you mean?"

"Do you intend to close me up in our house while you spend your hours here at the saloon?"

"My business takes a lot of my time. You'll have to understand that and be reasonable about it."

"Your business!" Susan sneered. "That includes your chattel of prostitutes, I suppose!"

"Are you jealous, Susan?" Dan was becoming quite aggravated.

"Jealous?" she remarked tartly. "No, I'm not jealous of these . . . these women who work for you, but I won't have my husband connected with prostitutes. Dan, what would our children think?"

"We'll decide how to handle that situation when it arises."

"No, we'll decide now!" Susan insisted angrily. If she had been more experienced, she'd have known that Dan was too mature to play the kind of game young lovers indulge in, and she'd never have given him an ultimatum. "Dan Butler," she pouted, "it's me or this distasteful saloon! Make your choice!"

254

For the first time, Dan saw Susan as she really was, and he didn't like her. He supposed he'd have seen her more clearly before if he hadn't been so consumed with guilt. He suddenly wondered whether he had actually seduced her that night in her room. He felt it might have been the other way around. Basically, he believed that Susan was a decent woman and that she probably loved him, but she would not be an easy person to live with. She would always insist on having everything her way, and she would pout and nag to make it so. This part of her makeup he disliked intensely. Yet he realized that she was very young. With maturity, she might become less selfish. But he was already thirty-eight, too damned old to wait for Susan to grow up with the hope that she might change.

When Dan did not reply to her ultimatum, Susan repeated it. "Make your choice, it's me or the saloon!"

"I'll take the saloon," Dan said calmly, moving to the edge of the bed. Standing, he walked to his closet and removed a robe, which he put on.

Dumfounded, Susan stared at him. "You can't be serious!" she exclaimed.

"I've never been more serious," he replied in an even tone, watching her carefully.

Realizing her blunder, Susan tried to undo her mistake. "Dan, I didn't mean what I said. Of course I don't expect you to make a choice between me and your business."

Dan placed Susan's clothes on the bed. "Get dressed," he said.

Then he left the bedroom and crossed the sitting room, heading for the door. Opening it, he stepped into the hallway and strode to the front staircase. When he glanced over the railing, he spotted his piano player, who was conversing with a customer.

"Adam!" Dan called loudly, so he could be heard

above the noise filling the saloon.

Looking up and catching sight of his employer, Adam replied, "Yes, sir?"

"In a few minutes, come up to my quarters," Dan told him; then he turned back toward his quarters.

Susan was almost dressed when Dan entered the bedroom. She hastily completed her toilet and then rushed to his side to plead her case, "Dan, I didn't mean what I said! Please don't be angry!"

"I'm not angry," he replied truthfully. "But, Susan, a marriage between us would be doomed to fail. It's best that we found out now, instead of after we were married."

"But I love you!" she cried desperately.

"Susan, you don't want to love me, you want to possess me. You're the kind of woman who is determined to run a man's life. With you there would never be a halfway mark, you'd always want everything done your way."

Hearing Adam's knock, Dan went to the door and opened it. As he looked back at the distraught Susan, he remarked, "This is my piano player. He'll escort you to Miss Rainey's."

"But, Dan . . ." she protested.

"Good night, Susan," Dan said with unmistakable finality.

Finding his curt dismissal insulting, Susan said defiantly, "The stage is due tomorrow at noon. You have until then to apologize."

"What does the stage have to do with this?" Dan asked.

"I intend to be on it!" Susan declared. "I'm going back home to live with my sister and her husband."

"I think that's a good idea," Dan retorted, undisturbed.

Susan tossed her head indignantly; then she strutted to the door where Adam was waiting.

The next day, the stage pulled out of Albuquerque on schedule and Susan Chandler was on it. She had hoped, and prayed, that Dan would try to stop her from leaving, but he had made no attempt to see her. As she climbed into the stage, she chastised herself for at least the hundredth time for giving Dan such a foolish ultimatum and then threatening to leave town. Surely he'll have a change of heart and come take me off this stage, she thought desperately. But to Susan's dismay, Dan Butler did not gallantly appear and sweep her into his arms.

When the stage rolled down the main street, Dan stood at the window in his quarters, watching it leave. In a very special way, he had loved Susan, and he knew it would be awhile before he completely got over losing her. But some things just weren't meant to be. There was no doubt in his mind that he had narrowly escaped making a big mistake. He and Susan Chandler did not belong together.

Chapter Twenty-Two

Observing Julie as she stood in front of the mirror, Hannah Lucas admired the way the light crimson gown complimented her hair and her dark eyes.

"Your beauty takes my breath away!" Hannah exclaimed. "When Mr. Ordaz sees you, he's going to fall even more deeply in love. Your sister was right when she said her dress would be lovely on you."

As she peered into the mirror, Julie tried to pull up the bodice of the gown, but it had been designed to reveal the fullness of a woman's breasts so her attempts were futile. "Oh, it's too . . . too provocative!"

Hannah's plump frame shook with good-humored laughter. Turning to look at the older woman and blushing, Julie asked, "Don't you think a wedding dress should be more modest?"

"Perhaps, if you were a young girl marrying for the first time."

Perusing her reflection, Julie ran her hands down the soft crimson folds of the gown. "I've never worn such a revealing dress," she replied.

Crossing her arms under her large breasts, Hannah said in her determined manner, "Well, if you ask me it's about time. You're a lovely woman, and it's a downright shame the way you've always tried to hide it."

Timidly, Julie murmured, "Hannah, I'm not beautiful."

"Heavens child! How can you be so blind?"

Shyly dropping her gaze to the floor, Julie said demurely, "Miguel thinks I'm beautiful."

"Then he can see a lot better than you can," Hannah remarked.

Julie laughed, and her laughter had an unmistakable ring of happiness. She sat on the vanity stool in front of the dressing table, and then turned to Hannah.

"Will you pin up my hair?"

"What?" Hannah exclaimed.

Startled by the woman's disapproving tone, Julie turned to look at her. "My hair, will you arrange it in a bun?" she requested hesitantly.

Stepping to the dresser, Hannah glared at Julie, but her hard stare couldn't completely conceal the kindness behind her gruff façade. "I most assuredly will not!" she declared.

Julie asked dubiously, "But why not?"

Standing behind her, Hannah told her to look into the mirror. As Julie complied, she declared, "Why would you want to hide all that beautiful hair in a bun? Sakes alive, child!" Shaking her head, she continued determinedly, "No, I insist that you wear it down." Taking the brush, she began to run it through Julie's extremely long hair.

Suddenly, Regina opened the bedroom door and rushed inside. "I found it!" she announced excitedly.

Julie turned to her. "You found what?"

"This!" Regina answered, holding up the lace mantilla in her hand.

Recalling that earlier Regina had left the room without an explanation, Julie said, "So that's why you left in such a hurry."

259

"The mantilla will look so nice with your dress," Regina replied. She handed it to Hannah and said quickly, "We must hurry. Everyone is waiting. It's time for the ceremony."

Hannah arranged the mantilla in Julie's hair, then stood back. "Honey, you are too lovely for words!" she said.

Julie didn't reply. She was too awed by her own reflection. For the first time in her life, she was aware of her own loveliness.

Hannah left the room, and touching Julie's shoulder, Regina said, "Dan is waiting in the hall. Are you ready for him to escort you to your future husband?"

Julie rose shakily, saying, "Oh, Regina, I'm so nervous!"

"Of course you are, but you look so radiant and happy!" Regina grasped Julie's hand and led her into the hall where Dan was waiting.

Julie stood by the window in the study. Through the closed door, she could hear Miguel giving instructions as he supervised the loading of her belongings. Four of his vaqueros had just carried her packed cedar chest down to the waiting buckboard. They planned to leave immediately for the hacienda. Although Miguel had said nothing about their hasty departure, Julie sensed that he had planned it in order to delay their first night alone as husband and wife. During the journey, there would be no real opportunity for them to consummate their marriage, and Julie was certain that Miguel wanted to give her time to adjust to her new life before she became his wife in every sense of the word. She appreciated Miguel's consideration, but she feared that when it came to the intimacies of marriage Miguel would find her lacking.

Turning from the window, she walked to the desk and sat in the large chair placed behind it. Reclining, she closed her eyes as she thought about her marriage ceremony. The wedding had been a simple one, but quite lovely. She smiled upon recalling the way Miguel had looked at her through the entire service. Why, it's almost as if he worships me, she thought with pleasure.

When she folded her hands in her lap, she became conscious of the ring on her left hand. Opening her eyes, she gazed down at it. With an expression of tenderness, she remembered the day Miguel had shown it to her. He had sent some of his vaqueros to his hacienda to inform his servants of his upcoming marriage and to bring back his buggy and buckboard for the journey home. Shortly after his vaqueros returned, Miguel had asked Julie if he could see her alone in the parlor. Julie smiled again as she recalled the almost shy way he had reached into his pocket and brought forth a small velvet box.

"I had one of my vaqueros bring this from my hacienda," he had said. "It belonged to my *madre*. It was her wedding ring. It is with all my heart that I ask you to please accept this ring as my pledge to love and honor you until the day I die."

If Miguel had been a diminutive, a less powerful man, perhaps his troth would not have seemed so humble, but such tender words coming from the huge Mexican had touched Julie deeply, making her seem sad.

Not understanding her distress, Miguel had questioned her urgently. "Angel, did I say something wrong?"

"Oh, Miguel, of course not!" she had replied.

"Then why did you seem so sad?" he had asked, confused.

Julie had smiled tenderly, "Miguel Ordaz, you are

261

so sweet!"

"Sweet?" he had pondered the words. "Angel, no one has ever said that Miguel Ordaz was sweet."

Julie had touched his cheek, and her eyes had shone with compassion as she told him, "Then no one has ever known you the way I know you."

Carefully, he had pried open the small box, and upon showing her the ring inside, he had asked, "It is beautiful, is it not?"

Julie had caught her breath in wonder as she'd gazed down at the ring. Observing the green emerald surrounded by a cluster of diamonds, her eyes had widened in disbelief. "Oh, Miguel, it's so exquisite . . . and so valuable!"

Placing his hand under her chin, he had turned her face to his. "But not nearly as exquisite or as valuable as the woman who will wear it."

Julie was brought back to the present by the opening of the study door.

Smiling at her, Dan entered and strode to the chair on the other side of the desk.

"I always knew you could be a lovely and provocative woman," he remarked. "You should wear dresses like that one more often." Relaxing, he removed a cheroot from his pocket, but instead of lighting it, he glanced at Julie. "But it's more than the dress or the hairdo." Grinning lazily, he asked, "Is it love that has made you so beautiful?"

Somewhat embarrassed, Julie blushed slightly, but before she could reply, the door burst open and Miguel bounded into the room.

"Angel," he began, "we must be leaving soon."

"Of course," she replied. "I'll change as quickly as I can."

As Julie got to her feet, Dan stepped to her side. "I

262

wish you happiness," he said sincerely.

"Thank you," she murmured.

Dan kissed her cheek, then embraced her warmly. He was happy for Julie, and he felt that she would have a good and satisfying life with Miguel.

When Dan released Julie she moved slowly toward the door. As she neared Miguel, he reached over and touched her hand. Pausing, she gazed at her husband, adoration in her eyes. Recognizing her expression, Miguel smiled tenderly, but Julie was not yet aware that she had fallen deeply in love with the vibrant Miguel Ordaz.

When María and Cort had gone to bed and the Lucases had retired to their quarters, Regina decided to take a stroll and enjoy the evening air. For a moment, however, she stood at the porch railing, thinking about Julie's wedding. She decided it had been a lovely ceremony. Frowning slightly, she wondered why Miguel had insisted on leaving for his hacienda immediately following the service.

"Regina?" Matt suddenly called softly.

She hadn't heard him come outside, and she whirled about, startled.

Moving across the porch, he studied her intently, appraising her beauty, which was enhanced by the golden moonlight. Her gown of pastel blue was fashioned to temptingly reveal only the beginning of a woman's ivory breasts, and her honey blond hair was drawn back from her face so her lovely features were clearly visible. Adoring his wife, Matt drew her into his arms and kissed her gently. Gazing down into her face, he asked, "How are you feeling?"

"All right," she replied, although, as always, his kiss

263

had sent her heart pounding rapidly.

"Did you go into town this morning and see the doctor?"

"Yes, I did," she answered. "And he said that I'm fine."

"Does that mean you are completely well?" Matt asked, his desire mirrored in his dark eyes.

Sensing his need for her, Regina told him happily, "I'm as good as new."

Matt's arms tightened about her, and he kissed the top of her head which was nestled against his shoulder. When he heard her sigh despondently, he wondered sadly if she was thinking about the twins. He knew time was supposed to heal all wounds, but he seriously doubted whether a mother ever fully recovered from the loss of a child, or, as in Regina's case, two children. Hoping to lift her spirits, he suggested, "It's a beautiful night, so why don't we take a ride?"

Stepping back so that she could look up into his face, she consented with a smile. "That sounds like a marvelous idea."

"While you change your clothes, I'll saddle the horses," he said, and as she turned away to head into the house, he called, "And bring a blanket."

"A blanket?" Regina asked, looking back at him. Then suddenly understanding his intention, she responded brightly, "My goodness, tonight you are full of marvelous ideas."

Anticipating the hours to come, Matt smiled as he watched his wife hurry into the house; then he went to the stable and quickly saddled his horse and Midnight. He was leading the horses around the corner of the house when Regina rushed outside. She had changed into riding apparel and held a folded quilt in her arms. Taking the colorful quilt, Matt placed it behind his saddle; then he helped Regina mount the stallion.

Regina began to feel wonderfully exhilarated. She hadn't ridden Midnight for months, and she was looking forward to giving him free rein so they could race with the wind.

They turned their horses away from the house and cantered to the end of the lane before encouraging the animals into a gallop, and by the time they reined in the horses at the west range, a short distance from the Rio Grande, Regina felt refreshed and vibrantly alive.

Matt helped her dismount, then he spread out the quilt beneath a ponderosa pine. Slowly, Regina moved over to stand at his side. As the moon's soft rays shone on Matt's ruggedly handsome countenance, she reached over to gently brush her fingertips across the faded scar on his cheek.

Her tender gesture touched Matt's heart more than anything she could have said. I love her! he thought desperately. God, how much I love her! He had known for some time now that he couldn't live with Regina and not tell her how deeply he loved her. But he had wanted to wait until she had fully recovered her health.

Regina longed for him to return her touch, but when he remained unresponsive, she lowered her hand.

Suddenly, moving with fantastic speed, Matt had her in his arms, his mouth crushing hers. Returning his kiss, Regina's lips parted, and relishing his closeness, she laced her arms about his neck and molded her body to his.

"Matt . . . Matt, my dearest," she sighed, then she brought her mouth passionately back to his in a long, demanding kiss.

Slowly, almost reluctantly, he broke their heated union to murmur, "I love you, Regina."

Stepping back, she gazed up at him with surprise. "You love me?" she asked, almost stunned by her happiness.

"How could you help but know?" he asked gently.

She flung herself back into his arms, and clinging to him, she almost sang her next words, "I love you, Matt—I love you with all my heart!"

Matt embraced her tightly, keeping her delectable body close to his. She had professed her love and he believed her, yet he didn't think that she loved him in the same passionate way that he loved her. Matt believed that Regina's love was the result of all they had shared together.

He lowered his head to kiss her once again, and her ardent response piqued his desire. Wanting her urgently, he began to remove her clothing, his hands trembling slightly with uncontrollable passion. When he had her completely disrobed, he bent his head to her soft breasts, and his warm tongue teased one taut nipple and then the other, making Regina moan with intense longing. Then, unexpectedly, he knelt in front of her and began to kiss her smooth stomach, causing Regina to gasp. Tantalizingly, his lips moved downward, finding her most secret place. Matt had never before loved her in this startling fashion, and shocked, Regina attempted to push him away. But he grasped her thighs, holding her firm while his lips and tongue worked magic, and soon Regina forgot that she had wanted to dissuade him. Excited beyond control, she entwined her fingers in his dark hair, pressing him even closer. Her fulfillment came to her effusively, sending shudders through her entire body.

Standing upright, Matt hastily shed his own clothes, then taking her hand, he eased her down onto the quilt. Lying at her side, he drew her into his arms.

"Oh, Matt," she murmured tremulously, "I never knew love could be like this."

"My innocent, you still have much to learn about making love, and I'm going to thoroughly enjoy teaching you."

"I'm a slow learner," she purred against his neck. "You may have to show me over and over again."

He grinned wryly.

"Cross my heart," she said gaily.

Rolling over, he pinned her slim frame beneath his, smiling lovingly before lowering his mouth to hers. She responded boldly to Matt's kiss, and his need for her building, he placed his hands under her hips, arched her thighs upward, and slid his manhood into her pleasurable warmth. As he moved powerfully against her, she clung to him equaling his driving passion until they reached love's blissful culmination.

Regina felt that she was slowly floating back to earth as Matt kissed her tenderly, then moved to stretch out at her side. Gathering her close, he asked soberly, "Regina, why did we have to go through so much before we could finally find each other?"

Thinking about the twins, Regina sighed mournfully, "Matt, sometimes my arms actually ache to hold my babies."

"I know." His voice was sympathetic. "I feel the same way." She rested her head against his shoulder, and he placed a brief kiss on her flushed brow. "But we have María and Cort," he continued. "And maybe someday, if the good Lord's willing, we'll have a child of our own."

Her feeling of melancholy dissolving, Regina smiled faintly as she snuggled next to her husband. "I love you, Matt Brolin," she whispered. "And now we are going to be happy."

Squeezing her gently, he admitted, "Darlin', I've never been happier than I am at this moment."

Chapter Twenty-three

Although Julie did not know it, she had effortlessly won the approval of Anna, the elderly servant who had worked for Miguel for many years. After his first wife had died, Anna had helped raise Miguel's daughter, Rosa, and she had loved her as if she were her own child. Anna also loved Miguel Ordaz and was totally devoted to him. When she'd heard that he was planning to marry again, the news had disturbed her greatly. The vaquero who had brought the news to the hacienda had revealed that Miguel's future bride was considerably younger than the *patron,* and Anna had thought that a shallow and frivolous woman might have turned Miguel's head with her youth and beauty. But upon meeting Julie, Anna knew at once that the *patron*'s bride was neither shallow nor frivolous. Julie was unquestionably a genuine lady, and Anna hoped that Julie would bear the *patron* a son. Being a religious woman, the elderly servant prayed every night for an heir to carry on the Ordaz name.

Now as she stood behind Julie and brushed the *señora's* hair, Anna reflected that the *patron* had been married for over a month, but it was doubtful that he was sharing his wife's bed. Miguel's bedchamber adjoined Julie's, and every morning when one of the servants straightened the rooms, both beds had been slept in. This news had traveled through the hacienda, and the servants all gossiped about the *patron*'s strange marriage. Soon rumors had spread over the walls to the vaqueros and their families.

Anna usually possessed extraordinary insight, but she was completely at a loss as to why Julie and Miguel hadn't consummated their marriage. It was obvious that they were deeply in love. One could tell that by simply looking at them. Anna wanted desperately to question the *señora,* but being aware of her place, she maintained her silence.

Looking into the mirror, Julie studied her reflection. Anna's brisk brushing was making her reddish brown hair shine radiantly. Julie knew that when Miguel came in to bid her good night, he'd gaze at her with adoration, and that thought made her smile dreamily. A becoming blush appeared on her cheeks as she visualized the powerful man who was her husband. She had been astounded when, on their journey to the hacienda, Miguel had informed her that he had no wish to pressure her and that their marriage would not be consummated until she came to him. Julie was not sure when she would dare to seek out Miguel, but the mere thought of doing so sent a warm flush running through her body.

She had to admit to herself that lately she had gone out of her way to touch her husband, finding any excuse imaginable to take his hand, grasp his arm, or brush her fingertips across his bearded cheek.

Placing the hairbrush on the dresser, Anna went to Julie's bed and turned down the covers. "Are you ready to retire, *señora?*" she inquired.

Rising, Julie straightened the folds of her white dressing gown as she answered, "I will wait until my

269

husband comes to see me."

"The *patron* is not at the hacienda," Anna informed her.

Surprised, Julie stammered, "Wh . . . where is he?"

"I do not know, *señora*. He left shortly after dinner and has not returned."

Disappointed, Julie said pensively, "Then I suppose I might as well go to bed."

Bidding the *señora* good night, Anna walked to the door, opened it, and left the room.

Julie then removed her dressing gown, placed it on a chair, and got into bed. Turning off the lamp she closed her eyes and tried to sleep, but she was unable to put her mind at rest. Miguel had never before left the hacienda right after dinner and not returned in time to tell her good night.

Restless, Julie threw off the covers. Propping her pillow against the headboard, she sat up in bed as nagging questions raced through her mind. Why hadn't he come home? Where was he? Who was he with?

She chewed apprehensively at her bottom lip. Was he with another woman? Had he already grown impatient with waiting for his wife to come to him? Had he taken himself a mistress? If his absence was due to another woman, how could she blame him? Her husband was a virile man. Why shouldn't he find an outlet for his masculine needs?

More than once Julie had been tempted to go to her husband and ask him to make love to her, but she had kept hoping that he'd come to her, even though she was terribly afraid that he would find her a disappointment.

She drew the covers up and snuggled beneath them. Reluctantly, she realized that Miguel would remain true to his word, and their marriage would not be consummated until she went to him and asked him to make

270

love to her.

Closing her eyes, Julie decided she would force herself to fall asleep. She settled herself comfortably on the soft mattress and resolutely pushed thoughts of Miguel from her mind. If he was with another woman, then so be it!

Her eyes flew open. Was she pretty? Was she young? Did she love Miguel? Did he love her? Was he holding her in his arms this very minute? Kissing her? Was she touching him? Perhaps even conceiving his child?

Bolting straight up, Julie cried out, "No! Oh, Miguel . . . no!"

The door to the adjoining room swung open, and Miguel asked urgently, "Angel, are you all right?"

Startled, Julie's eyes darted to her husband. "I didn't know you were home," she said breathlessly.

"I did not want to awaken you, so I was being very quiet." Concerned, he asked, "Did you have a bad dream?"

"Dream?" she questioned vacantly.

"I heard you cry out," he explained.

Flustered, she replied hesitantly, "Oh . . . yes . . . of course . . . I was having a silly dream." Trying to sound nonchalant, she continued, "Miguel, where have you been?"

"I was visiting an old friend who has a small *granja* not too far from here. Today, he became an *abuelo,* a grandfather. I went to his home to give him my congratulations." Miguel took a few steps into the room, and Julie noticed his gait was more relaxed than usual. "Together," he proceeded, "we drank many toasts to the new *infanta.*"

Relieved that he hadn't been with another woman, Julie asked pertly, "Miguel, are you tipsy?"

"Perhaps just a little, *señora.* But the best days to

271

celebrate are the days when babies are born. What better reason to drink and be merry, *sí?*"

"Did you see the baby?"

"*Sí.* He was all red and wrinkled, and screaming at the top of his lungs. But he was very beautiful."

The only light in the room was coming through the open doorway, and it shone on Miguel, making it easy for Julie to see him. Her gaze hadn't left him since he'd appeared. But then, Julie was always watching her husband. She was amazed that a man his age still had the physique of a man ten years younger.

Apparently, he had been in the process of preparing for bed because his shirt was unbuttoned. She could see the dark hairs on his chest, and noticed his hard muscles flex as he unbuckled his gun belt. Studying him intently, Julie knew she wanted to go to her husband. If only she weren't so afraid, and if only she didn't find the sexual act between a husband and wife so disappointing. Still, she couldn't bear the thought of Miguel being with another woman.

Holding his holster, Miguel looked over at his wife. When he saw that she was watching him, he smiled warmly. *"Buenas noches, Angel.* I will see you in the morning." Turning, he left the room, remembering to close the door behind him.

Julie leaped from the bed and reached for her dressing gown. She started to put it on, but, determined, she threw it back on the chair. Miguel was her husband, and it was certainly proper for him to see her in her nightgown. However, Julie's sudden determination had its limits, and she modestly made sure that her nightdress was buttoned all the way to her chin.

Decisively, Julie crossed the room. She felt a bit shaky, and she feared that her nerve would falter. Nonetheless, she knocked timidly on the door, and it was opened immediately. The bright light from Miguel's room shone on Julie's strained face. "Is something wrong?" he asked. "Are you ill, *señora?*"

She stepped back so that she could see him better. His shirt was now hanging outside his trousers and he had removed his boots.

"Miguel," she choked out, "I . . . I have something to say."

When she fell silent, he coaxed, *"Sí, señora?"*

She muttered faintly, "I . . . I want you to . . ." Her voice faded and she turned her face away.

Gently, he placed a hand under her chin and turned her face back to his. "Say it, Angel. Look me in the eyes and say the words."

Raising her head, she gazed into his eyes. Then, paling suddenly, she gasped in one quick breath, "I want you to make love to me." Instantly she lowered her gaze, too embarrassed to face him.

She waited anxiously for him to speak, but when he remained silent, she took a quick look at him. Her husband had one arm propped against the doorway, the other rested on his hip. He appeared to be totally at ease.

"Why?" he asked simply.

Julie's eyes widened.

"Why do you want me to make love to you?" he asked calmly.

"I . . . I don't understand," she replied uneasily.

"Señora," he began impatiently, "the question was quite simple. Why do you find it difficult to answer? I find it very easy to know why I want you to make love to me. You are my wife, and I love you very much. But those are not my only reasons for wanting you. Angel, you are a beautiful woman, and just looking at you as I am doing now makes me physically aware that my pas-

273

sion is rising."

Knowing the part of his anatomy to which he was referring, Julie's eyes sought the ceiling and then the floor.

Smiling at her modesty, he said, "*Señora,* I am still waiting for my answer."

Placing a hand over her fluttering heart, Julie confessed, "Tonight, when you didn't come home, I thought you were with another woman."

Still completely relaxed, he asked, "Did that bother you?"

Why was he making this so difficult for her? "Yes," she admitted weakly.

He moved swiftly, and taking her hand, he pulled her into his room. Losing her balance, she fell against him and he steadied her by holding her in his arms. As always, in his embrace she experienced a mysterious thrill.

Releasing her carefully, he went to the lamp beside the bed and turned down the flame. Julie glanced about the room as if seeing it for the first time. The huge four-poster bed rested on a raised platform. It was made of dark wood that matched the dresser and the wardrobe. On one side of the room there was a fireplace, with two overstuffed chairs placed in front of it. Over the mantel hung a large saber and two rifles.

Slowly Miguel moved back to Julie, and grasping her around the waist, he brought his hand up to the neck of her gown and undid the top button. Then his warm lips traveled excitingly over her neck, across her cheeks and down to her mouth.

Julie moaned, her feelings a mixture of fear and desire. Tenderly, he pried her lips open beneath his, and with his mouth still on hers, he whispered, "Do not be afraid, Angel. Put your arms around me."

274

Obeying, she wrapped her trembling arms about his neck, and his kiss grew more intense, demanding her response. Wanting to please him Julie accepted his feverish kiss, surprised to find that she was actually enjoying his dominant exploration of her mouth.

Holding her tightly, he thrust her thighs against his hardness, pressing her to him so forcefully that she felt she was becoming an inseparable part of him.

Once again his lips roamed to her ear, his warm breath sending chills down her spine. "I love you, Angel. So long, I have waited for this night. We will become as one, our marriage will be consummated, and you will learn what it is like to have a man love you passionately and aggressively."

"Aggressively?" she said fearfully.

Smiling tenderly, Miguel answered, "I am not Señor Edwards. You will not merely submit to me, *señora*. I will demand your passion, and I will not stop until you surrender it to me."

Swiftly he lifted her in his arms and carried her to the bed. As he placed her on the cool sheets, she gestured toward the lamp, "The light," she whispered.

"Only a blind man chooses to make love in the dark," he told her. Lying beside her, he began to unfasten the buttons on her long gown; then, removing the garment, he tossed it to the floor.

Never in her life had Julie lain completely nude beside a man. With Mace she had always remained beneath the covers, and he would simply lift her gown, taking his pleasure quickly.

Embarrassed, Julie closed her eyes, but Miguel ordered firmly, "Look at me." Slowly she obeyed, and looking into her beautifully flushed face, he spoke gently, "I love you, Angel. I love your heart, your soul, and your body. In time, you will know me as you know

275

yourself. Our hearts, our souls, and our bodies will become as one. Trust me, Angel." Kissing her cheek, he whispered, "Relax, and let my eyes take in your beauty."

Soothed by his tender words, she relaxed as he gazed lingeringly at her firm high breasts, her slim but feminine hips, and her shapely legs.

Sensing uncontrolled passion in his quick breathing, Julie was surprised that the mere sight of her body could so strongly affect such a powerful man, yet the knowledge pleased her.

Suddenly he gasped and his lips came down on hers. Remembering how she had enjoyed kissing him earlier, she submissively surrendered.

"You are so beautiful," he whispered. "Put your arms around me and hold me close."

Willingly, she did as he asked, and when his lips again met hers, she pressed her mouth tightly to his, moaning, wanting to become lost in his exciting kiss. While he relished her warm mouth, Miguel fondled her breasts, sending a pleasant sensation through her entire being, and finally his hand moved down, across her stomach and caressed the soft flesh between her legs. Julie stiffened.

With his mouth inches from hers, he groaned, "Let me explore your lovely body. Give yourself to me, Julie. Do not turn away." His lips suddenly devoured hers, and his fingers expertly evoked a need in her that she had never before experienced. When their desire was mutual, Miguel rose from the bed, hastily removing his cumbersome clothes.

Whenever Mace had been unclothed, Julie had always averted her gaze, but she was enthralled by Miguel's strong physique. In the dim light from the burning lamp his skin was the color of bronze, and his

276

muscles rippled as he impatiently removed his trousers. When his erect manhood was revealed, Julie caught her breath. Again she feared she would never be woman enough to satisfy him.

Kneeling on the bed, Miguel parted her legs and gently lowered his body to hers. "Later, Angel, I will teach you the pleasures of love, but I can no longer control my desire. I must have you now."

As he placed his lips on hers, he penetrated her deeply and smoothly. Thinking he would thrust a few times, then shudder, and withdraw, Julie waited patiently for him to finish.

But when he failed to do what she expected, she withdrew her mouth from his and looked into his face.

Sensing her confusion and inexperience, Miguel smiled as he explained, "We will take it very slowly, Angel. Together, we will reach fulfillment."

Lifting her legs, he penetrated her more deeply, moving smoothly inside her and arousing her. As Julie began to feel new and wonderful sensations, she gathered Miguel into her arms, and finally understanding her desire for him, she placed her lips close to his ear and said fervently, "I love you . . . Oh, Miguel, I love you!"

Sitting at the breakfast table beside her husband, Julie believed only she and Miguel knew the reason for her special glow. She was oblivious to all the whispering going on throughout the hacienda. For on this morning when a servant had entered the *señora*'s bedroom to awaken her, she had found the bed empty. The door to the *patron*'s bedchamber had been ajar, and taking a quick peek inside the room, the woman had seen the *señora* asleep in the *patron*'s arms. The news had quickly traveled through the hacienda, over the walls, and into the little village.

But no servant or vaquero was happier to hear the good news than Anna. Perhaps now her prayers would be answered, and Miguel would be blessed with a son to carry on his name and heritage.

Chapter Twenty-four

The driver removed Susan's luggage from the stage, then asked, "Where do you want your things delivered, ma'am?"

Susan's new gingham dress was flaked with dust, and brushing at the grime, she silently cursed the dirt that had blown through the open window during the jolting ride. The stage's passengers had spent the night at a wayside inn, and Susan had donned her new frock this morning so that she would make a good appearance when she arrived at her destination. Now her gown was almost ruined, and the matching bonnet, which was adorned with a dainty feather, was also layered with a film of dust.

"Ma'am," the driver said again, this time gaining Susan's attention, "where do you want your luggage delivered?"

Standing beside the coach, Susan shaded her eyes with her hand as she gazed down the sun-brightened street. Nodding toward a building a few doors away, she answered, "Take my luggage to the Trail Dust Saloon."

"It'll be a few minutes before your belongings can be delivered," the man replied flatly.

"That will be fine," Susan mumbled vaguely, her eyes still fixed on the saloon.

When Susan had left Albuquerque following her disagreement with Dan, she had returned to her hometown and had moved in with her sister and brother-in-law. Not one who easily gave up her dreams, Susan had hoped desperately that Dan would come to his senses and pursue her. Day after day, she had waited anxiously for him to appear on her doorstep and plead with her to forgive him. But as the weeks passed, Susan finally realized that he was not coming. She decided she had no choice but to return to him. Somehow, she'd find her way back into his good graces. He loved her; she was sure that he did!

Her stride self-assured, Susan walked quickly down the crowded sidewalk toward the Trail Dust Saloon. Pushing aside the swinging doors, she entered the establishment, and stepping to the bar, she asked the bartender where she could find Dan. Learning that he was in his office, Susan went to the rear of the room and knocked firmly on the closed door. It was midday, and the saloon was almost vacant, but the few customers standing at the bar watched her curiously.

Responding to her knock, Dan called out, "Come in," whereupon Susan strode directly into his office. Dan was working at his desk and did not glance up until he heard the door close.

"Susan!" he gasped, totally astounded.

Smiling with feigned demureness, Susan slowly moved farther into the room, and when she paused in front of the desk, she said softly, "Hello, Dan."

Rising abruptly, he demanded severely, "Why did you come back?"

Susan didn't need to force tears to her eyes. Dan's severity provoked genuine sobs. "Oh, Dan, please don't treat me so cruelly," she begged and she covered her face with trembling hands.

Dan hurried to her side, his old feelings of guilt once again plaguing him, and he drew her into his arms. "I'm sorry, Susan. I shouldn't have spoken so harshly."

Calmed by his apology, she stifled her distress, and when he pulled out the chair next to the desk, she allowed him to lower her onto it.

Keeping his deep voice on an even keel, Dan repeated his question. "Susan, why did you return?"

Gazing up at him through tear-filled eyes, she answered pleadingly, "I was miserable with my sister. Her husband is so domineering that it's impossible to live under the same roof with him. And he didn't want me there. He never said so, but I could sense it." There was not a word of truth in Susan's story, but she wanted to get Dan's sympathy.

"Why didn't you live elsewhere?" he asked.

"My hometown is so small that there was nowhere else to live. And if there had been, I had no income. I tried to find employment, but there was no work."

"That still doesn't explain why you are here," Dan responded patiently.

Susan said imploringly, "Dan, you loved me once and . . . and I think perhaps you still care. I was hoping you would help me. I need a job and a place to stay. I can't get a room at the hotel because I spent the last of my money to travel here. I thought maybe I could stay in the same room I used once before and you'd let me work in the restaurant."

"Wouldn't you prefer to live at Miss Rainey's?" he asked.

"Oh, I couldn't!" Susan moaned. "I left Miss Rainey's employment without giving her notice. She was furious with me!"

Dan sighed discontentedly. He had thought Susan Chandler was a permanent part of his past, but here she was back in his life again. He gazed down into her upturned face, and she looked so helpless and forlorn that his heart went out to her.

Susan could see his reservations crumbling as he continued to study her. Inwardly, she felt victorious, but her expression serene, she asked demurely, "Dan, will you please help me?"

Taking her hands, he drew her to her feet, assuring her gently, "Of course, I'll help you."

Flinging herself into his embrace and clinging to him, Susan murmured sweetly, "Oh, thank you, Dan!"

Deliberately, she arched her body so that her thighs were pressed against his, but the maneuver was so subtle that Dan was not aware she had planned it. As she nestled her head on his shoulder, she nuzzled her face against his neck.

When Dan's arms inadvertently tightened about her, enveloping her delicate frame, Susan lifted her head from his shoulder to peer up at him touchingly. Then, before Dan knew what was happening, her lips were on his. Sliding her arms about his neck, she urgently kissed him, her tongue darting between his teeth.

Suddenly feeling manipulated, Dan broke their embrace abruptly. His rebuff escaping her notice, Susan said excitedly, "This time, darling, things will be different. I promise you they will!"

A resounding knock on the door prevented Dan from telling her that she was taking too much for granted. "Come in," he called.

Taking a step into the office the bartender said to Susan, "Miss Chandler, your luggage has arrived, and the man from the stage depot wants to know where to take it."

Sweeping past Dan and going to the open doorway, Susan took charge, "I'll show him to my quarters."

When she left, Dan returned to his chair and sat

down. A worried frown crossed his handsome face as he pondered Susan's unexpected arrival. Opening the whiskey bottle on his desk, he tilted it to his mouth and took a large swallow. He wished Susan hadn't come back. He had a depressing feeling that her presence would turn his well-ordered life into a turmoil.

For the next three days, Dan tried to find an opportune moment to tell Susan that there was no future between them. He had no intention of resuming their former relationship, but each time he attempted to make her listen to him, Susan changed the subject or played upon his sympathy. Due to her evasive ploys, Dan had postponed the moment when he must make her face the truth.

When Dan did not put Susan to work in the restaurant, she believed it was because he planned to make her his wife. However, Dan didn't want Susan working for him because he was hoping to convince her to go back home. Her presence made him uncomfortable and he wanted her out of Albuquerque.

On the fourth day after Susan's return, Dan was standing at the bar talking to his bartender when he was pleasantly surprised by Regina's sudden entrance. Hastening across the floor, he bent over and kissed her cheek, then asked, "Gina, what are you doing here?"

She smiled, but Dan saw the worry on her face. "Dan, I need to talk to you."

"Of course," he replied. "We can go up to my room."

Placing an arm about her waist, he ushered her up the stairs, and as they moved down the hallway, he inquired, "Is something wrong?"

To reach Dan's private quarters, they had to pass Susan's room, and that young woman was just preparing to open the door when she detected Regina's voice.

"Nothing is wrong," Susan heard Regina answer. "I'm just a little worried."

"Well, you picked a good time to call," Dan told her, his reply carrying into Susan's room. "I need to talk to you too. Susan Chandler has returned."

"Susan!" Regina exclaimed, never imagining that she and Dan were being overheard.

As soon as Dan ushered Regina into his quarters, Susan quietly left her room. Noticing that Dan hadn't closed his door all the way, she crept down the hall to eavesdrop.

Regina, meanwhile, settled herself on the chair beside the sofa, then asked, "Why in the world did Susan come back?"

Seating himself across from Regina, Dan answered, "We'll discuss Susan later. First, I want you to tell me why you are worried."

Sighing heavily, she replied, "Matt is leaving a week from next Friday."

"Leaving?" Dan interrupted.

"He plans to visit Alan Garrett and discuss buying some cattle from him, and he also intends to let José know that María and Cort are well."

"I don't understand why you're worried," Dan said.

Moving to the edge of her seat, Regina declared, "Garrett's ranch is close to Santa Fe!"

"So?" Dan was puzzled.

"Robert Selman has a ranch outside of Santa Fe!" Regina declared.

Comprehending, Dan nodded. "Gina, I can see why you're upset. But if Selman had planned to avenge his son's death, he'd probably have done so before now. When he threatened Matt, he was most probably deranged by grief."

Unconvinced, Regina said gravely, "I was there when Selman swore to avenge his son, and I don't

284

believe he was temporarily deranged. I don't think that man will rest until Matt pays for his son's death."

"Gina, you're probably making too much of the incident. Apparently, Matt isn't worried about Selman."

"That's because Matt refuses to be intimidated!" Regina remarked testily.

"Does he plan to travel alone?" Dan asked.

"Yes. I tried to convince him to take along some of the ranch hands, but he said he wouldn't need them."

"Honey, I'm sure you're worrying needlessly," Dan said encouragingly.

In the hall, listening intently, Susan wished impatiently that they'd stop discussing Matt's trip and start discussing her. She was anxious to hear what Dan had to say about her return.

Regina, meanwhile, was still feeling uneasy about Matt's journey to Garrett's ranch, but it was apparent that Dan didn't share her concern. She had hoped to convince her brother to attempt to dissuade Matt from going to Santa Fe, but realizing Dan would be against the idea, she changed the subject. "Why did Susan come back?"

Hearing her name, Susan inched closer to the partially opened door, straining to hear Dan's reply.

Regina was very familiar with Dan and Susan's relationship. He had often confided in her, and she knew his reasons for breaking his engagement. During his courtship of Susan, Dan had brought her to the Black Diamond on several occasions, and as Regina had become better acquainted with the young woman, she had sensed something in her that she did not like. Regina had never been able to put her finger on exactly what that was, but she hadn't trusted Susan.

When Dan finished describing Susan's unexpected appearance at his office, Regina exclaimed with deep concern, "Dan, surely you don't plan to marry her!"

At hearing this a burning anger sparked in Susan's eyes, and she exerted all her will power to prevent herself from bursting into the room and telling Regina to mind her own business.

Rising, Dan began to pace back and forth; then he remarked, "I take it that you disapprove of Susan."

Leaving her chair and hurrying to Dan, Regina grasped his arm to halt his restless steps. "I don't trust Susan, and furthermore, I don't think she'd make you a good wife. She doesn't love you; she wants to possess you. If you marry Susan, she'll make your life a total misery. She's not only selfish, she's conniving."

At that moment, Susan detected footsteps climbing the stairs, and knowing she'd be caught eavesdropping if she didn't leave, she whirled away from the door. As she headed toward her room, she trembled with barely controlled rage. She hated Regina passionately, and she silently swore that if Dan took his sister's advice, she'd find a way to get even with her.

Regina's hand was still on Dan's arm, and placing his hand over hers, he smiled reassuringly. "Gina, I have no intention of marrying Susan. I'm not in love with her. Maybe I never was."

"Does she believe you two are still engaged?"

Dan shrugged casually, but his expression was grim. "I think she's convinced herself that we'll be married."

"You must tell her the truth!" Regina advised.

"I've tried but she always manages to evade the issue," he replied.

"Then you must be firm and make her listen. The longer you wait the more difficult it will be."

"Yes, I know," he answered somberly. "I'll talk to her tonight, and this time, I'll insist that she listen to what I have to say."

*   *   *

As Regina headed back toward the ranch, she gave the stallion free rein, letting him set his own pace. She was worried about Susan's return. She found the young woman manipulative, and she was afraid Dan might not find it so easy to break off his involvement with her.

Hearing a horse approaching from behind her, Regina glanced over her shoulder. When she recognized the rider as Antonio, she pulled up her stallion and waited for him.

Reining in his horse next to Midnight, Antonio smiled amicably. *"Buenos días, señora."*

"Hello, Antonio," she responded, her green eyes sparkling with friendliness.

Antonio silently noted that Regina looked ravishing. With her cream-colored suede riding skirt and matching bolero jacket, she wore a colorful long-sleeved blouse. Her blond tresses flowed freely and the dainty curls framing her forehead showed beneath her low-crowned hat. Her enticing loveliness prompted Antonio to sigh and wish he were the man she loved instead of Matt Brolin. Knowing he had no choice but to accept defeat, however, he suppressed his disappointment and asked cordially, "Do you mind if I ride with you?"

"Of course not," Regina replied brightly, never imagining that her presence made Antonio's heart ache with desire.

They urged their mounts into an easy canter, but when they had traveled only a short distance Midnight suddenly went off stride. Drawing back on the reins, Regina dismounted quickly, and hurrying around to the front of the stallion, she saw that he was keeping his weight off his left foreleg.

Getting down from his horse, Antonio joined her. "What seems to be the problem?" he asked.

"I don't know," Regina replied worriedly. "But it's

287

the same leg he injured once before."

Stepping to Midnight and grasping his harness, Antonio said, "It doesn't seem to be his leg, but his hoof. He probably picked up a stone." Calming the nervous horse, he patted the stallion's head and murmured soothingly to him. Then, kneeling, Antonio lifted the animal's hoof. Removing the stone, he rose and showed it to Regina. "It was merely a pebble."

She sighed with relief. "Thank goodness he isn't hurt."

Antonio and Regina were not aware that Matt was riding over a grassy incline not far away. He knew Regina had gone into town and he'd decided to ride out and meet her. When he saw Regina with Antonio, however, he pulled up his horse. He started to call out to them, but at that moment, Midnight nudged Regina's side causing her to lose her balance and fall into Antonio's arms. To steady herself, Regina grasped his wide shoulders.

From a distance, Antonio and Regina's accidental proximity looked intentional, and it made fury flicker dangerously in Matt's piercing eyes as he watched them.

Reacting impulsively, Antonio drew Regina against his chest. Her wonderful closeness compelled him to bend his head and press his lips to hers. Taken completely by surprise, Regina was too startled to break their intimate embrace immediately.

Matt's face darkened with rage as he observed the romantic scene taking place before his very eyes. For one wild moment, he considered confronting the pair, but afraid he might be tempted to attack them both, he jerked the reins and headed back toward the house.

Coming to her senses, Regina pulled away from Antonio's kiss. When she'd freed herself from his embrace, she said angrily, "How dare you!"

288

Immediately sorry for his impetuous behavior, Antonio apologized sincerely, "Forgive me, Regina: I am very sorry. I reacted impulsively and was not trying to force my intentions upon you."

She believed him, but she was quite perturbed. "Antonio, you must promise me that nothing like this will ever happen again; if you do not, I will be forced to terminate our friendship. I am deeply in love with my husband, and I could never desire another man."

"I promise you, Regina, that I will henceforth behave as a gentleman," he assured her, his expression apologetic.

Forgiving him, Regina smiled. "We'll forget what happened and never speak of it again."

When Regina arrived home and went to her bedroom to change for dinner, she was startled to find Matt resting on the bed. He was leaning back against the headboard, and he had a glass of brandy in his hand.

"Matt!" she exclaimed. "Why are you lying down? You aren't ill, are you?"

Keeping his stormy emotions well masked, he replied calmly, "I'm only relaxing."

Removing her hat, Regina placed it on the dresser. "I'm a little tired, I think I'll rest before dinner," she remarked. She was totally unaware that her husband was contemplating telling her that she was an unfaithful bitch, after which he intended to leave her, then beat Antonio to a pulp.

Matt watched Regina in furious silence. How far had Regina's relationship with Antonio progressed? Did it consist only of hidden embraces, or did Ramírez know Regina's body as well as he himself knew it?

If Regina's thoughts hadn't been centered on Dan

and Susan, Matt's unusual quietness might have registered with her, but because her mind was elsewhere, his peculiar conduct escaped her notice.

"Did you go into town?" Matt asked, his mild tone concealing his inner turbulence.

Going to the dresser and sitting on the vanity stool, Regina answered, "Yes, I did." As she brushed her hair, she told Matt about Susan's unexpected return.

"When you left town, did you come straight home?" he queried, despising himself for playing a game as deceitful as Regina's. He knew she had been with Antonio, so why didn't he just come right out and tell her that he had seen them together?

"Yes, I came straight home. Why do you ask?" Regina was still unaware of Matt's violent mood.

"I thought about riding out to meet you," he stated, watching closely for her reaction.

Remembering Antonio's kiss and imagining what might have happened if Matt had seen him take liberties with her, Regina blushed. "W . . . why didn't you meet me?" she stammered.

Misreading the reason behind her apparent discomfort, Matt took a large swallow of his brandy, then answered flatly, "I changed my mind."

Continuing to brush her hair, Regina sighed silently. Thank goodness, Matt had changed his mind. She didn't want hard feelings between Matt and Antonio. Antonio was their neighbor, and life was so much more pleasant when people lived in harmony. Besides, Antonio's kiss had not been one of passion, and he certainly hadn't tried to caress her intimately. She was more than willing to simply forget the incident.

Taking another drink of brandy, Matt continued to watch Regina. He could've sworn she loved him, but she had fooled him again, just as she had when she'd been trying to trap him into marriage. Maybe in her own way, she did care about him. Her feeling probably grew out of their mutual love for María and Cort, and losing the twins had brought them closer together. Yes, he was quite sure that she loved him in the same way one loved a close friend. Was that all he was to her? A companion? When they made love, were her fervent responses only make-believe? Did she save her true passion for Antonio? As these unanswered questions continued to plague Matt, he lifted the brandy bottle from the night table and refilled his glass.

But Regina's thoughts had returned to Dan and Susan, and placing the brush on the dresser, she declared, "I'm worried about Dan."

Matt was feeling his liquor. His muddled thinking led him to decide that his wife's first loyalties had always been to Dan, the Black Diamond, a stallion, and a damned dog! She was probably making as big a fool out of Antonio as she had made out of him! Mace Edwards had been right! Regina was incapable of truly loving any man! "Why are you worried about your brother? Susan's perfectly harmless," Matt muttered, his bitter tone beginning to reveal his mood.

"I'm not so sure that Susan Chandler is harmless," Regina replied seriously. Intending to slip into her dressing gown, then take a needed rest, she stood and removed her riding apparel. Underneath, she wore a lace chemise and silk pantalets.

Matt's eyes raked hungrily over Regina's tempting curves, and against his will, he responded to her striking loveliness. Deliberately glancing away from her, he tried to resume their conversation and ignore the passion stirring hotly within him. "What could Susan possibly do to Dan?"

"'Hell hath no fury like a woman scorned,'" Regina stated.

Or a man, Matt thought, his dark eyes suddenly

291

piercing hers. "I have a little fury of my own that needs releasing!" he said in a harsh whisper. "A fury only your delectable body can relieve." His temper exploding, Matt threw the glass across the room. Then as it struck the wardrobe and shattered, he leaped from the bed with the litheness of a panther, reaching Regina in two quick strides. His angry scowl frightened her, and instinctively she backed away from him. But his hands shot forward and grasped her arms, jerking her against him.

The threatening note in Matt's voice sent a cold shiver up Regina's spine, "You belong to me, Regina! If you value your life, it would be advantageous for you to remember that you are completely mine. I don't like to share what belongs to me!"

Regina felt as though she were staring into the cold eyes of a stanger, and when Matt suddenly ripped away her chemise, then lifted her into his arms, she protested feebly, "Matt, please put me down."

Roughly, he dropped her onto the bed. Then, grasping her pantalets, he drew them over her rounded hips and down her long, slender legs before hastily undoing his trousers to free his erect manhood.

She tried to ask him why he was so angry, but before she could, he lay over her and his lips brutally devoured hers, silencing her. His kiss was deep and demanding, and although Regina was wary of his strange mood, he aroused her desire.

His warm mouth moved to her throat, then down to her breasts as his hand cupped her womanhood, where her need for him was centered. When his fingers entered her feminine depths, her hips moved back and forth in rhythmic response to his erotic probing.

He sensed that she wanted him. Her response was too real to be affected. His wife was a deceitful little witch, but not when it came to passion.

"Oh Matt . . . I want you, my darling," she murmured.

Did she also murmur sweet endearments to Antonio? he wondered. Had she made love with him that very afternoon? Was his wife such a lustful creature that she needed two men in one afternoon?

His rage now out of control, Matt took her forcefully. His swift entry was so vigorous that Regina cried out, but her discomfort quickly dissipated and a feeling of ecstasy washed over her.

As Matt drove into her rapidly, Regina wrapped her legs about his waist, accepting his deep penetration with complete abandonment. His urgent thrusts soon had her tossing on tempestuous waves of rapture, and when they arrived at the peak of intense and utter pleasure together, she held Matt tightly, welcoming the love seed he released deep inside her.

Breathing heavily, Matt immediately left Regina's side, and, standing at the side of the bed, drew on his trousers.

Staring into his anger-filled eyes, Regina asked, "Matt, what is bothering you? Why are you so upset?"

Frowning irritably, he dismissed her questions and remarked resentfully, "Did I satisfy your sexual lust, Regina? Or do you still need more?" Envisioning her naked in Antonio's arms, he continued hatefully, "Should I go to the bunkhouse and get one of the ranch hands for you?"

Infuriated, Regina sprang from the bed, and drawing back her arm, she slapped Matt's cheek. He grabbed her and shoved her roughly down onto the bed.

"How dare you speak to me that way—what is wrong with you!" she exclaimed.

As his dark eyes bore into Regina's, he wondered how she could so convincingly play the role of the

293

wronged wife! Then he turned away brusquely and walked to the door.

"Where are you going?" she cried desperately.

Pausing and looking back at her, he replied coldly, "To the bunkhouse, but not to fetch you a lover. The men are having a poker game, and I plan to join them. It'll probably last for hours, so I'll skip dinner. And don't wait up for me because I'll sleep on the sofa in the study."

Before she could argue with him, he left the room, slamming the door. Regina was totally dumfounded. Why in the world was he so angry? He's returned to his old ways, she decided depressingly. Oh, I was a fool to think that our marriage was secure! Matt hasn't changed, he's insensitive as he ever was! Her heart breaking, Regina rolled onto her stomach, and grasping the pillow, she pounded it with her fists.

Chapter Twenty-five

Susan locked herself in her room and refused to see anyone. Not even Dan's two attempts could persuade her to open the door. The second time Dan had called on her, he had insisted that she let him in or step into the hall so that he could talk to her. But Susan had ordered him to leave her alone, saying she didn't want to see him or anyone else. Her sudden reclusive role had Dan baffled, and throwing up his arms in despair, he had stormed away from her door and gone downstairs to the saloon.

Susan's room was pitch dark, but she didn't bother to light a lamp. Sitting rigidly in a chair, she stared thoughtfully into the surrounding blackness. She knew why Dan wanted to see her: he had decided to take Regina's advice and he intended to tell her that he would not marry her—not now or ever!

Drawing her mouth into a thin, menacing line, Susan muttered with quiet rage, "Damn you, Regina Brolin! If it hadn't been for you, I could've convinced Dan to marry me. But you had to come here and stick your smug nose into my business. I'll get even with you. I don't know how, but I swear that I will!"

Susan was quite aware that sooner or later she'd

have to face Dan, and she knew that he would destroy her very reason for living. She loved him, but hers was a strange, obsessive love. Susan's father had been aware of her inflexibility and her willfulness. Indeed, he, too, had possessed these traits. But ordinarily Susan was not a malicious person. Losing Dan had brought out the worst in her, and she yearned for revenge. She was suffering terrible pain so she wanted Regina to feel the same kind of hurt. To Susan, it wasn't fair that she had lost Dan while Regina had Matt!

Now Susan was startled by a pounding on her door. She hadn't expected Dan to return until morning.

"Susan," he said testily, "I have found another key to this room. If you don't open the door, I'm going to unlock it!"

Dan waited a moment, and when Susan made no reply, he used the key to enter the room. Finding it in darkness, he lit a lamp. As the flame brightened his surroundings, he saw Susan sitting on a chair near the window. The shade was down, blocking out the night's fresh breezes. Crossing the stifling room, Dan raised the shade, and, immediately, a pleasant draft floated through the open window.

He looked sternly at Susan. "Why wouldn't you open the door?"

Slowly she raised her eyes to stare into his angry face. Then she replied caustically, "Are you so anxious to break my heart that it can't wait until morning?"

Dan was surprised. How had she known that he was planning to tell her it was still over between them?

Laughing harshly at his stunned response, Susan taunted him bitterly, "Well, go ahead, Dan. Tell me you hate me."

Stepping back, Dan sat on the wide window sill, and facing Susan, he replied gently, "I don't hate you."

"Oh?" she countered angrily. "Do you love me?"

"No. I don't love you either," he admitted. "Susan, your coming back was a mistake. I realize you have no funds so I want to help you financially. I can give you enough money to tide you over until you decide what you want to do. If you are dead set against returning home, then perhaps you might want to settle somewhere else."

"Are you ordering me to leave this town?" Susan remarked peevishly.

"I don't have the right to order you to leave," Dan countered. "But I'm asking you to leave, and if you refuse, then I'll move away."

"And give up your precious saloon?" she retorted.

As he had done several times before, Dan silently cursed himself for getting involved with Susan. He didn't want to argue with her, but she made it very difficult for him to remain civil. Deciding his best course was to cut this disagreeable scene extremely short, he stood and said emphatically, "In the morning you can give me your answer. But I meant what I said. Either you leave, or I will!"

The door was ajar, and at that moment Claire stepped cautiously into the room, calling tentatively, "Dan?"

Susan's head jerked around awkwardly, and she glared at the skimpily clad Claire.

"What is it?" Dan asked.

"Boss, I thought you might want to know that Robert Selman is downstairs in the saloon," Claire said softly. She knew all about Dan's past encounter with Selman.

"What!" Dan exclaimed, astonished.

"I casually made my way to his table," Claire explained, "and struck up a conversation with him. He's been away on business but he's on his way home now. He said he's staying at the hotel and will be leaving early in the morning."

"Thank you, Claire," Dan replied. "I'll be downstairs in a few minutes. I intend to keep a watchful eye on Mr. Selman."

As Claire left the room, Dan knelt beside Susan's chair. Taking her hand in his, he said sincerely, "I'm sorry, Susan. I never meant to hurt you, but by coming back here you brought all this unhappiness upon yourself."

Dan's gentleness gave Susan renewed hope, and throwing her arms about his neck, she placed her head on his shoulder and pleaded, "Dan, please don't leave me! I love you so much that I can't go on living without you!"

Untangling himself from her grasp, Dan quickly rose to his feet. "Damn it, Susan!" he bellowed. "What do I have to say or do to convince you that it's over?" His anger fierce, he stalked to the doorway and then turned back to shout furiously, "I want you out of my life! Do you understand, Susan? Get out of my damned life and leave me the hell alone!"

As Dan strode swiftly down the hallway and descended the stairs, he wished he could take back the words he had spoken so harshly, but he had lost his temper and his resentment had gushed forth before he could stop it. Well, in the morning he'd apologize to Susan, but he had meant what he'd said. If she didn't leave town, he would! Dan didn't want to sell his business and move elsewhere, but he did not intend to live in the same town with Susan Chandler.

When he reached the bottom of the staircase, Dan's gaze fell upon Robert Selman who was sitting at a corner table with two of his men. His thoughts turned exclusively to the vengeful rancher, and his confrontation with Susan was temporarily forgotten.

Meanwhile, Susan remained in her chair, gazing

unseeingly out the open window. Her thoughts were stormy. She didn't doubt that Dan meant everything he had said. She had lost him, and there was nothing she could possibly do to win back his love. Well, she'd take his money and leave town. All things considered, that was her best alternative.

Suddenly a malevolent smile distorted Susan's soft features. She had suddenly thought of the perfect way to get even with Regina. That could be taken care of tonight, and tomorrow she would leave Albuquerque. Susan knew her grief over losing Dan would remain in her heart for a long time, but she wouldn't be the only one suffering, she reflected spitefully. Regina Brolin would also be terribly distressed.

Shifting her chair closer to the window, Susan focused her gaze on to the nearly deserted street below. The moment she saw the man leave the saloon, she'd slip out by the rear stairway and go to his hotel room. Susan's face brightened. She was sure that Robert Selman would be very pleased to hear what she had to tell him!

Robert Selman was pouring himself a glass of brandy when there was a soft knock on his door. He had rented a suite, which consisted of two separate bedrooms, joined by a large, comfortable sitting room. His two most trusted employees were also in the sitting room, and gesturing toward the door, Selman said to the smaller man, "Answer it, and tell whoever's there that I've already retired."

Selman was leaving early the next day and he was in no mood to receive company. He stretched, picked up his glass of brandy, and headed toward the bedroom he occupied.

When the door was opened, Susan's voice carried

inside. "My name is Susan Chandler, and I must see Mr. Selman."

"Sorry, ma'am, but Mr. Selman has gone to bed," the man answered.

Placing his glass on the table beside the velvet-covered settee, Selman hurried across the carpeted floor. He wondered, why the hell Susan Chandler would call on him.

Brushing aside his man, Selman opened the door wider, and as his eyes scanned Susan curiously, he said, "Come in, Miss Chandler."

Susan entered hesitantly, saying, "Mr. Selman, may I please talk to you privately?"

"Of course," he quickly replied, gesturing his two men into the hall. Closing the door behind them, he asked, "What can I do for you, Miss Chandler?"

Susan studied him closely, wondering if he still wanted to avenge his son's death. Had his hatred of Matt diminished? Gazing uneasily into his austerely handsome face, she said coolly, "Mr. Selman, I came here to talk to you about Matt Brolin."

Susan detected a flicker of cold rage in Selman's eyes before he masked it.

"Brolin?" he queried, raising his eyebrows. She had his undivided attention.

"You once threatened him, didn't you?" Susan parried carefully.

"Come to the point, Miss Chandler," Selman said curtly, his interest now so aroused that his patience had worn thin.

"I happen to know that a week from this coming Friday Matt Brolin will be traveling alone to Santa Fe. If you should still want revenge, this will be an opportune time to get it."

He eyed her suspiciously, "Why are you telling me this? I should think Brolin would be a friend of yours."

300

"I have nothing against Matt," Susan assured him.

"Then why are you betraying him?"

Susan's expression hardened. "I despise his wife!" she replied.

Intrigued, Selman asked, "Why do you despise Mrs. Brolin?"

As quickly as possible Susan told Robert Selman about her relationship with Dan, concluding her explanation by letting him know that Regina Brolin had been the one to turn Dan against her.

"So you, too, seek revenge," Selman surmised, smiling contemplatively.

"I want Regina to feel the same pain I am feeling," Susan remarked resentfully.

Concentrating deeply, Selman moved away from her and stood by the window, gazing thoughtfully into the night. He still hated Matt, and he had not relinquished his plan to make Matt suffer for his son's death. But Robert Selman was a cautious man, and a patient one. He'd always known that if he bided his time the day would come when Brolin would pay dearly for killing his son. It was ironic, he mused, that Susan Chandler was the one to aid him in arranging Brolin's demise.

"Mr. Selman," Susan said, seeking his attention, "do you still plan to avenge your son?"

"Of course," he replied, glancing back out the window.

"Are you going to kill Matt?" she said weakly. Susan's fury was beginning to cool, and she was now having second thoughts.

Returning to her side, Selman dismissed her question by saying cordially, "Miss Chandler, I thank you for your information. If you will please wait, I will go into the hall and tell one of my men to escort you to your home. Where may I ask, do you live?"

"I'm staying in a room above the saloon," she

answered. "But, Mr. Selman, I think I should leave alone. I wouldn't want to be seen in the company of one of your men." As she stared deeply into Selman's eyes, Susan detected a ruthlessness that sent a shiver down her spine, and she began to feel very remorseful. Impetuous acts fueled by anger were not new to Susan, but she always regretted her bitter deeds.

"You need not worry, Miss Chandler. I will warn my man to be very careful." Placing a hand on her shoulder, he added considerately, "It's much too dangerous for you to walk alone at this time of night. Is there a rear stairway that you can use?"

"Yes," she replied, trembling inwardly. Dear God, why did I do such an evil thing? she thought. Fortunately, it wasn't too late to rectify what she had done. Tomorrow she would go to Dan and clear her conscience. When she realized that he would really hate her after he knew, she felt depressed.

"I'm sure you can return without being discovered," Selman commented. He stepped into the hall where his men were waiting, and closing the door behind him, he indicated that they should follow him down the corridor. Pausing a good distance from his room, Selman spoke to the taller man, "Jack, I want you to escort Miss Chandler back to her room above the saloon, but make damned sure that you aren't seen with her."

When Selman hesitated, Jack asked inquisitively, "Why did Miss Chandler want to see you?"

Hastily, he told Jack and the other man the reason behind Susan's visit. "I always knew," Selman said intensely, "that someday I'd find the ideal time to abduct Brolin. We'll surprise him on his first night out when he stops to set up camp."

Glancing at the closed door to Selman's suite, Jack asked, "Is Miss Chandler waiting for me to take her back to her room?"

Selman spoke with deadly quietness, "I want Susan Chandler killed, but I want you to make it look like suicide."

"Why do you want me to kill her?" Jack asked, his voice low, his question prompted only by curiosity. He had no qualms about ending a young woman's life.

"At the moment she's terribly angry, but tomorrow she's liable to have a change of heart and confess everything to Butler."

"Do you think the sheriff will believe she commited suicide?" Jack didn't mind committing a murder, but he wanted to be sure he could get away with it.

Selman nodded. "She just broke up with her fiancé, her heart is broken, and she feels that she has nothing left to live for. She's a perfect candidate for suicide."

Chapter Twenty=six

Walking unsteadily, Matt made his way down the hall and into the study. The poker game had lasted for hours, and he had lost heavily, which was rare for Matt. He was a good poker player. But tonight he hadn't been able to keep his mind on cards, and during the game, he had consumed an excessive amount of brandy.

Indeed, Matt was feeling his liquor as he opened the study door, he stumbled into the room. The lamp was burning, its soft rays illuminating Regina who sat in the chair behind the desk. She was wearing a sheer black dressing gown, and her long blond tresses fell gracefully to her shoulders. Noting Matt's awkward entrance, she folded her arms beneath her full breasts and eyed him reproachfully.

Matt closed the door and leaned against it. His smile was engaging as he murmured, "Good evening, Mrs. Brolin. Or should I say good morning? I'm not sure of the time."

"It's a few minutes past midnight," Regina answered flatly.

Quirking an eyebrow, Matt drawled, "Ah, the

bewitching hour. Is that why you are here, darlin'? Do you plan to bewitch me?" Moving away from the door and crossing over to the desk, he continued to taunt Regina. "My lovely wife, don't you realize that I am already bewitched? You bewitched me from the first moment I set eyes on you." He bent over and placed his hands on the desk, leaning toward Regina, and his dark eyes narrowed dangerously. "In that black negligée, with your hair falling sensually about your beautiful face, you look like a seductress. Are you a seductress, Regina?"

Becoming perturbed, she snapped, "Matt, stop it! I didn't sit in this study for the past two hours to listen to sly innuendos!" Regaining her self-control, she proceeded, "I demand that you tell me why you are behaving this way."

Matt's sudden laugh was harsh and short. "You demand? Do you think your superior Blakely blood gives you the right to demand whatever you please from a bastard like myself?"

Shocked, she gasped, "Matt, how can you even insinuate such a thing?"

Matt dropped onto the chair in front of the desk, and stretching his long legs, he rested his feet on the desktop. "Take a man like Antonio," he began evenly, "the name Ramírez signifies true Mexican gentry." Matt shrugged casually. "But the name Brolin, well we both know it isn't even mine. It was merely borrowed."

"Matt!" Regina said sharply. "What in the world is wrong with you?"

"Do you know your family tree?" he asked, his tone tinged with bitterness. When she made no immediate reply, he grumbled, "Of course you do."

"Will you please stop feeling sorry for yourself?" she pleaded.

Matt's smile failed to reach his piercing eyes. "I'm, not feeling sorry for myself. I'm simply discussing your bloodline, mine, and Antonio Ramírez'."

Standing, Regina remarked irritably, "Matt Brolin, you're drunk, and it is quite apparent that you are in no condition to carry on a rational conversation. I'll talk to you in the morning when you are sober."

"Well, excuse the hell out of me," he mumbled sarcastically.

Regina was baffled. Obviously, something was troubling Matt, but whatever it was, her presence only seemed to make it worse. Stepping around the corner of the desk, she said firmly, "Good night, Matt!"

As she moved past his chair, he sat upright and grabbed her arm. Roughly, he pulled her down onto his lap, and her flowing negligée billowed in soft folds about her slender form. She started to protest, but before she could, his mouth covered hers and he began to caress one of her breasts.

Demandingly, Matt pried her lips apart, and his tongue darted into her mouth, relishing her sweetness. He had treated her unfairly and Regina wanted to resist him, but his ardent kiss melted her defenses. Her body grew limp against his, and as he continued to fondle her breast, she trembled with desire.

Then Matt raised his head, and Regina looked into his eyes. She was startled by the cynicism in them. A sneer flickered across his lips, and the glow from the burning lamp emphasized the faded scar on his left cheekbone. Regina was seeing a callous side of Matt that she hadn't known existed. Good Lord! she cried silently, I feel as though I don't even know him!

He spoke huskily. "Be assured my bewitching seductress, that I fully intend to succumb to your irresistible charms. From the very beginning, you have always

306

gotten what you want from me by using your beautiful body as bait, so why should tonight be any different?" Standing with Regina in his arms, he began to carry her to the sofa as he asked gruffly, "What do you want from me now, Regina? My promise to stay at the Black Diamond and keep your ranch secure? Are you afraid that I might leave?"

Wary of his mysterious mood, Regina was speechless, and, as he lowered her to the sofa, she watched him with baffled eyes.

Grasping her negligée, he shoved the voluminous folds up to her waist. When the lower part of her body was exposed to his intense scrutiny, his eyes narrowed with desire. She trembled slightly as he caressed the golden vee between her soft thighs. Then, kneeling beside the sofa, he kissed her so demandingly that her pulse raced.

"Regina," he whispered bitterly, "you are mine, and the thought of another man touching you drives me crazy!"

She wanted to assure him that she would always be his alone, but suddenly his mouth was on hers, drowning her words.

Rising, Matt impatiently rid himself of his boots and clothing. Then he placed his well-muscled body atop Regina's, his lips seeking hers, his tongue exploring the recesses of her mouth in a demanding kiss of passionate intensity.

Drifting into blissful, sensual oblivion, Regina forgot Matt's foul mood and completely gave herself to this man she loved so desperately.

Parting her thighs, Matt entered her swiftly and masterfully. At first, his thrusting was tantalizingly slow, but as his need grew more urgent, his hips moved more rapidly. Against his own volition a brief picture of his wife with Antonio flashed before his eyes, and anger surged through him. Grasping Regina's slim hips tightly, Matt drove into her so aggressively that she gasped as she felt his manhood probing deeper and deeper. Matt's release came suddenly, and a violent shudder racked his hard body.

He remained on top of Regina for a moment before rising and immediately going to the chair in the corner where, earlier, he had placed a couple of blankets and a pillow. Picking them up, he returned to the sofa and looked down at Regina, who was still lying numbly as he had left her. "If you don't mind," he began tediously, "I'd like to retire. I'm sure you're well aware that I must be up and about at dawn so I can keep your beloved ranch prosperous, and in order to do that, I need my rest."

Pushing down the folds of her negligée, Regina rose quickly. Her green eyes blazing, she seethed, "Matt Brolin, at this moment I think I despise you!"

"The feeling is mutual," he growled, dropping the blankets and pillow onto the couch.

Her pain and anger out of control now, Regina struck at his chest with her fist. "Damn you! Damn you for hurting me this way!"

Capturing her fists in his hands and completely dismissing her attack on him, Matt asked mockingly, "Are you familiar with the old cliché, you made your bed, now you lie in it? Well, if you'll excuse me, darlin', I think I'll lie in the damned bed that I made for myself."

Wide-eyed, Regina gasped out, "That's it, isn't it? You are still bitter about living on the Black Diamond because you haven't gotten over losing your ranch in Wyoming!"

"You think I'm feeling bitter?" he asked, his voice

intense. He let go of Regina's hands. "Bitter is putting it mildly!"

Without a backward glance she left the room and slammed the door.

Regina sat alone at the kitchen table, drinking her second cup of coffee. She hadn't seen Matt since the night before. She had slept later than usual, and when she had finally decided to leave her bedroom, Matt had already ridden out to the range. Regina's lovely face was etched with worry as she sipped the coffee. Matt's perplexing behavior had her totally confused. Was he again feeling resentful over losing his ranch in Wyoming? She had come to believe that the Black Diamond and his family meant more to him than his dream of owning his own land. Had she been mistaken, or had Matt's unexplained bitterness been brought on by an entirely different matter? If only he would tell her what was in his heart and on his mind!

Her turbulent thoughts were suddenly interrupted by Hannah, who burst into the kitchen, exclaiming, "Regina, one of those women who work for your brother wants to see you! She's waiting in the parlor."

Regina was astounded. "Did she say why she is here?"

"She only said that her name is Claire and that she needs to see you at once."

Regina didn't really know the woman, but Dan had introduced them so Regina had a speaking acquaintance with Claire. Hoping that nothing had happened to Dan, she rose quickly from her chair and hastened to the parlor.

Claire was pacing restlessly, but when Regina entered the room her steps halted abruptly. Wringing her hands, Claire said urgently, "Mrs. Brolin, you must hurry to town!"

"Is my brother all right?" Regina asked, fear rising in her.

Claire's simple dress contrasted sharply with the skimpy gowns she wore at the saloon. Lifting the hem of her gingham skirt, she moved swiftly to Regina's side. "Susan Chandler committed suicide!" she proclaimed.

"Oh, my God!" Regina cried.

"This morning Dan went to Susan's room, and when she didn't answer his knock, he used the pass key." Her face paling, Claire exclaimed, "Susan was lying in bed drenched in her own blood!"

Feeling weak, Regina rasped, "How did she kill herself?"

"She slit her wrists and bled to death."

Regina could hardly believe what she was hearing. Trying to fully grasp the tragic situation, she started to turn away from Claire, but the woman reached out and clutched her arm.

"Mrs. Brolin," she said gravely, "I'm terribly worried about Dan."

"Is he blaming himself?" Regina asked, her heart aching for him.

"Yes, ma'am," Claire declared. "He needs you, Mrs. Brolin. I tried to console him, but I couldn't help him. He lost his patience and ordered me out of his room and told me not to come back."

Frowning, Regina replied, "That doesn't sound like Dan."

"He isn't acting like himself," Regina said.

"I'll have my horse saddled, then change my clothes and ride back to town with you," Regina stated briskly.

"Please hurry, Mrs. Brolin!" Claire seemed desperate. "I know how much your brother loves you, and you're probably the only person who can help him!"

Regina's face was pale and she was obviously worried as she walked into the saloon beside Claire. Going directly to the bar, she said to the bartender, "Where's Dan?"

"He's in his quarters. He's been closed in his rooms all mornin'. I tried to talk to him, but he wouldn't let me in. The boss is grievin' somethin' powerful. I feel damned sorry for him. He doesn't deserve what happened. The boss is one the nicest guys I know."

The man's words touched Regina, and thanking him, she hurried up the stairway. She walked apprehensively down the hall to Dan's door and knocked lightly.

"Go away!" He yelled sharply.

"Dan, please let me in!" she pleaded, rattling the doorknob.

"Regina?" he called.

"Yes, it's me. Dan, please unlock the door!"

Tense moments passed before she heard him release the bolt. As the door swung open, Regina caught her breath when she saw Dan's ravaged face.

Her knees weakening, she stepped into the room, and he closed the door behind her. For a long moment they stared at one another, each waiting for the other to speak.

It was Dan who finally broke the silence. "Oh, God!" he groaned. "What have I done?"

Taking him into her arms, Regina cried, "Hold tightly to me, Dan! Hold tightly!"

Clinging to her, he whispered pleadingly, "I need you, Gina! Stay with me! I don't want to be alone!"

"I won't leave you," she promised. "I'll stay here for as long as you need me."

Regina embraced Dan firmly; then, stepping back, she stood on tiptoe and touched her lips to his. Taking his hand, she led him to the sofa and urged him to sit beside her, but he whirled away brusquely.

Rubbing his fingers across his troubled brow, Dan remarked wretchedly, "She killed herself because of me!" His eyes shone hysterically as he went on. "Do you know what my words were to Susan? I told her to get out of my damned life and leave me the hell alone!" His broad shoulders shook violently, and covering his face with his hands, he moaned hoarsely, "Oh God, I can't forgive myself! But I never dreamed that she would take her own life!"

Standing rigidly in front of the sofa, Regina observed her brother's misery. "Dan," she implored, "you mustn't blame yourself!"

Abruptly, he moved back to her and somehow Regina ended up on the edge of the sofa with Dan kneeling at her feet. Clutching the loose folds of her skirt, he rested his arms across her bent legs. "God help me!" he cried, anguish in his voice. Then giving in to his sorrow, he placed his head on Regina's lap and cried.

Brushing her fingers through his hair, Regina crooned soothingly, "It'll be all right. Somehow, everything will be all right . . . in time, Dan . . . In time. It'll be all right. . . ."

Regina knew it was wrong to think ill of the dead, but she didn't understand why Susan had deliberately placed such guilt on Dan's shoulders. Regina was sure her brother would suffer from it for the rest of his life.

When Regina rode up to the ranch house, Ted was

walking down the porch steps. Halting the stallion at the hitching post and dismounting, she said, "Ted, would you please stable Midnight?"

"Of course I will," he replied, taking the reins from Regina. Noting her fatigue, he asked, "Ma'am, are you all right?"

Emitting a weary sigh, she answered, "I'm all right, Ted. It's just been a very trying day. Last night Susan Chandler committed suicide, but she wasn't found until this morning."

"Yes, I know. Hannah told me why that Claire woman came out here to see you. How's your brother?"

"He's taking Susan's death very hard. He blames himself, I'm afraid."

"That's too bad," Ted mumbled. "In time, though, he'll get over it."

Regina wasn't so sure, but not wanting to discuss Dan's emotional state with Ted Lucas, she went into the house.

As she walked listlessly down the hall, the study door opened suddenly and Matt remarked curtly, "I want to talk to you."

Regina followed him into the study, when he gestured to the chair in front of the desk, she sat down.

"Have you been with Dan?" he asked.

She nodded slowly, inquiring, "Did Hannah tell you about Susan?"

"Yes. I suppose Dan is taking it pretty hard," Matt commented. He leaned against the side of the desk, his arms folded across his chest.

Meeting Matt's gaze, Regina murmured, "I'm terribly worried about Dan."

"With time, it'll become easier for him," Matt predicted.

"I hope so," Regina replied. "You might not realize

313

it, but Dan's carefree and roguish attitude is merely a façade. Actually, he's very sensitive and compassionate."

"In a few minutes I'll ride into town and see him."

"In a few minutes?" Regina said. "But it's almost dinner time."

"I'll have a bite to eat in town. I'll be returning late, so I'll just sleep here on the sofa," he said calmly.

"Again?" Regina remarked, agitated. "Why don't you just move your clothes out of the bedroom and into the study? Apparently, you don't want to share the same bed with me!"

"That brings me to my reason for wanting to talk to you," Matt said matter-of-factly. "As you know, next week I'll be leaving to visit Alan Garrett and José. Until then, I intend to sleep here on the sofa. When I come back from Garrett's, we'll have a serious discussion about this marriage we're both trapped in."

"Trapped!" Regina exclaimed. "I don't consider myself trapped!"

Cocking an eyebrow, Matt said coolly, "No, I don't suppose you do."

"Matt, why do you want to end our marriage?" she asked anxiously.

"I didn't say I wanted to end it," he corrected. "I have an obligation to María and Cort, and before I make a decision, I must consider them."

Bounding to her feet, Regina demanded, "What about your obligation to me?"

Remembering her in Antonio's arms, Matt grumbled, "We'll discuss our obligations to each other when I return from Garrett's." He had every intention of confronting Regina with his knowledge of her behavior with Antonio, but first he wanted to give himself more time to think about everything. There was still a slim chance that she was innocent. The embrace she had

314

shared with Antonio might have been only an impetuous one.

Matt's unexplained bitterness and the exhausting hours she'd spent with Dan now took their toll on Regina. Wearily, she said, "Matt, do whatever you wish. I'm too exhausted to argue with you."

"Giving up so easily?" he retorted, wondering why he wanted her to put up an argument. Was it because a show of anger would make her look innocent? If she were truly guiltless, wouldn't his behavior make her furious?

Still reclining against the desk, Matt shifted his long legs to obstruct Regina's retreat, but she shoved her chair backward, thereby clearing a path for herself.

"I surrender to your ambivalence," she declared. "It's bigger than both of us." Keeping her hurt well concealed, Regina held her chin high as she walked out of the study.

Chapter Twenty-seven

The night was extremely warm, but as Regina stood
alongside the corral watching Midnight, the whisper of
a breeze fell across her troubled face, its refreshing
presence cooling her brow. The stallion was prancing
majestically, his graceful canter carrying him back and
forth from one end of the corral to the other. Smiling
wistfully, Regina murmured, "You want me to saddle
you, so we can take a ride, don't you?" As though he
understood her words, he tossed his huge head and
flared his powerful nostrils.

Feeling a sudden nudge against her leg, Regina
glanced down to find Blackie beside her, looking up
with adoring eyes. She patted the top of his head. "You
miss our nightly excursions as much as Midnight does,
don't you, boy?" The dog answered by wagging his
bushy tail.

Sighing discontentedly, Regina draped her arms on
the fence and gazed vacantly at the stallion. Matt was
leaving in the morning to visit Alan Garrett, and she
feared he might decide not to return. He had been
sleeping in the study for more than a week, and during
that time, he had successfully managed to avoid her
company. He had gone back to his old ambiguous

behavior, as if there had never been any real love between them. Their marriage, María and Cort, the loss of the twins—had it all meant so little to Matt?

While Regina pursued her disturbing thoughts, Matt, having concluded his business with Ted Lucas, left the study to seek his wife. Unable to locate her in the house, he stepped outside and his eyes turned toward Midnight's corral. The darkness blanketed his surroundings, and he could barely make out Regina standing by the circular fence. Thoughtfully, Matt observed her. He knew when she was troubled, she turned to the large black stallion. For some strange reason, the horse's presence seemed to calm her. Was she troubled because she had been unfaithful to him and was she hurt by his harsh treatment of her? Perhaps she feared that he suspected her relationship with Antonio. Matt did not know.

Descending the short flight of steps, he sauntered toward Regina. As he drew nearer, she became aware of his approach, and turning away from the corral, she watched him warily. Why was he seeking her out? Did he plan to confide in her and tell her what was bothering him, or did he intend to continue his strange behavior?

When Matt reached her side, Blackie welcomed him playfully. He stroked the dog affectionately, then told him to sit. Obediently, Blackie returned to a sitting position; then realizing that Matt wasn't going to give him any more attention, he lay down and placed his head between his front paws.

"Regina," Matt began evenly, "I've been looking for you to tell you that Ted will be able to take care of everything while I'm away."

"How long will you be gone?" she inquired, amazed that his mere presence made her so acutely aware of how much she loved him.

317

Stepping to the corral, he rested his arms on the fence and watched Midnight. The stallion was again prancing back and forth. "I'll be gone one week," Matt mumbled. He was quiet for a moment; then he asked softly, "Do you remember the evening we stood here and watched Midnight?"

Moving to Matt's side and facing the stallion, Regina replied, "Yes, I remember. You and Dan had returned from Mexico with Miguel." She hesitated, then said dreamily, "Midnight nudged me into your arms and you kissed me."

"A lot has happened since that night," Matt remarked quietly, recalling the happy times as well as the tragic ones.

Encouraged by Matt's gentle mood, Regina grasped his arm, urging him to look at her. "Why can't you tell me what has been upsetting you?"

Pulling away from her, he answered firmly, "We'll discuss it when I return from Garrett's."

"Why not now?" she pleaded.

His expression hardened, and his eyes glared darkly into hers. "It takes awhile for my temper to cool. If I talk to you now and receive answers I don't want to hear, I might be tempted to break your beautiful neck!"

Exasperated and baffled, Regina sighed despairingly. "If that's how you feel, then it's all right with me." Then, her anger surging, she added, "I'm tired of trying to reason with you. You're too bullheaded!"

She suddenly brushed past him, and he asked, "Where are you going?"

"To the house to change into riding clothes. I'm going to saddle Midnight and take a ride."

"I'll saddle him for you," Matt offered as she walked away.

"I'll tend to it myself! I don't want any favors from you, Matt Brolin!" Regina tossed the words over her shoulder, picking up her pace. Then, wondering if he was angry, she glanced fleetingly back at him, but Matt's face was inscrutable.

Regina went directly to her bedroom, where she changed hastily. When she left the house, she was surprised to find Matt waiting for her. He had saddled Midnight, plus his own horse. Blackie was sitting at Matt's feet, his tail wagging in anticipation of the jaunt that lay ahead.

One part of Regina was pleased that Matt had decided to accompany her, but the other part of her resented his impertinent intrusion. "I don't remember telling you that you could join me," she said coolly as she walked down the steps.

Intending to help her mount, he stepped to Midnight's side. "I don't remember asking your permission," he answered, his voice edged with irritation.

She allowed him to assist her into the saddle, but the moment she was seated, she jerked the reins and turned the stallion about. She dug her booted feet into Midnight's sides, and he took off with a start, leaving Blackie trailing in his wake.

As Regina raced down the lane, Matt mounted his own horse. He followed her for a short distance; then changing his course, he headed in a different direction. When Regina became aware that Matt was no longer following her, she was disappointed. She had hoped that he cared enough to pursue her.

Reining in the stallion, and slowing him to an even canter, Regina decided to ride to the west range where she could sit beside the river and be alone with her thoughts.

When she reached the designated area, she was

astounded to finding Matt sitting beneath a tree and leisurely smoking a cheroot while his horse grazed nearby.

Dismounting, she walked over and paused in front of him. Glancing up at her, he said flatly, "I took a short cut." A cocky grin curled his sensual lips as he patted the ground next to him. "Sit down and join me."

Complying, Regina sat beside him, and as Matt was doing, she leaned back against the tree trunk. Her shoulder touching his, she asked curiously, "How did you know I'd come here?"

"What makes you think I was expecting you?" he drawled.

His insolence made her frown; then noticing the flask in his hand, she prodded him. "What are you drinking?"

"Whiskey," he replied, putting out his cigar.

"Have you taken to carrying your liquor around with you?" she asked sharply.

"Maybe you're driving me to drink," Matt mumbled sarcastically, before taking a generous swallow of whiskey.

Piqued, Regina took the flask from his hand, declaring testily, "And you're driving me to drink!" She helped herself to such a large amount that the potent liquor burned her throat and made her cough.

Chuckling, he remarked, "It doesn't go down as smoothly as brandy."

Resenting Matt's laughter, Regina took another drink, then handed him the flask. Putting it to his mouth, he took a swig, then gave it back to her. His eyes challenged her to match him drink for drink, and accepting his unspoken dare, she placed the flask to her lips.

They continued the exchange several times before

Regina realized she was having difficulty keeping Mat in focus. In addition, she was beginning to perspire, and the night air seemed stifling. Getting awkwardly to her feet, she started unbuttoning her blouse.

Twisting the cap onto the half-empty flask, Matt asked, "Is there a special reason why you're undressing?"

Her glance sweeping toward the river, she answered, "I'm going to take a swim." Letting her blouse drop to the ground, Regina slipped out of her riding skirt, but as she leaned over to remove her boots, she lost her balance. Stumbling, she regained her footing.

"Mrs. Brolin," Matt taunted, "I do believe you're drunk."

Regina scowled. "Go to the devil, Matt Brolin!" she replied. Nonetheless, due to her tipsy condition, Regina found removing her boots a difficult chore. Finally she completed the task; then she quickly shed her underclothes.

Matt's dark eyes glazed with desire as they drank in her naked beauty, which was fully revealed to him before she hurriedly waded into the river. Blackie ran to the bank and scurried back and forth, barking loudly. Regina's steps were unsteady as she headed farther into the rippling water, and worried about her safety, Matt hastily removed his clothes and waded after her.

Regina had now ventured out where the water was over her head, yet she was swimming with comparative ease when Matt reached her. Keeping his strokes even with hers, he advised, "I think you should go back to shallow water."

"Why?" she asked, turning over to swim on her back.

"In your condition, you're liable to drown!" He was irritated.

321

"Nonsense," she objected casually. "I can swim like a fish."

"Fish do not get drunk before swimming!" Matt bellowed. Treading water, he reached for her, and capturing her around the waist, he pulled her smoothly against his strong frame. The cool water flowing against their bodies was stimulating and sensual. Matt used one arm to keep them afloat, while the other held her so close that she could feel his manhood harden against her thigh.

She looked into his face and his unexpected rage startled her. "Damn you, Regina!" he muttered between clenched teeth. "Damn you for this power you have over me!"

Grasping her securely, he maneuvered them toward the bank, but when his feet touched bottom, Matt swept her body to his. He locked one arm about her waist, then dipping his other hand beneath the water, he lifted her hips and thrust her against him. The swirling river made her so weightless that her legs seemed to part and wrap about his waist of their own accord.

Matt's hardness slid into her unexpectedly, his swift entry making Regina gasp as she was suddenly struck with a rapturous shudder. As her arms went around his neck, Matt gripped her wet buttocks, rocking her to and fro as the water splashed about them in gentle, cascading waves.

As his maleness filled her with ecstasy, Regina moaned throatily, "Oh, Matt . . . Matt, why must you punish me with loving torment?"

"Torment?" he mocked. "Don't you like it when I'm inside you?"

Tightening her legs about him, she said shakily, "Oh, yes . . . yes! But, Matt, why must you take advantage of my passion and then use it to torment me?"

322

Thinking of Antonio, Matt said gruffly, "Maybe you surrender your passion too easily."

His sarcastic reply angered Regina, and she tried to free herself. But he kept her pinioned against him, and as he continued their sensual rhythm, she quickly forgot that she had wanted him to turn her loose. Regina's yearning now inflamed, she clung tenaciously to her husband and her passion equalled his.

Matt's thrusting grew more demanding, causing waves to splash up onto their shoulders and faces. Enthralled by his exciting aggressiveness, Regina threw her head back and her long hair floated on top of the undulating water.

Matt then moved both his hands to her small waist, and grasping her firmly, he thrust her against him time and time again. His forcefulness brought them to the peak of pleasure; then total release left them both weak and breathless.

Gently, Matt cradled her in his arms and carried her to the bank where Blackie welcomed them with rapid barks. Taking Regina to their clothes, Matt placed her on her feet. Noticing a trace of tears in her eyes, he asked, "Why are you on the verge of crying?"

"Matt, you just made love to me and you never even kissed me. Men treat their whores with more respect."

Retrieving his clothes, and proceeding to dress, he replied dryly, "That's not true. Men don't marry their whores."

Raging inwardly, Regina hurriedly slipped into her apparel, and then declared tartly, "I'm returning home, and I prefer to ride alone!"

As she swept past him, his arm shot out and grasped her waist, and holding her flush to his solid frame, he bent his head and kissed her forcefully. Relinquishing her, he grumbled, "Now you have been soundly kissed.

323

Do you have any more complaints, Mrs. Brolin?"

Peering up into his expressionless face, Regina wondered how it was possible for her to love him when he continued to hurt her so mercilessly. But the fight had gone out of Regina, and not having the strength to bicker with him, she walked slowly to Midnight and rode home by herself.

Chapter Twenty-eight

Standing at the study window, Regina watched Matt ride away from the house. Her eyes became misty as he gradually disappeared from view. She had seen Matt only fleetingly that morning as he prepared for his trip to Alan Garrett's. She had tried to engage him in a serious conversation, but he had told her they would talk when he returned. He hadn't even bothered to kiss her goodbye, and his cold rejection had once again hurt Regina very deeply. She wondered if he really planned to come back, or whether he intended to ride out of her life forever. No! she thought decisively. He'll return! He might have no qualms about leaving me, but he won't desert María and Cort. Regina suddenly felt a prickling sensation at the back of her neck and her thoughts turned to Robert Selman. She hadn't been able to shake her uneasiness about Matt traveling so close to Selman's territory.

Depressed, Regina remained in the study for a long time. She was thinking about Matt's perplexing behavior when Hannah knocked lightly on the closed door. Clearing her mind, Regina bade her enter, and Hannah promptly did so, saying, "Antonio Ramírez is here."

"Antonio?" Regina responded questioningly. "Show him in, please."

Hannah brought Antonio to the study, then closed the door behind him. When Regina started to rise, he gestured for her to remain seated.

Taking the chair across from the desk, he said, "I came to see Matt, but Hannah told me that he left about an hour ago to visit Señor Garrett."

"Are you acquainted with Mr. Garrett?" Regina asked.

"I do not know him personally, but I have heard of him."

"Why did you need to see Matt?"

"I was in town this morning and I heard some news that might interest him. It's nothing important, but since Matt is not here, I will tell you instead."

In his elegantly Spanish attire, Antonio looked so handsome, that Regina couldn't help noticing what an attractive man he was. Smiling, she asked, "What is the news?"

"It seems that Billy the Kid is dead. The *Albuquerque Journal* received the story early this morning."

"Why would Matt be interested in Billy the Kid?"

"Your husband was once a bounty hunter. I am sure, *señora*, that he would find the story behind the infamous outlaw's death interesting."

"How did he die?" Regina asked, mildly curious.

"He was shot by Sheriff Pat Garrett," Antonio answered.

"Garrett!" Regina exclaimed. "Is he kin to Alan Garrett?"

"I do not think so," he replied, explaining, "The shooting took place at old Fort Sumner in a large house that had once been used by officers when the army was battling the Navajo Indians."

"How old was Billy the Kid?" Regina asked.

"Barely twenty-one. But he always claimed that he had killed as many men as he had years."

"How horrible!" Regina cringed. "He must have been very ruthless."

Antonio shrugged. "Billy did not have a bad heart; most of his killings were prompted by vengeance."

"Did you know him?" she gasped.

"No," he denied. "I did not know him, but I understand crimes that are governed by vengeance."

Regina was taken aback for a moment. She had almost forgotten that Antonio had once ridden with Comancheros.

Aware of her reaction, Antonio said quietly, "A man can change, Regina."

"Have you truly changed?" she asked intensely.

"Sí, señora," he assured her. "I am not the same man who was once a Comanchero."

"I believe you, Antonio," Regina declared. "I just wish . . ."

"What do you wish?" he coaxed.

"I wish that you and Miguel could resolve your differences," she replied carefully.

"Never!" he spat out harshly. "There is too much hate between us!"

"I don't understand why you two must continue your feud," she remarked with a note of impatience.

Antonio smiled charmingly. "Do not worry your pretty head about mens' affairs."

Regina frowned testily. She was about to extend their discussion when the study door opened and Cort bounded into the room. He hurried to his mother, and she lifted him onto her lap.

"Is anything wrong, darling?" she asked.

Leaning his head against her shoulder, Cort murmured, "I want my Papa to come home."

Positioning him so that she could look down into his large brown eyes, Regina said soothingly, "He'll only be gone a few days."

Studying Cort, Antonio said, "He is a very handsome boy. How old is he?"

"He'll soon be three." Upon hearing the clock in the parlor chime the noon hour, Regina said cordially, "Antonio, why don't you stay and have lunch with us? We'd love to have your company."

"Gracias, señora," he replied.

Matt was backtracking, and since he was anxious to return to the Black Diamond, he kept his horse at a fast gallop. He had been a couple of hours from home before he'd suddenly made the decision to return. This was not the time to visit Alan Garrett; he had merely been using this trip as an excuse to run away from his jealous suspicions. A confrontation with Regina was inevitable. He had only been delaying it because he dreaded the outcome. He didn't want to hear Regina tell him that she was in love with Antonio Ramírez. He knew about their embrace, so if she was guilty, she'd have no alternative but to admit that she and Antonio were having an affair. But it wasn't the thought of Regina's guilt that had compelled Matt to turn his horse around and head back to the ranch, it was his hope that she might be innocent. He had seen her kissing Antonio, but that didn't necessarily mean she was guilty of adultery. She might have a logical explanation for the embrace he had witnessed. The kiss could have been initiated by Antonio, and it might have taken her a moment to come to her senses. After all, he had ridden away at the very instant that she and

328

Antonio had kissed. If he had stayed, he might have seen Regina break the embrace.

Reaching the lane that led to the ranch house, Matt slowed his mount to an even trot. As he drew closer, he recognized Antonio's horse at the hitching rail and he pulled up abruptly. His dark eyes narrowed angrily as jealousy surged through him. He had only been gone a few hours and Antonio was already visiting Regina. It could be a coincidence, he said to himself. Maybe Antonio has a good reason for dropping by. He had a reason all right! Matt's thought. My absence!

Jerking the reins, Matt turned his horse around and headed back down the lane. To hell with Regina and Antonio! If she wanted Antonio, she could damned well have him! He'd pay a call on Garrett and José, and when he returned? . . . He wasn't sure what he'd do when he finally faced Regina, but he hoped a week's stay at Garrett's would cool the murderous rage he was now experiencing.

Matt stopped and set up camp when the sun was sinking in the west. He had unsaddled his horse, and set it to grazing nearby, and he was sitting by the small fire he'd just made when he heard riders approaching. Getting quickly to his feet, he stood with a tree at his back and drew his revolver. "Who goes there?" he called, cocking his pistol.

"Don't shoot, mister," a deep voice rang out as three men rode into sight. "We ain't lookin' for no trouble. We spotted your campfire and just dropped by to say howdy. We run out of coffee this mornin', and thought you might have some extra you wouldn't mind sharin'."

Keeping his pistol drawn, Matt replied, "I'm willin'

to share my coffee, if you're willin' to leave your holsters draped across your saddles."

"Sure we are," the man agreed heartily. "A man can't be too cautious in these-here parts. After all, there's three of us and only one of you."

"That's right," Matt answered. "Leave your guns and come on over to the campfire."

The three men dismounted, then placed their gun belts across their saddles. The man who had been doing all the talking reached into a cloth bag attached to his saddle and brought out three tin cups. Matt watched the strangers as they ambled toward him. They appeared to be cowhands and didn't look especially dangerous. Matt relaxed a bit and slipped his pistol back into its holster.

The men sat by the fire, and joining them, Matt looked on as one of them took the coffeepot and filled the three cups.

"We thank you for your hospitality," the man said cordially.

Matt nodded a welcome, then asked, "Where are you headed?"

Another man spoke up, "We're on our way to Santa Fe." He started to say more, but was suddenly struck by a coughing spasm. Dropping his cup, he crossed his arms over his chest and doubled over.

Matt hesitated for one critical moment, which gave the man who was feigning illness time to reach the revolver hidden beneath his shirt. He drew it out at the same second Matt's hand touched his pistol. Aiming his gun at Matt, the man warned, "Don't try it, Brolin!"

"Who in the hell are you?" Matt demanded, moving his hand away from his gun.

As the three men got to their feet, one of them ordered Matt to stand and unbuckle his holster. He did as he was told; then another man grabbed him and pulled him farther away from his pistol, which was now on the ground.

"Go get the boss," the man holding the gun on Matt told one of his companions. He was the one who had done most of the talking.

His comrade mounted and rode off quickly, returning momentarily with four men, one of whom was Robert Selman.

Dismounting, Selman sneered as he slowly approached Matt. "I told you, Brolin, that someday you would pay for killing my son."

"How in the hell did you know I would be traveling this way?" Matt asked, certain he hadn't been captured by chance.

"Susan Chandler told me," Selman answered. He enjoyed letting Matt know he had been betrayed by the woman he had once rescued so he described his meeting with Susan, and he told Matt why he had had Susan murdered.

"You must be real proud of yourself for ordering a woman killed," Matt remarked. Glancing at Selman's men, he asked, "Which one of you was brave enough to kill a helpless female?"

"Shut up, Brolin!" Selman shouted. Nodding to a couple of his men, he ordered them to hold Matt. Obeying, they pinned Matt between them, each grasping one of his arms.

Moving closer to Matt, Selman murmured threateningly, "Brolin, you're going to suffer greatly for murdering my son. A fast death is too merciful for you. Before I'm through with you, you'll be begging me to kill you and put you out of your misery." His icy eyes stared into Matt's as he continued sadistically, "You'll be sniveling and groveling at my feet, pleading for mercy."

"Selman, you're a sorry son of a bitch." Matt sneered. "I'll see you in hell before I kneel at your feet."

Selman's sudden rasping laugh was demonical. "Bring my whip!" he ordered, gesturing toward his men. Then nodding at the two men restraining Matt he said, "Strip off his shirt, and tie him to that tree! We'll see if a few lashes on his bare back will curb his insolence."

Selman quickly received his whip, and with a snap of his wrist, he made the long lash crack loudly. "Brolin, justice will be done and my son's death will be avenged!"

Matt's shirt was speedily ripped off, and his arms were bound about the trunk of a tree. The rough bark dug sharply into Matt's naked chest, but he knew that discomfort was nothing compared to the pain Selman would inflict upon his exposed back.

"I think a dozen lashes should subdue you and make you quite congenial on our journey," Selman taunted.

"Where are you taking me?" Matt asked, straining against the rope binding him.

"To your own private hell," Selman said evilly. He drew back the whip, and the sharp lash whistled as it cut through the air.

The cave was pitch black and damp, but Matt was not aware of the darkness or the moisture beading the jagged rock walls. Robert Selman's last blow to Matt's head had knocked him unconscious.

Selman and his men had taken Matt to a cave on Selman's property, where he was to be kept a prisoner until death finally prevailed. Selman was determined that his dying would be long and painful.

332

The twelve lashes Selman had inflicted upon Matt's bare back were merely the beginning of his cruelty. The moment his men had dragged the injured Matt into the cave, Selman had beaten him mercilessly. He had ended the punishment by striking the solid handle of his whip against the side of Matt's head. Then taking up the lantern, he and his men had left Matt lying unconscious. A large boulder had been placed in the opening of the cave, leaving the interior in total blackness.

Hours passed before consciousness slowly returned to Matt. He first became aware of a coldness that chilled him to the bone, and shivering, he crossed his arms over his naked chest. Still groggy, he wondered why he wasn't wearing a shirt. Was he in bed? He reached down to draw up the covers, but his seeking hands grasped only air. He tried to sit up but the agonizing pain that shot through his head made him clutch his temples and roll uncomfortably on to his side.

In jumbled pieces it all came back to him. The three men coming to his camp, Robert Selman's appearance, the stinging lashes across his back, and the trip to this cave.

His consciousness now fully restored, Matt became achingly aware of his bruised, cut, and battered body. There didn't seem to be a part of him that wasn't in excruciating pain—and he knew there was more suffering to come. Selman would be back to inflict some other sadistical tortures on him.

"Dear God," Matt moaned barely above a whisper, "what a hell of a way to die!" But maybe that wouldn't happen. Alan Garrett was expecting him, and when he didn't arrive, surely Garrett would send a wire to the Black Diamond. Then Regina would start a search for him—or would she? She might believe he had decided to quit their marriage and head for Wyoming instead of Garrett's.

He had to face the truth! There was a good chance that he was destined to die right here in this damned hellhole!

Chapter Twenty-nine

María had left for school, and Regina was in the kitchen having a late breakfast with Cort when Dan showed up unexpectedly. Hurrying into the house, and finding Regina, Dan said worriedly, "Gina, you received a telegram this morning from Alan Garrett. Mr. Ogden from the telegraph office brought the telegram to me."

"Why did he take the wire to you?" she asked anxiously, fear for Matt's safety gripping her heart.

Pulling out a chair, Dan sat down at the kitchen table and handed Regina the telegram. "Matt never reached Garrett's ranch," he muttered with consternation.

Quickly, Regina's eyes scanned Garrett's message. It simply stated that Matt had failed to arrive as expected.

"What do you think happened to him?" she asked, alarmed.

"I don't know." Dan was concerned for Matt's safety, but he was determined not to let Regina realize it.

"Robert Selman!" she suddenly gasped, rising quickly to her feet.

Standing, Dan replied, "The odds that Selman came upon Matt are very slim."

"I don't care how slim the odds are," Regina declared. "I tell you Robert Selman found Matt!"

"Gina," Dan began hesitantly, "is there a chance that Matt might have simply taken off? What I'm trying to say is . . . did you two have a quarrel?"

"Quarrel?" Regina repeated bitterly. "Matt doesn't quarrel! He keeps his feelings and thoughts to himself, but that's beside the point. Matt would never leave María and Cort. He loves them too much!"

Suddenly, they heard Antonio calling Regina as he headed through the house. Entering the kitchen, and seeing Regina and Dan, Antonio apologized hastily, *"Señora,* please excuse my intrusion, but the front door was open so I let myself in. I was in town and Señor Ogden told me about the telegram from Alan Garrett. I came here immediately to see if there is anything I can do."

"Oh, Antonio." Regina sighed. "I'm so afraid that something terrible has happened to Matt!"

Dan elaborated. "She suspects that Selman is behind Matt's disappearance."

"I agree with her," Antonio concurred. He knew about Matt's dealings with Selman and the threat Selman had made on Matt's life. Taking charge of the situation, he told Dan to ride into town and send a wire to Garrett, telling him to meet them in Santa Fe.

"What do you plan to do?" Regina asked Antonio.

"Señor Butler, my vaqueros and I will ride to Santa Fe. Along with Garrett's help, we will try to find Matt. Robert Selman may be holding him somewhere."

"I'm going with you!" Regina stated firmly.

"Gina," Dan objected, "I think you should stay here."

"Your brother is right," Antonio agreed.

336

"I'm going and that's final!" Regina insisted, her expression daring them to attempt to stop her.

Realizing it would be useless to argue with her, both men reluctantly assented.

Antonio had fifteen vaqueros riding with him, and as they approached Santa Fe, which was the Territorial capital, Regina rode in front of his men with Dan on her left and Antonio on her right. Before entering the bustling city, they rode parallel to the railroad tracks that lay on the outskirts of the capital.

The completion of the Santa Fe Railroad, on the ninth of February, 1880, had been an important event in the Territory. The people of New Mexico believed it to herald a new era. Through the development of its resources and the establishment of rapid communication with other parts of the country, the New Mexico Territory would soon assume a more prominent position in the American Union.

Mounted on her black stallion and surrounded by a large group of horsemen, Regina created quite a stir as they rode slowly into the city. But she was only vaguely aware of the attraction she and the others were attracting. Her thoughts were centered on Matt, and she gave her surroundings little thought.

Reaching the Santa Fe Hotel, where they were to meet Alan Garrett, the vaqueros remained seated on their horses as Regina, Antonio, and Dan dismounted.

As the two men escorted Regina into the tastefully decorated lobby, a tall, middle-aged gentleman crossed the room to greet them.

He addressed Regina. "Mrs. Brolin?"

"Yes," she replied, smiling faintly.

"I am Alan Garrett," he stated, realizing at once that he found Matt's wife extremely attractive. Although

337

Regina's beige blouse and dark riding skirt were layered with a thin coat of trail dust, and her face was etched with worry, she was strikingly lovely.

Regina quickly introduced Dan and Antonio to Alan Garrett, and after the men shook hands, Garrett invited them upstairs to the suite he'd rented upon his arrival the night before.

Regina was fatigued, but she climbed the stairs with haste. She was anxious to learn whether Garrett had learned anything about Matt's disappearance.

As she entered the sitting room in Garrett's suite, she was pleasantly surprised to see José. He was sitting on the sofa, but, at Regina's entrance, he hurried to his feet and moved across the carpeted floor to welcome her.

"Señora," he said his tone apparently troubled.

Fear seized Regina and she murmured, "Oh, José, I'm so worried about Matt."

"Señor Garrett and I, we have something we must tell you," José replied encouragingly, his words giving Regina sudden hope.

Quickly everyone was seated, but Garrett remained standing as he revealed what he and José had found out. "This morning José secretly watched Selman's ranch. At about ten o'clock, Selman left his house and rode away with a couple of his men. José followed them. They went to a cave a few miles north of Selman's home. Several men were guarding this cave. The boulder placed in front of it was pushed aside, and Selman entered with two of his men. A few minutes later they emerged, the boulder was replaced, and leaving the same men to stand guard, Selman and his two companions rode back to the house."

Antonio asked, "Do you believe they have Matt inside this cave?"

"I believe that's possible. I've already notified the sheriff. We decided that as soon as you arrived, we'd

338

ride out to this cave."

Bounding to her feet, Regina exclaimed, "Let's not waste any more time talking!"

Garrett was in complete accord. "Let's go; the sheriff is waiting."

Matt had been Selman's prisoner for seven days, but that week seemed like an eternity—an eternity filled with suffering and pain. Selman had imposed his cruelty upon Matt time and time again. He had physically tortured his captive every day, and he had allowed Matt barely enough water to keep him alive but no food at all. The dark cave was as damp as a dungeon, yet Matt was clad only in tattered trousers. His injured body was so weak that he hadn't the resilience to withstand the dampness and the chill, and he'd become very feverish. Finally as a result of his illness and the battering he'd suffered, Matt fell into a state of unconsciousness.

Entering the cave on the eighth morning of Matt's captivity, Selman was unable to rouse his prisoner. Realizing that Matt was on the verge of dying, Selman became enraged. It wasn't the thought of Matt's death that infuriated him, but the fact that his prisoner had never once begged for mercy, regardless of the torments he had inflicted upon him. And now, with Matt so close to death, Selman knew Matt would never really be broken.

Deciding his prisoner would soon be dead, Selman left the cave, but before heading back to his ranch, he informed his guards that he'd come back at dusk with a couple of shovels. If Matt wasn't dead by then, he'd put a bullet through his heart and have him buried where he'd never be found.

Approximately four hours after Selman's departure,

Regina and the others arrived at the cave. Selman's guards got off three shots before they realized that the sheriff was leading the advancing riders. Since they were outnumbered and their boss couldn't protect them from the law, they threw down their weapons and surrendered.

The gunshots registered vaguely on Matt's consciousness. Moaning feebly, he tried to fight his way back to awareness, but his injured, fever-racked body was too weak to cooperate and he quickly drifted back into the dark depths of oblivion.

Matt was not aware that the boulder was being moved away from the cave's opening, nor did he know people had rushed inside, hoping desperately to find him still alive. Alan Garrett and Regina reached Matt at the same time, and they knelt on the ground beside him. He lay on his side, his back turned toward his wife and his good friends. The cave was murky so Regina couldn't see Matt very clearly. But she could dimly make out the blood-clotted lacerations across his back.

"Oh, my God!" she gasped.

Alan glanced over his shoulder at Dan who was standing next to Antonio. "There was a lantern beside the opening. Light it and bring it to me."

As Dan was leaving, Alan carefully rolled Matt over, and even the gloomy darkness of the cave couldn't completely conceal his battered and bruised face.

Regina's sudden cry was shrill, although she was so shocked that she wasn't aware she had made a sound.

Listening for a heartbeat, Alan leaned over and placed his ear against Matt's chest. Within moments he sighed with relief, raised up, and looked over at Regina. "He's alive," he murmured gratefully.

Dan brought in the lantern and handed it to Alan, who held it over Matt. As Matt's terrible injuries were revealed Regina paled and then covered her face with

340

her hands.

Alan had brought a buckboard along, knowing it might be needed. To Dan, he now said briskly, while placing the lantern on the ground, "Let's get some blankets, then carry Matt to the buckboard and take him into town. I'll send a man ahead to tell the doctor to expect us."

They hurried away, leaving Regina kneeling beside Matt while Antonio stood by. Noticing that Regina was shaking, Antonio stepped to her side and, grasping her trembling shoulders, drew her into his arms. He studied the discoloration and swelling that grotesquely distorted Matt's features. Grimacing, he tightened his hold on Regina.

"Dear God," Regina said in a low voice, "he's hurt so badly that I'm afraid he might never recover." Moving so that she could peer up into Antonio's sympathetic eyes, she voiced the thought that terrified her. "He's been beaten so severely about the head and face that he . . . he could be permanently injured."

Antonio knew what she was thinking. He wished he could be optimistic and assure her that Matt would make a complete recovery, but he knew Matt might well have suffered brain damage. It was apparent that Selman had struck Matt about the head many times.

Regina waited a moment, hoping he would convince her that her fear was unjustified, but seeing her own suspicion mirrored in Antonio's eyes, Regina panicked. "No! . . . Oh God no! I would rather see Matt dead than see him completely helpless!"

Her terror uncontrollable, Regina clutched Antonio's arms and rambled insensibly. Her piercing cries began to bring Matt out of his unconscious state, but neither Regina nor Antonio were aware of the change in him.

Pleading incoherently, Regina sobbed, "If his brain is damaged then I . . . I wish Matt had died!"

341

At that moment, Matt's eyes opened and his blurry vision took in Regina clinging to Antonio. As his gaze focused, he picked up Regina's last words. "I wish Matt had died!" Matt's eyes closed and he plunged back into unconsciousness, but his wife's words were etched across his heart and imprinted in his mind.

"Regina," Antonio said strongly, "you don't mean that."

In an anguished voice, she replied, "Do you have any idea what it will do to Matt if he is an invalid?"

Antonio made an attempt to calm Regina, but she pulled away from him and knelt beside her husband. As tears streamed from her eyes, she took one of Matt's hands into hers, and holding it against her wet cheek, she pleaded, "Oh, please . . . please God, let him get well! I love you, Matt! . . . I love you so!"

Alan Garrett kept a supportive arm about Regina's shoulders as they climbed the stairs, then walked down the corridor toward his suite. They had just come from Dr. Carter's home, where they had left Matt in the doctor's care. Dr. Carter's diagnosis had not been encouraging. Matt was suffering from a concussion, multiple bruises and abrasions, two cracked ribs and congested lungs which, according to the doctor, might develop into pneumonia.

When they reached the door to his suite, Alan unlocked it and stepped aside so Regina could precede him. Then he followed her inside, and handing Regina her overnight bag, which he had been carrying, he told her, "The hotel has a bath at the end of the hall if you want to bathe."

Regina planned to freshen up, change her clothes, and then return to Matt's side. She was physically and emotionally exhausted, and sighing with fatigue, she murmured, "A bath sounds wonderful. I feel as though I could relax in a tub of hot water for hours, but I'll wash quickly because I want to hurry back to Matt."

"Mrs. Brolin," Alan said gently, "at the moment there's nothing you can do for Matt, so why don't you enjoy a leisurely bath and then let me take you to dinner."

"Thank you for the invitation, Mr. Garrett, but I'm terribly anxious to return to my husband. If he should regain consciousness, I want to be with him."

"Of course, my dear. I understand," he replied.

Then as a firm knock sounded on the door, Alan opened it and said, "Come in." When Sheriff Davis strode into the room, Alan asked, "Did you arrest Robert Selman?"

The sheriff, who was a middle-aged, rugged man, removed his hat, and toying with its weather-worn brim, he mumbled, "I'm sorry, Mr. Garrett, but Selman got away."

"What do you mean, he got away?" Alan exclaimed.

"Somehow he must've been warned, and when I arrived at his home, he was already gone."

"Damn!" Alan cursed.

Hastily, Sheriff Davis assured him, "He'll show up again, and when he does, I'll put him behind bars." He looked apologetically at Regina as he continued. "I'm sorry, Mrs. Brolin. By the way, ma'am, how is your husband?"

Regina was too upset to reply. Knowing that Robert Selman was free frightened her. She was sure that insane man wouldn't rest until he saw Matt dead.

Answering for Regina, Alan told the sheriff, "Mr. Brolin's condition is quite grave."

Sheriff Davis expressed his hope for Matt's full recovery, then making his excuses, he left. The moment the door closed behind him, Regina remarked decisively, "I'm taking Matt home where he'll be safe. Robert Selman has too many connections in Santa Fe, and I'm afraid he'll find a way to get to him."

"But Matt's too ill to travel," Alan objected.

Dismissing Alan's objection, Regina said hastily, "We'll leave early in the morning and travel straight through. I'll tell Dan to buy a wagon with a canvas top so Matt can be shielded from the sun, and as soon as I get Matt home, Dr. Henderson can take care of him." She thought of Selman's demented vindictiveness. "Tonight we'll keep Matt closely guarded, and we'll leave first thing in the morning."

Chapter Thirty

The Black Diamond was quiet. All the ranch hands were on the range rounding up the last of the cattle for the drive to Abilene, and Hannah had taken María into town to do some shopping. Regina was just tucking Cort into bed for a nap. The child was sleepy and put up no resistance. He cuddled his kitten close to his side as he snuggled into his pillow. Smiling tenderly, Regina leaned over and kissed the boy's forehead. Then she gently rubbed the gray kitten behind its ears. Mrs. Donaldson, who owned the general store in town, had given Cort the furry little creature while Regina was in Santa Fe.

Leaving Cort's door ajar, Regina moved down the hallway toward her own bedroom. As she entered it quietly, Ted Lucas was sitting near the bed on which Matt was sleeping. "Thank you for staying with Matt while I put Cort to bed for his nap."

Rising, Ted answered softly, "It was no trouble, ma'am." With a heavy sigh, he added, "He doesn't seem to be getting any better, does he?"

"Well, he's only been home a couple of days, and Dr. Henderson said he's doing as well as can be expected." Although Regina's tone was light, she was very worried. Matt awakened periodically, remaining conscious only long enough to be fed some warm broth before drifting back to sleep. During these wakeful moments, Regina had tried desperately to encourage Matt to stay awake and talk to her, but her attempts had proved futile. His failure to remain conscious for more than a few moments disturbed Regina despite Dr. Henderson's attempt to calm her anxieties by assuring her that Matt's body needed a great deal of rest.

Moving toward the door, Ted said in a lowered voice, "I think I'll ride out and meet Hannah. She and María should be on their way back by now."

As Ted stepped onto the porch, Antonio was tying his horse to the hitching rail. "How is Señor Brolin?" he asked.

"He's about the same." Ted replied. Then, hesitantly, he said, "Mr. Ramírez, why don't you see if you can talk Miss Regina into taking a walk? She's been closed up in that bedroom for two straight days. A little fresh air would do her a world of good."

"I will try," Antonio promised. He climbed the porch steps in two long strides and entered the house. Hurrying to Regina's bedroom, he knocked lightly.

When she opened the door, Regina smiled, "Antonio, what a pleasant surprise."

"Is Matt asleep?" he asked.

"Yes," she answeered.

"Señor Lucas told me that you have been cooped up in this room since we brought Matt home. It is a beautiful day, and I thought you might enjoy taking a walk with me."

"I don't want to leave Matt," Regina told him.

"But, *señora,* he is asleep and probably will not wake up for some time. We will not be gone very long."

"Well," she murmured hesitantly, "I could use some fresh air." She glanced at Matt. "He's sleeping very soundly, so I suppose it will be all right." Turning to face Antonio, she said, "Very well, I'll take a walk with you."

The kitten, becoming uncomfortable in Cort's vise-like grip, twisted its tiny body until it freed itself. Meowing, it stepped lithely across the boy and leaped to the floor. Waking, Cort tried to grab his pet, but he was too slow and the tiny cat ran quickly out of the room. Bounding from the bed, the child pursued the fleeing kitten, but the cat, a gray streak, disappeared down the hallway, moving with lightning speed. Racing into the kitchen, it spied an open window and jumped through.

Cort saw the cat leap through the window, and he darted onto the back porch, calling the kitten by name. "Here Whiskers! . . . Come back, Whiskers!"

Scooting across the yard, the kitten headed toward the corral that was packed with the cattle to be taken to Abilene. The penned animals mooed loudly as the small cat ran underneath the bottom plank, scurrying past their deadly hoofs.

Fearing for his kitten's safety, Cort ran to the corral. "Come here, Whiskers!" he pleaded.

Blackie had been resting on the front porch, but when he heard Cort's cries, he leaped to his feet and bounded to the corral.

Bending over, the child squeezed under the bottom plank and entered the perilous enclosure. The cattle moved about nervously as they eyed the little boy in their midst.

Venturing farther, Cort called again, "Here Whiskers! . . . Here kitty!"

The cattle began nudging against one another, their bodies drawing closer and closer to the child. Mooing,

347

they shifted their massive bodies, forming a circle around Cort.

Frightened, the boy cried, "Go away! Go away!"

As the playful kitten scooted back under the bottom plank to safety, Blackie cleared the fence in one, graceful leap. Running to Cort's side, he barked at the cattle, causing them to scatter, and positioning himself in front of the child, he growled deeply and lunged at any animal that attempted to approach them. The cattle continued to circle the boy and the dog, making escape impossible. Feeling threatened, the large animals instinctively would have charged the intruders, but the dog kept them at bay.

Becoming terrified, Cort yelled, "Mama, help me! . . . Mama!"

Regina and Antonio had strolled quite a distance from the house and were too far away to hear Cort's cry for help, but the boy's cries carried into the bedroom where Matt lay sleeping. Cort's screams roused Matt from his deep slumber, and his eyes flew open. As Cort's terrifying cry again rang through the quiet room—"Mama! . . . Mama, help me!"—Matt bolted straight up.

Throwing off the covers, Matt leaped to his feet. Then dizziness overtook him, and he grabbed at the bedside table to keep from falling. Glancing about, he spotted a pair of trousers draped across a chair in the corner, and on unsteady legs he went to the chair. He managed to pull the trousers on over his nightshirt; then, reeling weakly, he made his way out of the room and along the hallway. Halfway down it, he leaned tiredly against the wall. Although his cracked ribs were taped, a sharp pain shot through him, and bending over he clutched his chest.

Again Cort's cries pierced the silence. "Mama! . . . Mama!"

Straightening his aching body, Matt forced his weak legs to carry him down the hallway and outside. The urgent need to help his son drove him across the yard to the corral.

Cort's cries had grown more desperate, and as they headed back in the direction of the house, Regina and Antonio suddenly heard Cort. Immediately, they both began to run, but Regina wasn't able to keep up with Antonio's long strides.

Unlocking the gate, Matt made his way into the crowded corral. Desperation gave him strength and he pushed aside the cattle. Rushing to Cort, he lifted the boy into his arms, and shoving the animals out of their path, he carried his son out of the corral.

Now that the danger was past, Cort's fear had left him. He looked closely at Matt. He knew his father was sick, but he hadn't been allowed to see him. The unexpected sight of Matt's bruised and battered face was a shock to him.

"Papa!" he cried. "Are you hurt real bad?"

Tears came to Matt's eyes as he studied his son. "My God," he whispered, "I haven't been dreaming. I'm really home."

Cort's little face puckered into a baffled frown. Why would his Papa think he had been dreaming?

Nearing the corral, Antonio saw Matt with Cort, and realizing the boy was safe, he waited for Regina to catch up to him. By the time she did, she was out of breath and panting heavily. She looked toward the corral, and she could hardly believe what she was seeing. Placing a hand over her pounding heart, she gasped, "Matt!"

Happy for Regina, Antonio smiled broadly, "It seems, *señora,* that Matt will make a full recovery."

Regina's run had tired her considerably, so Antonio slipped his arm about her waist for support as they headed toward Matt and Cort.

Becoming aware of his mother's approach, Cort began to squirm in his father's arms, and carefully, Matt placed the child on his feet.

Running to Regina, Cort said excitedly, "I couldn't get out of the corral, but Papa came and got me!"

The sight of Regina with Antonio hit Matt hard. The picture of his wife clinging to Antonio in the cave flashed vividly before him, and Regina's words thundered in his mind. "I wish Matt had died! . . . I wish Matt had died!"

Antonio released his supportive hold on Regina, and with tears of joy streaming down her cheeks, she hastened past her son to Matt's side. She flung her arms about him, holding tightly. "Oh Matt! . . . Matt!" she sobbed happily.

When Regina realized that Matt was not returning her embrace, she stepped back and looked up into his eyes. Their cold expression startled her. "Matt?" she gasped feebly.

A dizzy spell came over Matt, causing his weakened body to sway unsteadily. He would have fallen had Antonio not moved swiftly to his side. Holding on to Matt, Antonio told Regina, "We'd better get him to the house."

Violent rage suddenly surged through Matt, giving him renewed strength. Breaking free of Antonio's grip, he muttered threateningly, "Ramírez, keep your damned hands off me!"

Regina was astounded. "Matt, he's only trying to help you!"

Gingerly, Regina reached out to touch her husband, but avoiding her, Matt turned away and headed toward the house.

"Antonio, help him!" Regina cried. "He's too weak to make it back by himself!"

Antonio agreed, and he was about to go after Matt when Ted Lucas returned with Hannah and María. Ted caught sight of Matt and hastily dismounted. Hurrying to Matt's side, he assisted him into the house.

Stunned by Matt's behavior, Regina remained standing by the corral. Why had Matt spoken so harshly to Antonio when Antonio had only been trying to help him? And, dear God, why had Matt treated her so coldly? Why must he always be so filled with bitterness?

"Regina?" Antonio called softly, stepping over to stand at her side. "Are you all right?"

Voicing her emotions, she murmured depressingly, "Matt has broken my heart time and time again, but this time is the worst. I'm afraid that someday he's going to hurt me so deeply that my heart won't mend."

Antonio was still in love with Regina, and her unhappiness touched him acutely. "Regina, I think it would be best if I do not come back here, if we do not see each other again."

"But why?" she questioned.

"I could see in Matt's eyes that he wanted to knock the hell out of me. Only his illness prevented him from doing so."

"I don't understand," Regina uttered.

"Matt is very jealous of you and does not want us to be friends."

"Jealous?" Regina scowled. "First you have to love someone before you can be jealous. Matt doesn't love me. If he did, he couldn't hurt me the way he does."

Studying her tenderly, Antonio replied, "I do not understand how he cannot love you. I should think any man would find it very hard not to fall hopelessly in love with you."

"Apparently, Matt is one man who finds it very easy not to love me," Regina replied, her tone edged

351

with agitation.

"I had best leave," Antonio remarked. "But if you need me, you know where to find me."

"I thank you for your kindness," Regina said sincerely.

Antonio was walking away, Cort went to Regina and tugged at her skirt. "Mama?" he said.

"Yes?" Regina glanced down at the boy.

"I can't find Whiskers."

"If he doesn't show up in a little while, I'll ask Ted to look for him."

The words had scarcely passed Regina's lips when Blackie came trotting toward them, holding the mewing kitten in his mouth by the scruff of its neck. He dropped Whiskers at Cort's feet, and picking up his pet the boy held it close.

"Blackie was in the corral with me and kept the cattle from gettin' me 'til Papa came."

Calling the dog to her side, Regina petted his large head, murmuring, "You're a good dog, Blackie."

Peering up at Regina, Cort asked, "Mama, will Papa's face get well?"

"Yes, in a few days he'll be completely healed."

"Can we go see him?"

"You go, darling. I think I'll just stay here for a few minutes longer."

"Don't you want to see Papa?" he asked.

"Yes, of course I want to see him," she replied, silently adding, but I don't think he wants to see me.

The door to the bedroom was open, and as Regina entered, María and Cort were talking to Matt. He was sitting up in bed, his back against the headboard. She could tell that Matt was physically drained, and although he was trying to conceal his discomfort,

352

Regina detected a look of pain on his face.

"Children," she began, "I think you should leave now so that your father can rest."

María and Cort kissed Matt, and telling him they'd visit later, they left the room.

Alone with Matt, Regina began to feel uneasy. She longed desperately to tell him how much she loved him and how thankful she was that he was alive and well. But believing he would spurn her display of affection, she merely walked to the foot of the bed and asked, "Is there anything I can get you? A bowl of broth, perhaps?"

"How did you find me?" he asked, dismissing her offer.

"Actually it was José who found you. He hid on Selman's property and then followed Selman to the cave. When Dan, the others, and I arrived in Santa Fe, Mr. Garrett was already aware of where you were being held captive."

"I take it that Alan notified you when I didn't show up at his ranch?"

"He sent me a telegram. I wasn't sure what I should do. It was Antonio who decided that we should go to Santa Fe and join Mr. Garrett in an attempt to find you."

"Are you saying I owe my life to Ramírez?" Matt asked flatly, his expression hard. How long did she plan to continue her deceitfulness? He knew damned well that she and Antonio hadn't wanted him to live. He had been a witness to their scene inside the cave. "I wish Matt had died!" Her words pounded in Matt's mind and ripped mercilessly at his heart.

"Yes, I suppose you owe your life to Antonio," Regina murmured. "And to José and Mr. Garrett."

"Where is Dan?" Matt abruptly chaged the subject.

"In town, but he was here last night. Before he left he

353

said he'd stop by late this afternoon."

"Good," Matt stated. "I need to talk to him."

"You need to talk to Dan?" Regina was curious.

"Susan Chandler didn't commit suicide," Matt said evenly. "Selman had her killed."

Shocked, Regina hurried to the side of the bed, and pulling up a chair, she sat down. "Why in the world did Selman have Susan killed?" she gasped out.

Matt explained why Susan had visited Selman, and he told her how he'd learned that Selman had had the young woman murdered.

Regina was shocked. "Good Lord! I never dreamed Susan would do anything like that."

"Well, I'm sure Dan will be relieved to learn that Susan didn't commit suicide because of him. By the way, what happened to Selman?"

"Robert Selman escaped," Regina replied regretfully.

Matt was furious. "That rotten son of a bitch!" Suddenly, he felt extremely fatigued, and sighing wearily, he said, "I think I'll try to sleep for a while."

"Matt," Regina began tentatively, "I must talk to you."

"About what?" he asked, looking at her suspiciously.

"About us," she replied firmly.

"I'm too tired for talking," he muttered, moving away from the headboard and lowering himself onto the bed.

Standing, Regina agreed. "Very well, Matt. But sooner or later, I insist that we have a serious discussion."

"Later," he mumbled rolling onto his side and turning his back toward her.

Regina loved Matt, but his cruelty so enraged her that she hissed, "Matt, you're an insensitive, cold-hearted bastard!"

"I'll admit to being a bastard," he droned. "But insensitive and cold-hearted? People who live in glass houses shouldn't throw stones."

For a moment, Regina glared at his turned back; then, whirling sharply, she headed for the door.

"Regina?" he called.

Pausing, she asked short-temperedly, "What do you want?"

"Since I am using your bed, where are you sleeping?"

She started to tell him that she hadn't been sleeping anywhere, unless you could call dozing in the chair next to his bed sleeping, but she wasn't about to give him the satisfaction of knowing she hadn't wanted to leave his bedside. She lied. "I've been using the guest room."

"Tell Hannah to prepare the guest room for me so that you can have your bedroom to yourself."

"I thought you preferred the study!" Regina retorted resentfully.

"I do," he concurred. "But considering my physical condition, I'm sure I'll find the bed in the guest room more comfortable than the study sofa."

Covering her hurt, Regina declared, "I don't give a damn where you sleep, Matt Brolin, so long as it's never in the same bed with me!" She darted into the hall and slammed the door behind her.

Chapter Thirty-one

When Regina entered her brother's restaurant, he was sitting at a table by the front window waiting for her. As his sister crossed the room, Dan watched her appreciatively. Regina's blond tresses were arranged in a flattering style—her golden curls were swept back from her face and held in place by two dainty combs—and her pink gown suited her well. It was a simple garment with a heart-shaped bodice and short bouffant sleeves, and white satin ribbon adorned the waistline.

Standing, Dan held out her chair, and when they were both seated, he inquired, "How is Matt?"

"Dr. Henderson saw him this morning and he said Matt is fully recovered."

"I'm amazed," Dan declared. "Matt's only been home a month. Considering his critical condition, I thought it would take a lot longer for him to get well."

Wishing to turn their conversation away from Matt, Regina said brightly, "I'm famished. What shall we have for lunch?"

Dan reached across the table, and taking her hand in his, he asked softly, "What's wrong, Gina?"

"Nothing." she replied, feigning a cheerful smile.

He gently squeezed her hand; then, releasing his

hold, he persisted, "Honey, you've never been able to keep your feelings hidden from me. Something is wrong and I want you to tell me what it is."

"Honestly, Dan," Regina mumbled evasively, "everything is fine."

He studied her speculatively and decided that he didn't believe her. Intending to question her later, he reached into his shirt pocket and withdrew an envelope. Handing it to Regina, he explained, "It's a letter from Julie. She sent it to me because she knows a week often passes before someone from the Black Diamond checks at the post office."

Taking the envelope, Regina asked urgently, "She didn't send bad news, did she?"

Dan grinned eagerly, and seeing him smile meant a great deal to Regina. Learning he hadn't driven Susan to commit suicide had lifted a heavy burden from his shoulders. "No, she didn't send bad news," he said enthusiastically. "Quite the contrary. She and Miguel are coming for a visit."

"How wonderful!" Regina's happiness showed on her face. She looked forward to seeing her sister.

"They'll be here a week from Wednesday," Dan revealed.

Regina read Julie's lengthy letter, while Dan placed their order for lunch. When Regina had finished, she folded the massive letter and returned it to the envelope, her face suddenly sad.

"Julie sounds very happy," she said.

"Yes, she does," Dan agreed, watching her closely.

"Miguel loves Julie very much." Regina sighed, wishing her marriage was as happy as her sister's.

Sensing her unhappiness, Dan insisted tenderly, "Gina, why are you so troubled? Is there something wrong with Matt?"

Dan was startled to see a look of bitterness cross

357

Regina's lovely face as she answered, "There's nothing wrong with Matt. He's just as stubborn and as unfeeling as he ever was!"

"So you and Matt are having problems," he surmised. "Surely you two can solve whatever it is."

"There is no solution!" Regina declared testily. She hadn't intended to blurt out her troubles, but against her own volition, her heartache flowed forth, "Matt doesn't love me, and I don't think he ever did. He showed me kindness when I was pregnant simply because of my condition. Then when we lost the twins, he felt so sorry for me that he mistook pity for love. But now he has come to realize that he doesn't care for me, and he is again bitter because he gave up his ranch in Wyoming. I'm sure he'd leave me if it weren't for María and Cort." Distress visible in her eyes, Regina confessed disconsolately, "Sometimes, I think he despises me!"

"I'm sure Matt doesn't feel that way," Dan said soothingly.

"No!" she moaned wretchedly. "You're wrong, Dan! He does hate me!"

"Gina," he began caringly, "when did Matt start behaving this way? Was he like this before leaving to visit Alan Garrett?"

"Yes," she said, sighing heavily. "I thought he was happy living with me, then, with no warning, he changed."

"If his changing didn't come about gradually, I'd guess something happened to cause Matt to turn against you."

"But what?" Regina asked.

He shrugged. "I suggest that you confront Matt and demand that he explain himself."

"Do you think I haven't tried to do that?" she cried desperately. "Time and time again, I pleaded with him to confide in me! But he's determined to keep his feelings to himself!"

"When was the last time you tried to get him to talk about it?"

"The day he found Cort trapped in the corral," Regina replied. Dan had, of course, been told about Matt's rescue of the child. "He treated me very cruelly that day and since then I have not given him the opportunity to hurt me again. During his convalescence, I never visited him unless I had the children with me. I knew he wouldn't mistreat me when María and Cort were present."

"Has he physically abused you?" Dan demanded, his anger rising.

"No," she said quickly. "Matt would never strike me. But the pain he inflicts goes much deeper than a physical one. He is tearing my heart to pieces."

"Gina," Dan said pressingly, "you must stop avoiding Matt. The longer you two postpone talking seriously, the more difficult it will become."

"I suppose you're right," she conceded hesitantly. "I'll talk to him tonight."

Encouragingly, he murmured, "Honey, I'm sure Matt still loves you and you two will solve your problems."

Regina nodded, but she didn't agree with Dan. She didn't believe that her husband loved her, nor did she think their problems could be solved. She was sure Matt's bitterness would only be cured when she set him free, and although it would break her heart, she was determined to let him go. Tonight, when she talked to him, she'd tell him that she wanted him to leave, and she would do so calmly so he couldn't see how deeply she was hurting.

*   *   *

Regina had taken a leisurely bath, and she was now sitting at her dressing table brushing her hair. She intended to dress, then find Matt and let him know that he was free to leave. Everything considered, she believed this to be the best alternative, but the thought of telling him to go was so depressing that she couldn't bring herself to actually confront Matt.

"But I must tell him!" she said to herself resolutely. "I can't go on living in the same house with Matt, not the way things are between us." The Lucases and María were well aware that Matt and Regina were not on good terms, and Regina knew they were worried, and uncomfortable about the situation. Only Cort was too young to understand what was taking place.

The door to Regina's bedroom opened suddenly, and whirling about, she was astonished to see Matt enter. Closing the door behind him, he locked it, and crossed the room to pause beside the vanity table. Regina was wearing a white chiffon dressing gown, and as Matt's dark eyes seemed to penetrate the sheer material, he asked casually, "Did you have lunch with Dan?"

His piercing gaze made Regina restless, and fidgeting nervously, she questioned him in return. "How did you know I was seeing Dan?"

"María told me. I asked her where you were because I had wanted to talk to you."

Hesitantly, Regina stated, "I also want to talk to you."

"Ladies first, Mrs. Brolin," he said, his tone mocking. Although Matt had every intention of telling Regina that he knew about her dalliance with Antonio, he decided to wait and hear what she had to say.

"Matt," she began, her heart pulsating irregularly, "I want you to know that I have decided to set you free."

"Free?" he repeated quirking an eyebrow. "You

talk as though I were your slave."

"You know what I mean." Regina was piqued. "You're free to leave our marriage."

"Is that what you want?" he asked, his outward calmness concealing inner rage.

"Yes!" she managed to get out, knowing full well it was the last thing in the world she truly wanted.

Regina waited intently for his response, but he didn't seem to be in any hurry to offer a comment. When he finally spoke, his voice startled her, "Do you plan to divorce me?"

Deciding to carry her decision through to the painful end, she answered, "Yes, of course." Isn't that what you want? she felt like screaming. Haven't you been hoping I would sever the bonds that tie you to me?

"I'll think about it," he remarked flatly. He didn't know why her revelation had taken him by surprise. She couldn't very well marry Antonio without first acquiring a divorce.

"You'll think about what?" Regina was confused.

"Leaving," he mumbled. Continuing, he explained, "I have an obligation to María and Cort, and before I can make a final decision, they must be considered. I'm sure María would prefer to stay here with you, but I suppose I could always take Cort with me."

Regina bounded to her feet, and her green eyes darted angry sparks. "I won't let you take Cort away from me!"

"You won't let *me?*" he countered. "If I decide to take my son, you will have no say in the matter!"

"But he's my son too!" Regina pleaded.

"He belongs to me!" Matt argued furiously. "He's the only person in this whole damned world who ever belonged to me!"

"I'll fight you for him!" Regina threatened. "The only way you'll take Cort is over my dead body!"

361

"That can be arranged!" Matt retorted, his tone fierce. Why should he give his son to Antonio? By God, Regina and her lover didn't deserve Cort!

Her temper now out of control, Regina flew at Matt, trying vainly to scratch his face and draw his blood. She longed to hurt him so that she wouldn't be the only one suffering.

Capturing her wrists, he twisted her arms behind her back, gripping her so tightly that she grimaced. Roughly, he jerked her against him until the soft contours of her body were flush with his muscular form.

"You damned little wildcat!" he grumbled. Regina's struggles had disheveled her hair, causing its long tresses to fall seductively about her flushed face. Matt's eyes dropped to her perfectly formed breasts, revealed by her half open dressing gown. Then, slowly, his gaze moved upward and he looked deeply into Regina's eyes. "Mrs. Brolin," he mumbled cynically, "we are not yet divorced, so I think I shall demand my husbandly rights."

Her better judgment warned her not to surrender, for she knew he would only use her to satisfy his lust, then cast her aside.

"Leave me alone!" she demanded.

Still holding her trapped wrists behind her back, he grasped them with one strong hand in order to use the other one to press her thighs against his hard arousal. "Can't you feel how badly I need a woman?" he taunted.

"Then go into town and relieve your sexual urge with Dolly. I'm sure she'd be only too happy to accommodate you."

"But she isn't the woman who is in my arms; you are. So I'll take you instead," he replied smoothly. Regina tried to protest, but his mouth was suddenly on hers, his lips taking hers almost brutally.

Moving swiftly, he lifted her into his arms and carried her to the bed, dropping her on it unceremoniously. Her dressing gown had come untied, and as she landed on top of the soft mattress, the garment parted exposing her bared curves to Matt's scrutiny. Admiring her flawless beauty, he murmured in a dangerously low tone, "As long as you are my wife, I will help myself to your seductive body whenever I please."

"It will be against my will!" Regina swore, intending to sit upright and shield herself with the dressing gown's protective folds. But before she could stir, Matt pounced on her, lithe as a panther capturing his prey. Straddling her and emprisoning her thighs between his tightly muscled legs, he placed his hands on her shoulders and pinned her to the bed. As he stared darkly into her face, he said quietly, "Whether or not you are willing is unimportant. You are still mine to do with as I see fit."

His cold insolence enraged Regina and she shouted, "I'm not yours! I'll never be yours! I hate you, Matt Brolin!" At the moment, she did feel that she hated him, so she continued to berate him. "Do you hear me, Matt? I detest you! You're a vile, inconsiderate, selfish, black-hearted devil!"

"And you, madam, are no saint," Matt snarled. Releasing his pressure on her shoulders, he grabbed her wrists and pinned her arms over her head with one hand. Then he stretched out his long frame at Regina's side, and his mouth crushed hers while his free hand cupped one of her breasts. Kissing her demandingly, his fingers kneaded her velvety flesh, his thumb working back and forth across her taut nipple.

Finally freeing his mouth from hers, he moved his hand downward to the softness between her delicate thighs. He stared intensely into her face as he fondled her where he knew her passion was centered, and a

363

triumphant smile curled his sensual lips when he felt Regina's response. "You are moist, my seductive wild-cat, and you want me. Don't you?"

"No!" Regina lied. She wished frantically that her body hadn't betrayed her.

"You lying little witch!" he growled. Bending his head, he once again kissed her aggressively while he continued to stimulate her.

Regina had no control over the rush of desire that surged through her, and when she began moving pro-vocatively against him, Matt freed her hands. Rising from the bed, he quickly discarded his clothes, and as he returned to his wife's embrace, Regina drew him to her. How is it possible to love him and hate him at the same time? she wondered fretfully.

Parting her legs with his knee, Matt entered her, and as he filled her, Regina trembled with intense longing. He drove into her powerfully, and his unleashed passion further aroused Regina. Clinging to him, she eagerly met his hard thrusting until he shuddered and collapsed on top of her.

His head was nestled against her neck, and Regina absently brushed her fingers through his dark, wavy hair. Matt found her touch soothing until thoughts of Regina and Antonio entered his mind. Does she run her fingers through his hair after they've made love? he asked himself bitterly.

Abruptly, he rose and began to put on his clothes. His brusqueness jolted Regina from her dreamlike state. Sitting up, she drew her dressing gown about her and tied the sash.

"What was it that you wanted to talk to me about?" she asked, remembering that he hadn't yet told her.

He finished dressing, then said curtly, "It doesn't matter."

"Why doesn't it matter?" she coaxed.

"I found out all I needed to know when you said you wanted a divorce," Matt answered evenly.

"Isn't that what you want?" Regina asked hastily. Could she have been mistaken? DIdn't Matt want his freedom?

"Well, it's less violent than what I had in mind," he drawled, then moved casually toward the door.

"Matt," Regina said, causing him to pause and turn back to face her. "Dan and I received a letter from Julie. She and Miguel will be here next Wednesday. They are coming for a visit."

"It'll be nice to see Miguel again," he commented.

"They will need the guest room," she pointed out.

"Which means I will have to vacate it," Matt responded dryly. "If my memory is correct, not very long ago you told me you didn't care where I slept so long as it wasn't with you. I guess that leaves me no choice but to move into the study."

"You can move into this bedroom," she said, feigning indifference, although she hoped desperately that he would.

Her suggestion surprised Matt. For a moment, he was caught off guard, but then the words Regina had spoken inside the cave flashed into his mind. "I wish Matt had died! . . . I wish Matt had died!"

Eying her severely, he replied firmly, "I prefer the study to your bedroom!" Afraid that he might be tempted to break her beautiful neck if he stayed one moment longer, Matt stormed out of the room.

Chapter Thirty-two

The moment Miguel and Julie arrived, Regina's spirits lifted. She had missed her sister, and Miguel was so vibrant and jovial that she couldn't help but respond to his cheerful presence.

Accompanied by an impressive escort of twenty vaqueros, Miguel and Julie had arrived at the Black Diamond as dusk was falling over the landscape. Shortly after warm greetings and embraces were exchanged, Hannah had insisted that everyone sit down at the dining-room table and eat the delicious meal she had prepared.

Now, after dinner, as Miguel and Matt were enjoying brandy and cigars, Julie asked Regina if they could talk privately. Complying, Regina suggested that they go to the study.

The moment the entered the room, Julie drew Regina into her arms and hugged her eagerly. "Oh, Regina," she breathed, "I have such marvelous news!"

"What is it?" Regina asked, stepping back and peering closely at her sister. Julie had never looked more beautiful. Her dark eyes were sparkling with vitality and her cheeks were rosy. She no longer wore her hair in a confining bun, but a lace mantilla now held her long tresses back from her face, allowing them to cascade radiantly past her shoulders to her tiny waist. Julie's brightly colored dress was a complete contrast to the dull, matronly gowns she had worn during her years with Mace.

Her voice ringing with happiness, Julie announced, "Regina, I'm going to have a baby!"

"Oh, Julie!" Regina exclaimed ecstatically. She knew how desperately Julie had longed for a child. "Are you sure?"

"Yes, I'm quite sure," Julie answered. "My time of the month is weeks overdue and I've been feeling nauseated."

"Does Miguel know?" Regina asked.

"No. I haven't told him yet. Only Anna knows."

"Anna?" Regina repeated vaguely before she recalled that Julie had written her about the elderly servant. "But why haven't you told Miguel?"

"Because I wanted to come home for a visit, and I was afraid if Miguel knew about the baby, he'd have canceled our trip. I had to practically beg Anna not to tell him. She didn't want me to travel. She said the journey might be too strenuous for my condition."

"She might be right," Regina remarked, her brow furrowed with worry.

"Nonsense!" Julie declared. "I have never felt better in my life! Anna thinks I should be coddled and waited on hand and foot as though I were sickly. My goodness, I'm not ill; I'm pregnant!"

Laughing gaily, Regina predicted, "When Miguel finds out about the baby, you may as well prepare yourself for being pampered. He'll probably be worse than Anna. And knowing that husband of yours, he'll have something to say when he learns you kept this from him so he wouldn't cancel your trip."

Picturing the upcoming scene with Miguel, Julie

367

said, "First he'll chasten me as though I were a naughty child; then he'll start worrying and I will have to convince him that I'm not a fragile doll but a strong and healthy woman."

"He has you on a pedestal, doesn't he?" Regina realized that she was envious of her sister.

"Yes, I suppose he does," Julie murmured dreamily. "I have never had a man love me the way Miguel does. He makes me feel special and beautiful."

"You are special and beautiful," Regina told her.

Clasping Regina's hands, Julie said intensely, "You can't possibly understand why I am amazed that Miguel can love me so deeply because you've never known what it's like to be unloved by a man. You had all of Papa's love. And Dan? Well, we both know that you've always been his favorite. Then, while I was trapped in a loveless marriage, you had a multitude of beaus proposing matrimony." Squeezing her sister's hands affectionately, she continued, "Now you have Matt, and he probably worships the ground you walk on."

Julie's last remark made Regina feel like laughing sarcastically, but she feared her laughter would soon turn into hysterical sobs.

Releasing Regina's hands, Julie said jubilantly, "I will tell Miguel about the baby tonight after we have retired." Beside herself with happiness, Julie's steps were buoyant as she walked toward the sofa. "Miguel will be so surprised and he . . ." Suddenly her words faltered, and whirling back to face Regina, she asked cautiously, "Why are there blankets and a pillow on the couch?" Julie remembered the last time bedclothes were kept in the study. That had been when Regina and Matt were first married. Refusing to sleep with each other, they had retired to separate rooms.

Regina sighed. "I knew there was no way that Matt

and I could keep this from you and Miguel. You were bound to find out sooner or later."

"Find out what?" Julie asked urgently.

"Matt and I are no longer sharing the same bed," Regina muttered.

"Why?" her sister cried.

"Please, Julie! I don't want to discuss my marriage, and I most definitely don't want to discuss Matt!"

Regina's bitterness was so apparent that Julie said anxiously, "It might help if you were to confide in me."

"Talking won't help," Regina stated firmly. "Matt and I are considering divorce."

"Surely you don't want to end your marriage!" Julie declared incredulously.

"It's not a question of what I want," her sister remarked sullenly. "Matt isn't in love with me and . . . and I'm not even sure I still love him."

"You'll never make me believe that you and Matt aren't in love," Julie argued.

"Well, maybe you'll believe it when Matt moves away and I legally end this marriage which was a mistake from the very beginning. In case you have forgotten, Matt only married me because I was pregnant. He didn't love me then, and he doesn't love me now!"

Tired from their long day of traveling, Miguel and Julie said their good-nights early and retired to the guest room. When he saw three pieces of luggage on the floor, Miguel asked, "Which one do you need opened?"

Julie pointed to the reticule, and lifting it, Miguel placed it on the bed. "Miguel," she began a little apprehensively, "I must talk to you."

Looking at his wife and taking note of her flushed face, he asked, "Is something wrong, Angel?"

Moving to his side, she murmured, "Darling, I have

369

good news." Then, sighing solemnly, she added, "But I also have some very disturbing news."

Watching her dubiously, he said, "Well, why don't you tell me the good news first."

Julie's brown eyes shone as she said happily, "Miguel, we are going to have a baby."

For a moment his face was expressionless, then a smile slowly appeared, starting at the corners of his mouth and spreading expansively. "A baby, Angel?" he gasped.

"Yes!" she assured him.

He swept her into his arms and hugged her vigorously, showering her face with light kisses, "Angel, you have made me very happy!" he declared, but suddenly he stepped back and looked at her reproachfully. "In your delicate condition you should not have made this trip. Why didn't you tell me about this before we left?"

"Because I knew you'd overreact and cancel our plans."

"We must return home immediately. We will leave in the morning," Miguel decided brusquely.

"I am perfectly healthy, and traveling is not going to make me lose our baby." Julie stated firmly. "I'm not as fragile as you think. Besides, we can't leave in the morning. Matt and Regina need us."

His brow furrowed with puzzlement. "What do you mean, they need us? You said you had disturbing news. Does it have to do with Matt and Regina?"

"Yes," she replied sadly. "They are considering divorce."

"What!" Miguel exclaimed, his deep voice resonant. "I do not believe this!"

Afraid that he might be overheard, Julie said hastily, "Darling, please keep your voice down."

Upset, Miguel bellowed, "I do not care if they hear me! I will talk to Matt, and if he does not listen, then I will knock some sense into him!"

Julie grasped his arm and attempted to calm him. "Why do you believe that Matt is to blame?"

"Because I have known him for years," Miguel replied. "He has always been moody and very stubborn. Many times, he has tried my patience."

"Darling, maybe you shouldn't interfere," Julie said hesitantly.

"You are probably right, Angel. But I cannot stand idly by and do nothing. Tomorrow I will ask Matt to ride into town with me. We will go to your brother's saloon and then we will talk."

Despondent, she murmured, "I don't think it will help matters."

"Why?" he asked.

"You didn't hear the hopelessness in Regina's voice when she spoke of Matt."

The next day, Miguel asked Matt to accompany him to the Trail Dust Saloon. During their ride to town, Miguel kept the conversation casual, deliberately conceding his knowledge that Matt and Regina were contemplating divorce.

When they entered the saloon, Miguel chose a corner table where they would have a certain amount of privacy. He then asked the bartender for two mugs of beer, and after the man had brought their order, he leaned leisurely back in his chair. Removing his wide sombrero, he placed it on the table, and his dark eyes perused Matt's as he asked quietly, "Why in the hell are you and Regina thinking about getting a divorce?"

Miguel's question didn't surprise Matt. He had

371

figured Regina would confide in her sister. Grinning humorlessly, Matt mumbled, "It's none of your business."

"You are right, *amigo,*" Miguel said lightly. "But I do not always mind my own affairs."

"Miguel," Matt said seriously, "stay out of this. It doesn't concern you or Julie."

"You are wrong," Ordaz argued. "We are family, so we are very worried about you and Regina."

"Damn it, Miguel!" Matt raged softly, losing his patience. "I don't intend to discuss my marriage with you."

"Regina is a good woman, and she loves you very much. Why must you hurt her?"

Snorting, Matt replied, "So you have already decided that everything is my fault."

"You carry a chip on your shoulder, *amigo.* It has always been there."

"Maybe," Matt admitted flatly. "But it helped me survive."

"*Sí,*" Miguel concurred. "When you were a boy fighting for survival, the chip on your shoulder, it kept you from getting hurt. You carried it as one would carry a protective shield. But you are no longer a boy. It is time to put away your bitterness. You must learn to accept the circumstances of your birth."

Matt smirked. "I can't believe you actually think my problems with Regina have anything to do with the fact that I'm a bastard by birth."

"Your problems have always stemmed from that fact," Miguel answered.

Matt laughed harshly. "Miguel, you don't even know what in the hell you're talking about. The trouble with my marriage has nothing whatsoever to do with my past." Crossing his arms on the table, Matt leaned forward and stared darkly into Miguel's eyes. "I'm

372

gonna tell you for the last time to butt out of my affairs!"

"For now, *amigo,* I will let the matter rest if you will answer one question for me," Miguel bargained.

"You're a persistent son of a bitch," Matt grumbled, but his gruffness couldn't completely conceal the fondness in his voice. His affection for Miguel was deeply rooted.

"Do you love Regina?" Miguel asked softly.

Matt's gaze met Miguel's without wavering. Did he love Regina? Was it possible for him to love a woman who had coldly wished him dead? "I can't answer that question."

"Why not?" Miguel pressed.

"Because I don't know the damned answer," Matt murmured dryly.

Shortly after Miguel and Matt rode into town, Regina decided to saddle Midnight. She was restless, and she hoped a vigorous gallop on the range might calm her fitful mood. Now, letting the stallion set his own swift pace, Regina found the ride refreshing. Midnight's strong legs stretched gracefully as he sped across the terrain, and the wind whipped about Regina, making her long hair stream out behind her.

Regina had ridden quite a way when she spotted four riders heading in her direction. They were too far off to be recognized, but taking for granted that they were ranch hands heading back to the Black Diamond, Regina didn't alter her course. As she drew steadily closer and the men became more distinct, she reached cautiously toward the rifle which was snug in its scabbard. But before she could remove the weapon, one of the advancing men drew his pistol and fired a warning shot. Quickly the riders approached and encircled her, and Regina gasped when she found herself staring into Robert Selman's ruthless eyes.

"Good afternoon, Mrs. Brolin," Selman said, his voice dripping with sarcastic cordiality.

"What do you want?" Regina demanded, watching him warily.

His humorless smile sent a cold shiver down her spine. "I want your husband," he answered calmly. "And I intend to get him through you."

"I . . . I don't understand," she stammered. It took great effort to keep her fear out of her voice.

"It's quite simple, Mrs. Brolin. Your husband will surrender himself to me, because if he doesn't I will kill you. My men and I have been watching him, and I know he's in town at the saloon."

Selman guided his horse close to Regina's. Grasping her wrist, he jerked her left hand upward and forcefully removed her wedding band. Then he studied it for a moment before handing it to one of his men. "You already know what to do," he said.

Dropping the gold ring into his pocket, the man replied, "Don't worry, boss. When I see you again, I'll have Brolin with me." He turned his horse and rode quickly away.

"Why did you give him my ring?" Regina asked.

"It'll convince Brolin that you're my prisoner. Your initials and his are engraved on it."

When Regina was pregnant with the twins, Matt had decided to have their initials engraved on her wedding band. At the time, she had believed doing so had been his way of telling her they would always be together. Now the gesture seemed ironic.

"Where are you taking me?" she asked tentatively.

"There's an abandoned cabin a few miles from here. We will wait there for Brolin."

Regina knew where the cabin was. When her Uncle

Carl had first bought a small tract of land, the log cabin had been his home. But when he became more prosperous and had acquired more land, he'd built the ranch house in which she now lived.

Selman reached over and took Regina's Winchester. He removed the bullets, then slipped the rifle back into the scabbard. "Shall we leave, Mrs. Brolin?" he requested, as though he were politely asking her to accompany him on a social ride.

As Regina edged the stallion forward, Selman rode close beside her and his two men followed closely.

Would Matt surrender himself in her place? Regina tried not to let the question plague her, nonetheless it kept nagging at her. Matt didn't love her, so why should he place himself in danger to save her? He knew Selman intended to kill him, so if he agreed to Selman's terms, he'd be signing his own death warrant. Realizing that Matt might die, Regina knew that regardless of how coldly he had treated her, she still loved him. And for the first time since she had become hopelessly enamored of Matt Brolin, Regina prayed with all her heart that he did not return her love. If Matt didn't, then he would not sacrifice himself. She adored her husband so deeply that his life was more precious to Regina than her own!

Chapter Thirty-three

When Selmam's man entered the saloon, Miguel was standing at the bar talking to Dan. Aggravated by Matt's refusal to discuss the problems in his marriage, Miguel had left his friend to seek out other company. Glancing about the room, Selman's man spotted Matt sitting alone at a corner table. He crossed the floor and, pulling out a chair, sat down beside him. He had been one of the guards at the cave so he had recognized Matt, but Matt had always been unconscious when the man had been present so he thought that a stranger had invited himself to share his table.

"Hello, Brolin," the man mumbled. He brought out Regina's wedding band and laid it next to Matt's beer. "You make one wrong move and your wife is dead."

Picking it up, Matt checked the engraved initials; then he slipped the ring into his shirt pocket. "Where is my wife?" he asked quietly, his eyes narrowing angrily.

The man's sudden grin resembled a sneer. "She's with Mr. Selman." Checking his pocket watch, he said, "It's now three. You have until four o'clock to exchange yourself for your wife. She's about an hour's ride from here, so I suggest we leave quietly—right now."

"Where are they?" Matt demanded, keeping his voice low. When the man made no reply, he said threateningly, "Answer me, or I'll beat the information out of you!"

Undisturbed, the man answered, "Go ahead, Brolin, but how can you be sure that I'll give you their true location? By the time you can get the sheriff and check out my story, it might be too late to save your wife." He smiled menacingly. "I could send you on a wild-goose chase."

"If you did, I'd kill you!" Matt seethed.

The man shrugged. "That wouldn't make your wife any less dead."

Matt's eyes met his. The man's appearance wasn't intimidating. He was older than Matt. His build was slim, and his face was clean-shaven. But his cold calmness was threatening, and Matt's acute ability to judge an adversary told him this man's loyalty to Selman would not waver.

"Well?" the man taunted. "Are you going to save that beautiful wife of yours, or do you intend to let Mr. Selman kill her? I can promise you that her death won't be a pretty one."

A nerve twitched at Matt's temple, and it took all his will power not to wrap his hands about the man's neck and try to choke the truth out of him. But Selman had him over a barrel. Matt knew he had no choice but to leave with this man. Fleetingly, he glanced at Miguel, who was still at the bar conversing with Dan. He had to find a way to get a covert message to him!

Facing Selman's man, Matt said evenly, "All right, I'll leave quietly with you, but first I need a drink. A stiff one!" Looking at the bartender, Matt yelled more loudly than necessary, "Bring me a shot of tequila!"

Alerted, Miguel broke off his discussion with Dan and watched Matt furtively.

"In fact," Matt continued blatantly, "make that a double shot of tequila!"

The bartender delivered the order, and Matt downed the drink in one quick swallow. Placing the glass on the table, he got to his feet. "Let's get the hell out of here," he mumbled.

The man stood, and gesturing for Matt to go first, he followed him out of the saloon.

The moment they stepped outside, Miguel said, "Damn!" He was furious because he had left his vaqueros at the Black Diamond. Quickly, he crossed the room, and peering outside, he took note of the direction Matt and the man had taken.

"What's wrong?" Dan asked, hurrying to Miguel.

"Matt, he is in trouble," Ordaz explained.

"How do you know?" Dan was confused.

"He ordered a double shot of tequila."

"So?" Dan queried.

"Matt hates tequila," Miguel declared. "Is your horse saddled?"

"Yes. He's right out front."

"Good!" he said briskly. "We will follow Matt and the man he left with."

"Don't you think we should notify the sheriff?"

"There is no time," Miguel replied, pushing aside the swinging doors.

As Miguel and Dan strode outside, Santos Ramírez was dismounting in front of the saloon.

Miguel felt no animosity toward Santos, but because he was Antonio's son, he did not acknowledge the young man's presence.

"Wait!" Dan shouted to Miguel who was heading swiftly for his horse. He nodded toward Santos. "We might need his help."

"I will not ride with a Ramírez!" Miguel barked stubbornly.

Determined, Dan declared, "This is no time for personal grievances!" Turning to Santos, he said quickly, "Matt's in some kind of trouble."

Santos liked Matt, and he immediately asked, "Do you need my help?"

"We might," Dan answered.

Already mounted, Miguel grumbled impatiently, "Let's go, we are wasting time!"

The two men who had remained with Selman were standing guard outside the cabin door when Matt arrived with his guide. The log cabin was situated in a desolate area, bordered on all sides by huge boulders. Scanning the surroundings, Matt hoped that Miguel had grasped his message and had followed them.

One of the men opened the door and said caustically, "Go right on in, Brolin. Mr. Selman has been expecting you."

The man who had accompanied Matt had already searched him thoroughly, relieving him of his pistol. Unarmed, Matt walked swiftly into the quiet cabin, followed closely by Selman's man who held a gun at his back. One of the guards shut the door behind them.

The dusty interior of the cabin was unfurnished, and Regina was sitting on the floor in a corner of the room. Selman stood beside her. She bounded to her feet as Matt entered, but when she stepped forward, Selman grasped her arm.

"Are you all right?" Matt asked Regina.

"Yes," she murmured, her heart pounding rapidly. He had come to save her! Did this mean he loved her?

Appearing to be quite relaxed, Matt turned his

attention to Selman. "How in the hell did you manage to escape the day I was found in your goddamned cave?"

"The man who rode here with you was one of my guards. As Sheriff Davis was arriving, he slipped away and came to the house."

"After you kill me, how do you plan to keep on evading the law?" Matt asked calmly.

"I never use banks, so all my money was in my safe. I have it with me, and as soon as you are dead, I'll head north."

"Are you going to let my wife go free?"

Selman grinned. "Of course not. She'll die too, Brolin. You're no fool. You know damned well I wouldn't leave her alive." Looking at Regina, he continued, "Mrs. Brolin, your husband is a very gallant man. He came here so that he could die heroically at your side."

Regina stared wide-eyed at Matt. "You shouldn't have come!" she said aloud, while she thought, Dear God, he does love me! He must! Otherwise, why would he be here!

Roughly, Selman shoved Regina, sending her stumbling into her husband's arms. Protectively, Matt drew her close.

Then Selman drew his pistol and said evenly, "This time, Brolin, I intend to kill you quickly, but before you die, you're going to see your lovely wife lie dead at your feet."

Moments after Matt and Selman's man had gone into the cabin, Miguel, Dan, and Santos left their horses nearby and, on foot, slipped up behind one of the large boulders overlooking the cabin.

Dan recognized the two guards as the same men who had visited his saloon with Selman on the night Susan was murdered. "They work for Selman," he said in a hushed tone. "He must be inside with Matt." Suddenly, Dan noticed Midnight tethered near the cabin. "Good God, Selman has Regina!"

Peering over the boulder's edge, Miguel said quietly, "We must find a way to kill the two men without making any noise."

"I'll be right back," Santos whispered. He hurried stealthily to his horse and returned quickly with a bow and a quiver filled with arrows. Noting Miguel's questioning expression, he explained, "Before I came to town, I had been practicing with my bow. As you already know, *señor,* my mother was an Apache. I often visit her people, and my Apache uncle taught me to be a perfect marksman with a bow and arrow. I can kill both men almost simultaneously and without making a sound."

Smiling, Miguel grudgingly admired the young Ramírez' shrewdness and skill.

Slinging the quiver onto his back, Santos crept quietly to the top of the boulder and loaded his bow as Miguel and Dan looked on. With practiced precision, he fired one arrow, then another. Both soared to their intended targets with incredible speed and accuracy. Their hearts pierced by Apache arrows, the two guards died at almost the same moment.

Moving silently, Miguel, Dan, and Santos rushed toward the cabin, but their strides slowed, then halted as they approached the closed front door.

"How do you intend to get inside?" Dan asked Miguel. "This time we don't have your shotgun."

"I will force the door open," Ordaz replied. "*Amigo,* you are not a gunman, so you had better stay here." Dan was carrying his rifle, and Miguel ordered, "Keep your gun aimed at the cabin, and if Selman or one of his men try to get away, shoot them." He then looked at Santos. "Can you shoot a pistol as well as you handle a bow and arrow?"

"Better." The young man grinned devilishly and then placed his bow and quiver on the ground.

Once again, Miguel felt a certain admiration for Antonio's son, but reminding himself that Santos was a Ramírez, he said gruffly, "We have no way of knowing what to expect when we barge inside, so shoot fast and do not miss."

"I never miss, *señor,*" Santos assured him, smiling self-confidently and drawing his pistol.

Pulling back the hammer on his revolver, Selman ordered harshly, "Brolin, step away from your wife. I wouldn't want to accidentally shoot you while I'm aiming for her."

"Go to hell, you rotten son of a bitch," Matt sneered, drawing Regina even closer. When he felt her tremble, his arms tightened about her. He admired her bravery, and was amazed that she could stand at his side and face death so courageously.

Suddenly the unbarred door was suddenly flung open. Selman's man was standing to the side, his pistol still drawn, but Matt and Regina were between Selman and the door, their bodies affording him shelter.

His reflexes alert, Matt dived to the floor taking Regina down with him, and Miguel's bullet slammed into the shocked Selman before he could react. At the same moment, Santos shot the other man. Hurrying to Selman, Miguel checked for signs of life. Finding him dead, he looked over at Santos and said briskly,

"Check the other one and see if he is alive."

"He is dead, *señor*," Santos replied, his voice cocky. "I told you, I never miss."

"Check him anyway!" Miguel bellowed, perturbed because the young man's insolence reminded him of the elder Ramírez.

Matt helped Regina to her feet, and, shaken, she leaned on his arms for support. When Dan walked up to them, however, Matt brusquely delivered her into her brother's embrace. His cold rejection hurt Regina, and she nestled her head against Dan's shoulder so Matt couldn't see how she felt. Oh God, she had been a fool to think that he loved her! Apparently, it was not love that compelled Matt to risk his life to save hers!

Midway between midnight and daybreak, Regina returned to the Black Diamond with Matt and Miguel. It had taken hours for the sheriff to fill out his report, but he had finally told them they were free to go home.

Because of the ordeal Regina had gone through, Hannah and Julie insisted that she go to bed immediately. Regina was reluctant to do so for she hoped to find an opportunity to be alone with Matt. Only when she learned that he had closed himself in the study with Miguel and Ted did she decide to take their advice.

Exhausted, Regina quickly fell into a sound sleep. The next morning, she was awakened abruptly when Matt entered her room and closed the door with a bang. Bolting to a sitting position, she watched him warily as he walked over to the wardrobe. Although Matt had not been sleeping with her, he still had clothes in Regina's bedroom. Now, opening the door to the wardrobe, he began to remove his belongings.

"Matt, why are you taking your clothes?" she

asked apprehensively.

"I'm leaving," he answered bluntly.

Getting out of bed and slipping into her robe, she hastened to his side. "Where are you going?"

"To Julie's former home. In case you have forgotten, it belongs to me."

Stunned, Regina was speechless. She wanted to beg him not to leave, but valuing her pride, she raised her chin and looked directly into his piercing eyes. "Very well, Matt. If you want to live elsewhere, I won't try to stop you."

"I didn't think that you would," he retorted. He wondered how long it would be before she flew to Antonio's arms and let him know that she was now free.

Regina was determined not to give him the satisfaction of seeing her fall apart, so she kept her voice cool as she asked, "You aren't taking Cort, are you?"

"I'll leave him here until I sell my ranch. Then I intend to move to Wyoming and take my son with me," he replied, his expression firm.

"But why are you selling the ranch?" she exclaimed.

"Because all my money is tied up in it. I can't very well leave for Wyoming without funds."

Regina sighed resignedly, "So you still intend to carry out your original plan. Our marriage and my pregnancy only delayed you."

Offering no comment, Matt turned back to the wardrobe and finished removing his clothes. Then he walked over and placed his things on the bed.

"Matt?" Regina said softly.

He faced her. "What?" he asked, his voice impatient.

"I don't want to lose Cort," she replied, her pain evident.

She was surprised to see a look of tenderness cross

384

his face. "I'm sorry, Regina. I'm not trying to hurt you or get even with you. I merely want my son."

"I want him too!" she pleaded.

"When I leave for Wyoming, he's going with me," Matt stated decisively.

Hurrying to Matt's side, she tried to reason with him. "But Cort's only a baby! How do you plan to take care of him? Do you really believe a three-year-old child can endure all the hardships you'll have to cope with? Good Lord, Matt! If you truly love your son, you'll leave him here!"

Matt knew she was right. How could he possibly give his son proper care? At a loss, he sat on the edge of the bed and his strong shoulders slumped. Never in his whole life had anyone truly belonged to him, so why did he think it was any different now? Letting down his guard, Matt mumbled discontentedly, "You can keep Cort. I know how much you love him. My reservations about leaving Cort here had nothing to do with you being his mother."

Regina had never seen Matt so vulnerable. Her heart ached for him, and she moved to the side of the bed and knelt at his feet. "What were your reservations?" she asked gently.

"Actually, I had only one," he admitted.

"Which was?" she coaxed.

"Antonio," he replied.

"Antonio?" Regina was confused. "I don't understand."

Suddenly Matt felt stifled, and he had an overwhelming urge to get out of that room, out of that house—to be away from Regina!

"Matt, I don't understand," she said again.

"The hell you don't understand!" he responded harshly, getting to his feet.

385

Standing too, she grasped his arm. Roughly, he flung off her grip, and gathering up his clothes, he hurried across the room.

As he reached the door, Regina cried out, "Matt, please don't leave without telling me what you meant!" But he left without saying another word.

Totally baffled, Regina stared at the closed door. Antonio! Why had he mentioned Antonio?

Chapter Thirty-four

Matt was now living in the house that had once belonged to Julie and Mace, and as he sat at the kitchen table, he was acutely aware of the lonely silence that surrounded him. The quiet was a drastic change. He had grown accustomed to Cort bounding through the house, yelping and shouting as he played make-believe games; and he longed for María's gentle presence. For the first time in his life, he'd had a family, and he missed them terribly. He hoped it wouldn't take too long to sell his ranch. He wanted to pack up and be on his way. The best cure for what ailed him was to put real distance between himself and the loved ones he had left at the Black Diamond.

An open whiskey bottle stood on the table, and as he picked it up, his thoughts turned to Regina. He hadn't known whether he still loved her until she'd been taken captive by Selman, but the moment Selman's man had dropped her ring onto the table, he'd known that he hadn't stopped loving her.

Matt took a large drink of whiskey; then he glanced at the mantel above the fireplace where he had laid Regina's wedding band. Fleetingly, he wondered why she hadn't asked about it. He decided resentfully that she was probably glad to be rid of it.

Against his will, Regina's words once again tore painfully into his heart. "I wish Matt had died! . . . I wish Matt had died!" How could she have wished him dead? Regardless of her feeling for Antonio, or of how desperately she might relish her freedom, how in the name of God could she have been so callous as to wish he had died?

Matt doubled his hand into a fist, then brought it down forcefully on the table. The solid blow resounded loudly throughout the quiet house. "Damn you, Regina!" he fumed viciously. "Damn you for the cold-hearted bitch that you are!"

Matt had been drinking for hours. He knew he was getting drunk, but he didn't care. He had every intention of drinking himself senseless so that thoughts of Regina would no longer plague him.

Holding the whiskey bottle by its neck, Matt tilted it to his mouth and helped himself to a big swig. Hoping to lose himself in a drunken stupor, he didn't hear the hoofbeats approach.

Halting Midnight in front of the silent house, Regina remained mounted as she debated whether or not she could confront Matt. Since he had left this morning to move into Julie's former home, Regina's mind had been in a turmoil. Why had Matt mentioned Antonio? She could think of no logical reason for him to do so. Taking a deep breath and mustering her courage, she dismounted and flung the reins across the hitching post.

The sun was setting and its last golden rays shone faintly on the porch as Regina knocked on the closed door.

"Who's there?" Matt called testily.

Deciding not to announce herself beforehand, Regina stepped inside and closed the door behind her.

388

Matt hadn't bothered to light a lamp, and the interior was dusky. The living area and kitchen was one room. Matt was sitting at the table. Noticing the bottle of whiskey in his hand, Regina hoped he was still sober and could participate in a sensible conversation.

"Come on over, darlin', and join me for a drink," he offered smoothly, while his eyes devoured the sensual curves that her attractive riding apparel accentuated.

"No, thank you. I don't want any whiskey," she murmured, as she tentatively approached the table.

Putting down the bottle, he asked cautiously, "Why are you here?"

"I want to talk to you," she said.

He stated calmly, "We have nothing to discuss."

"I think we do," Regina insisted shakily.

He quirked an eyebrow. "What do we have to talk about?"

"Antonio," she replied hesitantly, unsure of his reaction.

Matt's unexpected laugh was harsh. "So you've finally decided to confess! Regina, for God's sake, isn't it a little too late for you to bare your soul? Why don't you just spare us both an unpleasant scene and get the hell out of here!"

Regina's anger struck suddenly. "Damn you, Matt! You're a hateful, insensitive, unfeeling—"

"Bastard." He rose to his feet.

Her green eyes blazing, Regina continued her tirade. "You just told me what the problem is, Matt. Because you believe you are a bastard by birth, your heart is so filled with self-pity that there's no room left in it for love!"

He reached her in two long strides, and clutching her shoulders, he glared down into her flushed face. "Love?" he snickered. "What in the hell do you know about love?" His grip tightened painfully. "You lying, deceitful little wildcat!"

Releasing his hold, he headed toward the door, his unsteady steps revealing his tipsy condition. Swinging it open, he warned menacingly, "You had better leave, before I do something I may later regret!"

Regina strode to the door, and favoring Matt with a chilling glance, she said coolly, "Go to hell, Matt Brolin! You are a sorry excuse for a husband, and I'm glad to be rid of you!"

"I suppose a man like Antonio Ramírez would make an ideal husband," he said sarcastically.

So angered she could not think clearly, Regina declared feelingly, "I'd rather have him for a husband than you!"

Instantly, Matt slammed the door shut, preventing Regina from leaving. His expression turned savage, and, frightened, she reached for the doorknob, intent on escaping his wrath. But Matt swiftly lifted her into his arms and, holding her tightly, looked down into her face. When she met his gaze, the violent anger in his narrowed eyes was terrifying.

"Antonio is not yet your husband," he rasped. "You are still my wife, and since you surrender your passion so easily, I'm sure you won't mind accommodating the man who is your present husband."

As he carried her toward the bedroom, she tried frantically to squirm out of his arms. "Matt, put me down! . . . Let me go, damn you!"

Ignoring her resistance, he went to the bed and dropped her onto it. She made a desperate effort to rise but he immediately pinned her to the mattress by placing his muscular body over hers. His face mere inches from hers, he grumbled fiercely, "Regina, I know you for the lying little cheat that you are, yet I can't stop wanting you! By God, you bewitched me

390

the first moment I set eyes on you! How in the hell do I get you out of my thoughts?"

Lying little cheat? Regina wondered what had provoked him to say that. But before she could ask him to explain, his lips were on hers, and he was kissing her so sensually that her confusion was temporarily forgotten. Matt's passionate kiss stirred her desire, and with desire came hope. He couldn't get her out of his thoughts! Did this mean he didn't want their marriage to end? Was he willing for them to find a way to resolve their differences? Vulnerable, Regina responded to the warm mouth that was taking such wonderful possession of hers, and surrendering completely, she allowed Matt to undress her, then waited expectantly while he rid himself of his own clothes.

Enthralled by their burning need for each other, Regina and Matt both forgot what they believed was the other's cruel betrayal. They came together as one, and were totally engulfed by their mutual passion. This time, however, when their lovemaking ended and Matt quickly rose to don his clothing, Regina followed his example. When she had dressed, she sat on the edge of the bed, wishing desperately that Matt would say something.

Night was descending, and shadows darkened the bedroom. Stepping to the lamp on the bedside table, Matt lit it and adjusted the wick. Then he sat beside Regina. Leaning over and resting his crossed arms on his legs, he stared down at the floor.

Watching him intently, Regina silently pleaded for him to say that he loved and needed her.

"Regina"—Matt's deep voice penetrated the eerie quiet—"tomorrow I'll talk to Ted and ask him to sell this ranch for me. As soon as I'm settled in Wyoming, or wherever, I'll get in touch with Ted and let him know

391

where to send my money." Raising his head, he turned and looked at her. He would be a fool to think he could resist Regina while he was living so close to her. He had to put some distance between them, and he had to do it soon.

"I don't believe you are doing this," she whispered. "How can you make love to me one minute and, in the next, tell me you are leaving?"

Standing, Matt said irritably, "Damn it, Regina! Stop pretending that you care! You can go to Antonio and tell him that I have bowed out graciously. As far as I'm concerned, you two can have each other!"

"What are you saying?" she demanded shrilly, bounding to her feet.

"I'm saying I know all about you and Antonio!" he shouted. "I know you two are lovers, and I also know you once wished that Selman had killed me!"

His accusations left Regina incredulous. She opened her mouth to speak, but she was so astounded that her voice faltered. When she had regained a degree of composure, she asked hesitantly, "Why do you think Antonio and I are lovers? And why do you believe I wished you dead?"

In vivid detail, Matt told her what he had seen and heard. As his story unfolded, Regina's shock changed to disbelief and finally to anger. When she could stand no more she screamed, "How dare you accuse me of being so vile and cruel!" Shoving him aside, she headed for the bedroom door, but halfway there she whirled about sharply. "I was afraid that someday you would hurt me so badly that I couldn't recover. Well you finally did it, Matt! When you accused me of having an affair and then told me that I had wished you dead, you went too far! You have completely destroyed my love for you! I never want to see you again!"

Darting through the house, she flung open the front door and stormed outside, leaving Matt shocked by her unexpected response to his accusations.

Miguel was standing at the parlor window watching for Regina to return, and he spotted her the moment she entered the lane that led up to the house. Turning to Julie, who was sitting on the sofa beside María, he said, "Regina has come back."

Miguel and Julie were quite sure that she had ridden over to see Matt, although she had left the house without an explanation. "Darling, why don't you talk to her privately?" Julie encouraged. "Maybe you can help her."

Miguel wasn't too sure that anything he could say or do would help Regina, but at his wife's suggestion, he left the parlor and stepped onto the porch.

Regina was heading in the direction of the stable, but catching sight of Miguel, she changed her course and rode up to the house. "Miguel," she began as she dismounted, "would you mind stabling Midnight for me?"

"I will do it later," he replied. "But first I think we should talk."

Climbing the steps, she answered tonelessly, "I'm in no mood for conversation."

Taking her arm, Miguel ushered her over to the porch swing and urged her to sit down. Joining her, he asked quietly, "Did you see Matt?"

Regina scowled. "Yes, but I hope I never see him again."

"You do not mean that," Miguel stated gently. "You love Matt."

"I don't love him!" Regina declared angrily. "I used

to love him! God, I loved him with all my heart!"

The rage in her voice startled Miguel. *"Señora,* you sound as though you are serious."

"I am!" she insisted harshly.

Gingerly, Miguel placed an arm about Regina's shoulders, and wanting his comfort, Regina rested her head on his shoulder.

"Regina," he said firmly, "I want you to tell me why you no longer love Matt. Do not put me off, and do not become stubborn and refuse to confide in me. I am not only your brother-in-law, I am also your friend. And, very much I love you."

"But you also love Matt," Regina stated flatly.

"Sí, I love him as a brother. But I think he is to blame for what has happened between the two of you."

"Why do you think that?" she asked curiously.

"Because I know Matt very well. He has always been moody, hard headed. Usually he keeps his feelings to himself. On his shoulder, *señora,* he carries a very big chip." He paused for a moment, then continued soothingly, "You can trust me, Regina. Tell me what has happened to make you stop loving Matt."

Needing to open her heart and confide in someone who truly cared, Regina told Miguel why Matt believed that she and Antonio were having an affair. She also explained what had taken place at the cave, explaining that Matt had regained consciousness only long enough to hear her last words to Antonio. She finished her elaboration by saying with cold finality, "My love for Matt has been on the borderline for a long time, but tonight he pushed me over the edge. I can never forgive him for all the ugly accusations he flung at me."

"If you no longer love Matt, then what do you feel for him?" Miguel pried tenderly.

"I don't know for sure," Regina admitted. "Anger and resentment, I suppose."

"Those two feelings very often go hand in hand with love. Love can be a stormy emotion, *señora*."

Leaving the comfort of his arms and sitting upright, Regina argued, "Matt killed my love! It doesn't exist anymore! I hope he leaves immediately for Wyoming and never comes back!" Leaping to her feet, she hurried into the house.

Leaning back in the swing, Miguel rocked gently as he considered everything Regina had told him. Aggravated with Matt, he mumbled gruffly, *"Amigo,* you have acted very foolishly. I will have to set you straight." When he recalled Regina's coldness toward Matt, he thought gravely, Even if I do make Matt see the truth, it may be too late to save their love.

Antonio had been notified of Ordaz' visit, and as Miguel rode up to the ranch house, he was poised on the veranda waiting to receive his unwelcome guest. When one of Antonio's vaqueros has hurried into the house to inform him that Miguel Ordaz was arriving alone, Antonio had been astounded. Considering the hostility he and Ordaz felt for each other, he wondered why Ordaz hadn't brought his men with him.

Antonio had two of his vaqueros on the veranda beside him, but as Miguel drew closer, he ordered the men to wait inside the house. If Miguel Ordaz had the courage to confront him alone, he would meet him on equal terms.

It was fairly late, but the night was clear, the full moon made it easy for Antonio to keep a cautious eye on Miguel as he reined in his horse before the hacienda.

For a few tense moments, the two men stared heatedly at each other, neither acknowledging the other's presence. It was Antonio who spoke first, *"Señor,* I hope you have a good reason for being here."

"Ramírez," Miguel began coldly, "I will come straight to the point, for I do not like your company any more than you like mine."

"Politely said, but mildly put," Antonio replied.

"I am here to take you with me to see Matt," Miguel explained shortly.

"Take me?" Antonio questioned, his countenance hard. "Ordaz, you are either very brazen or very stupid."

It was extremely difficult for Miguel to carry on a civil discussion with Antonio. He would not even have attempted to do so if he hadn't loved Regina and Matt more than he hated this man. Keeping his composure, Miguel said calmly, "Matt thinks that you and Regina are lovers."

Astonished, Antonio exclaimed, "He is wrong!"

Miguel nodded. "I know that he is wrong, *señor."* As quickly as he could, Miguel told Antonio why Matt had come to believe that he and Regina were having an affair. He also described what Matt had seen and overheard at the cave. Concluding his explanation, Miguel said, "I want you to visit Matt and tell him the truth."

"Will he believe me?" Antonio asked skeptically.

"I think so," Miguel answered. "You would have no reason to lie. If you loved Regina, you would not try to save their marriage."

"That is not necessarily true. I do love Regina, but she does not share my feelings."

Miguel was taken aback. "I did not think you were capable of loving anyone. Does this mean you will not talk to Matt?"

396

"Not only am I capable of love, *señor,* but I am also capable of unselfish love. To help Regina, I will try to convince Matt that I am not involved with his wife."

"If you do not trust me and want to bring some of your men with you, I will understand. But you have my word that this is not a trap."

"Is this a temporary truce?" Antonio asked, smiling easily.

Miguel answered, *"Sí,* we will call a temporary truce." Grumbling, he added. "A very short one."

"Very well, *señor,* I will ride alone with you." Although Antonio's animosity toward Miguel was strong, he knew Miguel Ordaz was a man of his word.

Remaining mounted, Miguel waited impatiently for Antonio to have his horse saddled. He found this association with Ramírez very unpleasant and was anxious to end it.

For the first time in their acquaintanceship, Antonio Ramírez and Miguel Ordaz rode side by side. However, during the short journey to Matt's home, neither man spoke to the other.

Matt heard their arrival before they pulled up at the hitching rail. Opening the door, he walked onto the porch. The unexpected sight of Miguel with Antonio shocked Matt. Speechless, he simply stared at the two men as they dismounted and walked toward him.

"Let us go inside the house," Miguel said to Matt.

Stepping aside, Matt allowed them to enter first, and Miguel strode to the table and took charge, "We will sit here and talk."

As his visitors seated themselves, Matt continued to look on with amazement. Why in the hell was Miguel with Antonio?

Looking at Matt, Miguel insisted, "Sit down, *amigo.*"

Matt pulled out a chair and compiled. He was numb with shock. Seated between the two men, he waited for Miguel to explain himself as his eyes darted curiously from Antonio to Miguel. Apparently, Miguel was in no hurry to account for the situation, and as Matt's shock began to wear off, he began to resent Antonio's presence. Anger and jealousy surged through him, his eyes hardened, and turning his full attention to Antonio, he almost shouted. "Ramírez, get the hell out of here before I—"

Interrupting, Miguel said strongly, "Matt, for once in your life, I want you to sit quietly and listen!" Leaning forward, and crossing his arms on the table, he proceeded. "Earlier this evening, Regina came here to see you. When she returned to the Black Diamond, I persuaded her to confide in me. *Amigo,* you accused her of things that are untrue." Miguel detected Matt's sudden fury and continued hastily, "Matt, for your own sake, listen to what Ramírez has to say!"

Speaking up, Antonio said firmly, "Regina and I are not having an affair. I have never made love to your wife."

Matt said nothing and his expression was doubtful. Antonio decided to start at the beginning and to be perfectly honest. "I have been in love with Regina for a long time. I once asked her to marry me, but she refused because she was in love with you. She was hoping for your proposal. I pleaded for a kiss, and she consented only because she felt badly about turning down my marriage proposal. That day you came into the parlor and witnessed our embrace, Regina was kissing me out of compassion, love had nothing to do with it. I understand, *señor,* that you once again found us sharing an embrace. Regina was on her way home from town, and I happened to run across her. Her stallion

398

had picked up a stone, and I removed it. The stallion's head then brushed against Regina, causing her to lose her balance and fall toward me. My arms went about her, and her closeness was a temptation I could not resist so I kissed her. I took Regina by surprise and it was a moment before she pushed herself out of my arms. She was very angry. I apologized for my forward conduct, and because your wife is a very kind and compassionate woman, she accepted my apology. I promised her that it would never happen again, and I have kept my word."

Matt remained silent, although Antonio had his attention.

"When you were Selman's prisoner, he struck you many times about the head. Upon seeing your injuries, Regina was afraid that you had been beaten so severely that you would not make a complete recovery. She panicked and became hysterical. When you regained consciousness, I was trying to calm her because, believing you might have permanent brain damage, Regina was beside herself with grief. She would rather have seen you dead, than have you completely helpless. When she said "I wish Matt had died," it was because she was incoherent. She knew that you could not have coped with a permanent disability."

Deep in his own thoughts, Matt offered no comment. *"Señor,"* Antonio continued, "what I have told you is the truth."

Finally Matt spoke, his voice hoarse, "Why didn't you remain silent and wait for Regina to get a divorce so that you could pursue her?"

Antonio smiled slyly. "Maybe, *señor,* I do not want to be second choice," he said. Then he rose and looked directly at Matt, meeting his unwavering gaze. "Regina loves you and has not been unfaithful. And considering the way you have treated your wife, it is my opinion that you do not deserve her."

Gruffly, Miguel mumbled, "No one asked for your opinion, Ramírez."

Glaring, Antonio responded, "Our truce, Ordaz, is now officially over!"

"Good!" Miguel retorted. "I would rather share a truce with the devil himself!"

Matt knew it was extremely dangerous for Miguel and Antonio to be so close together. Their bickering could easily get out of control. Resonantly, Matt spoke to Antonio, "Ramírez, I think it's time for you to leave."

Agreeing, Antonio spun about and marched to the door. Before leaving, he looked at Matt and said, *"Señor,* you are a lucky man to have Regina's love. It is a shame that you do not know how to appreciate a good woman."

As Antonio left, closing the door behind him, Miguel leaned back in his chair. Relaxing, he muttered testily, *"Amigo,* I may never forgive you for making me associate with Ramírez."

"I didn't make you do anything," Matt grumbled.

"The hell you didn't!" Miguel retaliated. "You are a strain on my patience. I once slashed your cheek to remind you that it is foolish to rob, maybe now I should cut the other cheek to remind you that people are innocent until proven guilty."

Grinning fondly, Matt replied, "You might not find it so easy to make me turn the other cheek. I'm no longer an inexperienced, seventeen-year-old boy."

Reminiscing, Miguel smiled. *"Sí,* you were only a boy fresh out of prison." He hesitated for a few moments, then watching Matt closely, he asked, "Do you believe everything Ramírez told you?"

"Do you?" Matt retorted.

"Ramírez did not lie. Regina has always been faithful to you."

Sighing deeply, Matt admitted, "If that's true, then I have acted like a damned fool."

"If it is true!" Miguel snapped. "Why are you so skeptical where Regina is concerned?"

"I don't enjoy doubting Regina's sincerity!" Matt bristled. "But, damn it, Miguel, you're the one who instigated everything!"

"What did I instigate?" Ordaz demanded, perplexed.

"I've always known about the deceitful conspiracy you and Regina once shared," Matt admitted angrily.

"I think, *amigo,* you should tell me of this conspiracy so I will know as much about my life as you do."

In detail, Matt related to Miguel the conversation in which Mace had told him that he had eavesdropped at the study door and had heard Miguel advise Regina to trap him into marriage.

"Mace Edwards did not tell you everything, or perhaps he left before hearing Regina's reply. She flatly refused to entrap you and she was quite perturbed with me for advising her to do so. Julie has told me that Señor Edwards wanted the Black Diamond for himself. He was hoping that eventually Regina would give him the title. When you said that you were planning to marry Regina and stay at the Black Diamond, I am sure Mace realized the ranch would never be his if she accepted your proposal. When he told you about my conversation with Regina, he probably did so out of malice. He wanted you to feel manipulated so you would not ask Regina to marry you. Once again, *amigo,* you found her guilty when she was innocent."

Pushing back his chair, Miguel rose and began to pace back and forth. Irritably, he asked, "Is it only Regina that you do not trust, or do you distrust women in general? Do you judge all women by your mother?

Because she betrayed you, do you believe every woman will do likewise?"

Matt glared at Miguel. "What in hell does the woman who gave birth to me have to do with any of this?"

Pausing and looking at Matt, Miguel replied quietly, "Maybe everything, maybe nothing. I do not know. Perhaps the answer lies somewhere deep within your heart."

Moaning, Matt leaned over, and placing his elbows on the table, he rested his head in the palms of his hands. "I've hurt Regina so many times! How can I expect her to forgive me when I can't even forgive myself."

Deciding not to give Matt false encouragement, Miguel said solemnly, "She might not forgive you, *amigo*. It is possible that she no longer loves you."

Regina was in bed, but she wasn't sleeping when a firm knock sounded on her door. "Regina," Julie called from the hallway, "Matt is here to see you."

Sitting up with a start, Regina reached over and lit the bedside lamp. Matt! Why did he want to see her? Didn't he ever tire of hurting her? Well, he'll never break my heart again! she decided resolutely. I'll never let him get that close to me. "I don't want to see Matt," she answered loudly. "Tell him to go away!"

"Regina," Matt's deep voice suddenly responded, "please, let me in." He tried the doorknob, and finding the door unlocked, he entered Regina's bedroom.

Bounding to her feet, Regina grabbed her robe and donned it quickly. Then she glared at her husband and said coldly, "Get out of here!"

Matt ignored her order, and closing the door, he

crossed the room. Regina tried not to be affected by his physical proximity, but, as always, his rugged masculinity sent her pulse racing. Dressed in skin-tight dark trousers and dark shirt, his pistol slung low on his slim thigh, Matt's virility was blatant.

He paused in front of her, and she looked up into his eyes, surprised to find their expression tender. "Regina," he began quietly, "earlier tonight Antonio came to see me. He explained everything, and I now know that all my suspicions were uncalled for. I was wrong not to trust you." He hesitated, and sighing heavily, he admitted, "It has always been hard for me to say I'm sorry. I don't know why, most people find it quite easy." He placed his hands on her shoulders, and his fingers gripped her gently. "Regina, I'm sorry. I'm sorry for all my unfair accusations. I can only hope that you love me enough to forgive me."

Weakening, Regina almost went into his arms. She was about to tell him that all was forgiven when her resolution came to mind. Remembering that, she decided not to allow herself to become vulnerable; if she did, he'd only hurt her again! Hadn't her emotions made her defenseless time and time again, and hadn't he shattered her every time? I can resist him because I don't love him anymore, she told herself. He has destroyed my love!

Grasping his wrists, she flung his hands off her shoulders, and stepping back from him, she remarked coldly, "I'm sorry, Matt. But I don't love you enough to forgive you. In fact, I don't love you at all!"

When a hurt look appeared on his handsome face, she was tempted to ask him how it felt to be hurting for a change. Wasn't it about time he got a taste of his own medicine? Vindictiveness was not really a part of Regina's character, but it was the only defense she had against Matt.

"I don't believe you have stopped loving me," Matt murmured.

"How many times did you think you could treat me callously before you finally destroyed my love?" Regina shouted. "Did you think my love was invincible?"

"Yes, I do believe it's invincible," Matt replied firmly. "Just as my love is indestructible. Even when I was foolish enough to think you were having an affair, I couldn't stop loving you. I actually thought you had wished me dead, yet I still loved you."

She swept past him, and going to the bedroom door, she opened it. "I want you out of my life. As you said earlier to me this evening, "Isn't it a little late for you to bare your soul?" Why don't you spare us both an unpleasant scene and just get out of here!"

Hearing his own words flung back at him caused Matt to grimace. He walked over to Regina, and gazing down into her emerald green eyes, he said resolutely, "If you have stopped loving me, then I'll just have to make you fall in love with me all over again. I'll court you, I'll pursue you, and if it becomes necessary, I'll get a guitar and sing love ballads at your bedroom window. But I will win back your love. You have my promise."

"You can't revive what is already dead!" Regina said coldly.

Catching her off guard, Matt pulled her into his arms and his lips claimed hers. His demanding kiss caused Regina to become limp, and when he released her, she was trembling.

"Your love isn't dead, darlin'," he mumbled confidently.

Quickly, he left the room, and Regina angrily slammed the door behind him. She placed her fingers on her lips where his mouth had touched hers. She had actually melted in his arms! All he had to do was kiss her, and she responded as though she had no will of her own! Furious with herself for having such little resistance, she brushed the back of her hand across her mouth, wiping away his kiss. "I don't love him anymore!" she said aloud, trying to convince herself. "I merely responded because old habits are hard to break! If he tries to kiss me again, I'll react so coldly that he'll know it's all over between us. I will! I swear it!"

Chapter Thirty-five

It was late afternoon, and Regina was sitting on the porch swing and watching the sun dip in the west. It was a colorful sunset. The sun was a bright red ball against an orange and gold background.

Catching sight of Dan riding up to the house, Regina smiled and waved to him. He brought his horse to a stop, dismounted, and draped the reins across the hitching rail. Regina watched him as he sauntered up the steps and approached her. She had always thought her brother extremely handsome, and as he sat beside her, she wondered fleetingly if he was determined to remain a confirmed bachelor.

"Did Julie and Miguel leave this morning?" he asked, removing his wide-brimmed Stetson and placing it on his lap.

"Yes, they did." She sighed, already missing them. Remembering their early morning departure, a small frown crossed her face. Before they had left, Julie and Miguel had taken her aside, and both of them had advised her to accept Matt's apology and save her marriage. But that was easy for them to say; they hadn't been hurt by Matt time and time again!

Dan noted her look of irritation. "Is anything wrong?"

"No, of course not," she mumbled evasively, clearing her thoughts.

"I just had a talk with Matt," he stated, waiting carefully for her response.

"If you came here to talk me into forgiving Matt, then you are wasting your time," she remarked, vexed.

"Gina, don't be so damned stubborn!" Dan snapped.

Surprised, she exclaimed, "I can't believe you are actually siding with Matt!"

"It isn't a question of taking sides," he reasoned firmly. "You have a marriage, two children who need their father, and a husband whom you love, yet you're throwing it all away out of resentment."

Bristling, she replied sharply, "Oh, it's easy for you and Julie and Miguel to tell me what I should and shouldn't do! But their advice, and yours, is immaterial. I don't love Matt anymore!"

Dan grinned skeptically. "You can't make me believe that you aren't still in love with Matt." He reached over and took her hand. Squeezing it gently, he murmured, "Matt loves you very much, Gina. He told you he was sorry, what more do you want from him? Do you want him to get on his knees and beg for forgiveness? Do you plan to get even with him? Have you counted the times he's hurt you, so that you can repay him twofold?"

"Stop it!" she shouted, leaping to her feet. Her green eyes firing angry sparks, she stared down into his face. "I'm not playing some kind of spiteful game!"

Standing, he said impatiently, "All right, Gina, I won't try to pressure you. But I think you're behaving very foolishly."

"I don't care what you think!" she retorted. She didn't want to argue with Dan, nor had she wanted to argue with Julie and Miguel, but that discussion had

407

ended on an angry note. Damn Matt! Was he going to alienate her from her entire family?

Deciding to let the matter rest, Dan explained, "Gina, I came here to tell you that I'm going to be away for a few days."

"Are you leaving town?" she asked.

He nodded, answering, "When we were in Santa Fe, Alan Garrett invited me to visit. I'm taking him up on his invitation. I'll only be gone a couple of weeks. I need to get away from the saloon for a while. My bartender can take care of everything." He smiled engagingly. "My life has become monotonous. Santa Fe is a bustling town that will put a little excitement into my humdrum existence."

"Are you going by stage?" she queried.

"No, I'm traveling by horseback. I'll leave in the morning."

"I'll miss you," she murmured sincerely, her expression forlorn.

Placing his hand beneath her chin, he tilted her face up to his. "I hope when I return, I'll find you and Matt back together." Before she could get her dander up, he asked quickly, "Where are the kids? I want to see them before I leave."

"They're in the kitchen with Hannah," she replied.

"How are María and Cort taking your separation from Matt?" Dan's voice revealed his concern.

"Cort's too young to understand what is happening, although he often asks where his father is. I'm not sure how María feels. She's a very quiet girl and keeps her feelings to herself."

"Maybe you should try asking her how she feels," Dan suggested, his tone edged with impatience. Then not giving Regina an opportunity to respond, he turned away swiftly and strode into the house.

* * *

Regina wasn't able to get Dan's visit out of her mind, and later that night, she went to María's bedroom. Deciding to take her brother's advice, she intended to ask María how she felt about Matt's absence.

The door was closed, and Regina knocked lightly. "Come in," she heard María call softly. Entering, and closing the door, Regina saw María sitting on the edge of the bed. She was wearing a cotton nightgown, and her black hair was arranged in two long braids.

When Regina went to the bed and sat beside her, María's large brown eyes looked questioningly into hers. "Honey," Regina began tenderly, admiring the girl's loveliness, "I think it's time we had a heart to heart talk."

"All right," María agreed quietly.

Unsure of how to broach the subject, Regina mumbled, "How have you been feeling?"

"I'm fine," the young girl muttered, although she did not sound it.

Regina drew an apprehensive breath. "Do you miss Matt?"

"Of course, I do," she replied simply.

"How has our separation affected you?" Regina asked, waiting anxiously for a reply.

"I'm very sad," María said.

Rising, she began to pace back and forth. Her thin nightgown silhouetted her soft curves, and watching her, Regina was very aware that María would soon be a woman.

Halting, María turned and looked at Regina. "Everyone has treated me as if I were a child. No one has told me anything. But this afternoon, I asked Uncle Dan if I could talk to him alone, and he is the only one in this family who has treated me as an adult. I asked him to tell me what happened between you and Papa."

"What did he tell you?" Regina asked.

"He said that Papa thought you were involved with

Mr. Ramírez, and he also told me that Papa overheard you at the cave."

Regina wasn't sure whether she should be perturbed with Dan or not. Was María too immature to handle adult situations? Apparently, Dan thought she wasn't. "What else did he say?" she inquired.

"You are too bitter to forgive Papa," she answered.

"María, it isn't that simple," Regina said, frustrated.

Returning to the bed, the girl sat down. "Mama, I think you are wrong to stay angry. How can you not forgive the man you love?" Emotionally, she continued, "If Santos were my husband, I'd forgive him anything!"

Regina smiled tenderly. "María, you are still very innocent. Maybe someday, you'll understand how I feel."

"I hope not," she declared.

"W-why?" Regina stammered.

"I hope I never hate my husband so much that my heart will be filled with bitterness and spite."

"I don't hate Matt," Regina said hastily.

María shrugged. "Maybe not, but you're acting like you do."

Sighing discontentedly, Regina rose. "It's late, and you have school tomorrow so I'd better let you go to bed." Bending over, she kissed María's forehead. "Good night, honey."

Slowly, Regina walked to the door, and as she opened it, María said intensely, "I love you, Mama."

Her eyes misty, Regina replied, "I love you too."

When Regina awoke the next morning a heavy feeling of depression was weighing her down. Although she hoped her spirits would improve, she only became more melancholy as the day progressed. Matt came to the Black Diamond during the early afternoon, but she closed herself in the bedroom and refused to see him. She thought he would insist that she talk to him, but he graciously accepted her decision and left the house without creating a scene. But Regina knew he'd return, and the next time, he might not be so considerate. Patience was not one of Matt's stronger virtues. She was perfectly aware that, sooner or later, he'd demand that she face him. Afraid that it would be sooner instead of later, Regina impulsively decided to leave the Black Diamond for a while. She needed to get away, to be in a place where she could give her life serious thought without being so aware of Matt's influence. But where could she go? Where? Alan Garrett's, of course! She would follow Dan's example and visit Mr. Garrett. When she had met him in Santa Fe, he had also given her an open invitation to visit him whenever she pleased. Since the stage to Santa Fe wasn't due for days, and because she didn't want to wait that long, she decided to leave secretly that night. Knowing Hannah and Ted wouldn't want her to travel alone, and would probably stop her from doing so by informing Matt of her plans, she decided to leave after everyone had gone to bed. She'd write Hannah and Ted a note, letting them know where she had gone and telling them that she'd return with Dan. Regina knew it could be dangerous to travel alone, but once her mind was made up to leave, she wasn't about to let anything interfere with her plans. After all, she was a good shot with a rifle, and for added protection, she'd take Blackie with her.

Regina didn't stop to question why she was running away from her husband. To do so she would have had to search her heart for answers, and she was bound and determined to keep her heart closed.

Carrying through her decision, Regina waited until

after midnight; then she slipped quietly into the kitchen to pack food for her trip. Equipped with loaded rifle, provisions, and Blackie, she left the house and went to the stable. Quickly, she saddled the stallion, mounted, and with Blackie trailing, rode away from the silent house.

"Oh Ted," Hannah sighed gravely, following her husband out of the house and onto the porch, "I'm so worried about Regina. I can't believe she just took off by herself!"

Ted was also concerned, and he said hastily, "I'll ride over to Matt's and let him know what has happened."

The words had barely passed his lips, when he noticed Matt and Santos Ramírez rode into the narrow lane that led to the ranch house.

Santos had spent the night in town, drinking and enjoying Dolly's agreeable company. He had been on his way home when he'd met up with Matt. Aware of the younger man's hangover, Matt had suggested that he stop at the Black Diamond for a cup of coffee.

As the two men approached the house, Ted hurried down the porch steps to meet them. Not giving Matt time to dismount, he handed him Regina's note. "I think you'd better read this right away."

Matt scanned it quickly, then crumpling the note, he cursed, "Damn! How in the hell could she have done something so foolish!"

"What is wrong, *señor?*" asked Santos.

"Regina left last night to travel to Alan Garrett's," Matt answered.

"Alone?" Santos exclaimed.

Matt nodded brusquely. Looking at Ted, he said, "Pick ten hands to ride with me. If we leave within the hour, we should be able to catch up to Regina

412

sometime tonight. She has about seven hours head start on us."

"Do you think she'll ride straight through?" Ted asked.

"I doubt it," Matt replied. "Alan's ranch is about twenty miles north of Santa Fe. I'm sure she'll stop for the night."

"If you don't mind," Santos began, "I will go with you and your men."

"Of course, I don't mind," Matt answered, dismounting. As he climbed the porch steps, Hannah greeted him by murmuring, "I'm so worried about Regina."

"So am I, Hannah," Matt remarked, his tone revealing his anxiety.

Matt followed Hannah into the house, and a few minutes later, María came out onto the porch. Dressed for school, she was wearing a simple, calico gown, and her long hair was held back from her face with a white satin ribbon. Santos was standing alone when María stepped outside; Ted had gone to the bunkhouse. Matt hadn't told the girl of Santos presence, and surprised to see him, she gasped happily, "Santos!"

Turning to look at María, the young man smiled handsomely. He hadn't seen her for quite some time, and taking note of her blooming maturity, he knew she'd soon be a very beautiful young woman.

María rushed down the porch steps, and gazing up into his sensual face, she asked impulsively, "Santos, why have you stayed away so long? It's been ages since your last visit." Then she blushed, suddenly aware that she was behaving much too forwardly!

María's adoration of Santos was obvious, and recognizing her expression, he was pleased. From the first moment he had seen María, he had sensed that someday she would be his true love. But she was still

413

too young, and he had his wild oats to sow. Noticing her embarrassment, he smiled tenderly, "I promise, *señorita,* that I will visit again very soon." His eyes taking in her guileless beauty, he murmured, "You look very lovely. Are you on your way to school?"

"Yes," she answered. "I am looking for Mr. Lucas. He always drives me to school in the buckboard."

"Señor Lucas has gone to the bunkhouse, but he will be back shortly."

"Are you going with Papa to Mr. Garrett's?" she asked.

"Sí, I am," he answered. When María's pretty face clouded with concern, he asked, "What is wrong, little one?"

"Papa seemed very worried about my mother." Grasping Santos' arm, María said urgently, "Do you think Mama will be all right? She has her rifle and she took Blackie with her."

With an assurance that he did not really feel, Santos replied encouragingly, "I am sure she will be fine." Her hand was still on his arm, and placing his hand over hers, he continued gently, "Try not to worry, María."

At dusk, Regina had set up camp in a secluded area bordered by trees and shrubbery beyond which tall boulders loomed. Still wearing her suede trousers and fringed jacket, she now sat beside the small campfire, her knees raised and her arms crossed over them. As she watched the darting flames, she absently petted Blackie, and the dog snuggled closer to her side. Then, feeling sleepy, she looked away from the glowing fire, and lying back on her bedroll, she drew her Winchester close. She was just drifting into sleep when Blackie emitted a deep, warning growl. Sitting upright and bounding to her feet, Regina cocked her rifle at the

414

same moment that five riders emerged from the thicket. They had their pistols drawn, and spotting Regina's weapon, one of the men fired. The bullet grazed Regina's shoulder, but its powerful impact sent her spinning before she fell to the ground.

The man who had fired, drew up his horse and dismounted hastily. As he headed for Regina, Blackie's hair bristled, and baring his sharp fangs, he leaped forward to attack the stranger approaching his mistress. The man's pistol was in his hand, and as the dog jumped toward him, he aimed his gun at Blackie and pulled the trigger. He hit his target, and the dog's forward momentum was stopped in midair. Blackie's body dropped heavily, and blood oozed from his neck, its bright red color staining his white coat.

Regina was lying face down, so the man used his foot to turn her onto her back. Opening her eyes, Regina looked up into his bristly bearded face, and understanding his lustful sneer, she gasped.

"Well, ain't you a pretty little thing," he drawled. He glanced back at his companions. "Come see what we got here. I think we ought to get us some sweet lovin' before movin' on."

"We ain't got time," one of his comrades answered. "Come on, Chuck, let's get the hell out of here. That posse is hot on our trail."

Bending over, Chuck grabbed Regina and jerked her to her feet. His rough handling sent a sharp pain through her wounded shoulder. Grimacing, she placed a hand over her injury, and she could feel warm blood flowing through her fingers.

Glaring at Regina, Chuck ordered gruffly, "Get on your horse! I'm takin' you with me. After we lose that posse, I'm gonna take the time to get me a little lovin'."

When she made no response, he shoved her toward Midnight, causing her to stumble backward. Suddenly

415

catching sight of Blackie lying dead still, Regina cried piercingly, "Oh, no! Blackie!"

She moved so quickly that Chuck was taken off guard, and by the time he could reach for her, she had already passed him. Dropping to her knees beside the dog, she tried frantically to see if he was alive. But before she touched his blood-soaked neck, a barrage of gunshots erupted from the surrounding shrubbery. Regina immediately threw herself to the ground, draping one arm across Blackie. Feeling a heavy weight strike her side, she turned her head, and the sight of Chuck's bloody face and sightless staring eyes caused bile to rise in her throat. She wanted to move away from the grotesque body that was touching hers, but shots were still thundering around her.

Within moments, the firing ceased abruptly, and Regina cautiously raised her head. Looking around, she saw that three of the men who had come upon her were dead. The remaining two had surrendered. A group of riders materialized from the surrounding darkness, and remembering that a posse was chasing the five men, Regina assumed her rescuers were part of that posse.

Suddenly, Blackie whined, and happy that he was alive, Regina turned away from the mounted men to look at the dog. Patting his head gently, she murmured, "Blackie, thank goodness you aren't dead."

One of the riders dismounted, and hurrying to Regina, he clutched her arm and pulled her away from the dog. Angry at being treated so harshly, she tried to break free of his grasp, and she shouted, "Let me go!"

Still holding her, the man glanced at one of the riders and asked, "What should we do with her?"

He was answered by a heavyset, middle-aged man. "We'll hang her right along with her two friends."

Shocked, Regina gasped, "Hang me! But why?"

Swinging down from his horse, the heavyset man walked over to speak to her. "Do you think just because you're a woman, you can get by with murder?" he asked, his tone deadly cold.

"Murder!" Regina was astounded.

"After you robbed the bank, when you were shooting your way out of town, a little girl was wounded and a woman was killed. That girl is my daughter, and the woman was my wife."

"Bank robbery!" she replied strongly. "I don't know what you're talking about!"

At that moment, a man stepped up to them holding a saddlebag filled with money. "Here's the money from the bank, Mr. Delwood," he said to the older man talking to Regina.

Grasping the situation, Regina's heart began to pound rapidly as she stared into Mr. Delwood's angry eyes. Apparently, the men who had attacked her had robbed a bank and these men thought she was an accomplice.

Threateningly, Mr. Delwood said, "Maggie Fisher, I'm going to rid this countryside of scum like you."

"Maggie Fisher?" she repeated. "But I'm not Maggie Fisher."

His gaze moved to Regina's wounded shoulder. "I heard that you were shot when you were escaping from town, and now that I see it's true, I only wish your wound had been fatal. That would have saved us the trouble of hanging you."

When Delwood turned away, Regina cried anxiously, "Please, you must believe me! My name is Regina Brolin, and I'm traveling to Santa Fe to visit Alan Garrett. Please believe me! I'm not Maggie Fisher!" Regina had heard of the notorious Maggie Fisher. The woman was an outlaw who had committed several crimes in the New Mexico Territory.

417

"If you aren't Maggie Fisher," Mr. Delwood began, "then why are you riding with these men and why is the stolen money in your possession? I suppose it's merely a coincidence that you fit Maggie Fisher's description," he said ironically. "You're a tall, pretty blond dressed in a fringed jacket and trousers. That's exactly how the clerk described the woman who robbed the bank and told him she was Maggie Fisher." Abruptly, he turned away, and speaking to his companions, he ordered briskly, "Let's hang them before the sheriff and the rest of the posse show up!"

"The sheriff's goin' to be madder'n hell when he finds out we done lynched Maggie and her two men," one of the men remarked.

"I can handle the sheriff," Mr. Delwood assured him. "Hang those two murdering bastards, then we'll hang Maggie!"

Moving quickly, Regina clutched Mr. Delwood's arm. "Oh, don't you understand?" she said urgently. "Maggie Fisher must've died on the trail and they hid her body!" Receiving no response, her eyes looked wildly toward the two men who were soon to die. "Oh God, will you please tell them the truth? Tell them I'm not Maggie Fisher! It was your friend who shot me! I wasn't shot escaping town! For God's sake, tell them the truth!"

Stunned by the realization of their own impending deaths, the two men completely ignored Regina's cry for help.

Terrified, she watched as the two desperados were forced to mount their horses and ropes were swung over tree limbs. When a noose had been placed around each outlaw's neck, one of the men in the posse drew his pistol and moved closer to the horses carrying the condemned outlaws. As the blast of his pistol shot rang out loudly, the animals lurched forward, leaving their

418

riders swinging violently from the ends of the ropes.

Screaming, Regina collapsed onto the ground beside Blackie, and burying her face in the dog's thick fur, she began to weep hysterically. Blackie whined softly, and his wet tongue flickered across Regina's tear-streaked cheek.

At that moment, a pair of hands gripped her shoulders, and she held tighter to Blackie. "No! . . . No!" she begged. "Please don't hang me! . . . Oh, dear God, don't hang me!"

Roughly, she was forced to her feet, and with two men supporting her, she was led toward a horse. Growing faint, she fell to her knees, but they jerked her upright.

"Goddamn it, Maggie!" one of the men holding her said angrily, "Do we have to drag you to the damned horse?"

Suddenly, Regina found the strength to pull free of their grasps. "I am not Maggie Fisher! I am Regina Brolin!" she said forcefully. Then, lifting her head bravely and raising her small chin, she continued, "It won't be necessary for you to drag me to my horse!" As Regina's inborn courage took command, she glanced at both men with disgust, and her lips curled into a snarl, she ordered, "Don't put your dirty hands on me again!"

Swallowing back tears, she then began to walk steadily toward the horse that stood under a tree limb. Her steps faltered and she almost fell, but she regained her footing and resumed her slow pace. Deliberately, she kept her eyes turned away from the two bodies swinging back and forth at the end of the stretched ropes.

When she reached the horse, Mr. Delwood offered her his hand to help her mount, but brushing it aside, she stepped unassisted into the stirrup. The injury to

419

her shoulder made it difficult for her to swing into the saddle, but she was determined to do it unaided.

Regina could hear the rope being swung over the sturdy limb. Oh Matt, she cried inwardly, will you ever learn what happened to me, or will you and the others forever wonder why I never came home?

Involuntarily, she stiffened, and she once again felt faint as the noose was placed about her slender neck. She was vaguely surprised to find that it was so heavy and awkward as, jerking her hands behind her, Mr. Delwood secured them with a strip of rope.

Regina had never been so terrified. A paralyzing numbness came over her, and as she bowed her head to pray, tears streamed from her eyes.

Matt and the others had been some distance away when they'd heard the pistol shot that had sent Regina's attackers to their deaths. Now, cautiously, they made their way through the thicket, their horses' hooves muffled by the tall grass. As Matt neared the clearing, he caught his breath sharply when he saw Regina on a horse, a hangman's noose around her neck. As he watched one of her captors drew a pistol, and reacting alertly, Matt grabbed his Winchester from its scabbard. Instantly, he had realized that if he were to holler at Regina's captors, telling them to throw down their weapons, one of them might shoot, causing her horse to panic and gallop off.

As the man standing beside Regina slowly pointed his pistol upward, Matt gripped his Winchester and took careful aim through the rear sight for greater accuracy. The full moon's golden rays fell across the landscape, giving Matt the light he needed to see his target. Gently, he squeezed the trigger, and his rifle discharged simultaneously with the pistol shot. The bullet from the Winchester cut through the hanging rope, and, as Regina's horse bounded forward, the severed rope swung weightlessly in the air.

If he'd had time to think about what was happening, Matt's fear for Regina's life would have made his hands unsteady and his body tense. Then his horse, sensing Matt's unease, would have become fidgety, throwing off Matt's aim.

When Regina heard the shots that mingled into one blast, she'd braced herself and prayed that God would let her die instantly, but when she found herself still sitting on the galloping horse, her shock rendered her incapable of figuring out what had taken place. Almost immediately, because her hands were tied behind her, she lost her balance and began to slip from the saddle. But an instant before Regina would have fallen, Matt rode his horse up alongside hers. He grabbed her about the waist and swept her from her horse onto his own.

Still stunned by her sudden escape from death, Regina looked into his face a moment before she cried joyously, "Matt! . . . Oh God, Matt!"

Noticing her injured shoulder, he asked anxiously, "Darlin', are you all right?"

"Yes," she replied shakily. "I was shot, but the bullet only grazed me."

Holding her close, Matt turned his horse and rode back to where Santos and his ranch hands had the other men surrounded. Before he could find out why they had tried to hang Regina, the rest of the posse suddenly arrived, their horses breaking through the bordering shrubbery and entering the clearing.

Watching them advance, Regina recognized Sheriff Davis in the lead, and she realized the bank robbery had taken place in Santa Fe.

Pulling up his horse, the sheriff looked about with confusion. When he spotted the two men still hanging from tree limbs, his face reddened with anger. "What in the hell has happened here!" he bellowed fiercely. Then, seeing Regina with Matt, he rode over to them and demanded, "Mrs. Brolin, what are you doing here?"

Matt untied Regina's bound hands, and still in his arms she breathlessly explained everything that had happened. When she had completed her story, Sheriff Davis ordered his men to cut down the two bodies. Then, since Dr. Carter had accompanied the posse, the sheriff called him over to see to Regina's shoulder. When the doctor joined Regina, the sheriff left to talk to Mr. Delwood and the men who had carried out the lynchings.

So that the doctor could thoroughly examine her wound, Matt helped Regina down from his horse and assisted her to her bedroll. As soon as Dr. Carter had finished cleaning and bandaging her shoulder, she asked him to please see to Blackie. Complying, the doctor went over to the dog, and with Santos' assistance, he cleaned and disinfected Blackie's wound. After doing so, to Regina's relief, he told her that the dog would be all right.

Suddenly, wanting desperately to leave that place, Regina turned to Matt who was sitting beside her. "Please take me away from here. I want to go home."

"Of course," he said gently, rising and helping her to her feet.

Just then Sheriff Davis approached Matt and Regina. He eyed them thoughtfully for a moment before stating a little gruffly, "Mr. and Mrs. Brolin, I have now encountered you two twice, and both times you were involved in very dangerous situations." Arms akimbo, the sheriff grinned. "You two look like a nice couple, so why don't you return home and see if this time you can manage to stay out of trouble."

422

"We'll try," Regina replied, smiling, "By the way, do you know what happened to Maggie Fisher?"

He nodded toward a horse bearing a covered body on its back. "We found her on the trail. Apparently, she died from the gunshot she received in town."

Regina glanced across the short span separating her from Mr. Delwood. For a second his eyes met hers; then, too ashamed to face her, he averted his gaze. "What will happen to Mr. Delwood?" she asked the sheriff.

"That will be up to the judge. You understand, of course, that you can press charges against him."

"No," Regina answered quickly. "I don't ever want to see him again. I want to forget this horrible nightmare." Her voice almost breaking, she murmured. "I just want to go home."

Because of Regina's and Blackie's injuries, Matt decided to spend the night at a vacant shack located a few miles from the spot where Regina had set up camp. There was no furniture inside the deserted cabin, so Matt prepared a pallet on the wooden floor. The ranch hands and Santos, meanwhile, fixed themselves places to sleep outside, and taking care of Blackie, Santos settled the dog on a blanket close to his bedroll.

Considerately, Matt turned his back as Regina stripped down to her undergarments. Her shoulder was beginning to ache, and as she tried to make herself reasonably comfortable on the pallet, Matt turned around in time to see a flicker of pain cross her face.

Dr. Carter had given Matt a bottle of laudanum, instructing him to give Regina a small dose if her wound pained her, so, opening his saddlebags, Matt reached inside and withdrew the medicine. Taking it to Regina, he knelt beside her. The lit lantern was placed

423

next to her blankets, and moving it out of the way, he told her gently, "If you take a small drink of this, it'll help you sleep." He opened the bottle, filled the cap with medication, and handed the dose to Regina.

Sitting up, she reached for the medicine, but her hand was trembling so Matt helped her guide the cap to her mouth. As she swallowed the laudanum, her eyes sought her husband's. Then she lay back down. The glow from the burning lantern was reflected in Matt's dark eyes, and his piercing pupils shone like daggers, penetrating into her very soul. She wanted to look away, but his eyes mesmerized her. Despite her intentions, she could feel desire awakening. He only had to look at her and her defenses crumbled! Good Lord, had she no resistance at all?

The laudanum was beginning to have an effect, and Regina suddenly felt drowsy. Her vision blurred, and she seemed to be floating weightlessly. Matt was still gazing sensually at her, but she now saw him through a cloudy haze. An intense longing flowed over her, then became pinpointed where her physical desire was strongest.

"Matt," she murmured invitingly, drifting into a dreamlike state.

He dimmed the lantern, then lay beside her and took her into his arms. He knew she was affected by the laudanum, and as his maleness responded to her closeness, he was momentarily tempted to take advantage of her vulnerability. But he loved Regina too much to do that. When, or if, he again made love to his wife, she would be in full control of her faculties.

Snuggling next to him, Regina placed her head on his shoulder, and kissing her forehead, he mumbled, "Go to sleep, darlin'."

Her lips brushed against his ear, and her warm breath started a fire in his loins. "Matt," she whispered, her voice lethargic, "I want you to make love to me."

Matt groaned uncomfortably, his need for Regina demanding release. "Not tonight, sweetheart," he replied softly, as he desperately clung to his will power.

She ran a hand over his stomach, seeking his hardness. Even through his trousers, she could feel how badly he wanted her. She pressed her hand against him, her touch generating a heat in Matt that burned like wildfire. He removed her hand, and placing it on his chest, he insisted gruffly, "Go to sleep, Regina!"

Her mind muddled by laudanum, her voice slurred, Regina said, "Don't you want me, Matt?"

Matt grimaced. He wanted her with every fiber of his being! But not this way! He knew she'd soon be sound asleep, and tomorrow she probably wouldn't remember anything about tonight. Controlling his urge to relish her lovely body, he continued to hold her close, wishing desperately that she would fall asleep. When he suddenly became aware that her breathing had deepened, Matt sighed with relief.

Gently, so he wouldn't awaken her, he moved her out of his arms. Hastily, he shed his boots, trousers, and shirt. Then he rejoined Regina on the pallet. Pulling a blanket over them, he again took her into his arms and then closed his eyes, waiting for sleep to overcome him. But he had a feeling it would be awhile before his need for Regina would allow slumber to overtake him.

The next morning, Regina awakened before Matt. Her eyelids fluttered open, and for a moment she was disoriented. But, fleetingly, everything came back to her, the outlaw attack, the posse arriving, and her brush with death. Remembering the lynchings, she shuddered. If it hadn't been for Matt . . .

Her thoughts clearing, she became aware of Matt's

closeness. Sitting up, she looked down into his face which was relaxed in sleep. Then, glancing about, she spotted her outer garments on the floor next to Matt's. Thinking back, she recalled that Matt had given her a dose of laudanum, but after that her recollections were cloudy. Had Matt made love to her? She vaguely remembered that he had lain beside her and had taken her into his arms. She must have given herself to him. The laudanum had weakened her defenses. How dare he take advantage of her in that state! Now he probably believed she had forgiven him and was willing to resume their marriage. He was probably planning to move back into her life! Oh, he was so smug, so self-confident! Well, he was in for a rude awakening! She was not about to forgive him!

Matt began to stir, and remaining seated, Regina looked down at him. When he met her gaze, he started to grin, but noticing her irritable expression, his smile failed to materialize.

"Matt Brolin," she almost spat out, "you are despicable!"

He arched an eyebrow, and a cocky sneer concealed his inner hurt. "That's a strange way to say good morning to the man who saved your life."

Impatiently, Regina said, "You know what I mean! How did you dare to make love to me while I was under the influence of laudanum! If you think last night means I have forgiven you, then you are badly mistaken! Our marriage is over, Matt! Do you understand? It's over!"

Offering no comment, Matt flung off the blanket, and getting to his feet, he quickly slipped into his clothes. Then he sat down on the pallet and put on his boots.

Watching him silently, Regina waited for an explanation of his actions, but when he remained noncommital, she realized he had no intention of discussing last night or their marriage.

Reaching over, Matt gathered her clothes and placed them at her side. "Get dressed," he ordered.

Pressing the issue, she insisted, "You do understand, don't you? Regardless of what happened last night, there is no longer a marriage between us."

Matt stood and walked over to the unlit hearth. Taking his gun belt from the dust-coated mantel, he strapped it on. When he turned to his wife his face was emotionless. "Santos and the others are probably preparing breakfast, so as soon as you're dressed come outside and eat." Without another word, he stepped to the door and left.

Regina suddenly felt depressed. Had she been hoping that Matt would set aside his stubborn pride and plead for her forgiveness? Or was she sad because she had once again given herself to Matt when she had promised herself that she would continue to reject him? She wasn't sure what the answer was, but once more she silently swore that she would never again succumb to Matt. She would not give him the opportunity to hurt her as he had in the past. Shielding her heart with resentment, she told herself that if he was hurting, he deserved to suffer.

Chapter Thirty-six

Regina had now been home for two weeks and her shoulder was completely healed. Blackie's recovery was slower, however. He still hadn't regained his full strength but he was improving with each passing day. Although Matt continued to run the Black Diamond, he very seldom came into contact with Regina, and she was sure he was avoiding her deliberately. Did he feel guilty because he had taken advantage of her that night at the deserted cabin? She wasn't sure, and she kept telling herself that she didn't care why he evaded her.

Now, as she sat on the parlor sofa beside María, Regina was trying to keep from looking at Matt. Santos had been invited to dinner, and when Matt had dropped by to see the children, they had asked Regina to let him stay. Realizing Santos would enjoy a man's company at the dinner table, Regina had agreed. After the meal, everyone had retired to the parlor except Cort who had gone to bed. As Regina sat, silent, she finally glanced at Matt. He was sipping brandy and conversing with Santos. Once again, she told herself that it was all over between them.

Turning her gaze away from her husband, Regina studied María. She smiled tenderly when she noticed that the girl was looking worshipfully at Santos. Her adoration was apparent, and casting a quick glance at Santos, Regina wondered if he was aware of María's love. As she gazed at him, Santos put out his cheroot and thanked his host and hostess for a delicious dinner. When he rose to leave, Regina subtly suggested that María see him to the porch.

Complying gladly, the young girl escorted their dashingly handsome guest to the door. Once they were outside, Santos guided her to the porch railing and then studied her for a moment before asking, "How old are you, María?"

"Fifteen," she murmured, mesmerized by his dark eyes which gazed deeply into hers.

In her white dress María looked very lovely. The gown was designed to be worn off the shoulders and it accentuated the fullness of her young breasts. Her long black hair flowed gracefully to her waist, and the golden moonlight reflected its lustrous glow.

Santos found her very desirable, but he was too much the gentleman to take advantage of her youth and vulnerability.

Taking her hand, he raised it to his lips and kissed it gently. "You are very beautiful, María."

Her heart accelerating with joy, María breathed out, "Thank you, Santos."

Releasing her hand, he reached up and unhooked the gold chain that he was wearing. A tiny cross was fastened to it, and as Santos clasped it about María's slender neck, he said tenderly, "Wear this always, *señorita.*"

"I'll never take it off," she swore. "But why are you giving it to me?"

Smiling charmingly, he replied, "It is my promise that someday I will ask you to marry me."

Before María could respond, they heard a buggy

429

approach the house. Holding her hand in his, Santos led her to the porch steps, and as the conveyance drew closer, he recognized the visitor. "It's Dr. Henderson," he said, a touch of surprise in his voice.

While Santos and María were dallying on the porch, Regina had gone to Cort's room to check on him, and finding him awake and feverish, she had carried him into the parlor where Matt was still enjoying his brandy.

Her face etched with worry, she said, "Cort is running a fever."

Putting down his drink, Matt hurried to Regina. The child's arms were wrapped about her neck and his head was nestled against her shoulder. Touching Cort's brow, Matt said with deep concern, "He's burning up!"

As Matt started to lift Cort into his arms, the front door opened and María called, "Dr. Henderson is here. He wants to see both of you."

"Dr. Henderson!" Regina cried with relief.

"He couldn't have picked a better time to drop by," Matt said gratefully, as he ushered Regina and the sick child onto the porch.

The doctor had just alighted from his buggy, and he was poised at the bottom of the steps when Matt and Regina stepped outside. Before Matt had a chance to tell him of Cort's condition, Dr. Henderson revealed his grave news, "I'm on my way back to town from the Carlsons' spread, and I thought I should stop by and let you know that there is an outbreak of influenza. Mrs. Carlson and one of her children have contracted the disease. I've had four more cases besides this, so we are definitely in the midst of an epidemic. I advise you to stay close to home and avoid other people. Influenza is very contagious, and is often fatal, especially to the elderly and the very young."

Dr. Henderson's words hit Matt severely, but his reference to the very young caused him to pale. "Cort is running a fever," he told the doctor, his voice hoarse with fear for his son's life.

Moving quickly, Dr. Henderson grabbed his medical kit from the buggy, and leaping up the steps, he ordered briskly, "Take him to his room so that I can check him."

Matt turned to Regina, expecting her to obey the doctor and carry Cort to his bedroom. When she didn't move, he reached for the child, but clutching her son possessively, Regina stepped back. The loss of the twins was still too recent, and the thought of losing another child made Regina's eyes glaze with panic. A violent shudder racked her body, and her heart felt as though it were being torn from her chest. Losing control, she cried piteously, "No! Oh Matt! Not again! . . . Please tell me God won't take another of my babies!"

Fighting his own fear, Matt pried Cort from Regina's firm grasp and handed the child to Santos. Then, as the others hurried into the house, he clutched Regina's shoulders.

"You must get a hold on yourself," he told her, although his own grip was tenuous.

But she cried out hysterically, "No! . . . I'm not strong enough to lose another child . . . God, don't take Cort away from me . . . please!"

Shaking convulsively and on the verge of shock, Regina continued her frantic rambling until Matt drew her into his embrace and, holding her close, murmured soothingly, "Honey, you mustn't lose control."

"Oh, Matt, I'm so afraid!" Regina sobbed.

"I know," he whispered comfortingly. "Cort's going to get well, Regina. We won't lose another child." Gently, he moved her so that he could see down into

431

her face. Her eyes were lowered, and he said quietly, "Look at me."

She raised her tear-filled eyes beseechingly.

"You must be strong for Cort's sake. He'll need you," he explained compassionately.

The words had barely passed Matt's lips when they heard Cort cry for Regina, his summons so persistent that it carried clearly to the porch.

The sound of her son's voice gave Regina the strength she needed, and stepping back from Matt, she straightened her slim shoulders. She moved quickly to the door, but before entering the house, she turned back to her husband and said, "I couldn't love Cort any more if I had borne him. He may not be of my flesh and blood, but he's of my heart."

Regina entered the house quickly and she didn't see the tears that came to Matt's eyes.

Dr. Henderson diagnosed Cort's illness as influenza, and since the boy was only three years old, the disease posed a serious threat to his life. Since the doctor had to divide his time among all his patients, he described what must be done for Cort and then left the sick child in the hands of his parents.

Regina and Matt nursed Cort assiduously. One of them was always at his bedside, and they took turns catching a bit of restless sleep on the cot that had been moved into the bedroom. More than once, Ted and Hannah offered to relieve the weary parents, but neither Regina nor Matt was willing to leave Cort in the care of anyone else.

To protect María from the contagious disease, Regina had sent her to the Ramírez hacienda with Santos, along with a note asking Antonio to please let her stay at his home until the crisis was over.

432

It was very difficult for María to be away from her brother when he was so gravely ill, and not even Santos' company could console her. Several times a day, either Antonio or Santos rode over to the ranch to check on Cort's condition, only to bring back the depressing news that he was still critically ill.

In the evening, two days after Cort had been stricken, Santos returned from one of his rides to the Black Diamond to find María waiting for him in the parlor. As he entered the room, she bolted from her chair and fled to his side. "How is Cort?" she asked urgently.

"The same," he replied, wishing he could have brought her better news.

Feeling faint, María fell against Santos, who lifted her into his arms. Carrying her to the sofa, he laid her down.

"Papá!" he called urgently.

Hurrying from the study and heading toward the parlor, Antonio saw María lying on the sofa with Santos standing beside her. His son's face was clouded with worry.

Going to María, Antonio touched her brow. He was relieved to feel that she had no fever.

María's long lashes fluttered and, slowly, her eyes opened. Finding Santos and Antonio standing over her, she murmured feebly, "I must have fainted."

To Santos, Antonio said, "I will go to the kitchen and tell Carla to fix María a bowl of soup. She has not eaten in two days."

"No," María objected softly. "I can't eat. I'm too worried about my little brother."

Santos had not been aware that María had neglected herself so, and he told her quite firmly, "María, you will eat, and I will not take no for an answer."

As Antonio headed for the kitchen, Santos knelt

beside the sofa, and holding María's hand, he said gently, "You must take good care of yourself because when your brother is well, he will need you. I'm sure the doctor will insist that he remain in bed for some time, and you will need your strength to find ways to entertain him."

Clutching Santos' hand, María cried, "Oh, Santos, I pray that he will get well! I love him so much. And Mama? . . ."

"*Sí?* What about Regina?" he asked.

Gravely, she replied, "I don't know if she could survive losing Cort so soon after the twins."

"Regina is very strong," Santos said encouragingly.

María shook her head, insisting solemnly, "No, if Cort does not recover, I'm afraid that Mama's grief might destroy her."

"And Matt?" he asked, amazed that a girl as young as María could be so emotionally mature.

Tears flooded her eyes, and, as Santos took her into his arms, he said, "I don't know what it would do to Papa! Oh, Santos, Cort must get well! Please pray that he will!"

"I have prayed," he murmured, brushing his lips across her brow. "María, I have prayed with all my heart."

Cort's illness was now into its third and most critical day. Dr. Henderson had informed Regina and Matt that the disease usually reached its peak by seventy-two hours.

The doctor had come to the ranch in the late afternoon, intending to remain until Cort's crisis was over, but during the evening he was summoned to deliver a baby. Before he left, Dr. Henderson said that he'd return as soon as he could, and he told Matt and

Regina to take heart from the fact that Cort's condition hadn't worsened. No new cases of influenza had been reported, and to the doctor's great relief, it was beginning to seem that the epidemic was over. But he was genuinely concerned about Cort Brolin. The child wasn't improving, and during the epidemic's short duration, Dr. Henderson had already stood by helplessly as influenza claimed the lives of two children.

Night, like a heavy blanket, had descended over the quiet ranch house, and the glow from the kerosene lamp flickered softly across Cort's flushed face as he slept fitfully. Sitting in a chair beside his bed, Regina kept a constant watch on her ailing son, while Matt dozed on the narrow cot, his sleep haunted by worrisome dreams.

Dipping a cloth into the basin of water on the night table, Regina wrung it out, and leaning over, she placed the cool cloth on Cort's warm brow.

"My darling," she whispered maternally. "My precious, darling. Mama won't let anything happen to you."

She took one of his small hands in hers, and holding it tenderly, she rubbed her thumb back and forth across his fevered fingers. She smiled wistfully as her fatigued mind recalled the little game she and Cort always played at bedtime. She'd hold his hand, and he would wrap his fingers about her thumb. Whereupon she would kiss each dimpled knuckle, then open his hand and place a kiss on his palm, saying, "If you hold this kiss very tight, it will keep you safe throughout the night." Clenching his chubby hand into a fist, Cort's eyes would sparkle as he gleefully cried out, "I got your kiss, Mama! I got your kiss!"

Cort's growing restlessness brought Regina out of her reverie. Quickly she let go of his hand, and standing over the bed, she removed the cloth and checked his

435

brow. His fever was rising rapidly.

"Matt!" she called urgently.

Waking instantly, Matt leaped to his feet and he was at Regina's side in two long strides.

"His fever is higher!" she said anxiously.

Suddenly, the child was racked with severe tremors, his little body shaking convulsively. His eyes opened, and looking at his parents through a fevered haze, he moaned weakly, "Cold . . . cold . . ."

"Regina, take off your shoes and dress," Matt commanded hastily. As she did so without question, Matt quickly shed his boots, trousers, and shirt. Stripped down to his underclothes, he drew back the covers and lying beside Cort, he told Regina to do the same.

Hurrying around the bed, she placed herself at Cort's other side. The child was shaking violently, and his parents moved closer, trying to warm him with the heat from their own bodies. Within minutes his chills subsided, and he drifted back into sleep.

Regina brushed her lips against Cort's chestnut curls; then she kissed his fevered cheek. Gazing down into his sweet face, she whispered, "If only his fever would break." She looked over at Matt, and their eyes met, full of shared hope. Matt had a three-day beard, and his eyes were bloodshot. He looked wretched, and Regina knew she probably looked even worse. She hadn't even bothered to glance in a mirror for the past seventy-two hours.

"Oh, Matt, I'm so afraid," she said.

"Regina, take Cort's hand," he told her.

She did as Matt requested, and he, in turn, held the child's other hand. "Our love will give him the strength to get well. Hold tightly to his hand, sweetheart."

Regina knew that tonight the crisis period would be reached. Cort's fever would break or . . . ?

"Dear God," she prayed, "help us!"

Regina brought Cort's hand to her lips. She placed a trembling kiss on each small knuckle; then, opening his hand, she kissed his tiny palm. Closing her hand over his, she said softly, "If you hold this kiss very tight, it will keep you safe throughout the night."

Dawn was six hours away, and those proved to be the longest six hours Matt and Regina had ever spent. They dared not get up and move away from Cort. Nor did they release their holds on his hands. For some inexplicable reason they felt as though they would lose their son if they left his side. He needed his parents' strength, and they could only give it to him by holding onto him relentlessly.

The sun was just beginning to peek over the horizon when Cort's fever broke. Perspiration began to bead his brow, the wetness making his locks curl tightly about his forehead.

Regina was the first one to notice, and joyfully, she exclaimed, "Matt, his fever is gone!"

Sitting up, Matt looked down at his son. Cort had awakened and was watching him with eyes no longer clouded by fever. Gathering Cort into his arms, Matt showered the child's face with kisses, but as he gently released Cort, the boy's little face puckered into a frown.

"What's wrong, son?" Matt asked urgently.

"Your whiskers hurt," Cort complained, brushing his fingers over his tender cheeks.

Rubbing a hand across his bristly chin, Matt smiled, and getting out of bed, he muttered, "I guess I do need a shave."

"Mama," Cort mumbled, "I'm hungry." His eyes flitted curiously from one parent to the other as he wondered why they had been sleeping with him.

Regina kissed Cort's forehead; then, leaving the bed, she said happily, "I'll get you a bowl of broth."

437

Cort started to object to broth, but before he could do so, he quickly drifted back to sleep.

Regina walked around to the other side of the bed, and standing close to Matt, they looked down at their sleeping child.

"This time, darlin', we didn't lose," Matt murmured fervently.

"Thank God," Regina sighed. A faint smile touched her lips as she turned to face her husband.

He met her gaze, and noting her fatigue, he drew her gingerly into his arms. "Why don't you get some sleep?" he suggested. "Hannah can take care of Cort."

Giving in to her weariness, she leaned into his embrace. During Cort's illness, Regina had forgotten the bitterness and resentment she had been harboring toward Matt, and when he pulled her closer, she offered no resistance.

Hannah rapped softly on the door, then opened it. She was astonished to find Matt and Regina clad only in their underclothes.

Aware of Hannah's presence, Matt released his wife and stepped quickly to his clothes.

Averting her gaze from Matt's partial nakedness, Hannah asked, "How is Cort?"

Smiling, Regina answered, "His fever has broken."

"Thank the good Lord!" Hannah praised.

Having dressed, Matt moved to Regina, and taking her hand, he pressed it gently. "I'm going home to get some rest. I'll be back later."

Regina nodded agreeably, but she almost asked him not to go. She watched as he stepped to the bedside and kissed his son's brow, then gave Hannah an affectionate hug before leaving. Matt's departure brought a sudden loneliness into Regina's heart. Staring vacantly about the bedroom, which moments before had been filled with his presence, Regina missed her husband.

438

I still love him, she thought. I have never stopped loving him! I love him now more than when we married. In the beginning my love was based on passion and infatuation. Real love, the kind that can weather any storm, takes time to grow and mature. A man and woman must share much in life before their love can be impregnable.

"Hannah," Regina began briskly, her tired body rejuvenated by her new awareness, "I'm going to take a bath and then ride over to see Matt. Would you mind taking care of Cort until we return?"

"We?" Hannah asked with a knowing smile.

Her green eyes sparkling, Regina stated decisively, "I want Matt to come back home where he belongs!"

Matt had shaved and taken a bath before lying down for a nap. He intended to sleep for a couple of hours, and then ride out to the range to talk to Ted before returning to visit Cort. Making himself comfortable, he stretched, then fluffed the pillow beneath his head. He was about to close his eyes when his ears detected a horse approaching the house. Reluctantly, he sat up and got to his feet. He was extremely tired and in no mood for a visitor. But he hadn't expected Regina, and when she called his name as she knocked firmly on the door, he forgot his weariness.

Darting across the room, he prayed her appearance didn't mean that Cort had had a relapse. He flung open the door, and taking him totally unaware, Regina practically sprang into his embrace.

"Matt!" she cried. "Oh darling, I'm so sorry! Please forgive me!"

Stunned, Matt was unresponsive for a moment, then he slowly encircled her in his arms.

"Please say you'll forgive me!" Regina pleaded,

clinging to him desperately.

Gently, Matt moved her so that he could reach over and close the door. "Forgive you for what?" he asked, turning back to face her.

"For all the bitterness and resentment that I harbored," she replied.

"You had every right to feel that way," he said softly.

"No, I didn't have the right," Regina argued. "No one has the right to deliberately hurt someone they love."

Studying her carefully, he said deliberately, "Are you saying that you still love me?"

"Yes!" she admitted, her eyes filling with emotion.

"What brought about your sudden change of heart?" Matt asked warily.

Regina sighed deeply. "Cort's illness." Her excitement rising, she continued, "Oh, Matt, we are two adults who love each other, yet we have been negating love to "get even"! Dear God, how could we have been such fools? We placed too much importance on jealousy, suspicion, and passion. We completely ignored the only things in our lives that are truly precious."

"Which are?" he asked.

"María, Cort, and our marriage," she murmured.

Sweeping her into his arms, Matt groaned. "Darlin', you're right. We have been acting like fools."

Holding him close, she cried, "I love you, Matt. I love you with my heart and my soul. Please come back home! I need you!"

Embracing her tightly, he replied feelingly, "Of course, I'll come back home." Pausing, he added quietly, "Home. God, Regina, I never realized until this moment that the Black Diamond *is* home to me. It was never necessary for me to buy my own land and build a house on it to have a place to call home."

Stepping back and looking up into his face, she said teasingly, "Home is where the heart is."

Smiling tenderly, he replied, "My heart is at the Black Diamond with you and the children."

"Then let's go home, shall we?" she suggested, her eyes sparkling with happiness.

"First, we have some unfinished business to take care of," he told her, his tone edged with amusement.

"What kind of business?" she asked.

Grinning wryly, he replied, "That night at the cabin when you were under the influence of laudanum, you were a teasing little vixen. You tempted me quite strongly, but regardless of what you might believe, I was too much of a gentleman to take advantage of the situation." Taking her hand, he placed it against his male hardness. "Since that night I've had a continual ache."

Saucily, she asked, "Does it hurt terribly, darling?"

Frowning as though in deep pain, he groaned. "To say it is excruciating is an understatement."

"Poor dear," she purred soothingly. "What can I do to make the discomfort go away?"

Pressing her hand firmly against his rising hardness, he muttered, "I'm already beginning to feel better."

Rising on tiptoe, she kissed his earlobe; then, nibbling it gently, she promised seductively, "If you'll invite me to your bed, I'll make all your hurt vanish."

Chuckling, he lifted her into his arms. "You're the only medicine I need, you enticing little wildcat."

Taking her into the bedroom, he hastily helped her shed her riding apparel, and when she was completely unclothed, he eased her down onto the bed. As his eyes hungrily roamed her body, he whispered sensually,

"Regina, I love you. You're everything to me."

His need now urgent, Matt swiftly discarded his clothes, and Regina's eyes glowed with love as she watched her husband disrobe. I love him so! she thought. He's my life, my world.

She held up her arms to him, and when he entered her embrace, his lips claimed hers in a long, rapturous kiss while their bodies melded, bare flesh touching bare flesh. Then Regina's legs parted and Matt entered her moist depths, his penetration sending tingling chills up her spine.

"My darling," she murmured, locking her ankles around his waist.

"Regina," he moaned, his voice heavy with passion. "I need you, sweetheart."

Happiness enveloped Regina as she wrapped her arms possessively about his neck. She knew Matt's jealousy and suspicion had been put to rest, and he would never again doubt her sincerity.

"Make love to me," she whispered.

"It will be my pleasure to do so," he replied, and gathering her close, he drove into her with abandon.

Chapter Thirty=seven

As the months passed, life at the Black Diamond ran smoothly. Regina had never been happier. Her love for her husband had deepened, and she knew she was loved in return. That anything or anyone could possibly upset the contentment that she and Matt had found never even crossed Regina's mind.

On the sunny afternoon when she stepped onto the porch to see a buggy approaching, she never imagined that the people it carried were about to bring pain into Matt's life. Shading her eyes with her hand, Regina watched as the buggy drew closer. Seated upon it were an elderly couple that she had never seen before. Wondering why they were calling, she stepped off the porch to greet them. When the carriage came to a halt, the man stepped down from the buggy, then turned to assist the woman accompanying him. Holding her arm in a protective fashion, he led her to Regina.

"Mrs. Brolin?" he asked, raising his eyebrows questioningly.

"Yes," Regina murmured, her curiosity now aroused. Who were these people and why had they come to the Black Diamond? Their Eastern apparel made it quite apparent that they were visitors to the West.

Tipping the narrow brim of his felt hat, the man continued, "My name is Donald Richardson." Nodding toward his companion, he proceeded, "This is Ellen Davenport."

Regina looked at the woman and smiled. She was quite striking, and envisioning her as she had been in her youth, Regina imagined that she must have been beautiful.

"I am Mrs. Davenport's attorney," Mr. Richardson explained. "We are here to visit Matt Brolin. It is of the upmost importance that we see him as soon as possible."

"He's working in the study," Regina said, and gesturing toward the front door, she added, "If you'll come inside, I'll get my husband for you."

"Thank you, Mrs. Brolin," the lawyer replied. He grasped his client's arm and assisted her up the short flight of steps. Noticing how slowly the woman moved, Regina wondered if she was in poor health.

After showing the couple into the parlor, Regina hurried into the study to find her husband sitting at the desk and working on the tally ledger.

"Matt," she began, crossing the room, "you have visitors."

Glancing up from his work, he repeated vaguely, "Visitors?"

Pausing beside the desk, she replied, "Ellen Davenport and her attorney, Donald Richardson."

Perplexed, Matt mumbled, "I've never heard of them. Why would they want to see me?"

Smiling, Regina answered, "There's one way to find out, darling. Why don't you ask them?"

Matt grinned. "Are they in the parlor?"

"Yes," she answered.

"Why don't you bring them in here?" he suggested.

Agreeing, Regina returned to the parlor and asked

the couple to accompany her into the study. As Regina led the visitors inside, Matt got to his feet, and moving around the desk, he shook hands with Mr. Richardson. When Regina introduced him to Ellen Davenport, he nodded politely, but he noticed that the woman's dark eyes were studying him intently.

"Mr. Brolin," the attorney began, "my client and I must speak to you about something very personal." He stole a quick glance at Regina. "You might prefer that we talk alone."

"I have no secrets from my wife," Matt answered. He drew up two chairs and placed them in front of the desk, and when his guests were seated, he returned to his own chair. Regina walked over to stand at his side. They watched the couple curiously, waiting for an explanation of their visit.

Clearing his voice, Mr. Richardson spoke, "Mr. Brolin, it has taken us years to find you. We finally learned of your whereabouts from Alan Garrett."

Arching his eyebrows, Matt asked, "Why have you been looking for me?"

Mr. Richardson started to reply, but Ellen Davenport placed her slim hand on his arm. "Donald, let me explain," she said quietly.

He patted her hand consolingly. "Ellen, are you sure? Perhaps it would be easier for you if you let me do the talking."

"It's my place to tell . . . to tell Mr. Brolin the truth," she said in a low voice.

Stepping closer to Matt, Regina placed a hand on his shoulder. He glanced up at her, and as their eyes met, both sensed that Ellen Davenport was about to change their lives.

The woman removed a lace handkerchief from her purse and used it to dab at her eyes. Regina wondered if their visitor was crying, but she couldn't be sure. Then, resting her hands on her lap, Ellen Davenport toyed nervously with the handkerchief as she looked steadily into Matt's face. Her intense scrutiny made Matt uncomfortable, and he began to fidget impatiently as he waited for the woman to speak.

"Mr. Brolin," she finally said, "what I have to tell you will come as a shock, so please try to prepare yourself."

Matt nodded brusquely, wishing she would simply get to the point and tell him why she was here.

Ellen Davenport's breathing deepened, and, tensing, she moved to the edge of her chair, where she sat rigidly. Then she spoke slowly and quietly. "I am your mother."

Her words echoed thunderously in Matt's mind, but the room became eerily silent. The quietness hovered heavily over these four people who suddenly seemed incapable of movement or speech.

When Matt slowly got to his feet everyone stared at him with astonishment as though he had suddenly bounded from his chair. His expression was emotionless as he looked into his mother's face. He could see a strong resemblance between himself and the woman who had borne him. Her hair was gray, but he was sure it had once been the color of his own, matching her brown eyes and dark, olive complexion.

"Mrs. Davenport," Matt began, his tone unfeeling. "I don't know why after all this time, you have decided to find me, but I do know that you are thirty-four years too late. I don't like to be rude, but you leave me no other choice. You are not welcome in my home or my life." Glancing at Mr. Richardson, he said gruffly, "I want you both to leave immediately!"

"No!" Regina cried, clutching Matt's arm and getting his attention. "Darling, don't send your mother away!"

"Mother?" Matt sneered. "This woman isn't my mother. She gave up that right when she left me on the orphanage doorstep."

"You weren't left on the doorstep," Ellen whispered, so softly that Matt barely heard her.

"What?" he asked, turning to look at her.

She sighed deeply. "Please sit down and let me speak to you."

Noting Matt's hesitation, Regina pleaded with him. "Do as she says. If you send her away, you'll never forgive yourself. Oh, darling, don't you understand? This is your chance to find out who you are—to know your heritage, the circumstances surrounding your birth, who your father was!"

"Your wife is right," Mr. Richardson insisted. "You should listen to Mrs. Davenport, if for no other reason than to learn about yourself."

Reluctantly, Matt agreed. His shock was beginning to fade, and a feeling of numbness was coming over him. He returned to his seat, and Regina sat sideways on the arm of his chair. Taking her hand, he held it tightly.

Looking at his mother, Matt said tonelessly, "I'll listen to what you have to say."

"Thank you," she replied gratefully. Her hands were trembling, and she clutched at her handkerchief to quiet them. Then she leaned back in her chair, and drawing a deep breath, she began to unravel the mystery of Matt's birth. "I was born in Boston. My father, James Edwards, was an attorney. We were wealthy, but not extremely rich. My mother was Spanish. Father met her when he was touring Spain. They married, and he brought her back to Boston. You and I inherited our dark complexion and hair from my mother. She died when I was four years old, and I was raised by my father who was a very domineering man."

447

Ellen Davenport paused. "I loved him, but I also feared him. It was my fear of him that caused me to lose you and the man I loved. I'm not placing all the blame on my father; I must carry part of it on my own shoulders. I was weak, and I stood by helplessly and allowed others to manipulate my life."

Once again, she hesitated. Matt said nothing, but his hold on Regina's hand tightened considerably.

"Father was Thomas Davenport's attorney—the Davenports were very wealthy—and when I was seventeen, I became engaged to Thomas Davenport's son." Her voice became a little bitter as she continued, "Thomas Davenport the Second. Our engagement had father's complete approval, and after my fiancé took an extended tour of Europe, we were to be married. My father's sister was married to a Southerner. Her husband owned a home in Memphis and a plantation not far from that city. When my aunt came to Boston for a visit, she invited me to return home with her, since my fiancé planned to be in Europe for over a year. I'd never been to the South so I was anxious to visit that part of the country. Father agreed to let me accompany my aunt when she returned home, and I was to stay with her until it was time for me to return to Boston and prepare for my wedding. Deciding that I'd be happier living in the city, my aunt opened up the house in Memphis. Actually, I would have preferred to live on the plantation, since I was most curious about Southern plantations. But as I have already explained, I was weak. As I had allowed my father to run my life, I permitted my aunt to decide what I should and shouldn't do. In the beginning, she dedicated most of her time to me and we were together constantly. Then, gradually, she began spending more and more time away from me. I didn't suspect it at the

448

time, but I later realized she had a lover. Her husband wasn't staying with us; he was living at the plantation. Left alone, I began to take walks, always chaperoned by a Negro servant. But because I was not raised around slaves, I could never feel at ease in their presence. So I started taking walks by myself. During one of these outings I strolled down to the riverbank. The port was busy, and I was eagerly watching the activity when a very handsome man suddenly approached me. I could tell by his appearance that he worked on one of the boats. He was not of my social class, and I knew that I shouldn't talk to him."

A trace of sadness appeared in Ellen Davenport's eyes, and she looked at Matt strangely, suddenly aware of his resemblance to the lover she was recalling. "I took one look at him and fell hopelessly in love. I had never seen a man so handsome or so strong."

For a moment she was silent, and Mr. Richardson turned and patted her hand, smiling encouragingly. She took a deep breath and then continued, "To make this story as short as possible, I not only fell in love with him, but I also became his mistress. I don't know whether he loved me; he never said. At any rate our affair was into its third month, when I realized that I was pregnant. One of the female slaves became aware of my condition at about the same time I did, and she told my aunt. Instead of deciding to run my own life, I submissively allowed my aunt to take care of everything. I never went to the man I loved and told him I was pregnant. I don't know why. Maybe I feared he would reject me. Or perhaps Thomas Davenport's riches and my father's wrath were the reason I didn't try to see the man who had fathered my child. But my aunt did go to see him. I know nothing about their meeting. She never discussed it with me, and I never

449

bothered to ask. I was taken to the plantation, where I went into seclusion, and you were finally born in the middle of the night. There was no doctor; you were delivered by a slave woman. My aunt had already made arrangements with Miss Jones who was the head matron at the orphanage, so when you were two weeks old, you were placed in Miss Jones' care. She had been paid well to keep the truth hidden and to say that you had simply been left on the doorstep. When my aunt returned to the plantation, she informed me that Miss Jones would explain your presence by reporting that you had been found in a basket with a note stating your age, two weeks, and your name, Matthew."

"Why Matthew?" Matt asked, speaking for the first time since his mother had begun her story.

Ellen Davenport shrugged. "I don't know why. I don't even know whether it was my aunt or Miss Jones who gave you the name."

Matt scowled, but he offered no comment.

"Father never learned of your birth, nor did my husband. But after I had been married about a year I went to see Mr. Richardson who had joined my father's firm. I could not forget you, and taking Donald Richardson into my confidence, I told him all about you. He said that he'd correspond with Miss Jones and he would see that she kept us informed as to your welfare. We also sent her money periodically so you'd have special care. Later, we learned that Miss Jones kept the money for herself. During those years I hoped that you'd be adopted by a couple who would love you and give you a good home."

Matt frowned, remarking irritably, "Now I understand why I was never adopted. Miss Jones didn't want to forfeit the money she was receiving for my care."

"When we were notified that you had run away from

450

the orphanage, Mr. Richardson traveled to Memphis to try to find you. After making several inquiries, he learned that you had been befriended by a man named Silas Brolin and had gone West with him. Acting on that information, Mr. Richardson finally located the two of you. He never spoke to you, but he did speak with Silas Brolin."

Matt released Regina's hand, and crossing his arms on the desk, he leaned forward. His eyes bore into his mother's as he asked calmly. "Who was my father?"

Lowering her gaze from her son's piercing eyes, she murmured, "Silas Brolin."

Matt's breath caught sharply, and when his fist suddenly pounded against the desktop, Ellen looked up quickly. The anger on Matt's face made her gasp. Concerned, Mr. Richardson reached over and clasped her hand snugly.

"Silas!" Matt spat out, his rage barely under control.

Regina's heart ached for her husband. She longed to be able to console him, but at the moment, she felt completely helpless. Why hadn't Silas Brolin told Matt that he was his father?

Suddenly, Matt laughed harshly. "So Brolin is actually my name. And all these years, I thought I had borrowed it." His tone hard, Matt asked his mother, "Why in the hell didn't Silas tell me who he was?"

"I can best answer that question," Mr. Richardson replied. "When I talked to Silas Brolin, I asked him if he intended to tell you that he was your father, and he replied that he had no intention of ever telling you. I don't know why; he refused to explain his reasons. Perhaps he was suffering from guilt, or maybe he didn't want a father and son relationship with you."

"When he found me on the river front, did he know I was his son?"

451

"Yes, he knew," Mr. Richardson answered. "He had also been giving Miss Jones money to be used for your benefit. When you ran away from the orphanage, she contacted him."

"Well, I guess I should be grateful to my parents." Matt's voice was laced with sarcasm. "They both contributed so unselfishly to my upbringing." He stared coldly at his mother. "Mrs. Davenport, I still don't know why in hell you are here. Surely you don't expect me to forgive you and welcome you with open arms."

"Of course not," she said hastily. "To explain why I'm here, I must finish my story."

Waving a hand impatiently, Matt said ungraciously, "By all means, continue."

"When Mr. Richardson returned to Boston and told me that you were with Silas, I believed you would be properly taken care of, and I was happy to learn that you two were together. My husband and I never had any children. I often felt that perhaps God was punishing me. Then, four years ago, my husband passed away. In his will, he left everything to me, but when I die, there is no one to inherit my money. That is why Mr. Richardson and I decided to try to locate you. At times we believed our search was futile, but we never gave up. Eventually our inquiries led us to Alan Garrett. When we visited him and explained who we were, he told us where you were living."

Mr. Richardson cut in. "We are here, Mr. Brolin, to inform you that your mother is making you her beneficiary."

Sensing Matt's reaction, Regina rose quickly from the arm of the chair and stepped to the side. Matt bounded to his feet, and shoving the chair backward out of his way, he glared furiously at his mother and her lawyer. "I don't want the Davenport fortune!" he shouted. "Give the damned money to charity!"

Knowing he would become violently angry if he remained in the room, Matt stormed out of the study, slamming the door behind him.

At his departure, Ellen Davenport burst into tears, and Regina looked on silently while Mr. Richardson tried to console her. Despite how Regina felt about what Matt's mother had done, she couldn't help but feel sorry for the woman. But when Ellen's tears had subsided, Regina said collectedly, "Mrs. Davenport, I think it would be best for all of us, if you and your attorney leave immediately for Boston. Matt will not change his mind and accept your money."

Mr. Richardson got to his feet and offered Ellen his hand. When she made no move to accept his assistance, he murmured, "Come, Ellen. It's time for us to go."

Again she did not respond, and this time he studied her with deep concern. He had always been afraid that it would be a mistake for Ellen to locate her son, but she had pleaded with him to help her find the child she had abandoned. Now, gazing into her grief-stricken face, Donald Richardson emitted a weary sigh. He had suspected that their long search would end this way.

Her eyes pleading, Ellen looked at Regina. "It sounded as though I was trying to buy his love, didn't it?"

Regina nodded slowly. "Yes, in a way."

"I wasn't," Ellen declared.

Once again, Regina found herself feeling sorry for Matt's mother. Although she believed that she would never give up her own baby, she tried to refrain from judging Ellen Davenport.

"I'll talk to Matt," Regina offered. "Maybe I can persuade him to see you again before you leave for Boston. But, Mrs. Davenport, if he does agree to meet with you,

453

don't mention your money. He doesn't want it, and if you insist on discussing it, you will be making a very big mistake."

Suddenly, the study door swung open and Cort scampered into the room. Surprised that his mother had company, he stopped abruptly.

Rising, Regina walked around the desk to the boy. "I'd like you to meet Mr. Richardson and Mrs. Davenport."

Cort smiled politely at Mr. Richardson, but when he glanced at Ellen Davenport his grin faded and he wondered why the woman's face was so pale.

Aware of Ellen's condition, her attorney grasped her arm and helped her to stand. Her eyes fixed on Cort, the older woman asked raspingly, "Matt's son?"

"Yes," Regina answered, placing an arm about Cort's shoulders.

"He looks very much like his father," Ellen Davenport said, her voice quivering. Dear God, she had lost so much by giving up her son! She had chosen wealth over her child, and now when she should be enjoying her grandchildren, she was alone.

Noting Ellen's distress, Regina gave Cort a gentle shove toward the door. "Run along, darling. I'll see you later."

The moment Cort closed the door behind him, Ellen said with great pain in her voice, "My grandson . . . and I don't even have the right to hold him!"

Mr. Richardson started to embrace her, but unsure of how to console her, he stepped aside. It was Regina who took Ellen Davenport into her arms.

After Matt stormed from the study, he left the house and rode out to the range to work alongside his ranch hands and Ted Lucas. The sun was dipping far into the west before he decided to return home, but when he rode up to the house, Regina was standing on the porch, waiting for him.

Dismounting, Matt draped the reins over the hitching post. He then quickly went to his wife and gave her an eager hug. "What's for dinner?" he said. "I'm famished!"

Regina looked directly into his eyes, and taking his hand in hers, she said carefully, "Matt, don't do this to yourself."

"Do what?" he asked, his brow furrowing.

"Don't pretend your mother's visit never happened."

He drew his hand from hers, remarking testily, "Surely you don't expect me to forgive her!"

"Darling," she began tolerantly, "it's not a question of forgiveness. You must learn to accept what she did and lose your bitterness."

His dark eyes flickered angrily. "Damn it, Regina! It's easy for you to give advice, you don't know what it's like to be abandoned."

"No, I don't," she admitted softly. Touching his arm, she suggested, "Why don't you tell me what it was like?"

"I've already told you about my childhood," Matt replied impatiently.

"You've never told me about the little boy who grew up without a mother or a father. Please tell me about him, Matt."

Matt shook his head and started to move past her, she grasped his arm. "Why can't you talk about it?" she pleaded.

Matt replied gruffly, "What exactly do you want to hear? Shall I tell you how I used to lie in bed and long for my mother? I actually convinced myself that she

455

had been abducted by gypsies, that after I was born, they took me away from her and left me at the orphanage. I used to dream that she would escape and come back for me."

"Didn't you ever think about your father?"

"Sure." Matt's voice revealed his irritation. "He was with my mother when she was kidnapped, and when he tried to protect his wife and his unborn child, the gypsies killed him."

"How did Miss Jones treat you?" Regina asked.

"She was a cold-hearted bitch. She was the reason I decided to run away," he snapped.

"Matt, now that you know the truth, how do you feel about Silas Brolin being your father?"

"I don't know." He sighed. "Maybe I haven't quite grasped the fact. In a few days, after the shock has worn off, ask me again."

Tentatively, Regina broached the subject she had wanted to discuss with Matt alone. She had waited on the porch for him in order to do so. "Your mother and Mr. Richardson are returning to Boston, but they plan to stay in Albuquerque for the remainder of the week. Ellen wants you to come visit her, and, darling, I think you should. You two have so many things you need to discuss."

"No!" he shouted severely. "I have nothing to discuss with Ellen Davenport! I never want to lay eyes on the woman!"

Brusquely, Matt stepped to the front door and flung it open.

Desperate, Regina cried, "But, Matt, she's your mother!"

Looking back at her, Matt remarked emphatically, "I don't have a mother, and, Regina, I never again want to hear the name Ellen Davenport!"

When Matt entered the house, Regina went to the

pine rocker and sat down. She knew her husband, and she didn't doubt that he meant what he said. She sighed deeply; then she decided her loyalty lay with Matt and not with Ellen Davenport. If Matt didn't want to discuss his mother, she would abide by his wishes and not bring up the woman's name again.

Chapter Thirty-eight

Regina was in bed reading when Matt entered their room. Placing the book on her lap, she watched her husband thoughtfully as he closed the door and walked over to his side of the bed.

"I'm bushed," he remarked wearily. He had worked hard all day at rounding up the cattle on the east range for market.

For a moment, his gaze met and held Regina's. She wondered if thoughts of his mother were on his mind and she was tempted to ask, but remembering her decision to remain loyal to her husband, she suppressed the urge. It had only been two days since Ellen Davenport and her attorney had arrived unexpectedly at the Black Diamond, and Regina was sure their visit was still very much in Matt's thoughts.

Sitting on the edge of the bed, Matt started to remove his boots when the sounds of a horse and buggy nearing the house caused him to get back to his feet. "Who in the hell would be calling at this time of night?" he grumbled.

As he headed out of the bedroom, Regina rose, slipped on her dressing gown, and followed him. When Matt opened the front door, Regina was poised at his side.

"Mr. Richardson!" she exclaimed.

"Mr. and Mrs. Brolin, please excuse me for this late intrusion," he apologized.

"What do you want?" Matt demanded short-temperedly, refusing to invite the man inside.

"I'm afraid that I am the bearer of bad news," Donald Richardson replied. "Mrs. Davenport had a heart attack this evening."

"Oh no!" Regina cried. "How is she?"

"She's recovered somewhat," Mr. Richardson replied. "Dr. Henderson is with her now, at the hotel. This isn't the first time she's had such an attack." Looking directly at Matt, he continued, "Mr. Brolin, your mother is in very poor health. She hasn't long to live. In fact, she may not make it through the night."

When Matt did not reply, Mr. Richardson pressed on. "It would mean a lot to Ellen if you'd come back with me to the hotel." Still receiving no response, he became angered. "Good God, your mother is dying! Don't you even care?"

"I don't have a mother," Matt mumbled.

"Yes, you do!" Regina cried, clutching Matt's arm and turning him in her direction. "Matt, you must leave with Mr. Richardson! Darling, for your own sake, as well as your mother's, don't let it end this way. Go to her, Matt! Please!"

"All right," he conceded, knowing that Regina was right. There were times when the past had to be faced, and Matt was aware that this was one of those times.

He drew Regina into his arms and kissed her soundly; then, grabbing his hat from the rack beside the door, he stepped outside.

Regina watched him as he followed Mr. Richardson to the buggy. As he got into it, he turned to her and waved. It was too dark for her to see Matt's face, but

459

she didn't need to see his expression to know that somewhere deep inside him the little boy who believed his mother had been abducted by gypsies was still very much alive.

"Dear God," Regina prayed, her heart aching for her husband, "please be with him tonight."

Mr. Richardson and Matt were greeted by Dr. Henderson as they entered Ellen's suite. She was occupying the same rooms that Robert Selman had once rented. The doctor had left her bedroom door open, and Matt could see his mother. The huge oak bed, much too large for her delicate frame, made her look very small and helpless.

"How is she?" Mr. Richardson inquired urgently, removing his hat and placing it on an end table.

"The same," Dr. Henderson replied. Then he turned his full attention to Matt. Mr. Richardson had taken him into his confidence, and the doctor knew that Ellen Davenport was Matt's mother. Studying Matt carefully, he tried to catch his eye, but Matt's gaze was still centered on Ellen Davenport. Addressing him, Dr. Henderson said, "She's been asking for you."

Matt's face was inscrutable, and the doctor wasn't sure whether he had even heard him. He was about to repeat himself, when Matt turned his head and looked at him. "She's been asking for me?" he mumbled vaguely.

"Yes," Dr. Henderson assured him. "She's awake, so why don't you go in and talk to her." Matt started to walk past him, but the doctor put a hand on his arm. "Matt," he began, his voice stern, "you are my good friend, but at the moment, Mrs. Davenport is my patient. I am concerned for her, so I must insist that you say or do nothing to upset her."

460

Brusquely, Matt flung off the doctor's hand, and strode swiftly to his mother's bedroom. As he moved to the side of her bed, his strides slowed.

Ellen's eyes were cosed, but sensing his presence, she opened them and looked up at him. Her voice was feeble, "Please pull up a chair and sit down."

Complying, Matt drew the small hard-backed chair forward and sat down. He gazed closely at his mother. Her face was drawn and pale. It was odd, but his heart ached for this woman who had abandoned him thirty-four years ago.

"Matt," she whispered weakly, "I am so glad that you came." She waited a few moments, hoping he would say something that might make this time easier for both of them, and when he remained silent, she asked tentatively, "Why did you come here?"

He spoke truthfully, "I don't exactly know why."

"Do you hate me?"

Ellen Davenport's question caught Matt off guard, causing his strong frame to tense. Remaining honest, he murmured, "I don't think so."

She smiled faintly. "Matt, I didn't look for you all these years only to leave you the Davenport money. I merely used that as an excuse to come into your life."

"Why did you want to come into my life?" he asked, his tone dry.

It wasn't easy for Ellen to tell Matt what was in her heart. She feared that he might reject her, and she knew there was a good chance that he might unleash the anger he had bottled up all his life.

She spoke slowly, in a weakened voice, "I searched for you because I wanted to see my son before I died."

"Son?" Matt scowled. "The term *son* implies more than merely giving birth. You saw me the night I was born. Wasn't that enough?"

"No, I didn't see you," Ellen explained. "Your birth

was difficult, and I passed out moments before you were born. You were taken to a slave cabin, where a slave woman nursed you."

"When you woke up, did you ask to see me?"

"Yes, I did. But my aunt was afraid that if I saw you or held you, I might decide to keep you with me."

Matt frowned a little irritably. "So you accepted your aunt's decision with no argument."

"Yes." His mother sighed regretfully. Then, feeling desperate, she pleaded, "Oh, Matt, please try to understand. I was so young and so frightened."

"Frightened?" he repeated questioningly.

"Of my father. He had a terrible temper."

Suddenly, Ellen noticed a small smile touch the corners of Matt's mouth. "What are you thinking about?" she asked softly.

"Now I know where I inherited my short-fused temper," he answered.

When Matt's smile faded as suddenly as it had materialized, his mother said, "Please tell me your thoughts."

"I was thinking about bloodlines," he replied.

"When I am feeling better, I'll tell you about my side of the family, but I know nothing about Silas' family."

"It doesn't matter," Matt declared testily. "I'm not interested in my family tree. The only family I have is at the Black Diamond—my wife and children."

"Children?" she questioned.

"I have a daughter and son," he answered.

"I saw your son," she told him. "He's a very handsome boy." Pleadingly, she added, "I'd like to know my grandchildren."

Matt offered no response, but a harshness came over his face. His icy severity hurt Ellen. "I'm sorry," she said quickly. "I don't have the right to be with my grandchildren. As soon as I'm well, I'll return to

462

Boston, and I promise you that I'll stay out of your life."

She really wanted him to tell her she was welcome to stay, but his look of relief told her that he wanted no contact with her. "Matt," she began, her voice growing weaker, "I have only one thing left to say and then you are free to leave and go back to your family. I know you are here only out of compassion for an old woman who will soon die, so I will not impose on you any longer. But I do want you to know that I am very grateful to you for coming to see me."

Matt glanced away. Why in the hell was he suddenly feeling guilty? Covering his confusion, he muttered flatly, "You said you have one thing left to say."

"Since the night that you were born, the night my aunt took you away, I have never known a moment of complete happiness. In my mind, you didn't exist. I had never seen you, never held you in my arms. It was as though you weren't real. But in the deep recesses of my heart, I never forgot the baby I abandoned. I was plagued by guilt and regret. I know your life has not been an easy one; neither has mine. But, Matt, you now have a lovely wife and family. You have found happiness, whereas I never did. I had a mansion to live in and money to spend, but never a day went by that I didn't wish I'd had the courage to give it up for the child I had borne."

"Why didn't you?" Matt demanded gruffly. "You knew where I was. Why didn't you come to the orphanage and claim me?"

"I couldn't," Ellen sobbed. "Thomas would have divorced me, and Father would have disowned me. I had no way to support us. At least at the orphanage, you were sheltered and fed. For your own well being, I had to leave you where you were."

Matt stood abruptly, and thinking over his mother's

words, he stepped to the window and gazed into the night. Although nothing could erase the aloneness of his childhood, he was now able to think of it without bitterness. He had suffered, but so had Ellen Davenport.

Dr. Henderson came into the room and went to Ellen's bedside. He saw that her eyes were closed, and noticing that her breathing was failing, he quickly checked her pulse.

"Matt," the doctor said gravely, "her pulse is very weak."

Turning away from the window, Matt exclaimed, "But she was just talking to me and she seemed fine!"

"I'm sorry," Dr. Henderson murmured, "but I'm afraid we might be losing her."

"No!" Matt cried, suddenly realizing that he didn't want his mother to die. He knew that they could never make up for the thirty-four years they had lost, but he'd felt that they might find a way to share the time Ellen Davenport had left.

He hurried to her bedside, and Dr. Henderson stepped back. Taking her hand, Matt held it firmly. Tears moistened his eyes, and his deep voice was filled with emotion as he said, "Mother . . . mother, don't leave me! I want you in my life!"

Her son's words penetrated Ellen's fogged consciousness, giving her renewed life. She fought her way back to full awareness, and finally her eyelids fluttered open.

"Mother," Matt groaned, looking directly into her eyes. "You can't leave me now. We just found each other." Seeing color begin to return to her face, he smiled gratefully. "You must get well so that you can get to know your grandchildren."

"You called me mother," she whispered.

"Yes, I did," Matt murmured, although he hadn't

464

been aware of it himself until she brought it to his attention.

Ellen smiled. "For the first time in thirty-four years, I know complete happiness. Thank you . . . my son."

Stepping to the bed, Dr. Henderson once again checked his patient's pulse. "It's much stronger," he said to Matt. "But she needs rest. Why don't you go home and come back in the morning."

Matt immediately agreed. He didn't want his mother to become overtired. Bending over the bed, he kissed her forehead. "Good night, Mother. I'll see you in the morning, and I'll bring Regina with me."

"God bless you," she said softly; then, closing her eyes, she drifted into sleep.

Sitting at the kitchen table, Regina smiled happily as she watched Matt swallow the last of his coffee and then place his cup beside his empty plate. He had eaten a hearty breakfast and his mood was cheerful. Last night when he had left the hotel and returned home, Regina had been waiting up for him. She had been delighted to learn that Matt wanted his mother to become a part of his life.

Regina was still wearing her dressing gown, so she pushed back her chair, saying, "I'll go dress so we can go into town and see Ellen."

Matt nodded his approval, and she was about to stand when, suddenly, Dan barged unannounced into the kitchen. Smiling, he went to Regina and drew her to her feet. "I just received a message from Miguel!" he exclaimed. "Julie had a baby boy!"

"How wonderful!" Regina cried, embracing him. Then, stepping back and looking at him questioningly, she said, "Julie and the baby are fine?"

465

"They are fine," Dan assured her.

"Oh Dan, I'm so happy for Julie!" Regina replied.

"So am I," he answered with a large grin.

Rising from his chair, Matt congratulated Dan on becoming an uncle; then he took Regina into his arms and kissed her.

Dan's marvelous news had made Regina momentarily forget Ellen Davenport, but she suddenly remembered the forthcoming visit. Excusing herself, she went to dress.

Matt invited Dan to join him for a cup of coffee, and as they waited for Regina, Matt told his brother-in-law about his mother's unexpected visit and her illness. He was just finishing his explanation when Hannah came into the kitchen to inform Matt that Mr. Richardson had arrived and was waiting in the parlor.

Hoping his mother hadn't taken a turn for the worse, Matt rushed out of the kitchen. He was hurrying toward the parlor as Regina came out of the bedroom, and noting his haste, she followed him.

Entering the parlor behind her husband and seeing Mr. Richardson poised beside the sofa, Regina stopped to Matt's side.

"Mr. Brolin," he said heavily, "I am the bearer of bad news. I'm sorry, but your mother passed away early this morning. She died in her sleep."

Regina grasped Matt's arm. For a few moments he didn't move and his expression was emotionless. Then, groaning deeply, he took Regina into his arms and held her close.

"Oh, darling," she whispered. "I'm so sorry."

Releasing her gently, he turned to Mr. Richardson. "I don't want the Davenport money," he said firmly.

"There is no money," Donald Richardson said quietly. "Thomas Davenport the Second was a poor business man and a compulsive gambler. When he died, very little of the Davenport fortune was left. But your mother never knew. The other lawyers and I did not tell her."

"Why not?" Matt asked.

"We hadn't the heart." Richardson sighed. "Ellen had lived a very sheltered life. She'd gone from an extremely dominating father to a dominating husband. They'd made her like a helpless child. I don't think she could have coped with poverty."

"The money she spent searching for me, where did it come from?"

Mr. Richardson hesitated. "It was your money, wasn't it?" Matt asked.

"Yes," Richardson replied quietly. "But she never knew."

"Mr. Richardson," Regina began, "are you married?"

"No," he replied.

"Have you ever been married?" she asked.

"No, I haven't."

Looking sympathetically at Donald Richardson, Regina said, "You were in love with Ellen Davenport, weren't you?"

He smiled wistfully. "Yes, I was."

"Did she know?" Regina queried.

"No. I never told her." Richardson's face became quite sad. "She was a married woman, and after her husband died . . . well, she wasn't interested in a December love, she was completely immersed in finding her son." Looking at Matt, he asked, "Do you prefer that she be laid to rest in Albuquerque, or shall I make arrangements to take her body back to Boston for burial?"

"Boston," Matt decided. "That was her home."

Mr. Richardson nodded brusquely. "If you'll excuse me, I think I'll go back to the hotel."

"I'll come to town this afternoon and we'll take care of everything that has to be done," Matt told Richardson as he walked him to the door.

Within moments, Matt returned to the parlor, and drew Regina into his embrace. Her love was the only comfort he needed.

Chapter Thirty-nine

It was now the month of July, and due to the intense heat, Matt and the ranch hands worked on the range from early morning until midday. Then they returned to the ranch and did not venture back out until the late afternoon when the sun wasn't so unbearably hot. As were most houses in New Mexico, Regina's home was constructed of adobe, a sun-dried brick commonly used in environments having little rainfall. During the summer months, it kept the inside of the house comparatively cool in contrast to the scorching heat outside.

On this day, following their midday meal, Regina asked Matt to join her in the study. She had something very important to tell him. As Matt was opening the study door, however, he heard riders approaching the house. He headed down the hallway. "Who would be coming here in the heat of the day," he grumbled.

When he reached the front door and swung it open, he called back, "It's Miguel and Julie!"

Regina rushed to greet them, and as she and Matt stepped out on the porch, Miguel was assisting Julie from the buggy. Anna was still in the back seat, holding the baby, and the fifteen vaqueros accompanying them remained mounted.

Hurrying to her sister, Regina embraced her warmly before turning to Miguel, who hugged her so vigorously that Regina wondered how her ribs survived the huge Mexican's display of affection.

Shaking hands with Miguel, Matt asked, "Why the sudden visit? You should have told us you were coming."

"We did not know we would be making this trip," Miguel explained. "It came up very unexpectedly."

"Is anything wrong?" Matt questioned.

"*Amigo,*" he began, "let us get out of this hot sun, and then I will tell you why we are here."

"Of course," Matt replied. "Tell your men to turn their horses loose in the corral before they go to the bunkhouse."

After giving the order to his vaqueros, Miguel helped Anna from the carriage. Regina immediately went to the servant and took the baby from her arms. Hugging and kissing him, she exclaimed, "Oh, Miguel, he looks so much like you!"

Flattered, Miguel replied, "He is as you *gringos* say, a chip off the old block, *sí?*"

Laughing, Regina answered, "*Sí, Miguel!*"

Telling Anna and Julie to follow, Regina carried her nephew into the house and headed directly to her bedroom.

"Where are the children?" Julie asked.

"Hannah and Ted are spending the day visiting friends, and they took María and Cort with them."

As Regina placed the infant on the bed, Julie touched her arm. "Let Anna take care of him. I think we should join Miguel and Matt."

For the first time, Regina became aware of her sister's anxiety. "Is something wrong?" she asked.

Leading Regina from the room, Julie answered, "I'm

470

so worried about Miguel."

Halting their steps, Regina studied her sister. In spite of Julie's distress, she had never looked more beautiful. Her hair was drawn up and held in place by two pearl-adorned combs, but a few loose strands framed her face with reddish brown ringlets. Her dress was patterned with bright, colorful flowers that contrasted attractively with Julie's dark brown eyes. "Why are you so worried?" Regina asked.

"I'm so afraid that Antonio Ramírez will kill Miguel!" Julie cried.

Regina started to question her, but at that moment, the door to the study was opened. His large frame filling the doorway, Miguel called to them, "Come inside. We are waiting for you."

Regina and Julie did as he asked, and leaving the door ajar, Miguel followed them. Matt was sitting at his desk, and Regina walked over to stand behind his chair.

After seating Julie on the other side of the desk, Miguel paced across the room as he began to explain the reason for their sudden visit. "Pedro is one of my oldest and most trusted vaqueros, and his granddaughter is unmarried and with child. Esperanza, she says the papá is Santos Ramírez."

"What!" Regina blurted. "Are you sure?" Regina grew apprehensive. What would this do to María?

"Pedro, he believes Esperanza would not lie about something so serious."

"What do you believe?" Matt asked.

Miguel shrugged. "I do not know, but I aim to learn the truth. Pedro and Esperanza are at the hotel in town."

"But if she lives on your hacienda," Matt began, "how could she possibly have been with Santos?"

"Esperanza has not lived on my hacienda for the past

471

three years. She has been living with a cousin. Her parents have been dead many years, and Pedro thought she should have a woman's influence, so he sent her to an older cousin."

"How old is Esperanza?" Matt asked.

"She is seventeen," Miguel replied.

"If Santos is the father, what do you intend to do?" Matt inquired.

Forcefully, Miguel replied, "Santos Ramírez will take full responsibility for his actions!"

"Is this a private conversation, or can anyone join in?"

Dan's presence had gone undetected until he spoke, and, they all turned toward the doorway. Grinning, Matt remarked, "This seems to be the day for unexpected guests."

"But welcome ones, I hope," Dan replied as he sauntered into the room. "The front door was standing open, so I let myself in." Smiling at Miguel and Julie, he continued, "You two are a pleasant surprise. But what's going on? Why does Santos have to take full responsibility for his actions?"

Quickly Matt told Dan what had happened, and when he finished his explanation, Dan said to Miguel, "If you want to talk to Santos, he's at the saloon."

Crossing the room, Miguel decided hastily, "I will send one of my vaqueros into town to tell Santos to be expecting me, and to inform him that if he tries to run away I will hunt him down and drag him back to town."

"If you let Santos know you plan to confront him," Regina warned, "he'll send a message to Antonio."

Pausing in the doorway, Miguel eyed Regina shrewdly, "That, *señora,* is the idea!"

* * *

472

Matt and Miguel tried to talk their wives into staying at the ranch, but Regina and Julie were determined to accompany them. Finally the men conceded to their wishes on the understanding that both women remain in the buggy.

Santos had been told of Miguel's arrival, and he was standing in front of the saloon doors as they rode into town. Regina brought the buggy to a stop close to the saloon, while Miguel, Matt, Dan, and the vaqueros guided their horses to the saloon's hitching rail. Miguel ordered his men to remain outside; then to one vaquero, he said heartily, "Go to the hotel and get Pedro."

As Miguel dismounted, Santos remarked casually, "I understand you wish to speak with me, *señor*."

"Let us go inside," Miguel replied. He reached up to his saddle and removed his rifle from its scabbard.

Dismounting, Matt and Dan trailed them into the saloon. As they entered they found the room was almost empty, except for the four men with Santos. There were two customers at the bar, and three men were seated at a table playing cards.

Santos nodded at his companions. Gesturing toward the doors, he said, "Get out!" They were hesitant to leave the *patrón*'s son alone with Miguel Ordaz, but when Santos once again ordered them to leave, they did so with reluctance.

Miguel cocked his rifle, then aimed it at Santos. Fearing a gunfight, the five remaining customers fled the saloon so quickly that the swinging doors flapped loudly behind them.

Grinning carelessly, Santos pulled up a chair. Sitting, he asked, "Do you plan to shoot me, *señor?*"

Placing the rifle on the table next to him, Miguel replied, "It is the best way to empty a room."

Chuckling, Santos agreed, "So it would seem."

Dan noticed Matt move quietly to the front of the saloon, close the shutters, and then stand beside the doors. He leaned against the wall in a relaxed manner but Dan knew he was there to keep a close vigil on Miguel's exposed back. Not knowing what else to do Dan went to the bar, and along with the bartender, he watched Miguel and Santos.

"What is the reason for all this?" Santos asked, a though he were bored with the entire incident.

Placing his foot on a chair, Miguel leaned his arm on his raised knee. "Do you know Pedro's granddaughter, Esperanza?"

"Sí, I know her," Santos answered.

"Are you the *papá* of her unborn child?" Miguel asked.

Astonished, Santos exclaimed, "Is that why you are here, *señor?* The *puta* is with child, and she has named me as the father?"

Enraged, Miguel grabbed Santos by the front of his shirt, jerking him roughly. "You do not call the *señorita* a *puta!*"

Santos was no longer a boy, but a man full grown who had the strength to break Miguel's grip. His eyes narrowed dangerously as he warned, "Listen to me *señor!* I do not wish to kill you, but make no mistake, will if I have to!"

Miguel was not angered by Santos' threat; instead he admired him for his refusal to be intimidated. "I will ask you again. Are you the *papá?"*

Pointing his finger at the older man, Santos lips became taut. "And I will tell you again, *señor!* She is a *puta!"*

"For God's sake!" Dan yelled to Santos. "Just answer the damned question, will you?"

Glancing at Dan, Santos said coolly, "You are my friend, *amigo.* To you I will answer. No, I am no

474

the father."

"You did not defile Pedro's granddaughter?" Miguel asked.

"You have not been listening to me," Santos replied tolerantly. "Esperanza has not been a virgin for two, maybe three, years. If you do not believe me, ask your younger vaqueros. I am sure, *señor,* at one time or another most of them have been with the *señorita."*

Before Miguel could reply, Pedro entered the saloon with his granddaughter holding onto his arm. Esperanza was not a pretty girl. She was much too heavy, and her features were unbecomingly broad.

Leading Esperanza to Miguel, Pedro asked, "Did he confess, *patrón?"*

"He claims he is not the father," Miguel answered.

"He lies!" Pedro yelled. The elderly Mexican was short and slender, and his skin was heavily lined from aging and from exposure to the sun.

Standing, Santos looked down into Pedro's angry face. "I have never been with your granddaughter!"

"You know Esperanza, do you not?" Pedro demanded.

"Sí, I know her. I have known her for years. But I have never made love to her." Glaring at Esperanza, Santos commanded, "Tell him it is the truth!"

Esperanza had been staring down at the floor, but she slowly raised her gaze and forced herself to look at the man that she wanted dead. Suddenly out of the corner of her eye, she caught Miguel studying her thoughtfully. Things weren't working out the way she had planned. She hadn't considered the possibility that Pedro would go to Ordaz. She had thought her grandfather would simply confront Santos, and that when Santos lost his temper and called her a *puta,* Pedro would kill him.

Esperanza hated Santos Ramírez. At one time she had loved him and had done everything within her power to make him love her in return. Finally, to find some release, she had turned to other men for solace. She was a homely girl, so young and handsome vaqueros had never noticed her, until she offered them her body. Having done so, she foolishly gloried in her new popularity, but deep in her heart, she still longed for Santos Ramírez. Finally, one night at the cantina in the small Mexican town where her cousin lived, Esperanza had had too much tequila, and kneeling at Santos' feet, she had begged him to make love to her. Disgusted, he had shoved her aside, and calling her a *puta,* he had left the cantina. Then everyone had laughed at Esperanza. She had never forgiven Santos for publicly humiliating her. Her love had turned to hate which grew until, at last, she wanted him dead. Esperanza was not pregnant. After Pedro killed Santos, she had planned to tell her grandfather that she had miscarried. But, now, with Miguel Ordaz taking a part in her deceitful scheme to destroy Santos, she feared he would keep delving until he learned the truth.

Touching Esperanza's shoulder, Miguel spoke so softly that no one else could hear his warning. "Esperanza, I am going outside to question my vaqueros. They will not lie to me, *señorita.* If what Santos has said about you is true, then my vaqueros have not remained silent to protect you, but only because they have not been questioned."

Tossing her head, she said smugly, "And you will take their word over mine, *señor?"*

Miguel's dark eyes looked into hers without flinching. His voice was inflexible. *"Sí, señorita.* And so will your *abuelo."*

Esperanza knew her plan to have Santos killed was now ruined. And all because Pedro had to run to the *patrón!,* she thought resentfully. Wildly her eyes flew to Santos. He was watching her, a cunning grin on his handsome face. He's laughing at me! she decided angrily. Well, she would see to it that he would never laugh at her again! Swiftly, she drew the pistol from the holster strapped to her grandfather's hip, and cocking the weapon, she aimed it at Santos. But as she pulled the trigger, Miguel's hand gripped her wrist, forcing it downward and sending the bullet into the floor.

Shattered splinters flew about Esperanza's feet, and as she moved to dodge them, the frustration of her revenge made her enraged. In a mixture of Spanish and English, she spouted insults and obscenities at Santos. Then, ranting almost incoherently, she revealed her plan to have her grandfather kill him. Finally, wanting to destroy Santos' cool mien, Esperanza then placed her hands on her hips, and declared loudly that his mother had been a dirty Apache whore.

Watching Santos carefully, Miguel detected the violent rage apprearing in Santos' eyes, and he reflected that all Santos needed was a breechclout and war paint to be one with his mother's people. As Santos, his Apache blood coming to the fore, moved swiftly toward the girl who was still spouting filthy insults, Miguel stepped between them, preventing Santos from reaching her.

At that moment Esperanza's piercing voice penetrated Miguel's ears, nerve-racking and shrill, and he spun about. Facing the hysterical girl, he drew back his arm and slapped her so powerfully that she staggered across the room before hitting the floor. Her obscenities and insults immediately turned into bawling shrieks.

"Get her out of here!" Miguel ordered Pedro.

Hanging his head in shame, the old Mexican murmured, "I am sorry, *patrón.*" Hurrying to Esperanza, he seized her arms and pulled her to her feet. Shoving her toward the doors, he declared in Spanish that she

477

was no longer his granddaughter, and he added that if his eyes ever fell upon her again, he would kill her.

Turning to Santos, Miguel said, "I owe you an apology, *señor*."

When Santos made no move to accept his apology, the room suddenly became dangerously quiet, and the two men stood motionless, staring at each other. Matt knew neither would concede, so he slowly crossed the room. Pausing beside them, he spoke calmly, "I don't know about the rest of you, but I could sure use a drink." He didn't turn to look at the bartender, he simply called out, "Bring a bottle of whiskey and four glasses," and pulling out a chair, he sat down. Eying Santos and Miguel, he said irritably, "Damn it! Do I have to drink alone?"

Taking the whiskey bottle and glasses from the bartender, Dan went to the table, and seating himself, he said clearly, "Santos, Matt is offering to buy you a drink. Are you going to refuse his hospitality, *amigo?*"

The two men continued to eye each other with silent rage. Finally, disgusted, Matt drew his pistol. "Sit down, damn it!" he shouted furiously, getting their attention. Aiming the gun at Miguel and then at Santos, Matt continued firmly, "We're all going to have a drink together if it kills us!"

Reluctantly, Santos and Miguel sat at the table, and Dan quickly filled the glasses with whiskey.

Raising one of the glasses, Matt said coolly, "Here's to friendship."

Slowly, Santos' hand moved toward his glass. For as long as he could remember, he had been taught to hate Miguel Ordaz, but his father's war with Ordaz had begun years before he was born: Santos had never harbored a true hatred for Miguel. As a boy he had simply, and unquestioningly, followed in Antonio's footsteps. But Santos Ramírez was now a man with a

478

mind of his own, and for the first time in his life, he broke his strong alliance with his father as he lifted his glass. He believed the time had come to end the long feud between Antonio Ramírez and Miguel Ordaz.

Responding, Miguel joined in the toast. He would not hold Santos responsible for his father. So, ironically, Miguel Ordaz drank a toast to friendship with Antonio Ramírez's son.

When Regina heard the first shot, she almost broke her promise to remain in the buggy. It took all her self-control not to rush into the saloon.

Turning pale, Julie cried, "Where is the sheriff? Surely he heard the gunshot!"

"He's out of town, and his young deputy is too afraid of Antonio to interfere," Regina explained. "I'm sure he intends to stay in his office until it's all over."

When Pedro suddenly walked out of the saloon with Esperanza, Regina had had to force herself not to run to them and ask what had happened. It was obvious that Pedro was terribly angry at his granddaughter. He was shouting at her, and it surprised Regina when he shoved the girl into the street. Crying convulsively, Esperanza fled across the road and into the hotel.

The waiting had become almost unbearable when Regina suddenly heard approaching horses. Looking down the street, she saw Antonio and his men arriving, and her promise to stay in the buggy was completely forgotten. Lifting her long skirt, she bounded from the carriage at the same moment Antonio and his large group of vaqueros raced past the buggy. Their horses stirred up loose dirt, sending it flying into Regina's face and on her clothes. Whirling, she turned back to the buggy. The gritty particles stung her eyes, and she could feel the loose earth settling on her lips and cheeks. Lifting the hem of her skirt, she wiped vigorously at her face.

Antonio pulled up his stallion so abruptly that the powerful animal had to lean back on its haunches in order to come to a stop. As Antonio dismounted, Regina called to him, but he was so preoccupied that he did not hear her.

Running toward the saloon, Regina yelled again, "Antonio!"

Becoming aware of Regina, he paused long enough for her to reach him and his arm. "Antonio, please don't start trouble!" she pleaded breathlessly. It wasn't until she had said the words that she realized how foolish they sounded.

"The trouble, *señora,* has already started, but I intend to end it . . . permanently!"

"No!" Regina cried. "I'm begging you! Antonio, please!"

"Does Ordaz's life mean that much to you? It is not like you to beg, *señora.* Why aren't you carrying your rifle so that you can simply shoot me? That is more your style, is it not?"

Finding his arrogance intolerable, Regina replied irritably, "But I'm not only pleading for Miguel's life, I am also pleading for yours!"

"You do not want me to die?" Antonio asked with sudden tenderness.

"Of course not!" she exclaimed.

Antonio's order was arrogant, but gentle, "You are a woman, *señora,* and your pretty nose does not belong in a man's business. Go back to the buggy where you belong."

Before Regina could voice her angry response, Antonio turned and walked into the saloon. Folding her arms, Regina paced back and forth in front of the doors. She did not intend to return to the buggy, and she decided that if she heard another gunshot she would go into the saloon! Good Lord, how much did a woman have to live through before men considered her more than a silly female! Feeling eyes on her, Regina paused, and glaring at Antonio's and Miguel's vaqueros, her hard stare dared them to utter one objection to her presence.

Barging into the saloon, Antonio was so startled that he came to a sudden stop. He didn't know what he had expected to find, but he certainly hadn't expected to see his son sitting at a table drinking with Miguel Ordaz.

The four men were aware of Antonio's entrance, but not one of them bothered to acknowledge his presence.

"Santos!" Antonio shouted.

Glancing up, Santos smiled pleasantly. "Hello, Papá."

Reclining his chair, Matt balanced it on its back legs. "Join us for a drink, Antonio?" he asked casually.

Moving slowly, Antonio neared their table. Miguel's back was turned, so Antonio had to walk around and stand beside his son's chair to see Miguel's face.

"Ordaz!" he said sharply.

Miguel looked up, straight into Antonio's eyes.

"I understand that you threatened my son!"

Miguel nodded calmly. "That is true, señor. But only if he ran away. He did not run." Turning to Santos, Miguel grinned slightly. His speculations had been right. Santos had sent a message to his father.

"Ordaz, I'm going to kill you!" Antonio raged.

Speaking as if the threat were nothing more than a mild aggravation, Matt mumbled, "Aw hell, Ramírez. I wish you wouldn't do that. If you kill Miguel, then I'm gonna kill you because you killed my good friend."

Santos spoke next, "But then, amigo, I would kill you because you killed my father."

Dan stated calmly, "But, Santos, then I would kill

481

you because you killed Matt, and of course, one of your vaqueros would promptly kill me."

Laughing heartily, Miguel refilled their glasses. *"Amigos,* let us drink up before we are all dead!"

Taking a generous swallow of whiskey, Matt chuckled, "Besides, Santos, what makes you so sure you could kill me? I just might blow you away with Antonio." Santos laughed. "That is true, *amigo."* He looked at Dan. "And what makes you think you could kill me? You are not a gunfighter."

Grinning shrewdly, Dan replied, "I'd wait until you had your back turned."

Holding his silence as long as he could, Antonio's face turned beet red with rage. *"Madre de Diós!* Santos, have you gone completely *loco?"*

"No, Papá," he answered quietly. "I am merely having a drink with my two friends, Señor Brolin and Señor Butler. And also, Papá, I am having a drink with the man who saved my life."

"Ordaz?" Antonio choked.

"Sí, Papá." Hastily, Santos explained what had happened with Esperanza. "And that is why you cannot kill Miguel Ordaz. He saved my life." Turning his attention to Miguel, Santos asked, "How do you feel about everything, *señor?"*

Miguel took a large drink of whiskey before answering, "I have seen and inflicted more violence in my lifetime than I like to remember. Now, I want nothing more from life than to live in peace. I want only to love my beautiful wife and watch my son grow. But I have never backed down from a fight, and I will not back down this time." Miguel looked at Antonio. "Ramírez, if you do not think this country is big enough for both of us then, *señor,* one of us will walk out of this saloon. The other one will be carried out."

Antonio was furious, but how could he kill the man

who had saved Santos' life and still be respected by his son, his vaqueros, and himself?

"My son is my life," Antonio began in a strained voice. "I love no one the way I love Santos." Bowing stiffly to Miguel, he stated, "This country is big enough for both of us, *señor!*" Then, turning swiftly, Antonio marched out of the saloon.

Regina longed to question him when he stepped outside, but the hard glare in his eyes dissuaded her. She watched him as he mounted and headed his stallion down the street, his vaqueros following. Then, hearing chairs being pushed back, she realized the others were coming out. It was all over, and no one had been killed! Regina was so elated that the moment Matt came through the swinging doors, she threw herself into his arms.

As Miguel stepped into the street, he smiled broadly and called to his wife, "See, Angel, I am all right." Heading toward the carriage, he remarked heartily, "You will not be rid of me for many more years. I am too mean for the Devil to want me, and God thinks I need more time to mend my ways."

Smiling radiantly, Julie stepped down from the buggy, and lifting the hem on her long skirt, she ran into her husband's outstretched arms.

Chapter Forty

Matt, Dan, and Miguel were enclosed in the study, drinking brandy. As Regina sat on the porch steps admiring the golden sunset that colored the far horizon, she could hear their hearty laughter. She smiled. When her home had belonged to James Blakely, it had never known such joy and warmth.

Suddenly, the front door opened and closed loudly as Cort bounded out onto the porch. Turning, Regina watched her son as he scampered to her side to sit next to her. Placing her arm around his shoulders, she drew him close.

Once again the front door was opened, but this time it was done quietly. Glancing behind her, Regina smiled at María. Responding, the girl also sat beside her mother.

"Where is Julie?" Regina asked.

"She's helping Anna put the baby to bed."

Hearing a rider advance, they all looked down the lane leading up to the house, and María immediately exclaimed, "It's Santos!"

As he reined in his horse at the hitching post and dismounted, María, Cort, and Regina stood to welcome him.

Smiling, Santos tipped his black hat. "Good evening, *señora,*" he said to Regina.

Hesitantly, she inquired, "How is your father?"

Santos chuckled good-humoredly. "To be indebted to Miguel Ordaz has put Papá in a foul temper. But, with time, he will come to know that their truce is for the best."

Looking away from Regina, Santos' eyes fell upon María. She was wearing a pink calico dress, and the bodice had been designed to accent her delicate bosom. It was apparent to Santos that her developing breasts would soon be full and sensual. Since she wore only one petticoat, due to the summer heat, her skirt clung to her hips, and he also could see that her thighs were no longer slim like a girl's, but had become curvaceous and feminine.

Raising his gaze, Santos studied María's pretty face. Her long black hair was held back from her face with a pink ribbon, and its silky tresses fell smoothly to her tiny waist. Her eyes held steadfast to his, and in their dark pools, he could see her adoration for him.

Noticing the interplay between Santos and María, Regina smiled, and taking Cort's hand, she said, "Let's go into the house."

"I wanna stay and talk to Santos!" the boy insisted stubbornly.

"You can talk to Santos later," Regina said firmly, and reluctantly, Cort allowed his mother to usher him into the house.

Still entranced by María's beauty, Santos moved up the steps to stand at her side. Then, placing his hand under her chin, he tilted her face upward. Recognizing his look of desire, her heart began beating rapidly.

Santos' fingers gently traced María's features, touching her high cheekbones, her small nose, and her full lips. His hand finally moved down to her neck, his

485

fingers following the length of the gold chain until they reached the miniature cross he had given her. "I see you still wear my gift."

"I will always wear it," she murmured.

Caressing the cross, he looked deep into her eyes. "Are you in love with me?" he whispered sensually.

"Yes, Santos!" she replied. Then, taking a quick breath, she asked hesitantly, "Do you love me, Santos?"

Carefully, he considered her question before answering, *"Sí, señorita.* But you are still too young to know a man's love. We must wait."

Bursting with happiness, María declared, "Oh, Santos, I'll wait forever if I must!"

Smiling tenderly, he replied, "It will not be necessary to wait forever, little one. Very soon now you will be a woman, and a very beautiful one."

Placing his hands to her shoulders, he drew her closer, and bending his head, he touched his mouth to hers. His kiss was gentle, parting her lips only slightly beneath his.

María had dreamed of this moment, and sliding her arms about his neck, she responded to Santos' kiss sweetly, but with an awakening passion that caused him to feel a stirring within his loins. Releasing her, he stepped back. *"Señorita,* it is not yet the right time for us," he said quickly. Then, gazing deeply into her large eyes, he promised, "Someday, María. Someday, you will be my wife."

In the guest room, Julie turned off the lamp and slipped into bed beside her husband. Nestling close to him, she said with intense feeling, "Darling, this afternoon I was so worried. I was afraid that Antonio would kill you."

Placing his arm around her, Miguel drew her closer. "Do not think about it, Angel. I am well and very much alive."

Struck anew by how deeply she loved her husband, Julie murmured, "Miguel, let's have another baby very soon. I want a large family."

He chuckled reminiscently. "I remember you once told me that I should remarry and start a family. Do you remember?"

Smiling dreamily, she answered, "Yes, I remember. And you said, 'At my age I should start a family? *Señora,* you flatter me.' Then I told you that you were the kind of man who would never grow old."

Turning toward her, he ran a hand over her soft thigh. "With such a beautiful wife to share my bed, I will stay young forever."

"I love you, Miguel Ordaz," Julie whispered before her lips sought his and they were lost to the exciting ways of love.

Sitting on the stool before her vanity table, Regina looked into the mirror as she brushed her hair briskly, giving her blond tresses their customary hundred strokes.

Already in bed, Matt leaned back against the headboard and took in his wife's beauty. She was wearing a sheer white gown, and underneath it, nothing at all. As he admired her silhouetted breasts and soft thighs, Matt felt desire awaken in him.

"When are you coming to bed?" he asked impatiently.

Counting aloud with each stroke of the brush, Regina finished, "Ninety-eight, ninety-nine, one hundred." Putting down the brush, she turned to face her husband, and smiled. "Matt, I have something to tell you."

"Can't it wait?" he asked, anxious to have her in his arms.

Regina rose and walked over to the bed. Sitting on the edge, she gazed at Matt, and her eyes were shining radiantly. "I've already been waiting all day to tell you. I was planning to tell you this afternoon after lunch, but Miguel and Julie unexpectedly arrived."

Slipping a hand beneath her dressing gown, Matt slowly moved it up her slender legs until it rested between her soft thighs.

Smiling mischievously, Regina grasped his hand and placed it back on the bed. "Matt Brolin," she began, "I want to tell you my wonderful news!"

"All right," he agreed, this time placing his hand on one of her full breasts.

Pushing his hand aside, she clutched his wrist and held his arm to his side. Grinning, he showed her his other hand. "I still have this one," he teased.

Laughing, Regina locked her fingers around his other wrist, then straddling him, she pinned his arms to the bed. Looking down into his face, she declared, "You are going to listen to me, Mr. Brolin!"

Easily he freed his arms and swiftly grasped her waist. Rolling her to his side, he leaned over and kissed her demandingly. As he slowly took his mouth from hers and looked into her eyes, she said, "You're going to be a father."

"Are you sure?" he exclaimed.

She nodded. "Yes, darling, I'm sure."

Smiling happily, he replied, "Honey, that's wonderful!"

Suddenly Regina's face saddened, and understanding why, Matt held her tightly. "The twins," he murmured.

"Oh, Matt, my heart still aches for my babies."

"I know," he whispered. "But, Regina, God has blessed us with this child. Let's be thankful."

It took her a moment to set aside her melancholy. Then, moving her lips to his ear, she said softly, "I'm not restraining your hands anymore, darling. So why don't you put them to good use?"

He grinned. "If you'll remove your gown, I'll see what I can do."

Hastily she discarded the flimsy garment, flinging it to the floor, and drawing back the covers, she slid her body close to her husband's. Matt always slept nude, and as she pressed her thighs to his, she could feel his male hardness touching her womanhood. Forcing her hips against his, she said seductively, "Mr. Brolin, I am all yours."

"For always," he added, while his hand traveled down her back to her rounded buttocks.

Her lips finding his, Regina kissed him with deep passion as her fingers traveled downward to his aroused flesh, provoking a pleasurable moan in response.

As he eased her onto her back, Matt brought her hand up to his lips, kissing it lightly. "Regina," he said fervently, "you have always had the power to excite me. Your touch is like magic."

"So is yours, darling," she murmured.

Bending his head, his mouth found her breasts, kissing one and then the other, before moving tantalizingly over her stomach and then downward. Regina responded by provocatively arching her hips, and moving his sinewy frame upward, Matt's mouth claimed hers as his fingers entered her female warmth.

Matt deftly aroused Regina's need of him to fever pitch before he pulled her thighs up to his and drove deeply into her.

"Darling," she whispered, locking her ankles over his back.

"Regina . . . I love you," he confessed hoarsely.

Wrapping her arms about his neck, Regina matched her husband's demanding thrusts, and lost in their need of each other they reached a plane of ecstatic fulfillment. As they descended from it with luxurious ease, Matt kissed her passionately before moving to lie at her side.

Placing her head on his shoulder, Regina said softly, "I love you, Matt."

"I know you do, Regina. But I like to hear you say it. Don't ever stop telling me."

"I won't," she promised.

They were quiet for a long time, content to be close to each other. Then, suddenly, Regina sat up and leaned back against the headboard. "Matt," she said eagerly, "before Miguel and Julie leave, let's have a barbecue."

"Sounds good to me," he agreed.

"We'll also invite Santos and Antonio," Regina decided.

Chuckling, Matt admitted, "I never dreamed I'd live to see the day that Miguel Ordaz and Antonio Ramírez would call a truce."

"Since Miguel will be here, do you think Antonio will accept our invitation?"

Matt shrugged. "I think so. Antonio has changed a lot in the past few years."

"Miguel and Antonio must learn to be civil to each other because in about two or three years we are going to be related to both of them. Which means, Miguel and Antonio will be together on quite a few occasions."

"How are we going to be related to Antonio?" Matt asked.

"By marriage," she replied.

"Marriage!" he exclaimed.

"María and Santos."

Frowning, Matt mumbled, "María is a child."

Regina smiled. "She's not a child. She'll soon be sixteen years old. I think Santos has merely been waiting for her to grow up. Take my word for it, in about two or three years, they will be married."

"Oh yeah? Well, Santos will have to wait three years," Matt decided gruffly.

Giggling, Regina remarked, "Oh, Matt, you sound like a typical father."

"Since you have María's future all planned, what about Cort's?"

"When he comes of age, we'll give him the deed to Julie's ranch, and considering the size of the Black Diamond, I think that we should also give him more land. The entire northern range, for instance."

Grinning, Matt inquired, "And the baby you're carrying?"

"If it's a boy, he'll inherit this ranch, and someday it will be handed down to his son."

"And if we have a daughter?"

Smiling romantically, Regina said dreamily, "Someday a handsome stranger will come into her life and sweep her off her feet. If not she can inherit this ranch. I did."

"What about our future, Mrs. Brolin?"

Gazing into his dark eyes, she replied pertly, "We will spend the rest of our lives loving each other. How does that sound to you?"

"You won't get an argument from me," he answered. "Talking about love," he added, "why don't you move back down here beside me? I want you in my arms where you belong."

Regina knew there was no way to tell what the future would bring, but she had learned a valuable lesson from the past. She would live each day as it came, and savor every moment of happiness; moments such as this one.

She slid down into her husband's arms.

Dear Friends,
   All authors love to hear from their readers, and I am
no exception. If you'd care to write, please send your
letters to the following address.

Sincerely,
Rochelle Wayne

Rochelle Wayne
c/o James B. Finn Literary Agency, Inc.
P.O. Box 28227A
St. Louis, Mo 63132

CAPTIVATING ROMANCE FROM ZEBRA

MIDNIGHT DESIRE   (1573, $3.50)
by Linda Benjamin
Looking into the handsome gunslinger's blazing blue eyes, innocent Kate felt dizzy. His husky voice, so warm and inviting, sent a river of fire cascading through her flesh. But she knew she'd never willingly give her heart to the arrogant rogue!

PASSION'S GAMBLE   (1477, $3.50)
by Linda Benjamin
Jade-eyed Jessica was too shocked to protest when the riverboat cardsharp offered *her* as the stakes in a poker game. Then she met the smouldering glance of his opponent as he stared at her satiny cheeks and the tantalizing fullness of her bodice—and she found herself hoping he would hold the winning hand!

FORBIDDEN FIRES   (1295, $3.50)
by Bobbi Smith
When Ellyn Douglas rescued the handsome Union officer from the raging river, she had no choice but to surrender to the sensuous stranger as he pulled her against his hard muscular body. Forgetting they were enemies in a senseless war, they were destined to share a life of unbridled ecstasy and glorious love!

WANTON SPLENDOR   (1461, $3.50)
by Bobbi Smith
Kathleen had every intention of keeping her distance from Christopher Fletcher. But in the midst of a devastating hurricane, she crept into his arms. As she felt the heat of his lean body pressed against hers, she wondered breathlessly what it would be like to kiss those cynical lips—to turn that cool arrogance to fiery passion!

Available wherever paperbacks are sold, or order direct from the Publisher. Send cover price plus 50¢ per copy for mailing and handling to Zebra Books, Dept. 1762, 475 Park Avenue South, New York, N.Y. 10016. DO NOT SEND CASH.

SWEET MEDICINE'S PROPHECY
by Karen A. Bale

#1: SUNDANCER'S PASSION   (1778, $3.95)

Stalking Horse was the strongest and most desirable of the tribe, and Sun Dancer surrounded him with her spell-binding radiance. But the innocence of their love gave way to passion—and passion, to betrayal. Would their relationship ever survive the ultimate sin?

#2: LITTLE FLOWER'S DESIRE   (1779, $3.95)

Taken captive by savage Crows, Little Flower fell in love with the enemy, handsome brave Young Eagle. Though their hearts spoke what they could not say, they could only dream of what could never be. . . .

#3: WINTER'S LOVE SONG   (1780, $3.95)

The dark, willowy Anaeva had always desired just one man: the half-breed Trenton Hawkins. But Trenton belonged to two worlds—and was torn between two women. She had never failed on the fields of war; now she was determined to win on the battleground of love!

#4: SAVAGE FURY   (1768, $3.95)

Aeneva's rage knew no bounds when her handsome mate Trent commanded her to tend their tepee as he rode into danger. But under cover of night, she stole away to be with Trent and share whatever perils fate dealt them.

Available wherever paperbacks are sold, or order direct from the Publisher. Send cover price plus 50¢ per copy for mailing and handling to Zebra Books, Dept. 1762, 475 Park Avenue South, New York, N.Y. 10016. DO NOT SEND CASH.